THE

RELUCTANT

DETECTIVE

AND OTHER STORIES

MICHAEL Z. LEWIN
(Photograph by Elsie)

MICHAEL Z. LEWIN

THE
RELUCTANT
DETECTIVE
AND OTHER STORIES

Crippen & Landru Publishers
Norfolk, Virginia
2001

Crippen & Landru Publishers, Inc.
P. O. Box 9315
Norfolk, VA 23505
USA

www.crippenlandru.com
CrippenL@Pilot.Infi.Net

This book is dedicated to Alan Lebowitz, who began it all

CONTENTS

In the beginning was a story…

MY FIRST MYSTERY prose was conceived as a story to amuse family members while I was in LA on a visit. This was 1969, and my mother was being given her first wakeful tastes of grannyhood. I never read mysteries as a kid, but my then wife, a Brit, had been told by her high school English "master" that if she would insist on reading junk then she should at least read good junk. He introduced her to Raymond Chandler. She passed this favo(u)r on to me. I have a fond memory from the summer of '65, scootering to the seaside hearing *The Little Sister* read to me aloud from the pillion.

The Chandlers led to Hammett, those early Dick Francises, and MacDonald's McGees — all rather like taking that first aspirin leads to heroin addiction, according to some theorists. By '69 my detective drug of choice was Ross Macdonald.

By that time I was already a "writer," with a non-fiction book commissioned (by E.L. Doctorow just before he gave up the day job.) Therefore my contribution to the family entertainment should be some writing, right? I figured I'd do something detectivey, with some jokes. I figured it would play out at about twenty pages.

But when the LA sojourn was finished, the story wasn't. I carried it back to New York and I was curious where it would lead. Then, as now, I hadn't planned it out. When the central character, Albert Samson, wondered what he ought to be doing next, it was because I was wondering what he ought to be doing next.

I worked on the story in libraries at Columbia University that I had no right to be in. We lived in the neighborhood (where Daniel Lewin in Doctorow's *Book of Daniel* lived: writers are such scavengers …) and I had this theory that if I walked into a university library frowning, people would think I belonged there.

I liked the Philosophy Library best. Its wooden tables rested in a valley of books. And slowly the story grew into *Ask the Right Question*.

❖ ❖

I'm not one of those people who wrote from childhood. I only began attempting fiction in my junior year at college.

I was a science major — Chemistry and Physics, ackshully (in fact the first time my name appeared in print was in a book on chemical thermodynamics.) During my first two and a half years I'd made some poor choices when I picked electives, so during the '62-'63 Christmas break I gave my father the college course book and asked him to pick my elective for the spring. He picked Creative Writing, a course I would never have found for myself.

At the time my father said he picked it because I wrote good letters. I'm appalled to think I might have been the kind of kid who wrote letters to his parents or took their suggestions seriously, even when he'd asked for them. But I guess I was and I guess I did because, come February, I'd prepared the writing sample that was required for entry into the course. And I had picked the course I would enroll in when I was rejected. But I wasn't rejected.

Later, much later, I found out why. The only reason the course teacher, Alan Lebowitz, required writing samples was so he'd have an excuse to reject the applicants he knew he didn't want to teach. And, of course, he didn't know me.

I remember that first class meeting. Alan was — as he still is — funny, charming, electrically smart. And one of his riffs was about how there are a lot of good reasons to write fiction, only one of which is to be published. Over all the years I've been doing it since, I've learned how right he was. I would write now even if I knew I wouldn't be published.

Which is not to say that I was the kind of kid who listened and accepted everything a teacher told him. Near the end of the time Alan taught me we had a meeting in his office and he must have seen a glint in my eye. He put the current story down and leaned forward and said, "Mike, you really must never be tempted to give up science for writing."

He don't remember sayin' that. I remind him every time we get together nowadays. I surely do.

✣ ✣

I've been trying to remember the first crime short story I ever finished as such. I think it was also the first published. "The Loss Factor" appeared in the British *Penthouse*, and was perhaps notable there because of its utter lack of sex. (Then as now I only write what I know about.) I wrote the story in the early seventies. No way is it appearing in this collection.

The next crime story to surface (in English) was "Wrong Number" which won me a very welcome $500 in a competition run by the Swedish Academy of Detection in association with the 1981 International Crime Writers Conference in Stockholm. In fact the story had an earlier, crimeless, incarnation, for a BBC radio program(me) — "Not Now, I'm Listening" in 1978. When I received the competition details I was in the middle of a novel so I looked through the stories I already had in stock to see if I could crime any of them up. And with "Wrong Number" — a story of lovely love — I got this idea ... (Writers are such scavengers ...)

✤ ✤

Stories are at the core of everything I do: novels, plays, poems, songs, criticism, letters, fatherhood, loverhood, or the form of storytelling that is "the short story."

My short stories are usually triggered by a single idea. A line of dialog will occur to me, or I'll overhear a fragment of conversation, or I'll read a newspaper story. What happens then is that a part of my brain will click it into a different reality from the one that happened. Something that strikes me as unexpected. Mostly likely then is that I'll write the notion on a scrap of paper and put the scrap into a drawer.

Hours, days or months later, when I'm feeling in the story way, I'll sit myself somewhere comfortable with the kind of pad I like writing on and a pen or pencil I like writing with, and on the pad I will talk to myself. I might begin, "So, sunshine, whatcha got in the tank today?" And soon I'll be going through my scraps of paper to see which fragments appeal to me (if I can read them) and whether any seem to go together. In this way, having been pregnant with story, one or more will pop out.

✤ ✤

First drafts of stories usually don't take more than a few days to write. Turning the first into the final draft is another matter, and isn't a function of the story's length. For example the story "Suicide Note" is only a wee thing, but it took weeks to finish.

But however many times I may rework stories, they're always quicker than novels. In a story I can explore characters and situations without the time commitment that a novel requires. And occasionally writing a story leaves me feeling that I'd like to write more, or longer, about the people in it.

The Lunghis are the prime example so far. Six of the stories in this book are about this family of private detectives who live and work in Bath. I've also written two novels about them. This is how they arose.

I'd been encouraged to submit a story for a collection edited by Hilary Hale. Still one of the great British crime editors, Hilary edited an annual *Winter's Crimes* when she worked at Macmillan. "The Reluctant Detective" had already appeared in an earlier winter.

On January 5th, 1987 I sat down with a pad and a fountain pen. "OK fans, here we are again. Today's needs have to do with short stories — for Hilary H. 1st to mind this moment is old man spots a young shoplifter — takes her aside and tells of his tragedy re shoplifting ..." (That later became "You Pay For Everything.")

On January 10th, I returned to the pad — I have it before me even as I write this. "OK friends, back again ..." The idea I had in mind "has to do with the fact that although there have been PI stories around for a long time ... there have been no on-going PI agencies. I mean, father passes trade to son, etc. So what I have is A Small Family Concern, Family Ties, Family Problems, Family Cases, Family Practice. PIs always have security or police backgrounds. Never brought up in the trade as kids: hang around Dad's office while he's interviewing clients, out on tails. So: hypothesis is a 2nd generation PI (or even third) who has his own kid around. Out on surveillance — whatever — talk about work over the kitchen table. That's it: wife is involved: very much presented as a small Family Business."

And there it is. First appearance of "Family Business," the title of the first story (as well as the first novel.) In the story dad takes his son out on a surveillance job.

Oddly — given how the series progressed — I did not have Bath in my head as a setting in 1987. Maybe I was too focussed on the idea of familyness in the PI biz to trouble myself with anything as mundane as a setting. Maybe I just thought it would be easier to do alternative UK and US versions if the story wasn't set anywhere in particular. Dunno. But now Bath is intrinsic to the Lunghi ethos and culture. Curiously — maybe bizarrely — I've recently moved to Bath and have an apartment that overlooks the doors on Walcot Street that I think of as the Lunghis'. In any case, I'm sure the stories get better as the Bathness in them gets stronger.

✢ ✢

The last thing that I want to say here is that although I work hard at my stories, I've never reread a published story of mine without wanting to change it. And so it is with this collection. Give me the book back and give me some time. I can make it better.

Michael Z. Lewin
Bath, Sept 2000 through July 2001

The Reluctant Detective

IT STARTED AS a tax fiddle. Well, give it a little semantic gloss: call it a tax avoidance structurization. Uncle Edward would have preferred that, I think.

It was Uncle Edward — Mom's brother — who was responsible for my coming to England in the first place. Me, I'm American by birth and by upbringing but sometime in Uncle Edward's relative youth he moved over here and he stayed. I never actually met him, though I did play postal chess with him.

We did that over a period of more than ten years, so while I didn't know him at all, I felt I knew him fairly well. You get a sense of people by their chess games.

When Uncle Edward died I was sad. He was one of my few fixed points, a focus for a little contemplative time no matter where I was or what a shambles I was making of the rest of my life.

When I learned that Uncle Edward had provided for me in his will, I was astonished. What I inherited was a house over here. Also a small income to be sent to me every month from the States. Just about enough to live on.

At first I didn't know what to do. Sell the house, or what. But when I thought about it, it occurred to me that if I thought I could tell about Uncle Edward from our chess games, maybe he could tell about me. Perhaps he was suggesting that it would be good for me to live in England for a while.

The only thing Mom ever told me about why he'd moved to England was that he said, "Britain is the closest thing there is left to a civilized English speaking country." "He was never very good at languages," she said.

The more I thought about it the better an idea it seemed. So I decided to give it a try, and over I came.

2

The tax fidd ... tax avoidance structurization didn't come up till I had been here a year or so. In fact, it was Dawn's idea, so in a way everything that's happened is down to her.

Dawn is the lady friend I've made. She is very civilized and if she is what Uncle Edward meant, I understand better why he spent his life here. It could happen to me, though that's not something I think about a lot.

13

Dawn agreed to move in after I'd been here about six months. We live in my house, and on my income. It gives us a lot of time to enjoy life. And think about things. We're not quite what they call drop-outs back home, because we intend to get into careers when we're sure what we want to do. But if we have no need to rush a decision … well, we didn't make the rules.

I see I'm already talking as if I am staying forever. Well, there are worse fates.

And, it turns out, we've already done something along a career line, even if it was strictly by accident. That's what this story is about.

OK, get the picture. I come over here to my house and an income. After six months Dawn and I are friends enough to live together. After six more months we realize that comfortable as my income is, maybe there are things it would be nice to do if there were a little more money around.

Get a car for one. Nothing flash, but some wheels to see some of the rest of the country with.

Have I told you where I am? It's a little town in Somerset called Frome. (They pronounce it to rhyme with broom, by the way.) And it is pretty enough and in a lovely part of the country. But there are other places to see. Yes, it was thinking about getting a car that set us thinking in the first place.

Or set Dawn thinking, actually. She is the one who cooked it all up.

The idea was this. If I set up in business, as a self-employed person I could save money in taxes by deducting a lot of what we spent as necessary commercial expenses. Part of the house as an office; proportion of rates and heat and repairs and insurance; even a salary to Dawn as my secretary. And all the costs of my business vehicle.

Dawn worked it all out, and there was no question, it would pay for the car. And maybe a little bit more as we went along.

Then the question was what kind of business to supposedly set up in. That was Dawn's idea too. Well, not all ideas are necessarily bright.

3

I set up as a private detective. See, in Britain you don't need a licence of any kind. And, I have to admit we yielded to a certain pleasant absurdity attached to the notion. I mean, a private detective, in Frome! As well, the chances of anybody coming to us for business were, of course, nil.

Which was the idea. We didn't want the business to succeed, or, indeed, for there to be any work at all. What we wanted were the deductions. It was a tax fiddle. As I've mentioned.

So, I bought a notebook and a pen, and a small sign to put on the front of the house. It gave my name and said under it "Private Inquiry Agent" which is what they call private detectives here.

And that was it. No advertisements, no listing in the Yellow Pages.

And no business. We bought a little yellow Mini. Life as planned. It worked like a charm. For a while.

4

It was a Tuesday, I remember, because I was reading the basketball column in *The Guardian* — I try to keep up with some of my old interests from the USA — when the doorbell rang. It was about ten o'clock. I thought it might be the gas man. Dawn was out visiting her mother — she's got as many relatives here as I have none, so to speak. A lot is what I am saying.

At the door was a sallow faced little man — well, I suppose he was about average height, but I am awkwardly tall, about two meters, so I have a distorted perspective on people. He had a jacket and tie on and he looked unhappy.

I thought, not the gas man but maybe a local government official.

"Are you Mr. Herring?" he asked.

"Yes."

"May I talk to you?"

"What about?" I asked.

He looked momentarily at the sign on the house by the door. It's so small you can hardly see it even if you know it's there. "Are you the Mr. Herring who is a private inquiry agent?"

And I suddenly realized he had come on business. I was stunned. I began to shake though I don't know if he noticed.

"Yes, yes, of course," I said. "Fredrick Herring. Do come in."

I led him to the living room. It wasn't much to look at. Not for a detective's office. It was just a living room, and lived in at that.

I sat him down. I didn't know what to say. But he made the running.

"My name is Goodrich," he said.

"Hi."

"I don't know whether I should even be here."

"It's not a step to take lightly," I said.

"I'm not," he said. "I'm not."

"Oh."

"I am a solicitor with Malley, Holmes and Asquith, but I need someone to make some inquiries for me on a private matter."

"I see."

"Well, you do that kind of thing, don't you?"

He looked at me. There was something devious in his eyes. And I had a sudden shock of suspicion.

You see, Dawn and I had talked about what to do if someone did actually come to us for work. We would just say that we were too busy to take the case on. But there was something about this man. The same thing that made me think he might be a council official. I got this idea that he was from one of the tax offices and that he was checking up on us.

It's just that on all these tax forms we'd been sending in we always had expenses listed, but never any income. It looked funny, of course. But economic times are hard and we assumed our amounts were so small, relatively, that nobody would notice.

But when you think you are being checked on, you suddenly feel the cold draught of accusation, prosecution.

"Of course," I said.

5

Dawn was not pleased when she returned to the house and found that I had taken a case. But I explained my worries and she accepted the situation as a fact.

"It's about his brother-in-law, a guy named Chipperworth, who is a crook," I said.

"Chipperworth … ," Dawn said. She was thinking. She's lived in Frome all her life and knows a lot of people.

"He has a company that manufactures beds, up on the trading estate. The brand name is Rest Easy."

"Ah."

"You know it?"

"Rest Easy, yes."

"And this man Goodrich says that Chipperworth set fire to a warehouse next to his factory up there and collected the insurance for it."

"I read about the fire," Dawn said. "But not that it was on purpose. How does Goodrich know?"

"He says Chipperworth was bragging yesterday that he had just collected a cheque for over three hundred thousand pounds and it was for beds he wasn't going to be able to sell."

"Good heavens," Dawn said. "But why doesn't Goodrich go to the police?"

"Because that's not what he's trying to sort out."

"Oh."

"What he's worried about is his sister. That Chipperworth is a crook, and that he's dangerous. He wants his sister to divorce Chipperworth."

Dawn cocked her head.

"But his sister doesn't believe the stuff about the insurance fraud."

"What are we supposed to do about that?"

"Goodrich wants us to prove Chipperworth has a woman on the side. If we can do that then the sister will divorce him and will be safe. Goodrich is sure that his sister will get a divorce in the end anyway, but if he precipitates it at least she'll be well off financially. If he waits till Chipperworth's activities catch up with him then it might ruin the sister too."

"Oh," Dawn said.

"I agreed to try."

She nodded. Then she looked at me.

And I looked at her. We were thinking the same thing.

I said, "What the hell do we do now?"

6

Well, we had to go through the motions. The first motion was to find Chipperworth and identify him.

That wasn't hard. Mr. Goodrich had given me a photograph and we decided to wait outside Rest Easy Beds toward the end of the work day. Rest Easy was not a big company. We counted about twenty people coming out after five-thirty. Chipperworth was the last and got into an A registered Sierra.

"OK," Dawn said. "There he is. What do we do now?"

"Drive along after him, I guess," I said.

So we did. He went straight to a house on the Prowtings Estate. He pulled the car into the driveway. Got out. Went to the front door. Was met by a woman at 5.46 pm. Then Chipperworth went into the house and closed the door.

That would have wrapped the case up if the woman hadn't been his wife.

Dawn and I sat.

"At least we know the registration number of his car now," I said after ten minutes.

But we were both sinking fast.

After half an hour Dawn said, "This is no good. What are we going to do, sit out here all night without any food or anything?"

And after some consideration of the situation, we decided to get fish and chips from Pangs. Even detectives have to eat.

When we got back, Chipperworth's car was gone.

7

Solicitor Goodrich rang up at 9 the next morning. He seemed annoyed that I didn't have anything to report.

I explained that progress is not always rapid, that we'd had less than a day on the job.

But Goodrich knew that Chipperworth had been out the previous night. He'd called his sister and she told him.

"If you want to do the surveillance yourself," I said, "please say so. Otherwise, leave it to us."

He took a breath, then apologized — rather unconvincingly I thought — and we hung up.

I told Dawn about the call. "If we don't sort this out quickly," she said, "it's going to mess up our lives for weeks."

"I know."

"I'm going to see a couple of my cousins."

I looked puzzled.

"Nigel is a telephone engineer," she said. "He's a nut case and would probably be willing to work out a way to tap the Chipperworths' telephone. And Paul works in the photographic section at B & T." Butler and Tanner is the big local printing firm. "He is a camera buff. He'll lend us a camera with a telephoto lens."

"Right," I said. "We may have to borrow another car too, so we can cover Chipperworth the whole day. If it goes on for long we'll have to do shifts. I ought to be able to use Adele's Reliant. You remember Adele?"

"No."

"She's the small one with the big — "

"I remember now," I said.

Biggest feet I'd ever seen on a woman.

"I just wish I knew someone who could lend us a two-way radio."

"There's your Uncle Mike," I said.

"So there is," she said. Then made a face. "But he pinches and pokes whenever I get close enough and what he'd want for doing me a favour ..."

My mind boggled. "We'll get along without," I said firmly.

8

In the end it only took a day.

It was the afternoon of my first shift. I was rigged up with a thermos, sandwiches and a radio. Even a specimen jar — from Dawn's friend Elaine, the nurse — in case time was short and need was great.

When Dawn and I get down to it, we're impressive.

I took the afternoon shift because Dawn had to see her Auntie Wendy who was having troubles with a neighbour boy picking on her son Edgar.

The camera was one of those instant print jobs. We'd talked it over with Paul and he figured that would be best. No time waiting for the film to come back from the developers. And, he said, "Considering what kind of pictures you may get, a commercial firm might not print them." Does a great leer, does Paul.

He also gave us a foot long lens for the thing. "It'll put you in their pockets," he said. "If they're wearing pockets."

Cousin Nigel jumped at the chance to plant a tape recorder up a telephone pole to tap the Chipperworths' home phone. He volunteered to do the company phone too. Well, you don't turn down offers like that.

It's always struck me that all of Dawn's family are just that little bit shady. I offer it as an observation, not a complaint.

Anyway, after an hour's lunch at home, Chipperworth didn't go back to his office. He drove instead out Marston Road and pulled into the driveway of a detached brick house just beyond the end of speed restrictions. I drove past but parked immediately. I left the car and got the camera aimed and focussed just in time to see Chipperworth open the door to the house with a key.

The picture came out a treat. I stood there in the road looking at it. And wondering what to do next.

But Dawn and I had talked it through. First I made a note of the time, date and location on the back of the photograph. Then I set about trying to find out who lived in the house.

I went next door and rang the bell and had a little luck.

A tiny old woman with big brown eyes answered it. I said, "Excuse me. I have a registered letter for the people next door but nobody answers when I ring."

"That's because Mrs. Elmitt has her fancy man in," the old woman said. "And she wouldn't want to be disturbed now, would she? Some of the things I've seen! And they don't even bother to draw the curtains."

Old women can do pretty good leers too, when they try.

9

Dawn was pleased as punch with me. I was pretty pleased myself. It meant that the wretched case would soon be over and we could get back to life as usual. I resolved to try to arrange for my income to arrive from America as some kind of retainer so that it looked like proceeds of the business. Then we wouldn't have to worry about being inspected by the tax people. Worry is a terrible thing.

But just about the time that we were getting ready to be pleased with each other, Cousin Nigel showed up at the front door.

He punched me on the shoulder as he came in, and gave Dawn a big kiss. A hearty type, Nigel.

"I've got your first tape," he said jovially. "Went up to see if it needed changing and blow me if there hadn't been a lot of calls. Thought you would want to hear them sooner rather than later, so I put another cassette in the machine and brought this one right over. Got any beer while we listen to it?" He dropped into our most comfortable chair. "Hey Dawnie, how about something to eat? Egg and chips? Hungry work, bugging telephones."

✢ ✢

The tape was a revelation.

Right off, the very first phone call had things like the man saying, "Darling, I can't wait until I see you again."

And the woman: "I don't know whether I'll be able to bear not being with you full time for very much longer."

"It will be soon. We'll be together, forever. Someplace nice. Away from your wretched husband."

"I don't know what will become of me if our plan doesn't work."

"It will work. We'll make it work."

"Oh darling, I hope so."

And on and on, that kind of mushy stuff. There were a lot of slobbering sounds too. I would have been embarrassed if I hadn't been so upset.

"Wow!" Nigel said. "All that kissy-kissy, and before lunch. They must have it bad."

Dawn said, "Isn't that great! We've got all we need now, Freddie, don't you think?"

But I was not happy, not even close.

Because, unlike my two colleagues, I had recognized one of the voices. The man's. The conversation was not between Mr. Chipperworth and Mrs. Elmitt. The man on the telephone was our client, Mr. Goodrich, and the object of his affection was, presumably, Mrs. Chipperworth, his "sister."

10

We got rid of Nigel before we talked it out.

"I guess this means that our client was not being completely open and frank with us," Dawn said.

There was no law that a client had to tell us the truth. But neither of us liked it.

"But what do we do?"

We had a long chat about it.

✛ ✛

What we did was go the next morning to Dawn's Uncle Steve, who is a police sergeant. We asked him about the fire in the Rest Easy Beds warehouse.

"Always knew it was arson," Uncle Steve said. "But we couldn't prove who did it. The owner was the only possible beneficiary, but he had an airtight alibi. Not quite as good as being out to dinner with the Chief Superintendent, but he was at a function with the mayor and he was at a table, in full sight, the whole evening."

"I see," Dawn said.

"I interviewed Chipperworth myself," Uncle Steve said, "and he was quite open about being delighted about the fire. Business wasn't very good and he was having trouble moving the stock that was destroyed. Personally, I don't think he did have anything to do with it. I've been at this job long enough to get a good sense of people and that's the way he came across."

"I see," Dawn said.

"But we never got so much as a whiff of any other suspect. Checked through all current and past employees for someone with a grievance. Sounded out all our informants in town for a word about anybody who might have been hired to do the deed or who heard anything about it. But we didn't get so much as a whisper. It's very unusual for us not to get some kind of lead if something's bent and we try that hard. In the end, it was written off to kids. There are so many around with nothing to do these days that we are getting all sorts of vandalism."

"Thanks, Uncle Steve," Dawn said.

"Helps you, does that?" he asked.

"I think so."

"If you know anything about the case, you must tell us. You know that, don't you?"

"Yes, Uncle Steve." He looked at her and shook his head. Then he said to me, "Young man, there is a look in her eye that I don't like. There's something tricky about all her people. You watch yourself."

He was right, of course. Dawn was cooking something up, and it wasn't chips.

❖ ❖

When we got home we sat down over a nice cup of tea. She hadn't said a word for the whole drive. I couldn't bear it any longer. I said, "All right. What is the significance of that funny look?"

"I've decided we're going to get Mrs. Chipperworth that divorce our client wants after all."

"We are?"

"It's what we were hired to do, isn't it?"

11

I called Solicitor Goodrich to tell him that we had had success in our investigation and did he want our report.

He did. He was with us within twenty minutes.

I explained what I had seen the previous afternoon. I gave him the photographs I had taken of Chipperworth entering Mrs. Elmitt's house with a key and, later, adjusting his flies as he came out. I reported what the neighbour had told me.

"She is willing to testify to what she's seen in court, or to swear out a statement," I said. "But she would like some money for it."

"I think that can be arranged," Goodrich said.

A little ready cash might help the old woman get some curtains for her own windows.

Goodrich wrote out a cheque for our fee and expenses on the spot.

"Of course if we have to testify," I said, "there will be an additional bill."

"I don't think it will come to that," Goodrich said.

❖ ❖

After he left I rang Rest Easy Beds.

I explained to Mr. Chipperworth that we wanted to come over to speak to him.

"What is it that is so urgent, Mr. Herring?" he asked.

"We wanted to tell you about your wife's plans to sue you for divorce," I said.

As soon as we arrived we were ushered into Chipperworth's office.

"But she's known about Madeleine for years," he said when I explained what we'd been hired to do. "It's an arrangement we have. She doesn't like *it*, you see. So Madeleine keeps me from making ... demands."

"She doesn't seem to mind the demands of her lover," Dawn said.

"Her *what?*"

"Why don't you ask her about her telephone calls recently," Dawn suggested. "We have to be going now. Ta ta."

❖ ❖

We stopped at Nigel's and then we went on home.

We didn't have long to wait.

A few minutes after noon the bell rang. Before I could get to it, pounding started on the door. When I opened it I faced Solicitor Goodrich, in a fury. He swung fists at me. For the most part being as tall as I am is an inconvenience. But at least I have long arms and could keep him out of reach. When he finished flailing, he started swearing. The rude language seemed particularly unseemly for a member of the legal profession. I would have been very embarrassed for Dawn if I hadn't heard as bad or worse from her family. But they are foul mouthed in a friendly way. Goodrich was vicious.

Also defamatory. He claimed that we had sold information to Mr. Chipperworth.

I was about to deny it when Dawn said, "What if we did?"

"I'll have you for this," Goodrich said. "It's illegal. I can put you in gaol."

"That's fine talk from somebody who set fire to a warehouse."

Goodrich was suddenly still and attentive. "What?"

"You're the arsonist responsible for the fire at Rest Easy Beds."

"That's silly talk," Goodrich said. But he wasn't laughing.

"The idea was that when Mr. Chipperworth collected the insurance money Mrs. Chipperworth would start divorce proceedings which would entitle her to claim half of it. With your help she could probably settle out of court and between the insurance cash and her share of the rest of the joint property, you and Mrs. Chipperworth would have a nice little nest egg to run away on."

"Prove it," Goodrich said.

"Oh, I think it's a very clever plan," Dawn said charmingly. "I suppose you have an alibi for the night of the fire?"

"Why should I need one?"

"Well, if we went to the police ..."

"Why the hell should you do that?" Goodrich burst out.

"Ah," Dawn said. "Now we're getting down to the serious questions." She batted her eyelashes. "We never actually gave our evidence to Mr. Chipperworth, you know, and as long as Mrs. Chipperworth has denied everything ..."

You want money, I suppose," Goodrich said.

"Well, poor Freddie is terribly tall, and a bigger car would be so such easier for him to get in and out of."

"All right," Goodrich said. "A car."

"And there are so many little improvements that ought to be made on this house."

"How about just getting to a bottom line figure."

"I think thirty thousand would come in very handy, don't you Freddie?"

"Oh, very handy."

"Thirty thousand!" Goodrich said.

"Yes," Dawn said. "See how reasonable we are!"

12

When the trial came along it was plastered all over the local papers. Frome is not so big a town that we get serious court cases involving local people every week.

Especially not cases involving solicitors and arson, not cases with a little titillation in them. Goodrich pleaded guilty, but the local reporter, Scoop Wall, tracked down Mrs. Elmitt's neighbour who was photographed pointing to some of the uncurtained windows she had been forced to witness indescribable acts through. Well, the descriptions didn't make the papers anyway.

Uncle Steve was not pleased at first when he heard what we had done.

Heard is the operative word because we had tape recorded the entire conversation with Goodrich on equipment we borrowed from Cousin Nigel.

But Dawn explained. After all this time the only way Goodrich's arson would be proved was if he confessed to it. But the police couldn't have used the threat of exposing his relationship to Mrs. Chipperworth the way we did because that would have transgressed legal niceties. "So it was up to Freddie and me," Dawn said.

Eventually Uncle Steve laughed. "I warned you about her," he said to me.

But it worked out all right in the end.

❖ ❖

Except … Scoop Wall tracked down Dawn and me too.

We begged her not to put anything about us in the paper. But she refused. We were key figures in bringing a dangerous solicitor to justice. It was news. And besides, Dawn has good legs and photographs well.

It's not that we weren't proud of what we — or let's be fair — what Dawn had done. But it meant that the Fredrick Herring Private Inquiry Agency burst from its quiet and planned total obscurity into the glare of public attention. We started getting calls. We started getting visitors. We started getting letters. Find this, look for that, unravel the other. And it wasn't actually the attention which was the problem. The problem was that we found we quite liked it. See, some of the cases we were offered were pretty interesting. Rather like chess problems … So, we decided, maybe one more. Or two.

Rainey Shines

ALEX RAINEY, arms occupied with groceries, shouldered his way through the front door of Homeleigh Guest House. Once inside, he eased the door closed with the heel of a shoe and carried his burden through the foyer, past the office, and into the kitchen. As he set the bags on the table, a voice, wafting like a fragrance, tickled his eardrums, or so he mused. It asked, "Hello? Is that you, Alex?"

" 'Tis I."

"I'm finishing up the accounts."

Happy for an excuse to leave his labours, Rainey retraced his steps as far as the Guest House office. "I wouldn't have thought there was that much to —" he began, but he hit his head on the doorframe as he entered the room.

"Not again!" Pru said, without looking up.

"God damned England. Just because it's little and its cars are little and its people are little and its ambitions are little it thinks it can get away with its doors being little."

"You always sound so much more American when you — "

"Smug, self-satisfied, undersized, little island. Calls itself Great Britain? Well, I just think it's Cramped and Inconvenient Britain, and you can quote me all the way back to the seventh Viscount. This country is just too damn small."

"Don't rub your pate, darling. It will get all shiny again. You know how you hate people using your forehead to see if their ties are straight."

"As well as being physically small, you people have dwarfism of the compassion."

"You've hit your head six times in the last five days. How often am I supposed to shed tears?"

"Remind me. Warn me. Help me." Rainey rubbed his head. "Is it *only* five days?"

"Yes, yes. Just two days to go."

"Feels like forever," Rainey said. "And half of today yet as well."

"As I recall, it was you who convinced me, that we should look after this place for Wendy and Terry after they'd been let down."

"Well, she looked so sad."

"Sweet, kind, sympathetic man that you are."

"Mmm." Rainey picked up Pru's handbag and began to hunt through it.

"Hey! What do you think you're doing?"

"Going through your bag," he said.

"I keep all my love letters in there!"

Rainey found what he was looking for and took the mirror out. He held it up and looked at the reflection of his bald head.

"Just a scuff," Pru said.

"A scuff! There's blood up there."

"If you want me to apply a tourniquet to your neck …"

"Heartless. Heartless."

"Do you think you could get the groceries in and check the bar stock before you expire. It would help so much."

"The groceries are in the kitchen and I'm sure the bar is all right for a mere three guests, unless they turn into alcoholics with the full moon around here.

"We have five guests, Alex."

"I thought there were three."

"We have a couple coming in tonight. Compatriots of yours."

"But I thought those Frenchies were leaving."

"They're staying another night."

"Nice to be told."

"I did tell you. Before you went shopping. I reminded you so that you would get enough food for breakfast."

"Mmmm."

"For someone who is supposed to be a genius, you can be the most exasperatingly stupid person!"

"I think a further short sortie into the depths of town is indicated. A bit of fresh air for my wound."

"Do you want me to pin a list to your shirt, or can you manage?"

"I think I'll cope." Then, "Do you think it will leave a scar?"

"If it doesn't," Prudence Rainey said, "then I think maybe I will."

2

"Eight years," Alex Rainey moaned behind the bar. "Eight long years."

"You do not like living in England, then, Mr. Rainey?" asked Monsieur Hirou.

"Lord no. Terrible place. I don't know how human life manages to sustain itself."

"Is it just the food you are meaning?" Madame Hirou asked. "Or the weather, or are there other things more subtle?"

"There is a fog of the soul," Rainey said, and he lifted his eyes in melancholic posture.

After glancing at her husband, Madame Hirou said, "But it is beautiful too, especially here in the West Country."

Rainey shrugged.

"But say to me, Mr. Rainey," said Monsieur Hirou, "if you don't like it so much, why do you live here?"

"Ahhh," Rainey said, with another theatrical gesture. "My downfall. An uncontrollable passion for a beautiful woman who refuses to live anywhere else. *D'accord*. What can one do?"

Monsieur Hirou nodded understandingly. And, as if on cue, Pru entered the small bar from the foyer. The Hirous and Rainey all watched her carefully. "Is something wrong?" she asked.

"No alas, no," Rainey said. And sighed.

"Well, actually, there is," she said. "Mr. Bates, in number seven, is having some trouble with his plumbing."

"Ah, his plumbing," Madame Hirou said knowingly.

"Is surgery required?" Rainey asked.

"Well, why don't you go up and make a diagnosis."

✛ ✛

Pru did not remember to ask the outcome of Mr. Bates's plumbing difficulties until she and Alex had been in bed for an hour.

"Ah, a quick plunge saw it right," Rainey said. "I think I have an aptitude. The perfect wrist."

"Perhaps you should take it up professionally."

"I would have thought," Rainey said speculatively, "that there were a number of improvements which could be made in basic plumbing design."

From elsewhere in the house they heard a door slam.

"That must be the Maxwells," Pru said. "They said they would be coming in late, so I gave them a key."

"How long are they staying?"

"She wasn't sure. Maybe only tonight, but perhaps another day or two. Her husband had some business in Bristol so she checked in and then met him there. I gather they were going to the theatre tonight."

"The theatre …" Rainey said wistfully. "I can remember when we went to the theatre of an evening."

"All right. All right. Two more days, that's all. Just two more days."

✛ ✛

Pru was washing the breakfast dishes when Rainey came into the kitchen and closed the door. In a serious voice he said, "Has anybody left yet?"

"Left?" she asked, without looking up.

"As in checked out. Departed."

"Only Mr. Bates"

"Well, don't let the others leave."

"Alex, what's wrong?"

"The police would smack our little fingers, naughty, naughty."

"Alex?"

"Because there is a dead woman in number 23."

"Good heavens! Who?"

"Never seen her before in my life," Rainey said.

3

"You're of American origin, I believe, Mr. Rainey."

"I have that good fortune, yes, Inspector Mothersole."

"And how long have you been with us?"

"My wife and I have lived in this country for the last eight years."

"And you are hoteliers by trade?"

"We are not." Alex Rainey drew himself to his full and considerable height as if the idea of a life in guest house proprietorship was repugnant to him.

Pru said, "We are filling in for friends who have gone on holiday, Inspector. Wendy and Terry Peverall."

"Ah yes, the Peveralls. And where exactly have they gone to, Mrs. Rainey?"

"They're spending the week skiing in Austria."

"I see. And if you are not in the hotel trade, how do you normally make your living?"

"Alex has an independent income."

"Does he now?" Mothersole looked at Rainey. "That must be very pleasant for you both."

"He also acts as an electronics and computer consultant for a number of companies and he dabbles in other activities some of which have commercial applications."

"Dabbles, does he? All sounds very comfortable, very comfortable indeed," Inspector Mothersole said. "Myself, I and the wife have quite a job to scrape by with three teenage children. But then, that's life for you."

"If you wish me to look at your investment portfolio," Alex Rainey said stuffily, "then I might be able to suggest some appropriate changes."

"I see," Inspector Mothersole said.

"Inspector?"

"Yes, Mrs. Rainey?"

"She is not Mrs. Rainey," Alex Rainey said. "She is Lady Prudence Elizabeth Scott-Rainey. And I would hope that — "

"Oh shut up, Alex! Please excuse my husband's bad manners. He can be dreadful and imperceptive boor, and he thinks that being intelligent entitles him to special treatment."

"I assure you that I am quite used to dealing with flawed personalities, Lady Prudence," Inspector Mothersole said with positiveness.

Mothersole looked at Rainey, as if expecting him to speak. But Rainey said nothing.

"Perhaps, Mr. Rainey, would would be so good as to tell me exactly how you discovered the dead woman."

"I looked in the room and saw her in the bed."

"Why did you look in the room?"

"While my wife washed the breakfast dishes, I went upstairs to conduct the morning routine: clean sheets, towels; soap, glasses, toilet paper, tea makings. The things which are generally changed or checked each day."

"You do this all yourselves?"

"The Peveralls have a woman who comes in during the busy season, but this is the quiet time of year for them," Pru said.

"Do you know the woman's name?"

"Mrs. Witcombe."

"Ah yes. Paula and Darren Randall's girl that married Andy Witcombe's oldest boy." Mothersole turned back to Rainey. "So, you looked in the room and saw the woman in bed."

"I knew that the room was meant to be unoccupied so I went farther into the room and — "

"Excuse me, Mr. Rainey. You leave unoccupied rooms unlocked?"

"That was the Peveralls' instruction."

"Go on."

"I went far enough into the room to see that the woman was dead. Then I went to the kitchen to tell Lady Prudence to prevent those guests remaining on the premises from leaving and I called the police."

"You are able to tell by looking that someone is dead, Mr. Rainey?"

"I know asphixiation when I see it, Inspector Mothersole."

"First hand experience?"

"My sister is a forensic pathologist in Hartford, Connecticut. In the course of our chitter chatter we speak about her work. I have also read one or two books, and I attend a fair few autopsies."

"As part of your dabbling?"

"As part of my dabbling."

"Where we live," Pru said, "Alex is friendly with the coroner. He is often invited to autopsies. They have a little game in which each sees if he can notice a detail which the other misses."

"And do you often win this little game, Mr. Rainey?"

"I hold my own, Inspector."

"You sound quite a fellow, Mr. Rainey," Inspector Mothersole said. "Perhaps as a mere small town policeman I should enlist your assistance on this puzzling case."

"Perhaps you should," Rainey said.

"Of course you could save us all time by explaining now why you killed this woman."

For the first time in several minutes Rainey smiled and looked interested.

"But that would be telling," he said.

Pru was less amused. "Certainly you don't seriously think ..."

"He was the first one to the body, Lady Prudence. Maybe he knew which vacant room to look in. If he was upstairs refurbishing the used rooms, why look into one which wasn't booked?"

"Why indeed," Alex Rainey said.

"So, Mr. Rainey, if you were me, what would you do next?"

"When your medical representative had finished, I would go upstairs to have a look at the body."

"Well, just let me go ask Dan how he's getting on."

4

Inspector Mothersole hesitated outside the door of Room 23. He turned to Pru and said, "It's not a very pretty sight, Lady Prudence."

"I'll be all right," Pru said.

Mothersole held the door open and the three of them went in.

"Is this how you found the body, Mr. Rainey?"

"No. The covers were tucked neatly up to her shoulders and she had a nightie on. The one now on the table, I presume." Rainey looked slowly around the room. "I don't notice any other changes."

"I see."

"May I look at the body, Inspector?"

"Please do," Mothersole said.

Rainey went to the foot of the bed. "I like to start at the feet and work up," he said.

"Likes to start at the feet, does he?" Mothersole asked Pru.

But Pru said nothing. They both watched as Rainey examined the dead woman slowly.

After a few minutes Rainey said, "May I turn her over, Inspector?"

"Please do."

Shortly afterwards he turned back to the watching pair.

"Examination complete," Rainey said with some lightness. "I've done what I can without a scalpel and saw."

"And have you decided that you knew the woman?"

"Good heavens no. Never saw her alive."

"What a pity. I think it would help us a good deal to know who she was. Don't you?"

"I think," Rainey said slowly, "that it would."

On the room door there was a sharp knock. Inspector Mothersole called out, "Enter," and a tall, angular young constable came into the room.

"What is it, Howell?"

"I got Mrs. Witcombe here, Inspector. You said to let you know when she come."

"Please show her in."

Inspector Mothersole turned back to Rainey and Pru. "It crossed my mind that Mrs. Witcombe was the best source close at hand to tell us whether the dead woman had been a guest here before. What do you think, Mr. Rainey?"

5

Constable Howell led a slight woman in her mid-thirties into the bedroom. Inspector Mothersole took her hands for a moment. "Sorry to have to ask you to come in, Janet."

"That's all ..." She stopped as she noticed the body. "Oh my!"

"As you see we have a little problem."

"Oh, Tony. Such a nice looking woman too. But shouldn't she — I was about to say, shouldn't she be covered up, but I was thinking that she would get cold."

"Bit past that now, Jan."

Mrs. Witcombe looked at the body again and took a deep breath. Turning back to Inspector Mothersole she asked, "And how's Christine?"

"Fine thanks."

"The boys?"

"Being boys. And how is your Mum?"

"Much as ever, thanks."

Inspector Mothersole hesitated before he said, "What I wondered was if you had ever seen this woman."

Mrs. Witcombe frowned. "As a guest you mean?"

"Anywhere."

Mrs. Witcombe looked at the Raineys.

Mothersole said, "The Raineys are here while the Peveralls are on holiday. They've never seen the woman before."

"Dead in the hotel and they never saw her?" Mrs. Witcombe looked at the couple again. "That's a bit funny, isn't it?" She moved to take another look at the body, but it was brief. "No, Tony. I've never seen her before. Certainly not from town, and I'd swear I never saw her as a guest here either."

"OK, Janet. Thank you very much for coming in."

"That's all right," she said.

To Howell Mothersole said, "Take Mrs. Witcombe downstairs and get Ashwell to run her home. Then bring the American couple up."

"Yes sir. And Inspector?"

"Yes, Howell?"

"Dickie said to tell you that they got the accountant from where he was working and they got him waiting downstairs with the Froggie couple and the

Yanks."

"Good. We'll see him after the Americans."

As the door closed behind Constable Howell and Mrs. Witcombe, Mothersole turned to the Raineys. "Sounds a reasonable question, doesn't it?"

"What do you mean, Inspector?" Pru asked.

"I think," Rainey said, "that he is referring to Mrs. Witcombe's wonderment that a woman could enter an unused room, and get herself murdered in a hotel without the people in charge even knowing she was on the premises. Would I be right, Inspector?"

"You weren't under instruction to leave the front door unlocked by any chance were you?"

"No," Pru said. "We have been scrupulous and careful about locking up. We've never left the premises empty and unlocked."

"Can you hear people coming in and out of the hotel?"

"Generally yes."

"And what time did you go to bed last night?"

"A little after eleven."

"And did you hear anything?"

"Only Mr. and Mrs. Maxwell when they came in about quarter past twelve."

"You expected them to be that late?"

"Yes," Pru said. "The other guests had night keys too, but the Maxwells were the only ones who came in after we closed up."

"I see," Inspector Mothersole said. "And Mr. Rainey? Any comment on how this woman managed to get herself killed here without either of you knowing about it?"

Rainey, who was thinking about something else, took a moment to focus on the question he was being asked. "Comment? Only that I think you will find that the woman was murdered elsewhere and put into this bed."

"Oh yes? Why do you say that?"

"People who die stressfully generally at least partially evacuate bladder and bowel. There is no sign of that here. For similar reasons I doubt she was wearing that nightie when she was killed."

"You are suggesting that she was dead when she was brought into the hotel?"

"Or killed elsewhere on the premises and brought into this room."

"But why?"

A knock on the door was followed by Constable Howell entering with a robust man of about forty-five, and a well-dressed woman in her late twenties.

6

"These here are Mr. and Mrs. Maxwell, Inspector," Howell said.

"How do you do, Inspector?" Chester Maxwell said, as he came forward and extended a hand for shaking. "I'm Ches Maxwell and this is my little woman, Candy."

"Mr. Maxwell," Mothersole said, shaking the proffered hand limply. "Mrs. Maxwell."

"A terrible thing to happen. Terrible. What can Candy and me do for you?"

Mothersole said, "You look uneasy, Mrs. Maxwell."

"It's just ... I've never seen a dead body before. I'll be all right."

"Be brave honey. We got to do our best to help these folks."

"OK, Ches."

Mothersole said, "I would like you both to take a good look at the dead woman and tell me whether you think you've ever seen her before."

"Not like that or I sure would have remembered," Maxwell said lightly, referring to the corpse's nakedness. Then he seemed to feel that a light tone was not appropriate and said, "Sorry."

The couple spent a short time looking at the body and turned back to Mothersole.

Maxwell shrugged. "Sorry. Never saw her before."

"Mrs. Maxwell?"

"I don't know her. I don't remember ever having seen her."

"You are both certain?"

They looked at each other and both nodded. "Sure as shooting," Chester Maxwell said.

"Where was your room last night?"

"Down the other end of this hall, at the front," Maxwell said.

"And did you hear anything unusual, or anything at all after eleven-thirty?"

"We only got in from Bristol a little past midnight, but I didn't hear a thing. Did you, Candy?"

"Nothing, except your snoring," Mrs. Maxwell said.

"We tried to be real quiet, because I guess folks aren't so used to staying up late in little towns over here," Maxwell said.

"Are you sound sleepers?"

"Reasonably sound," Mrs. Maxwell said. "Aren't we, Ches?"

"Wouldn't sleep through a tornado or one of your bombings, but we like our shuteye."

"All right. Thank you. But I must ask you not to leave the hotel for the time being."

"We understand, Inspector. You got a problem. Can't be easy for you."

"Thank you for your consideration, Mr. Maxwell."

7

George Bates needed hardly a glance at the body to say definitively, "I've never seen this woman before in my life, and I certainly didn't kill her."

"I didn't suggest that you had," Inspector Mothersole said.

"Well, what did you have me pulled out of an important meeting for then?"

"What is your job, Mr. Bates?"

"I am an auditor with the Trimsgate Group."

"They own Victar Brothers on the edge of town, don't they?"

"That's right. I am conducting the Group's annual audit of each subsidiary. Well, that's not quite accurate because I have responsibilities which are not, strictly speaking, part of the audit. Relating to other records, production, efficiency, personnel."

"Something of a company hatchet man?"

Bates allowed himself a slight smile and said, "I like to think my rôle is rather more positive than that phrase suggests."

"How long have you been in town?"

"They will have told you," Bates said, indicating the Raineys. "I've been here since Sunday night. I was due to leave tonight. And I still will, if I am allowed to get back to work shortly."

"I wish to get this matter cleared up as soon as possible too, Mr. Bates. But I can assure you, none of us will be going very far unless I make progress today."

Alex Rainey began to speak, but then stopped as George Bates said, "Do we have to stay in this room? I hate illness."

"The woman is not ill, Mr. Bates," Mothersole said.

"Yes … well."

"Are you married, Mr. Bates?"

"What's that got to do with anything?"

"Are you married, or not?"

Somewhat sullenly Bates said, "I am not. I was, for a while. But not now. Not for four years."

"What have you been doing with your evenings since Sunday?"

"I spend nearly half the year in strange towns, Inspector. I have spent the evenings this week the way I always do. A certain amount of my work can be taken back to my room. I watch that small amount of television which is bearable. And each evening I go for half an hour's walk."

"Bit unpleasant for walking lately."

"It has been cold and wet, yes. But it is my routine," Bates said.

"What time did you return from your walk last night, Mr. Bates?"

"I was there from just before ten. I took a bath, or did so as soon as Mr. Rainey sorted out my plumbing. Then I went to bed. I was asleep before eleven."

"How can you be so sure of the time?"

"I listen to Book at Bedtime on the radio. I don't remember the end of the episode."

"And during the night, did you hear anything or anybody?"

"Nothing whatsoever. I woke at seven sharp, as I always do. Between times I was dead to the world."

8

Michelle Hirou was the first to answer. "No, *Inspecteur*. I am sorry. I have never seen this woman before now."

"Mr. Hirou?"

Gérard Hirou stood looking at the body.

Inspector Mothersole asked again, "Have you seen her before?"

"What? Oh, no. Never. I was just thinking what a shame it is. A good looking woman like this."

"You're both absolutely certain? You didn't see her in a tea shop or at Nunney Castle or at any of the places you've been visiting?"

They looked at each other and agreed. "No, we are certain."

"And you say you were in bed shortly after ten-thirty."

"That's right," Michelle Hirou said.

"May I ask how long have you been in England?"

"This is now the end of the second week," Gérard Hirou said.

"And why did you choose this time of year to come over?"

"It has been a kind of second honeymoon for us, *Inspecteur*."

"That's not quite correct, Gérard," Michelle Hirou said.

"It is all they need."

Michelle Hirou continued, "Not so much a second honeymoon. We have come away together to find out whether we can still get along one with the other."

"I see," Mothersole said. "A kind of marital recuperation."

"Yes, I think," Michelle Hirou said.

"Your English is very good," Mothersole said.

"Thank you, but we would hope it to be so because we are both teachers of it in our French schools. It is how we met."

"Is language why you picked England to come to?"

"Well," Michelle Hirou said, "Gérard is passionately fond of holidays in the sun, on the beach *avec tous les nus*."

"And Michelle," Gérard Hirou continued, "she loves the skiing, or shall I say *l'après ski* and the ski *instructeurs*."

"But you won't get either here," Mothersole said.

"Exactly."

9

As Constable Howell opened the door to lead the Hirous back downstairs he said, "Dickie told me to say that they turned somebody up on the house to house. Somebody who saw something."

"I see," Mothersole said.

"They got her downstairs. It's an old lady and he says you ought to come down instead of making her come up."

"We'll come down then," Mothersole said.

"May I have a word first, Inspector," Alex Rainey said.

"What can I do for you, Mr. Rainey?"

"Did I gather from what you told Mr. Bates that you would be preventing people from leaving town until substantive progress on the case has been made?"

"I think you agree with me that identification of the dead woman is crucial. It will be hard for me to rule anybody out until that identification has been made."

"And that restriction on leaving would apply to us as well?"

"Most certainly, Mr. Rainey," Inspector Mothersole said, and he left the bedroom.

10

Mrs. Westerbeck, a diminutive woman of nearly eighty, sat calmly on a chair in the Guest House office.

"So you see I do have this what they call jet lag," the old woman said in a surprisingly strong voice. "Only it be permanent, and I never been on a jet. What happens is I stay awake in the night and what sleep I do get is in the day."

"It must be very trying for you, Mrs. Westerbeck."

"It be hard to keep my mind occupied."

"So you sit at the window."

"Since it were double glazed. That's right. What I do is turn on the radio and I sit by the window."

"And you saw something?"

"I'll tell you what I saw. You can decide whether it do mean anything to you or not."

"All right."

"Full moon last night. After it stopped raining I saw pretty clear. Well what I saw was first a car drive up and a couple get out. Man and a woman it was."

"About what time was that?"

"Ten or eleven past midnight. I thought to myself, 'That's a late time to be coming in. Stunt your growth, that will,' I thought to myself."

"What did the people do?"

"They come in the front door, with a key."

"I see. And was there anything else?"

"There was the other woman."

"Was there now?"

"Only she didn't drive up. She walked in from the road. She let herself in with a key too, and I said to myself, 'Hello hello,' I said. 'That's a pretty time of night for a woman to be out alone. Can't be up to no good, that one.' That's what I said to myself when I saw her."

"And what time of night was that, Mrs. Westerbeck?"

"Just gone two-thirty a.m."

<h2 style="text-align:center">11</h2>

"You're keeping very quiet, Mr. Rainey," Inspector Mothersole said.

"I think," Pru said, "that Alex is depressed by the idea of having to remain here after the Peveralls get back on Sunday. Either that or he is thinking. Depression and thought are the only two reasons he is ever quiet."

"Not grown fond of our little town, then, Mr. Rainey?"

"No."

"Which? Depression or thought?"

"What I have been doing, Inspector, is giving your fertile imagination time to mull over your suspicion that my wife and I were involved in the murder of the woman upstairs."

"Now why would I think something like that, Mr. Rainey? Not just because of the mark on your forehead. There are other ways you could have got that than by fighting with a woman as you were suffocating her. There must be." Mothersole made much of scratching his head as if trying to think of some.

"You must be very pleased that Mrs. Westerbeck has such staying power."

"Knowing exactly how many people and of what gender went in and out through the course of the night does considerably restrict the field of possible scenarios."

"And it spares us an unknown woman appearing, as if by magic, dead in a bed."

"Funny to think of someone arriving at two-thirty a.m., entering with a key, and being murdered before morning though."

"Mmmm," Alex Rainey said, and was silent for a while.

"Thinking again, Mr. Rainey?"

With an extravagant sigh and a rub of his forehead, Alex Rainey said, "Yes. I was thinking what a grim little town this is, and how I don't want to spend a single minute more in it that I have to."

It was Mothersole's turn for silence.

Alex Rainey sat down behind the Guest House office's desk. He leaned forward with his elbows on the blotter and he said, "Your main line of consideration, am I right Inspector, that the dead woman was given a night key by one of our residents and that she was killed here after she arrived. And you are giving special thought to our accountancy expert Mr. Bates, are you not?"

"Am I?"

"Because you ask yourself, if he retires to his room each night so early, why would he ask for a night key? Is he a plotting man? Unmarried, alone in a strange town. Perhaps a man who arranges a little treat for himself on his last night in a town. A treat which went wrong this time."

"The possibility had occurred to me, Mr. Rainey."

Smiling, Alex Rainey leaned back and said, "Would you like a cup of coffee, Inspector?"

"Not just now," Mothersole said quietly.

"Alex," Pru asked, "do you think Mr. Bates did it?"

"No," Rainey said casually. "I think Mr. Bates is just a prudent man, protecting himself against the eventuality of finding himself locked out one night."

"So, one of the couples? The Maxwells or the Hirous?"

"Or us, my dear. Mmmm."

"Oh!"

"But I certainly agree competely with the good Inspector."

The Raineys looked at Mothersole who again said nothing as he watched what was growing into a performance.

"The good Inspector said that identification of the body was crucial, and I think he's absolutely right. Now, in the ordinary run of events I wouldn't dream of interfering in his case. But the idea of spending any extra time in this noxious little town ... Well excuse me, Inspector, but it would drive me bananas."

Mothersole continued his silence.

"Which leads me to consider a number of factors."

"Like what, Alex?" Pru asked.

"The body is left in an unbooked room in a small town hotel in a new nightie from a chain store. No other clothing. No jewelry. It's really a highly anonymous situation. Am I right, Inspector?"

"You are, Mr. Rainey."

"And by arranging circumstances this way the killer is telling us loud and clear that identification of the body is important."

"Just so."

"Yet, nevertheless, the face is not interfered with, apart from a little faint brusing around the eyes. Nor are the fingerprints. Nor are the teeth. All things which are among the best means of identifying someone. You see, Pru?"

"What?"

"It means that the woman is not local. The good inspector is virtually invited to splash the dead woman's picture over newspapers and TV screens. But it will be to no avail. And given that newspapers and television here get national distribution, it is almost a guarantee that the woman is not even British."

"I see," Pru said.

"Which again brings us to people with foreign associations."

"Like the Maxwells or the Hirous?"

"Or us, my dear," Rainey said.

"I trust this is not the end of your little discourse, Mr. Rainey," Mothersole said.

"Oh, by no means, Inspector. For instance I will tell you that the woman was killed by someone who knew her well."

"Oh yes?"

"I said she was lightly bruised around the eyes. I think this damage came as the result of contact lenses being taken out, and none too gently. Perhaps in a hurry, but by someone who knew that she wore them which is hardly obvious to a stranger." Rainey paused. "No comment?"

"Go on."

"The woman was also relatively wealthy."

"And why do you say that?"

"Apart from generally being well kept, there are more specific signs of affluence. And I don't just mean that her fingers show that she wore several rings. You will find — and no doubt your medical examiner will tell you this when he completes his report — that there are signs of two operations."

"So?"

"Operations which were cosmetic in nature. The scars under her breasts are in a location which suggest either an enlargement or a reduction. I'm afraid I am not adequately familiar with the two procedures to be able to tell the difference. There are also scars on each leg, which relate to some kind of thigh reduction. Are these things not suggestive?"

But Rainey hardly gave Mothersole time to respond.

"In addition you will already have noticed that the woman enjoyed a deep tan, which is well defined in what one might call the bikini region. Or shall I say, the monokini region, as there is no equivalent shading on the chest, indicating that the woman sunned topless, as they rather misleadingly describe such activity. At this time of year maintenance of a dark tan, whether by natural or artificial means is at least consistent with a degree of affluence."

"Please don't stop now, Mr. Rainey."

"All things considered ... affluence, cosmetic surgery ... I would be inclined to think that the woman is of American origin."

"Are you leading me to Maxwell and his wife?" asked Inspector Mothersole.

"Yes," Rainey said sharply. "But not in the sense you mean, Inspector. I think that the dead woman is Chester Maxwell's wife."

"Alex!" Pru said.

"The sheerest, most impudent speculation of course." Rainey leaned back relaxedly, enjoying the moment of revelation enormously.

"I think," said Inspector Mothersole, "that you have made something of an existential leap to your conclusion, Mr. Rainey."

"Mmmm, perhaps, perhaps," Rainey said. Then, "Still, we were led initially to the Maxwells if you consider that the Hirous are quite completely wrapped up in their struggle with each other, that Mr. Bates is preoccupied with making trouble for other people, and that I would not have been involved in murdering anybody in such a boring and prosaic manner however puzzling the circumstances."

"Not exactly evidential, however," Inspector Mothersole said.

"No. But I am able to embroider my speculation in such a way as to offer you a number of points at which to test my hypothesis. Consider the overview first. Suppose Chester Maxwell and the real Candy leave their home for a period of extended foreign travel. If Candy were to disappear, or be replaced, there are no friends, neighbors or relatives around to notice. Maxwell and the new Candy can live as man and wife in obscure foreign countries like this one for as long as they like. For a motive to murder rather than divorce, we might guess that the couple's money was Candy's rather than Chester's."

"Is that an example of one of the places to test your hypothesis?" Mothersole asked.

"In a moment," Rainey said dismissively. "Pru, you said that it was Candy who checked in and picked up the night key yesterday afternoon."

"That's right."

"Well, suppose Chester and the real Candy were together yesterday and that our Candy had the night key copied. That by some prearrangement Candy left the original key for Chester to pick up and that Chester and the real wife returned to the hotel using that key. Did your Candy ask what time we were likely to go to bed?"

"Why yes. I told her about eleven."

"And they get here at a quarter past twelve. They get upstairs without meeting anybody. He tucks Candy in — maybe she even has a sleeping pill — and he suffocates her after she has fallen asleep. Our Candy lets herself in at two-thirty to help put the body in the spare room and help tidy up. When Chester and Candy come down to breakfast this morning, you recognize Mrs. Maxwell as the woman who picked the key up from you yesterday and all the bits and pieces fit."

"Yes, I see," Pru said.

"Points to check out," Rainey said. "First, the new Candy would need a signal to show that everything had gone smoothly and she could enter the hotel. You might ask Mrs. Westerbeck whether an upstairs light was still on here at two-thirty. Second, I would think that a close examination of the Maxwells's luggage would turn up the duplicate night key. Of course, a photograph of the dead woman sent to police in the Maxwells' own town, for showing to the Maxwells' friends and neighbors will sort things out in a definitive fashion."

12

Rainey lay in bed with his eyes closed and a pained expression on his face.

Seeing this, Pru said, "Come on now, it wasn't that bad. You're just tired from all that thinking."

"It's raining again," Rainey said. "What a bloody awful dark dank little country this is. One season to the next the only thing that changes is that the rain is colder or warmer."

Pru sighed, then said, "Though Inspector Mothersole tried to pass it off, he was impressed. He was definitely impressed."

"Oh, he would have got it in the end," Rainey said. "He may be steeped in the dung of English rural life, but there are no flies on Mothersole. I wouldn't have butted in, but I just couldn't bear to wait. Imagine! Extra days here!"

"Oh, it's not so bad."

Rainey was quiet for a moment before he said, "What do you mean it's not so bad?"

"Just that I rather like running a guest house. A lot of people passing through."

"Yes," Rainey said, mimicking, "Mr. Rainey, there's a fly in my cider. Mr. Rainey, the honeymooners next door are keeping me awake. Mr. Rainey..."

"Maybe I'll have a little chat with Wendy and Terry when they get back."

"I need a drink," Rainey said mournfully.

"That's a smashing idea," Pru said. "We'll drink on it."

Reluctantly, Rainey got out of bed.

"Mine with ice please, dear," Pru said. And then, "Alex, watch — "

But the warning came too late as Rainey's forehead made a solid contact with the top of the bedroom door frame.

Danny Gets It Right

BEING VICE PRESIDENT is not nearly as time consuming as people seem to think.

Oh sure, I have to defend freedom and democracy, but not that many people die around the world. Not important ones. So I get time to try to be interested in things and to go places and to meet people. Geo thinks it's very important to get a feel for the common people so I do whenever I can.

And they appreciate it. Just last night, for instance, Wayne — he's one of our numerous bodyguards and very common — he said, "Excuse me, sir, but Mrs. Quayle asked me to remind you about going to Swan Lake tonight."

"Gosh," I said, "it's a little on the cold side for swimming."

Wayne laughed and said, "Hey, you're grooved in there a lot more than people think, sir."

And I laughed along and said, "I do my best, Wayne."

We go out a lot of nights, Maddy and me. In fact, there are a lot of misconceptions about the Vice Presidency. The time thing is only one of them.

Of course I had a lot of things going for me when I ascended to my high office. For one thing, Geo had already done a lot of Vice Presiding so he could explain all the stuff he wanted me to do.

For another I already knew my way around Washington. I was a Senator for eight years, remember, like Jack Kennedy.

Washington is not nearly as hard to learn your way around as a lot of people think. Of course I had an advantage there too. Way back years ago they hired the same guy to build Washington as built Indianapolis and he used the same plans. So I'll tell you a little trick I use. Whenever I have someplace to go in Washington, I just think of the name of the street it would be in Indianapolis and that way I know where it is.

But what you really want to know about is that murder I solved, isn't it?

Well, it was just one of the things that results from the fact that being Veep doesn't take all the hours that God sends, bless Him.

I mentioned the trip to Swan Lake already because I wanted to show that Maddy and I do a lot of social engagements. Although I don't have official duties at most of them, often as not people ask me to comment on one thing or another and because I am important they take a lot of notice of what I say. So even when I'm not being VP, I can't get away from it, if you know what I mean. So it's a full time job all right. I may get a lot of spare time but it's not as spare as other people's.

Of course I do have a lot of specific jobs and not just to go to funerals or to generals in South America. I am in charge of the Senate and that helps me keep in touch with a lot of my old friends and use my influence. And I am Head of the National Space Council. That takes some time.

Not that I know everything there is to know about space. Well, nobody does, do they? Space is a huge area. There's a lot of uncharted waters in space and one of our jobs is to draw a map of them. But I read about space when I get a chance and I get a lot of experts to read even more about it. Nobody expects me to know where all the streets are out there and I'm sure they weren't designed by that great guy who did Indianapolis and Washington. I mean, they were designed by God, of course. Now there *is* a great guy.

But I mentioned space because it's an example of how when I have to do something I don't know all about I get to have experts. In fact I have a lot of experts.

In fact I even have an expert on being Vice President. That's Pete. He's a real talented young lawyer and he's a great guy and a friend of Geo's and of Jim Baker's. That's one of the things about being in this team. Everybody cares. Important guys like Geo and Jim take time from their busy schedules to show an interest in just about everything I say and do. Not that they're more important than me. Well, they are, but not in the fundamental kind of way because everybody is equal really, and that's one of the things that made this country great.

But they do care and that helps me care about them. Especially Geo, of course, because he's the one who took me out of Indiana and put me into the world. I really love the guy. Well, you know what I mean. It's OK for a guy to love a guy that way. I mean, I would really miss him if he was gone. I mean, for instance, if Geo died or something, well I just don't know what I'd do.

But the murder I solved, you want to know about that.

It began, I think I'd have to say, when Maddy and I went to this dinner at the Fortesques in Georgetown. I remember it because I had just been to a track meet at Tucker's school and all the arrangements went wrong. First the camera crews got there late. Then my limousine, VP-1, wouldn't start so I had to catch a cab from the kids' school.

And I remember the taxi driver, a fully equal person of color, and I talked to him, because it was a chance to talk to a common person and there also wasn't much else to do.

So I said to him, "Hey, how about that deep doodoo Marion Barry's in?"

The driver didn't say anything at first, so I waited. He might have been a little confused — which often happens when I speak to common people. Or maybe he even hadn't heard about it, because not everyone watches television, you know.

But at the next red light he turned to me and he said, "Did you hear the latest Dan Quayle joke?"

I was a little surprised, but I said, "Hey, you know, I *am* Dan Quayle."

"That's OK," he said. "I'll tell it slowly."

But then the light turned green and I guess he can't drive and talk at the same time. Before long we arrived at the Fortesques.

Marilyn — that's Maddy, my better half, well, not better but equal but different half — she was already there. And as soon as Pete and I walked in the door Maddy and Wayne — he was guarding Maddy's body that day — they came over to me. And with them was another woman. Well, Maddy said, "Oh Danny! The most terrible thing has happened."

"What is it?"

"Robin Fortesque has had another stroke. He's dead."

"He was in a wheel chair anyway, wasn't he?"

"Honey," Maddy said, "I'd like you to meet his daughter, Janine." And she nodded to this other woman.

"How do you do, Mr. Vice President?" the woman said, and she was a pretty cute lady for her age. Not that I would look at another woman than Marilyn, except when I was being introduced or something.

"I'm fine. How are you? Oh, sad I bet because of your Dad."

"Yes," she said.

"We first met Mr. Fortesque last month," Maddy said.

"That's right," I said. I knew it was right, because Maddy's got a heck of a head for stuff like that.

"He told me," Janine said. "You made quite an impression."

"Janine. That's an unusual name," I said. "Is it foreign? Not that there's anything wrong with that, of course. Some of the best names are foreign. Or at least they were."

Geo taught me that: talk about them instead of yourself when you meet them. It's one of the little tricks that's good to do as Veep. He's one great guy, Geo and I'd really really miss him.

"We met in Milwaukee," Maddy said. "There was a convention for stroke victims that Danny was invited to."

And then I remembered, there had been this big party with all these people in wheel chairs. I'd talked about wheel chair basketball and the technological advances that had been made and how good for the game it would be when they made wheel chairs that could jump.

"I remember," I said. "Your dad was the one whose wife kept giving him licorice, wasn't he? That's your mom, right?"

"He certainly seemed to like his licorice," Maddy said, not without a certain pride in her spouse's memory.

But this lady Janine looked at me in the strangest way. In fact it was so strange I turned to Pete and whispered, "Do I have a pimple on my nose or something?"

But before he could say "No sir, Mr. Vice President, sir," or "Yes sir, Mr. Vice President, sir," Janine grabbed me by the lapels.

Wayne was about to kill her when I said, "It's all right, Wayne."

You see, I didn't think that Janine meant it personally. And two deaths in one family on the same day would be a real shame.

Anyway she said to me, this Janine — and she was shouting — "Did you say that my father's wife gave Daddy licorice?"

"Yeah. Lots of it. In fact, he didn't eat anything else at this party, did he, Maddy? Even though it was a buffet and all the food was free and it was on a low table so guys like him could get at it. Isn't that right, Maddy?"

"Yes," Maddy said. "He ate a lot of licorice."

Then I said, "I like licorice all right even though it's black, but I wonder whether eating so much is good for a person."

Well, at that, this woman Janine screamed. She did! A real scream. And she ran away.

"Boy," I said, "her daddy ought to teach her some manners."

Of course people of foreign origination have different ideas of manners. That's one of the things you have to learn real fast when you're Vice President. I remember Geo told me, almost first thing, "Danny," he said, "you're going to have to get used to the fact that not everybody is like you."

And it's true. You do have to get used to it.

Well this Janine had no sooner run away screaming than she came back leading this old guy by the arm.

"Tell him," she said to me. "Tell him."

"Please don't shout at me, lady," I said. "You may be an orphan but that's no excuse to shout because I'm not deaf. In fact I don't allow anyone to shout at me unless they're my superior officers in the National Guard or members of the Cabinet. And," I added stingingly, "you aren't either one of those."

"Tell him about Daddy and the licorice!"

Pete whispered, "That's the Surgeon General, sir."

"Oh," I said. I turned to the old guy. "Sorry sir," and I saluted. "What was it I can do for you?"

"Janine has just told me that you saw her father being fed a lot of licorice last month."

"That's right."

"Well spotted, Mr. Vice President. I congratulate you."

"Uh, thank you sir."

Another thing Geo taught me was when someone congratulates you, thank them. You don't get congratulated that often in life that you can afford to turn one down.

Then the General and Janine went away again.

I took Maddy to one side and I whispered to her, "I know I am supposed to be friendly to everybody, but that Janine is really a pain in the neck, don't you think?"

But just about then I was introduced to the Botswana Ambassador, so I had to concentrate. In fact he looked like a chauffeur my Uncle Gene use to have. The chauffeur was pretty prickly so I said to this guy, "I don't want to offend you, so maybe the best thing is for you to tell me up front just what kind of ambassador a Botswana Ambassador is."

And that was the last I heard about Janine until I got the letter.

"Dear Mr. Vice President," it began. "My stepmother got sentenced to Life Imprisonment this morning and I wanted to thank you."

And then there was a lot of technical stuff. In fact, I was busy reading up on space and I thought about just sending a standard "You're Welcome" letter but then Maddy came in and I showed it to her.

"Oh my," she said.

That kind of annoyed me. Not in any significant way, because a love like ours is too strong for anything significant, but anybody can get annoyed sometimes. "Your what?"

"Do you remember Janine Fortesque?"

Well, of course I did.

"She's written to thank you for telling her about the licorice."

"Oh," I said. "What about it?"

"Well Janine is a doctor."

I hadn't realized that, but of course we are getting more and more foreign doctors over here these days.

"It turns out that what you said about her father being fed licorice *proved* that his wife murdered him."

"Murdered him? How?"

"With the licorice."

"They were only little pieces."

"Being a doctor," Maddy said, "Janine knew that licorice raises the blood pressure."

"It does?"

"It's all here. Glycerrhizinic acid in the licorice affects the adrenal gland and stimulates aldosterone production which promotes sodium absorption, hence fluid retention and elevated blood pressure."

"Oh," I said.

"Janine's stepmother was feeding Mr. Fortesque licorice in order to keep his blood pressure up so that he would have another stroke and die. And he did. And so the stepmother just got convicted of murder so Janine will inherit seventy-five million dollars."

"Wow!"

"So Janine's written to thank you. Without you, her stepmother would never have been convicted."

"Those stepmothers can really do it to you sometimes, can't they?"

"Danny," Maddy said, "you ought to let the world know about your part in bringing this murderer to justice."

"Do you think so?"

"Definitely."

So, world, that was the story. And boy, I'll tell you this: am I glad I never really liked licorice all that much anyway!

Danny Pulls His Weight

No SOONER HAD I walked in the door that day in May than Pete ran up and said, "Where have you *been*, Mr. Vice President?"

Pete is a real nice guy and he's a great help to Geo, but he seemed upset so I tried to calm him down. That's one of the things I've had a lot of practice at in my first four years, calming people down. I said, "No place public, Pete. Don't worry." In fact, I was just back from my lip-reading class, and that's about as private as you can get.

"We've been looking all over for you, Mr. Vice President. The President wants to see you, *now!*"

"But I haven't done anything," I said. And that's exactly what Geo asked me to do, what with the start of the election campaign. Anyhow I followed along after Pete and, sure enough, Geo was waiting for me, and he was with another man.

Geo said, "Come in, Dan. Sit down," so I did. I try to do everything Geo says, which is an important part of my job, as I see it. The reason I signed up for the lip-reading class was because Geo told me to read his.

"I don't think you've met Harmon Kettlemeyer," Geo said.

"No, sir, I haven't."

"Harmon is our nation's finest spin doctor."

"Wow!" I said. One of the neat things about being Vice President is you get introduced to all kinds of important people. "Pleased to meet you, Dr. Kettlemeyer. But I sure hope you being here doesn't mean our nation's spin is sick."

"We called you in," Dr. Kettlemeyer said, "so you don't worry about a rumor you may have heard."

"What rumor would that be, sir?"

"The rumor that the President is going to dump you and find a vice presidential candidate who would strengthen the ticket."

"I want you to know, Dan," Geo said, "that I will only do that over my dead body. You can count on that. No new vice presidents."

"In fact," Dr. Kettlemeyer said, "to show the President's continuing confidence in you, we have a whole campaign issue we want you to handle personally."

"A whole issue? Me?"

"Mr. President, perhaps you'd care to explain what we have in mind."

"Dan, you know that the safety aspect of life in the states of our union has gone through hell, coming off a pinnacle, you might say, of being lower. Personal safety is a little furry-feathery kind of guy who needs protecting. We've got to find a proper balance between the excesses of the regulatory movement and the excesses on the rape, pillage and plunder side. I'm not asking you to cry for Argentina, you know, or anybody else, but I'm getting sick and tired of hearing those carping little liberal Democrats jumping all over our you-know-what."

"Me too, sir," I said.

Dr. Kettlemeyer said, "To reiterate, Mr. Vice President, we want you to be at the forefront of the fine work this administration has done to promote the issue of law and order."

"Law and order? But that's important!"

"It sure is, Dan," Geo said.

Dr. Kettlemeyer said, "You're going out to Indianapolis next week, I believe, Mr. Vice President."

"That's right, sir," I said. "They have a big car race out there and because I'm such a famous Hoosier, I get to be the Grand Marshal."

"Perfect." Dr. Kettlemeyer smiled and he nodded to Geo.

"And after the race there's a banquet at a hotel and somebody gives a speech there, which might be me, though I'll have to amplify on that." `

"Good," Dr. Kettlemeyer said. "They are both big, public occasions, aren't they, Mr. Vice President?"

"Yes, sir, they are."

"Now put your thinking cap on, Mr. Vice President. At these big, public occasions, how do you think that you could show the greatest possible confidence in George Bush's safer, more law-abiding America?"

"I give up, sir. How?"

"By going to Indianapolis without your bodyguards, Mr. Vice President."

❖ ❖

The day of the 500 Mile Race is a big day in Indianapolis — though I'd be the first to say that Indianapolis has lots and lots of big days, every single year. It's not a one-big-day town, no way.

But the 500 is such a big day that there's a parade before the race, and that's what has to have a Grand Marshal, which was me. Being a Grand Marshal is probably not the job that a person who hasn't been a vice president thinks it is. There's no badge and no gun either. However, Dr. Kettlemeyer did give me a big white stetson hat. He said it would remind everybody of law and order and of good guys. And he made me promise I'd wear it all the time I was in

Indianapolis.

And I did, I wore it every minute through my Grand Marshalling which, to tell the truth, was mostly riding around in an open car and waving at everybody. Well, not *everybody* in the sense of every specific body. There were far too many bodies to wave at them individually. If I did that, it would take much too long, probably the whole day, and there wouldn't be time left for a race at all, which is not the point.

It all went OK, praise the Lord, and I didn't fall out of the car, even though it was open. Then I went to the Grand Marshal's bulletproof box seat and that's where I got to watch the race.

But after the race cars started their engines a surprising thing happened, which was a knock at the door of the box. I didn't know what it could be, but it turned out to be a man knocking on the door. When he came in he said, "Don't get agitated, Mr. Vice President. Harmon Kettlemeyer sent me. He thought you might be getting bored without your bodyguards to talk to, so I'm here to make your visit more interesting."

"If you're from Dr. Kettlemeyer," I said, "then you'll know I'm supposed to be proving Geo's America is safer. Are you *sure* you're not a bodyguard?"

The man smiled and said, "Scout's honor, Mr. Vice President. I am no bodyguard."

To tell the truth, it does get pretty boring when you sit in a box wearing a stetson and waiting to see if a car that went past a minute ago is going to come past again. I know that was not the most diplomatic thing I could have said, but I didn't say it loud and after all, I'm not a diplomat, I'm a vice president.

And the man from Dr. Kettlemeyer, whose name was Euple, understood immediately. He said, "You know, sir, I think I could find a little action for you."

I didn't see exactly what he was getting at, but one of the tricks I've picked up now that I am more mature as Vice President is not to let on right away when I don't understand something. Instead I say, "Would you care to amplify on that?" which is what I said to Euple.

"Oh, don't get me wrong," Euple said. "I'm not talking about anything that would interest the Drug Enforcement Agency."

"I should think not," I said. "I'm not a senator now."

"Or anything immoral," Euple said.

"I never claimed that I was *completely* like Jack Kennedy."

"But what I had in mind was that we could go for a ride tonight after your official engagement."

"I can't get mixed up in any engagement either," I said. "I'm already married."

Euple looked at me for a minute and then he laughed. "They told me you didn't have any sense of humor, Mr. Vice President, but they were wrong."

"They sure were," I said. "I went to Arizona quite a few times when I was a kid because my grandad, Eugene, lived near there. So I think I have quite a good sense of Yuma."

"Yup," Euple said, "you're a lot sharper than they say, aren't you, sir?"

"Would you care to amplify on that?"

He laughed again and he said, "The ride I had in mind was in a special police car."

"You mean I might be able to get a hands-on seat-of-the-pants taste of law and order?"

"That's the idea, sir. It's what Harmon Kettlemeyer said you were here for."

"That's a great plan, Euple," I said. "Because there's nothing I want more than to do my bit for Geo's re-election. If Geo isn't re-elected, boy, I'd be so upset! I just don't know what I'd do, except maybe go onto the Supreme Court!"

"Sir, what I thought was that after the big 500 Dinner tonight, I'll wink at you twice and that'll be the sign that you should follow me and we'll pretend we're going to the men's room."

"You're not from the National Endowment for the Arts are you, Euple?"

"Me? No, sir. Not me. No way. Chill out. Uh uh."

"Even so, do you think that we could come up with some other sign?"

"OK I'll tug on my left ear lobe."

"And what happens then?"

"We'll go out back and that's where we'll meet the special police car that'll take you for the ride."

∗ ∗

Euple's great plan almost went wrong because I was nearly missed the Dinner. The first thing that happened was I spotted a neat golf course inside the oval at the race track and I probably would have succumbed to temptation except I couldn't work out a way to fly there.

Then I realized I'd left my invitation back in Washington. That was because it's Marilyn, my precious but equal wife, who looks after our invitations. What I forgot was that she wasn't with me in Indianapolis because she desperately needed some quality time at her word processor. So when I showed up at the hotel for the banquet, the guard wouldn't let me in.

"I'm sorry, sir," he said. "I can't let you in without your invitation. We have Vice President Quayle here tonight."

"But I *am* Vice President Quayle."

"That's what you say, sir, but how can I be sure without seeing your invitation? Suppose I let you in and you turn out not to be who you say you are and then you bump off who you say you are because you're not. Think of the trouble I'd be in."

"But those two guys who got here just before I did didn't have invitations."

"Ah," the guard said, "but they proved who they were."

"How did they do that?"

"Well, the first gentleman said he was Placido Domingo and he sang me a few notes and I could tell right away he was the real Mr. Domingo and I let him in. And the next guy said he was Yo-Yo Ma and he played me a few bars on his cello, and I could tell right away he was the real Mr. Ma and I let him in."

"That's not fair," I said. "Who *are* these Domino and Mom guys?"

"Ah!" the guard said, "please enter, Mr. Quayle."

⁜ ⁜

The banquet was more fun than the Marshalling. I sat next to a man who made tires and he told me a fact I didn't know: that in a racing car tire they use enough rubber on the tread to make more than 350 condoms.

When it came time for someone to speak it turned out to be me. I decided to use what I had just learned, but it seemed only right to give credit where it was due. I said, "I am here in Indianapolis to help remind people of law and order in our kinder, safer America. And speaking of safety, did you know they use enough rubber on the tread of a tire to make more than 350 condoms? Of course that's in a Goodyear."

Then the Master of Ceremonies said, "Sounds like a *really* good year to me."

"Would you care to amplify on that?"

And he said, "Maybe you'll need a pocket calculator to keep track."

"No, I won't," I said. "I already know how many pockets I have."

Anyway, people seemed to get the message.

After I made my speech Euple pulled on his ears and winked at me too and I thought, what the heck. I excused myself and went to the restroom with Euple and he led me out of the hotel by a back way. But there was no special police car waiting there, so I asked where it was.

"I'm sure it'll be here any minute," Euple said. "But, Mr. Vice President, where's your stetson?"

"I left it at the banquet."

"Go and get it!" he said.

But to tell the truth, the stetson had started chafing the tops of my ears, which is why I took it off. Besides, it wasn't as white as it was before, due to a little accident during the soup. "It'll be all right," I said. "They'll save it for me."

"But you've got to have it!" Euple said, and I was surprised at his bossy attitude, which is not what I am used to away from home.

I said, "I'm sure Dr. Kettlemeyer will understand. I'll take full responsibility."

Just then a big, dark car turned into the alley from the street, and Euple got even more excited and he started jumping and signalling to it. Sure enough, the car slowed down when it got near us, but then it suddenly speeded up again and drove away, so it must not have been the special police car after all.

Euple was still upset, so I tried to calm him down. I said, "Pull yourself together," but it didn't seem to help.

We waited in the alley another fifteen minutes, but the special police car never came. By that time I was getting nervous too, and I said, "I don't think it's smart waiting any longer, Euple. Downtown Indianapolis is a dangerous neighborhood, you know. Guys standing around are sitting targets."

But Euple didn't seem to comprehend what I was saying, so I said, "You have a car, don't you? Why don't you just take me for the ride yourself?" And in the end that's what he did.

Even so Euple never relaxed. Probably it was because he wasn't used to having a vice president in his car. For the whole time his voice was husky and tense.

My voice used to get that way, but that was before I had so much experience at being the Vice President. It happened most when I had press conferences all by myself. These days, though, I am a lot stronger with the media, which is how you have to handle them. For instance I'm on record for making it clear to critics of Geo's that when there's unfair criticism going his way I will respond in kind.

✣ ✣

Euple drove away from the center of town but he didn't drive very fast, like he was making up his mind where to go. That was understandable because Indianapolis has many, many fine sights to sightsee, even at night, and some of them as late as 1.30 or 2 in the morning.

But we didn't get very far at all. Just about the time Euple seemed to make a decision and start driving faster, we came to a big obstruction in the road, and it was made up of police cars. We came around a corner and there they were, and it was all Euple could do to dent only the one car just a little bit.

A lot of policemen crowded around and they were not very happy with Euple and, to be perfectly honest, some of the language they used was the worst I'd heard since I was in the National Guard.

But fair's fair, so I got out and said, "Don't blame him. He was only trying to keep me from getting bored."

"And who in tarnation are you?" one of them said.

"I'm Dan Quayle," I said, and it was very exciting for them.

The police were all together because there had just been an FBI raid on some notorious interstate criminals and one of the feds had been murdered. A call had gone out on the police radios which is why there were so many police cars in the street. They'd all been in a hurry and hadn't had time to park neatly.

The corpse was in the middle of a room and a whole crowd of people were questioning each other and looking around in case the murderer was still there. I went to have a look at the body, which I have to say was not nearly as well done as on TV, because the blood was spattered all over everything and very messy. I even got some on my shoe. "Ugh, look at that," I said.

The policeman next to me said, "Look at what, sir?" and he bent down. But right away he stood up again. He said, "Tank! Come here!"

Tank, who was another policeman, came over and the first policeman said, "Mr. Quayle has spotted something red under the fed." Tank looked and then he pulled out a red baseball cap.

The first thing that occurred to me was that maybe it would cheer Euple up if I put it on, even though it wasn't a stetson. I said, "Can I see?" and Tank gave me the cap.

I turned it over to see if it was my size and it was then I saw that there was blood on the hatband. In this day and age it's not a good idea to put a hat like that on, not if your ears are chafed. But it was a real nice cap and the label said, "J.C. Pennies," so when I gave the cap back to Tank I said, "I bet a nice cap like this costs more than pennies."

Tank looked at the cap real hard, and he suddenly said, "Well spotted, sir!"

And rest of the story is history now.

❖ ❖

When I got back to Washington Dr. Kettlemeyer was terribly upset when I called to tell him about the murder, but he is the kind of guy who tries hard to make the best of things. Elections are won and lost from lots of issues, but I certainly think I did my bit for law and order.

It turned out that the baseball cap was part of a batch for "J.C. Penney's" but the cap company took the order over the phone. When they delivered the order, Mr. Penney wouldn't accept it because the spelling was wrong. What the company did then was sell the caps to a mail order catalogue and when police asked the mail order company how many caps they'd sold in Indianapolis, it was only the one and they had the address. Then the police drove over and picked up the killer.

The whole thing was a very great coincidence and a very handy one because, as it happened, that very same night another murder took place in Indianapolis, and almost at the very same time.

Tank drove me back to town — because we couldn't find Euple anywhere — and he told me all about this other murder on the way. It seems that a man dressed like a waiter was shot in an alley, and nobody knew why. With there being two murders the same night, it was lucky for the police that the first was an easy one. The police hadn't identified the dead man in the alley but Tank said he had a white hat and that was probably a good clue.

It seemed like another big coincidence to me. That very same night I had told Euple how dangerous it can be in an alley, even though America is a wonderful, safe place with Geo. But even a great man like Geo can't be everywhere at the same time which is another reason why it's important to have a Vice President who does everything he can to help.

The Stranger

A S THE BUS pulled into Jesper, Indiana, the stranger took his Gladstone bag from the overhead rack. Almost alone on the bus, he was the only passenger to alight. As he passed the driver he said, "Thanks awfully. You gave us a smashing drive." The driver turned his head toward the voice, but the stranger had already begun to descend the steps to the new town.

Four people waited on the curb. The bus would continue in the direction of Bedford and Bloomington, eventually arriving in Indianapolis before dark. The fat man at the front of the line made space for the stranger, but not a lot. Even so the stranger smiled and nodded to the man, and then he nodded to each of the other would-be passengers, all women. None gave him a second glance.

❖ ❖

The bus stop in Jesper is on the main street. The stranger considered which direction to walk in and picked what seemed to be toward the middle of the town. As he walked he shifted his bag from one hand to the other and, later, back again. Finally he found a motel that seemed to be the only accommodation not part of a national chain. It was called the Sunrest and outside the door marked "Reception," he took a breath, lifted his chin, and muttered "Jolly good." Then he walked in.

A middle-aged couple shared a couch as they watched an early afternoon game show. Once they noticed the stranger the woman turned the sound down by remote control and the man rose, walked to the reception counter, and said, "Do something for you, mister?"

"I believe you can, my good man," the stranger said. "But first may one say this is a remarkably lovely town you reside in?"

The man took a moment to consider this unexpected response to his question. The stranger's voice caused the woman to look, and then rise from her chair.

Cautiously the man said, "You think so?"

"Oh I do!" the stranger said with enthusiasm. "The more one travels, the more one comes to appreciate the virtues of small, honest towns in the heartland of this wonderful country of yours. The people in such places recognize what's important in life and they concentrate on it. Family. Business. Hospitality. It's wonderful, truly refreshing."

"You talk funny," the man said.

From behind his shoulder the woman's head appeared. "You're English, huh?"

The stranger smiled broadly. "I am, madam, I am. You are remarkably perceptive, if one may say so."

"I've heard your kind of talk on the TV," the woman said. "He is, Glen. He's English!"

"English, huh?" Glen said. The tone of Glen's nasal voice was neutral but the face was welcoming. "My daddy was over there during the war. He was somewheres called Pontyfrat. You ever been to Pontyfrat?"

"I certainly have," the stranger said. "What an astonishing coincidence! I know Pontefract well."

"Well I'll be jiggered," Glen said. "Did you hear that, Edie? This here fella knows Pontyfrat."

"Welcome to Jesper, mister," Edie said. "So, what can we do for you?"

"To tell you the truth," the stranger said, "it's a slightly delicate matter."

"No credit," Glen said.

"It's nothing like that," the stranger said. "But my circumstances require considerable discretion. Although, if one may speculate, I'd wager that you both know how to be discreet. You strike one immediately as discreet people."

"Yeah, well maybe," Glen said.

"What's this about, mister?" Edie said.

"I am taking a brief holiday, a vacation as you good folks would say. I need to get away from all the hurly-burly for a while, family pressures. You know the sort of thing?"

"We sure do know about family, all right," Edie said.

"And I must say," the stranger said, "I feel I have come to the right place. I *feel* it. Precisely the right place."

"You have?" Edie said.

"Because you've already shown me exactly the kind of discretion that I shall need if I am to spend a week or two in your best room."

The couple glanced at each other. Glen said, "And what discretion have we shown, mister? 'Cause so far Edie and me have treated you the same as we'd treat anybody that come through that door."

"That's it exactly!" the stranger said. "I will need your assurance that you will treat me precisely as you would treat any other resident in your establishment."

"I don't get you, mister," Glen said. "Is there some reason why we wouldn't't?"

Edie studied the stranger's face.

"Excellent!" the stranger said with a smile. "No reason. No reason at all."

"Now you mention it," Edie said, "you do look kind of familiar."

"Please, madam, don't scour your memory any further." The stranger tugged at an oversized ear. He scratched his beaky nose. He rubbed the bald area at the top of his head. "I really do need to remain entirely incognito. No newspapers. No television. Just your best room for a week, or perhaps two."

"Lord love me, I've got it!" Edie said.

"Please stop!" the stranger said. "Don't even say it. If you do, I shall have to find other premises and that will be a great disappointment, because we were getting along so well."

"Naw," Edie said, changing her mind and shaking her head. "It can't be. Not here in Jesper."

"Thank you for your understanding and your cooperation, madam. Truly, it is most appreciated."

⁜ ⁜

The best room at the Sunrest was only better than the others because it was farther from the street. The stranger unpacked his few clothes and hung them in the closet. Next he enjoyed a hot shower. Then, with a clean shirt, he dressed again, suit, waistcoat, tie. With toilet paper he buffed up his shoes. Then he sat for a while on the bed.

Before long there was a hesitant tapping at his door. Immediately the stranger rose and opened to find Edie standing outside his room.

"Why hello," the stranger said. "What can I do for you?"

"Sorry to bother you, Mr. … Hey, is there something I can call you. I don't know what I'm supposed to say."

The stranger raised a hand and smiled. "Please. My friends call me Chuck."

"No kidding."

"And it would be my pleasure if you and your good husband were to do the same."

"Chuck. Wow!" Edie was giggly with pleasure. "And y'all call me Edie, and my husband's Glen."

"How do you do, Edie," the stranger said. He took one of her hands. He raised it and touched it lightly with his lips. "It is my very great pleasure to make your acquaintance. To tell you the truth, I was on the verge of coming to the office to ask you and Glen for another favour."

"You were?"

"But you've come here first. What can I do for you?"

"For me?"

"You knocked on the door for some reason."

"Oh, yeah. That. I wanted to check everything in the room was OK. You got enough towels and soap and stuff?"

"Everything is spiffing."

"Spiffing?"

"Perfect."

"Oh, great," Edie said. "But if anything goes wrong, you run out of paper or you want another towel, anything at all, you let me know, hear?"

"I will," the stranger said. "I won't hesitate. Thank you."

"So, why was you coming to the office?"

"I wanted a word with you and Glen. I'll meet you there in a couple of minutes. OK?"

✤ ✤

As the stranger entered the Sunrest Motel office, Glen and Edie stood behind the reception desk. Glen said, "Chuck, hi. What can we do for you?"

"First," the stranger said, "I want to refrain from taking advantage of you."

"How's that?" Glen said.

"Is it not customary, when an unknown traveller comes to a motel, for the traveller to make payment arrangements? I don't know how long I shall be able to stay here, of course, but it's only right that I pay in advance for my room tonight." From his wallet the stranger took a one hundred dollar bill. "Do you have change?"

Glen hesitated, but Edie said, "Shucks, we don't need that, Chuck."

"Well," the stranger said, "if you're sure." He put the money away and said, "There is also a favour I would appreciate, if you don't mind my asking."

"Y'all ask away," Edie said.

"I'd like some guidance."

"Guidance? About what?" Glen said.

"When I am away from home, what I enjoy, more than anything, is meeting people. Now, of course, in my situation it's rather difficult, but I thought that perhaps you two kind people could introduce me to a few of the local residents."

"You want to meet folks?" Edie said, eyes widening.

"Only if absolute discretion can be maintained," the stranger said. "But yes, I'd love to meet some of the good citizens of Jesper. Perhaps people in business like yourselves. Or people who entertain."

Edie said, "So you wouldn't mind going to folks' house for dinner or a little party?"

"I wouldn't mind at all," the stranger said, "as long as — "

"No newspapers, no TV. Am I right?" Glen said.

✣ ✣

"Hi. I'm Phil Hoechstadtler, Glen's second cousin and Commissioner of Oaths. Glad to have you aboard."

"It's very gracious of you to extend the invitation at such short notice, Phil," the stranger said.

"Oh hell, no problem with a barbecue. Just throw on another steak. All I got to know is what to call you when it's ready."

"Just call me Chuck," the stranger said. "And make mine medium-rare."

"Come on through, Chuck," Hoechstadtler said. "Everybody is just dying to meet you."

✣ ✣

"This is the most wonderful thrill for us," a woman said nervously as they shared the shelter of a maple upwind of the grill.

"Now now, please!" the stranger said.

"No, it is. We read all about England and everybody and we love them, every one. Though of course some of them we love better than others."

"And what do you do … ?"

"Connie."

"Connie."

"Oh, I'm just a housewife."

"Don't say *just* a housewife. One can hardly have a more complex and intricate task than organising the daily running of a modern household."

"It can be quite a handful," Connie said. "Especially with three teenage boys."

"Don't I know it," the stranger said.

"You got kids?" Connie asked.

"Yes, boys."

"Of course you do. Silly old me." Connie laughed nervously. "Of course, our house is no palace, or anything."

✣ ✣

"So tell me, Chuck," Lenny Kahlenbeck said, "how come you chose a little dump like Jesper to honor with a visit?"

"You do Jesper a serious unkindness," the stranger said. "I think it's most attractive, and in a beautiful part of the state."

"You been through southern Indiana before?"

"Once or twice. Never Jesper, however."

"And you really like it?"

"I certainly do, what I've seen of it."

"You … want to see around? I sell real estate, so I know my way around pretty good."

"Real estate? Property, you mean?"

"That's right," Kahlenbeck said proudly. "I'm not the biggest in Dubois County yet, but I'm on my way."

"Might that include holiday cottages?"

Kahlenbeck squinted. "You mean a vacation home?"

"That's it," the stranger said.

"You interested?"

"I certainly wouldn't mind looking at one or two."

"Hey, you're talking to the right man if you're looking for property in Dubois County. And take it from me, there's not a better part of the state to invest in right now."

❖ ❖

"I read somewhere that you like horses," said an elegantly dressed woman in her thirties. She carried a cocktail glass, but no paper plate of food.

"I can't imagine where you read that," the stranger said, "but it's true. I do like horses, very much."

"I'm Elvira Klingerman," the woman said. She offered her free hand.

The stranger lingered as he shook it. "I'm pleased to meet you, Elvira."

"They say I should call you Chuck and they say I shouldn't ask personal questions."

"I can see you've been well briefed, Elvira. And, I must say, you are an extremely lovely woman."

Elvira laughed. "They also said you were Mr. Charm. I can see why now."

"I do meet quite a lot of women, but it's such a pleasure to meet someone I can compliment sincerely."

There was a moment when neither of them spoke.

Then the stranger said, "Did you ask me about horses for a reason? Do you own some?"

"I do," Elvira said. "Would you like to see them?"

"I would," the stranger said. "Very much."

❖ ❖

"Chuck, this here is my wife, Loretta."

"Hi," Loretta said, nearly spilling her drink.

"How do you do, Loretta," the stranger said. "And what a gorgeous bracelet, if I may say so."

"Diamonds and opals," Loretta said.

"It is good, isn't it," Loretta's husband said. "I can tell you have an eye for good jewels. Of course you would, wouldn't you."

"I try," the stranger said. Delicately he lifted Loretta's arm and looked at the bracelet more closely. "Yes," he said with genuine approval.

"I'm Ben Hanna," Loretta's husband said. "I'm a trained lawyer, but I inherited a jewelry business from my old man and I run that too. It means Loretta gets to wear some real good stuff, and I can write off the insurance because she's advertising it."

"So you might have some pieces that would be suitable for gifts?" the stranger said.

"I sure do. Hell, you've seen this little wrist full of sparklers. Hold it up again, honey."

Loretta Hanna raised her arm unsteadily. At the same time she said, "I think they ought to do laboratory experiments on lawyers instead of rats, don't you? For one thing there's more of them, and for another you can get attached to a laboratory rat."

"Shut up, Loretta."

"Well, excuse my butt, mister smooth talker."

"No more to drink. Understand me."

"Well I *no habla Engles* anymore all of a sudden."

"Excuse me, Chuck," Ben Hanna said. "You come down to the store, see if something grabs you where you can't say no. Anybody can tell you how to get there. Maybe catch you again later, after I sort out this little problem."

❖ ❖

Mrs.Dexter put her arm around the stranger's waist and said, "Hey tell me the truth, will you, Chuck?"

"What about, Mrs.Dexter?"

"About Margaret. I always thought she was the cutest little thing, but then she got a real raw deal over that Captain. And now I hear she's a lush. Is that the truth? 'Cause that would be so sad."

"I'd really rather not talk about that kind of thing, if you don't mind."

"Oh, they told me not to. But c'mon, tell *me* anyhow." She winked. "If you do, I'll have you to dinner. I know all the recipes. You'll go away satisfied. I've never had a complaint yet."

The stranger extricated himself from Mrs.Dexter's grasp. He said, "Please don't press me."

Mrs. Dexter drew back. "Well, excuse *me!* I guess after all those years with a goddamned peroxide alfalfa salad, you're just not up to a *real* meal."

"Margaret is *not* a lush," the stranger said stiffly. "In fact, she has one of the finest minds you would ever care to encounter." He walked away.

❖ ❖

Near the end of the evening the stranger found Glen and Edie watching the Hoechstadtler's television. Edie looked up and said, "About ready to go?"

"Yes, thank you," the stranger said.

"Have you had a good time?"

"Very nice indeed," the stranger said. "Your friends are fascinating people."

"I'd have called them just plain folks," Glen said.

"And they are extremely hospitable. Two even invited me to stay in their homes as their guests. People here are most marvellously friendly."

Edie's face wrinkled up. "Does that mean you're moving out of the Sunrest?"

"No, Edie, I'm not. I never feel that I'm my own man when I'm staying in a house as a guest. Do you know what I mean?"

"I sure do, Chuck," Edie said. "And let me just say, Glen and me are honored to have you in our little motel."

"You've made me feel very comfortable, and very welcome. And I continue to count on your discretion and cooperation."

⁜ ⁜

The next few days were very busy ones for the stranger, and increasingly Edie acted as social secretary, taking messages and keeping track of when the stranger was available for lunch or dinner, for this excursion or that.

The stranger went out several times with Lenny Kahlenbeck to look at substantial homes in various parts of Dubois and adjoining counties. Isolation, as they discussed at length, would be essential because of the need for privacy. Kahlenbeck offered to help with a hi-tech security system too, through a cousin.

The area the stranger found most attractive was near Patoka Lake in the Lick Fork State Recreation Area. But there were tempting houses too in Celestine, Riceville, Bacon and in the ironically named English and Ireland.

By the third afternoon, however, it was clear that the stranger could not be easily satisfied and would not make a hasty purchase.

"But don't get me wrong," Kahlenbeck said. "I respect a careful man, I truly do."

"It *is* beautiful country," the stranger said. "And I certainly appreciate your generosity with your time. I particularly like the modern log cabins. Do you have any more on your files?"

"You've seen everything," Kahlenbeck said.

"But if something else came up, you wouldn't mind my coming back for a look?"

"I sure wouldn't," Kahlenbeck said.

"Good."

"Chuck?"

"Yes?"

"I wondered if I could ask you a little favor."

"What's that?" the stranger said.

"I don't begrudge a minute of it, but I've put in a lot of time with you the last few days."

"And I am very grateful, truly."

"What I was wondering was, would you mind if my little secretary, if she took a picture of the two of us together."

"Oh, I don't know about that," the stranger said.

"It would be just for me, maybe to hang on the wall behind my desk. I know how you want to make sure it didn't get in newspapers or anything."

"Even so," the stranger said. "It's a matter of ... Well, how things are done. What we call protocol."

"Don't you ever have your picture taken with people you meet?"

"Oh, sometimes. For instance, when I'm at a charity function."

"Charity?" Lenny Kahlenbeck's eyes narrowed.

"If, say, a local philanthropist were to make a large charitable donation to one of the causes I espouse. Organic farming, for instance, or population control. Well it would be churlish in such circumstances for me to object to a photograph being taken with the benefactor."

"A donation, huh?" Kahlenbeck said.

"Yes," the stranger said.

"Like, how big a donation is 'large'?"

Having had considerable opportunity to assess the best answer to such a question, the stranger said, "On the order of, say, two thousand dollars."

"I see," Kahlenbeck said.

"So you understand," the stranger said affably, "it's probably best all around to forget the picture, because even if you wanted it I'd need the money in cash."

"Cash?"

"Well think about it. Suppose I took a check. The charity could see immediately where I'd been. And then there would be no chance of my ever being able to buy a secret vacation home here, would there?"

"No," Kahlenbeck said. He considered. "I spose not."

"With no receipt, you wouldn't be able to deduct it as a charitable donation," the stranger said. "But since you'd have the photograph you *could* deduct it as advertising. Especially if it were taken, the two of us together, in front of your real estate office, showing the name in the background."

The photograph was taken the next day.

❖ ❖

The price to Ben Hanna, the lawyer-jeweler, was five thousand. If the stranger had worried that Hanna's legal training would make him balk at dealing in cash, he needn't have. Hanna agreed immediately, making the stranger wonder if, perhaps, he had pitched the level of the charitable contribution too low.

❖ ❖

Elvira Klingerman made her charitable donations in an altogether different manner and the stranger agreed to appear in several photographs with her, all Polaroids. The best were taken in the stables.

❖ ❖

Although the stranger declined to dine with Mrs. Dexter, he twice ate with Connie, her three teenaged sons, and her trucker husband. Connie was "just" a housewife, but she was a marvellous cook.

❖ ❖

In the late afternoon of his fifth day in Jesper, Edie appeared at the door of the stranger's room at the Sunrest with a boy of about five.

"Hello, Edie," the stranger said. "And who is this?"

"This here is Georgie," Edie said. "Georgie's my grandson."

"Is he really a prince, gramma?" Georgie said to Edie. "Are you really a prince?" Georgie asked the stranger.

The stranger kneeled so that he could speak face to face with his chubby, energetic little visitor. "Am I really a prince?" The stranger winked up at Edie. "No, Georgie, I'm not a prince. Not today."

"My mommy says you're a prince."

"That's very nice of her," the stranger said. "But I'd say that *you* were mommy's little prince, wouldn't you?"

"What do you have to do to be a *real* prince?" Georgie asked.

"Well, gee," the stranger said, "I don't know. I guess you've got to be real good. Are you going to do that? Are you going to be real good and see if you can be a prince too?"

"OK," Georgie said, and then a horn sounded behind him and his grandmother.

"There's daddy," Edie said.

The stranger shook Georgie's hand, but the boy pulled away and ran to his father's car. Both Edie and the stranger waved until the vehicle pulled out onto the street.

Then Edie stepped away and faced the stranger. She said, "I know."

"Excuse me, Edie?"

"I said that I *know*."

"What do you know?"

"I know what you've been doing."

The stranger said nothing.

"I have trouble sleeping sometimes," Edie said. "I leave Glen where he's laying and I watch the all night news. Last night they had some news from England. They showed the Queen of England and all her kids, and the program was about how hard it is on all of them, being royal."

The stranger was ready with a speech about the use of doubles, lookalikes, hired to enable members of the Royal Family to get time to relax away from home, away from the paparazzi.

But Edie said, "You never claimed to be him, did you? Not in so many words."

"No, I didn't" the stranger said.

"I've been thinking about it all day long. Glen even asked me what's the matter, but he knows I'm funny sometimes when I don't sleep, so he stopped asking."

The stranger considered saying he was sorry.

Edie said, "Thinking about it, I can't see as there's a lot of harm you've done. A lot of folks have had a good time because you was around, though I expect there's some that's paid for it. No more than they could afford, I shouldn't wonder."

The stranger said, "Thank you Edie. You're a generous hearted woman."

"Oh no, I'm not," she said. "And I'm also not the only one in town that can't sleep sometimes."

"What do you want me to do?"

"I want you to pack your bags."

"All right."

"And then I want you to go down to the office. I want you to shake Glen's hand, and I want you to pay your room bill. You got enough money to do that?"

"Yes."

"You pay that bill in full, because it would about destroy Glen if he gave you credit and you didn't pay."

"I'll pay the bill in full," the stranger said.

"And then you get the hell out of Jesper," Edie said.

"Is there a bus? Or a train?"

"I don't know, and I don't care. But I want you out of this town before the sun goes down, and I don't you stop moving till you're a hundred miles away. And don't you never come back. Most folks, when they're leaving, I say to them, 'Don't be a stranger now.' But you *be* a stranger, mister, or I'll have your hide, Glen or no Glen."

"I'll be on my way inside the hour," the stranger said

Night Shift

"ALL RIGHT," Powder said as he closed the shift's announcement book, "now get out there and be *good* cops."

The second half of Night Shift pushed its chairs back and began to rise. As they did, many spoke to their neighbors. Powder heard more of what was said than they thought, including, "So only he gets to be the 'bad' cop?"

"He" smiled. To the room in general and no one in particular he said, "God, I hate the noise those chairs make when they scrape across the floor. It makes me think of dentists. You guys ought to have better equipment, including better chairs."

"We're not all 'guys'," Kaneesha Williams said. "In case you hadn't noticed, Lieutenant."

"The word is used generically these days, in case *you* hadn't noticed, Allopetia," Powder said. Although it was wrong to say that Powder hadn't noticed that the shift was not all "guys" in the old way the word was used. He had noticed Williams in particular. She worked hard. He liked her.

She, however, didn't like his comment. He could see it in her face.

Well, tough titty.

From the right side of his desk someone said, "Maybe what we need isn't better chairs but a better floor." This was Kirsh, one of the fast-track kids.

"Yeah, deep pile carpet," Kirsh's fast-track buddy said. "To go with recliners."

Powder frowned as he tried to remember the buddy's name. He wasn't expected to know, it being only his second night with the shift, but that was all the more reason to. He struggled to fit a name with the face. Damn. He'd do another run through the personnel files before he went out on patrol. Was there time before the rider arrived? Could he make time?

"Or maybe, Lieutenant, huch-huch, maybe you ought to have, a better dentist, huch-huch."

The name of the owner of the stupid huch-huch laugh Powder did remember. "Stay for a minute, Mitchell."

"What?" Huch-huch Mitchell was tall, young, bulky and the shift's most recent graduate from the Police Academy. He was also not the brightest spark in the campfire.

67

"Stop moving toward the door," Powder said.

"Sir?"

"Do I have to superglue your feet? Do not leave the room, Officer. Cease exiting. Got it? ¿*Entiendo?*" There was muffled laughter from those of Night Shift who had not yet left for their cars.

"Yes sir," Mitchell said. The tone of his voice transparently asked, "What have I done wrong?"

Powder shuffled the documents on his desk to allow Mitchell's anxiety to increase. Then he picked up a sheet of paper and turned to the young man.

"Is there a problem, sir?"

"Do you think there is a problem?"

Mitchell's frown showed plainly that he couldn't think of any problem he wanted to admit to.

"Well?" Powder said.

"I don't know, sir."

"That's good, Mitchell."

"It is?"

"Never be too certain of yourself."

"Sir?"

"A good cop always questions things. Could I have done that better? Did what I just say mean what I meant it to mean to the person I just said it to?"

A pause. "Sir?"

"Now," Powder said, as he waved the paper in his hand, "do you know what this is?"

"Uh, no."

"It's a waiver."

"Oh."

Not a clue, Powder thought. "For a rider. What would you say if I asked you to take out a rider tonight?"

"A rider? Tonight? Me?".

"Do you have a problem with that, Officer Mitchell?"

"Uh well ..."

"Is your hesitation because it would interfere with collecting bribes from the drug dealers in your sector?"

"I don't take bribes!" the shocked, young Mitchell protested.

Mildly Powder said, "So everything's copacetic then."

"It's what?"

Powder knew a lot of words that began with "cop" but he opted to delay elaboration to another time. The rider was due to arrive at any minute. "You'll be able to cope."

"It's just ... I never had a rider before, sir."

"But you know about the program."

"People can ride with us on a shift to see how we work."

"To help members of the community understand our work better, Mitchell. As long as they sign away the right to make a claim if something nasty should happen to them." Powder waved the waiver again.

"But ..." Mitchell began.

"Why you?"

Mitchell nodded.

"Because the Chief asked me to pick the best man for the job."

Mitchell frowned, transparently torn between asking about why he was the "best man" and asking about the Chief's involvement.

"The new Chief and I are like that," Powder said. He wrapped two fingers over each other. "Haven't you heard the rumors?"

"Uh, not that one, sir."

"He's a fine man, Mitchell. Don't let any of the complainers tell you different just because he didn't come up through the ranks. Chief Cody wants nothing more than to make this a better, more effective police department, and anyone dedicated to doing that should be all right by you."

"Sir."

"In fact the new Chief is setting me up a special assignment so I can help him."

"Yeah?"

"It's something he thinks only I can do because nobody in the department likes me."

"Sir?"

"If I have no friends then I can be impartial. But until the special assignment is worked out, I am filling in by taking charge of roll calls on shifts where the regular officer is away, for whatever reason. Like your Lieutenant Turk."

"Oh."

"For a fine man like the Chief, I'll help out wherever I can. And you should too. Which is why you should be glad to let this foreign visitor ride with you tonight."

"Foreign?"

"Didn't I mention it? Your rider's Japanese."

"Japanese?"

"That means 'from Japan', Mitchell. Televisions ... Cars ... The Nobel prizewinner, Kawabata ..."

"Uh, sure, sir, but I don't ... Well I never was much good at languages."

"Pity. I guess we'll just have to make do with the amount of English you already know then, won't we?"

✢ ✢

Powder was looking at personnel file pictures and testing himself on the names that went with them when there was a knock on the open door behind him. He ignored it. Echiaverra, Carla. The left-handed one. And Flaherty. Tony? Something with T. Tim. Yes.

"Lieutenant Powder?" The voice was female and unfamiliar.

"One sec," he said with a sigh. He flicked through five more cards and got all the names right. Good. It was always possible that Turk's shoulder wouldn't heal as quickly as she expected and that his assignment to her Roll Call would last more than just the one week. "Good," he said aloud.

He turned around and found himself facing a small woman with black-rimmed glasses and a dark blue suit. Maybe five feet even, Asian. "Who are you?"

"You are Lieutenant Powder?"

"I know who I am. That wasn't the question."

"I am Reiko Yamaguchi," the woman said with a bow. "I believe that your Chief Cody arranged for me to have a 'ride' with you tonight?"

"I wasn't expecting a woman."

"Oh, so sorry," Reiko Yamaguchi said. "But I am unable to change at so short notice."

Powder rubbed his face. Was that a joke? "Pleasure to meet you, Ms Yamaguchi. *Hajimemashite. Dozo yoroshiku.*"

Reiko Yamaguchi's face burst into a beautiful smile. "You speak Japanese!" she said. But in English.

"Only a few words."

"Have you been to Japan?"

"No. What I know is from a book."

"A book! But that is wonderful and so surprising to me."

"Why? Don't policemen in Japan know how to read?"

Reiko Yamaguchi was momentarily silenced. Then she said, "To tell the truth, Lieutenant, my knowledge of police in America comes from the movie pictures in which the police men and women do not have such cosmopolitan interests."

She didn't know anything about American police? Why was she here? "Are you a cop in Japan?"

"Me?" The smile again. "No, no."

"So why are you here?"

"I am a writer, Lieutenant Powder. I am here at invitation from your Mayor who hopes to promote tourism and investment from Japan to Indianapolis with the article I will write in my magazine."

Powder rubbed his face again.

"Lieutenant? I have not made my self clear? I am sorry. My English is so poor."

"Your English is excellent, Ms Yamaguchi. Very impressive."

"Oh, thank you so much."

"But I don't understand how riding on Night Shift could promote tourism and investment."

"It is because," Reiko Yamaguchi said, "our Japanese tourists and businessmen also watch the movie pictures."

"So?"

"And what they see is American cities full of shooting and beating and robbery and explosion and police who do not obey their own rules."

"I don't go to the movies much," Powder said.

"The reason I 'ride' with you tonight is to make it so I can write it from real experience — and not from public relation — that your city is safe and not like the movie picture."

"Or that it isn't safe."

"Or that it isn't safe. Exactly!" The smile. The smile almost made Powder regret having decided to send Ms Yamaguchi out with Mitchell. Almost.

❖ ❖

Mitchell's face when he saw that his rider was to be not only foreign but female would have been worth a TV crew. Why aren't the media ever there when you need them?

Ms Yamaguchi didn't look much happier. "I am not to ride with you, Lieutenant Powder?"

"The ride request that came through to me said you were to ride with Lieutenant Turk." He understood why it had come here now — that this *female* foreigner would ride with the *female* Lieutenant Turk. Pity Turk got her arm nearly torn off. Ah well, stuff happens.

"But," Ms Yamaguchi said, "do you not replace Lieutenant Turk? I do not understand."

"I do not work regularly on this quadrant so I don't know the area well. And, I have documents to work on that will delay my getting out on patrol. So I selected Officer Mitchell for you to ride with. He is regularly assigned here, and he is our newest graduate from the Academy which means that all the correct policing procedures will still be fresh in his mind."

"I see," Ms Yamaguchi said. And it was clear from her eyes that she understood full well that she was being fobbed off.

Smart as well as the beautiful smile. Powder was in danger of falling in love.

"Mitchell?" Powder said.

"Sir?"

"I want you to answer any question Ms Yamaguchi asks you, as truthfully as you can. Any question whatever, no matter how embarrassing to the force. And I want you to take her wherever she wants to go. If she wants to see drug dealers, show her drug dealers. The same for gangs, transvestite hookers, whatever. Hide nothing. Do you understand?"

"But I don't know where — "

"Anything she asks for. Do you understand me?"

"Yes sir."

Powder turned for a moment to Ms Yamaguchi. "OK?"

"Thank you, Lieutenant Powder." But no smile.

"Once I'm on the road myself, I'll come and find you. Meanwhile, Mitchell, if there's anything you're uncertain about, radio me."

✣ ✣

Powder waved the odd couple off to the parking lot and then he returned to the personnel cards' pictures. He sailed through those that remained, which pleased him.

He considered going through the cards once again, but it would be better to go out and see if he could match some names to real faces.

As a replacement Roll Call Lieutenant, no one would have complained if he'd just hung around the station, going out only if there was an important "run", a shooting, say, or a robbery. But it wasn't Powder's style to dog a job. It had been a long time since he'd gotten access to patrolling officers and they were, after all, the core of policing. If during his stay on Northside Night Shift he could make even one officer do the job *better* then Powder would take away some satisfaction from this marking-time assignment.

Besides, Turk was a more-rather-than-less performer herself, a ground-troops Lieutenant with a reputation for trying hard to help her less experienced soldiers. Like Huch-huch Mitchell. Who struck Powder as likely to have difficulty functioning competently and confidently even when he didn't have a rider in the seat beside him and scrutinizing his every move and word.

"I'm going out now, Becky," Powder told the civilian who ran the office side of the station.

"Fine," she said, without looking up.

He handed her a sheet of paper.

"What's this?"

"Tonight's message for the Chief."

"Haven't you gotten your meeting with him yet?"

"How can I if you never send through my requests?"

She leaned back. "I send all your requests through."

"You better. I'm going to check this one. Bye now."

Powder headed for the parking lot and his own patrol car thinking, No smile?

✥ ✥

Powder found Mitchell and Ms Yamaguchi in an apartment in an attractive block on Washington Boulevard. The run had been to an architect who returned from an evening out to find that he'd been burgled.

"This is Mr. Briggs, sir," Mitchell said. "He's been burgled. TV, DVD, Hi-fi."

Is life all alphabet these days? Powder wondered. "And PC?" he asked.

"No," Briggs said. He was about forty and wore a well-cut three-piece suit comfortably, "*Fortunately*, I left that at the office. *But*, but the scumbag did take my food processor."

"Your food processor?"

"It was top of the range, and a gift. And, worst of all, the *very* worst of all, he took my briefcase."

"And what was in the briefcase?"

"Nothing of value to anyone, except me. Well, there was a cell phone and a solar calculator. But those are nothing compared to the drawings and the notes, which represent absolute hours of work and are of no earthly use whatever to anyone but me. It's heartbreaking."

"Drawings?" Powder asked.

"I'm an architect," Briggs said. "I don't know *what* I am going to do."

"Mitchell?"

"Sir?"

"What are *you* going to do?"

"Well, next — "

"Don't tell me, son. Just do it."

"Sir," Mitchell said with a nod. "When you feel you're able, Mr. Briggs, I need you to continue going through the house to see if anything else is missing."

"I don't know if I can *bear* to look in the bedroom."

"Can I get you something?" Mitchell asked. "A drink of water?"

Briggs pulled himself together and stood erect. "If you look in the fridge, you'll probably find that he stole the Perrier. I'm ready, officer. Let's check the other rooms."

As Mitchell followed the architect down a hallway, Powder turned to Ms Yamaguchi. "How has your ride been so far?"

But before she answered, Powder saw that her eyes — frosty at the end of their last meeting — were now shining and bright. "It is so unexpected," she said. "That I should be standing inside the home of a complete stranger who has not questioned who I am or why I am here."

"You are with a uniformed police officer. That validates you."

"I understand, but still it is amazing for me."

"Just don't steal anything, all right?"

A look of horror passed over Ms Yamaguchi's face. "I would never conceive to do such a thing."

"I didn't mean to suggest that you would," Powder said. "It was a joke."

Ms Yamaguchi gave a slight bow. "Of course. But a joke was so unexpected in this context."

"And from me?"

"I am sure that you are very humorous," Ms Yamaguchi said. "But humor, especially the humor of my region in Japan, depends so much on familiarity with the situation."

"What is your region?"

"Have you heard of Kobe?"

"I know of the earthquake, and the beef."

Ms Yamaguchi smiled and bowed. "Also, we are known for humor."

"But not, perhaps, in this situation," Powder said.

"But the poor man, Mr. Briggs. How upset he is. Is such a thing to happen commonplace?"

"I'll have to check, but from reading the recent records I don't remember any other petty burglaries in this neighborhood."

"So that makes you thinking what?"

"That it might be … say, a kid in the area who's decided he needs some money to supplement his allowance."

"And for money he robs a neighbor? How distressing."

"It'll be even more distressing when he tries to sell what he's stolen, unless he knows how."

"But he must be feeling so ashamed of himself."

"Who? The burglar?"

"Yes."

"Ashamed?"

"To commit a theft, from someone else's home, a neighbor."

Briggs and Officer Mitchell returned to the living room as Powder was saying, "Is that what a burglar in Japan would feel? Shame?"

"Of course. To do such a thing is terrible."

"And what would happen if he got caught?"

"Well, it is not the same at all times, but he could be taken to his victim, so that he could to apologize for what he had done. And he could take a small gift of atonement."

Mitchell said, "Sir, the burglar doesn't seem to have taken anything from the rest of apartment."

"Thank *God*," Briggs said.

Powder said, "Ms Yamaguchi thinks that in Japan your burglar would be feeling ashamed of himself about now. What do you think about your burglar in Indianapolis, Mr. Briggs?"

"I think he would be feeling a baseball bat if I caught up with him. It's such … such an invasion!"

"So you don't think he's feeling ashamed? Or that he's likely to come back here and apologize for what he's done, and bring you a gift of atonement?"

"What are you talking about?" Briggs said. He looked at Mitchell. Who said, "Sir?"

"Well, I think we should ask him," Powder said.

"What?" Briggs said.

"It's the only way we'll find out?"

"You know who the little scrotum is?"

"Mr. Briggs, may I use your phone?"

"Of course you can use my phone. It's over there."

"Thank you. And now, may I have the number of your cellular phone?"

✣ ✣

Of course it was a bit of luck that the thief actually answered the cell telephone when it rang. But once he did …

"Hi," Powder said in his friendliest tone. "Am I speaking to the person who stole this phone earlier this evening from an apartment on Washington Boulevard?"

There was a pause.

Powder said, "Gee, I hope I am, because one of the things you took tonight was a briefcase with some papers in it. The papers aren't worth anything to you, but if I could get them back it'd sure help me out of a jam at work."

"I … don't have your briefcase." The voice was young and pathetic.

"But if, maybe, you threw it somewhere then I could get the papers back. It'd sure save my ass, and maybe even my job."

There was another pause.

Powder said, "Hey, I need those papers real bad. If you tell me where they were I promise I won't call the cops or anything."

"The briefcase, it's in the trashcan outside the drugstore at … at 49th and Penn."

"Oh thank you," Powder said. "I really do appreciate it."

"Uh, OK."

"And, while you're on the phone, I've got someone here who'd like to know whether you feel any shame about what you did tonight?"

A silence.

"And do you think it's likely that you'll come back to my apartment to apologize, and to bring me a present of atonement?"

The line went dead.

Powder turned to Ms Yamaguchi and shook his head. "No shame. No atonement. Life's a bitch, ain't it? I blame society."

"The briefcase?" Briggs said. "My briefcase?"

However Powder addressed Huch-huch Mitchell. "Officer, the said briefcase is said to be in a trashcan outside the drugstore at 49th and Penn."

"Got it."

Powder waved a finger. "But make sure you preserve any fingerprints on it. If there's any chance we can identify Mr. Briggs's scrotum, or log some evidence to use against him in the future, we want to do it."

"Yes sir."

"You're getting my briefcase back?" Briggs said. "And my drawings?"

"Sounds like," Powder said.

"Why that's *wonderful!* I swear I'll never say a bad word about the police again for the rest of my life."

"You see, Mitchell," Powder said, "do a good job for the public and there's no limit to the gratitude they'll lavish on you."

"So now," Briggs said, "do you think that you'll be able to get me back my TV and DVD and food processor?"

❖ ❖

Powder met and left Huch-huch and his rider several times during the night. Ms Yamaguchi was privileged to share many adventures. She was present when the K-9 people used a dog to flush a homeless man out of a warehouse. She was at Mitchell's side when he stopped a woman for a traffic offence and then identified her as a bail absconder, using the in-car computer. She was there when officers heard gunshots fired in the distance as they were chatting at the scene of a traffic accident. And she watched as a teenage girl, reported missing, was found waiting at a bus stop on 34th Street.

Only one incident reflected badly on Mitchell. Near the end of the shift Powder received a radio message from a Lieutenant Lane urgently requesting that they meet in the parking lot of a Village Pantry on 38th Street.

Lane turned out to be in an unmarked car. Powder didn't know him, but he wasn't given time to get acquainted and bond. Lane rolled down his window and said, "One of your patrol cars is about to screw up an undercover narcotics operation that took six months to set up."

"Yeah? How?"

"The jerk-off is driving up and down the streets and alleys south of Fall Creek. He's got a civilian in the car, and maybe he's trying to get her to ID someone, but it's a bad time for him to be doing that — do you get me? Whatever he's up to, pull him off it."

Powder twitched a finger in Lane's direction. "I don't have any jerk-offs on my roll call."

"No?" Lane said. "Well if he looks like a jerk-off and acts like a jerk-off and drives like a jerk-off, that's a jerk-off in my book. And if you don't pull him out of there now, him and the lady could very well find themselves in the middle of something very nasty."

"I will pull him out since you guys can't keep your situations under control," Powder said, starting his engine, "but get this straight, Lane. If you ever want something from me again, calling members of my roll call names is unacceptable. And next time you better remember to say 'please'."

As Powder roared away he reached for his radio to ask Mitchell where he was.

"23rd and Alabama, Lieutenant. I've been showing Reiko the customized cars the drug dealers have."

"That's well and good, but take her up to 58th and Guilford now. There was a robbery reported there a while ago and I think that might turn out to be interesting."

"Yes sir."

So, it was "Reiko" now, was it?

❖ ❖

Given the hour — nearly 4 a.m. — "Reiko" looked very bright when she and Mitchell arrived at 58th and Guilford. "Have you enjoyed your ride?" Powder asked her.

The beautiful smile broke loose almost instantly. "Oh yes, very very much, Lieutenant Powder. But ..." She turned to the tavern they were outside. "... what have we here?"

"Let's find out." He led her to two officers who were talking in front of the tavern window. "Horgan," Powder said, greeting one officer. "Krezewski," the other. Score two for his time with the personnel files. "What have we here?"

Krezewski said, "It's a high-incidence premises, Lieutenant."

"This is the fifth break-in in about twelve months," Horgan said. "It's on my list for special attention, which is why I spotted it."

"What did you spot?"

"Broken window, sir."

Powder looked at the large intact window they were standing by and frowned. "What broken window?"

"It was broken when I got here," Horgan said. "But because of the history at this address, the owner's details are on file. I called him and he sent over an emergency glazier rather than leave the premises unsecured for the rest of the night. I wish I could get a window replaced so quick when my kid breaks one."

"So why are you and Krezewski still here?"

"The glazier's only just gone," Horgan said.

"I happened to be in the vicinity when the call came through, Lieutenant," Krezewski said. "I checked that the back of the tavern is secure, which it is — a solid door and two small windows with heavy wire mesh."

"And the owner?" Powder said.

"A Freddy Franklyn," Horgan said. "He said he'd check out what's missing in the morning."

"I see," Powder said. He was not happy. He heard a car and glanced behind him to see Kaneesha Williams pull up. "And what about you, Mitchell?"

"Uh, what about me, sir?"

"How do you think our guys did? Well?"

"Uh, I guess so. Yeah. Especially getting the window fixed and the premises secured again."

As Kaneesha Williams joined the group she said, "Hey. What's happening?"

Powder said. "Your timing's perfect."

"It is?"

"I got a little test for you."

"Oh yeah? What kind of little test?"

"Basically, to see how good a cop you are."

Williams looked from Horgan to Krezewski to Mitchell, her face asking someone to explain what was going on. The three men stood impassive.

"I said 'basically' which means it's about basics," Powder said. "So it can't be hard, right?"

Having gained no support from her fellow officers, Williams turned her eyes to Reiko Yamaguchi.

"How do you do?" Ms Yamaguchi said with a bow.

"I couldn't have put it better myself," Powder said. "How do you do … it?"

"Do what?" Kaneesha Williams asked.

Powder went through the chain of events as they had been reported to him.

"OK," Williams said. "So what's the question?"

"The question is, how do you do it from here? What's next? If you were in charge."

"You been giving this test to everybody?"

"They tested themselves," Powder said, "and they all failed."

There were sounds of protest from Horgan and Krezewski but Powder waved them away. "What's next, Kaneesha?" he said. "Help these guys become better cops."

"The guys all failed, huh?" Williams set herself to the task with a smile. "Well I'd be glad to help, Lieutenant. Just give me a minute here to check this out."

"Exactly!" Powder said.

"What?"

"What'd she say?" Krezewski asked.

"She said, and I quote, 'check - this - out'."

"I don't get it," Horgan said.

"Let me make it simple for you," Powder said. "Which of you guys went inside?"

"Inside?" Horgan said. He looked at the tavern.

"To check it out," Powder said. "For all you know, your burglar's still in there."

Horgan and Krezewski turned to look at the tavern front again. "But," Krezewski said, "now that the window's fixed, how are we supposed to get in?"

"I think it may be time for you to call the owner back and get some keys, don't you? Unless you'd rather wait till the burglar decides to break out again, though I wouldn't want to be around when you explain to the owner why he has two glazier's bills for the one window." Powder turned to the women. "Well done, Ms Yamaguchi. And well done, guy."

✣ ✣

Back in the station as Powder readied himself to go home at the end of the shift, he was joined by Reiko Yamaguchi. "I wondered if I was going to see you again," he said.

"I wish to apologize for my rudeness, Lieutenant."

"What rudeness?"

"I was displeased when you sent me out with Norman. Excuse, with Officer Mitchell. But now I am pleased that you did so, and I should never have doubted your judgement. It was discourteous."

"Apology accepted," Powder said. "One of the things I admire about your country is that it's a place where courtesy matters."

"Yes, for us courtesy is important."

"And tell me, did you find Indianapolis to be safe?"

"Yes, very safe, in the hands of you and your fine officers. To retrieve the stolen briefcase, and to retrieve the criminal from inside the tavern, that was most impressive."

A pathetic little burglar cowering in a corner, Powder thought. Who was nearly as pathetic as a bar owner who's burgled over and over and still doesn't improve his security.

"Yes, most safe," Ms Yamaguchi said.

"I wonder," Powder said, "if I might I ask you a favor? Something that might help Indianapolis to become even more safe."

"A favor? Yes, of course," Ms Yamaguchi said with a bow. "It would be my pleasure."

"Will you be seeing the Mayor again?"

"Why yes. I have an appointment is this afternoon and it will be my happy job to tell how very well was the result of my ride."

"Well, the favor is to tell him that I treated you badly."

"Tell him … what?" Reiko Yamaguchi seemed stunned. "I must not have understood properly. My English is so poor."

"Please tell the Mayor that he must order the Chief of Police to see me himself, about my rudeness to you."

"But you were not rude. Not at all."

"It would be a great favor to me if you say that I was," Powder said.

"Truly, you *wish* me to say such a bad thing?"

"Yes," Powder said. "And to say that you won't write nice things about Indianapolis until the Chief has talked to me himself."

"But I find this so hard to understand."

"You must trust me about that."

"If it is a truly a favor to you …" Ms Yamaguchi acknowledged her acquiescence to the request with a bow.

Good, Powder thought. This would demonstrate resourcefulness to the new Chief. Request after request for a meeting had been ignored but he'd found another way to get to pitch for the special assignment that would let Powder help populate the whole force with better cops.

"Thank you, Ms Yamaguchi. I hope you have a good journey home and continued good health."

What a Woman Wants

"**J**OHN?"

John's head was hanging over the stack of roll call documents on the table in front of him. But his was mind bright with an outboard on Sagamore Lake, with what he would do in it with Lizzie if he could just get her there, with how he might accomplish that particular goal, with whether she liked him at all. There *were* signs of improvement in that direction: she didn't dump on him all the time now. Maybe she was playing it cool, keeping her options open, not committing herself in public. Maybe ... maybe he could say he'd won a competition. He heard her tell Vince how bad she needed a vacation. Maybe that was the way ...

"*John?*"

John's head jerked up. "Lieutenant?"

"We've got to get started. Do you know where Maxwell is?"

"Maxwell?" John looked around the room. "Isn't he here yet?"

The lieutenant tapped her roll call clipboard impatiently.

From behind him John heard one of the patrolmen say, "Maxwell is got to be late tonight, Lieutenant."

"Why's that, Vince?" the lieutenant asked good-humoredly.

"Because his girlfriend's daddy says how she's got to do her homework first."

Laughter grew in the room as another officer said, "No homework tonight, Vince. She's out trick-or-treating."

John turned to the twenty faces behind him and grinned. "Especially tricking, huh?" he said.

John heard someone say, "You wish." He couldn't tell who it was, but he smiled to show he was a good sport. And he used the moment to allow his gaze to linger on Lizzie. She was laughing with the rest, but without looking at him. He waited as long as he dared, in case she glanced his way. Eventually he turned back to the lieutenant.

At that moment Maxwell walked in, making his entrance with customary swagger. "The man sublime as you ring your chime, Lieutenant," he said.

The lieutenant looked at her watch but did not play angry. Maxwell saw the others laughing. "What's up? Why they got the giggles, Lieutenant? Don't they know this is a *police* station?"

"They laughing 'bout your love life," Vince offered from the back.

"Ain't no laughing matter, *my* love life," Maxwell said. He made his way down the side of the room and he slid into a chair next to Vince's.

"Just how big *is* her daddy?" someone else asked. "Bigger than you?"

Maxwell looked around, searching for the speaker. He made a face suggesting he didn't like some of the ways one could take that question, but then the lieutenant began roll call formalities. Vince winked. Maxwell smiled. Each man made a fist. The fists touched lightly.

"I want to remind those of you who are blind as well as deaf and stupid that tonight is Halloween," the lieutenant said. "Which is a pain in the butt because of all the kids on the streets. Even so, I've got a good feeling about tonight. I think you all know what I'm talking about."

From two or three places in the room the phrase "smash-and- grab" was spoken aloud, and it was not said with any humorous content. Another officer said, "Cutlass."

The lieutenant said, "Damn right. He is due, that sucker. He is *overdue*. Time the ghost of a police uniform rose up and haunted him into custody."

The room ceased to be individuals and became a team. Their enthusiasm and determination was genuine. The serial smash-and-grabber was top of the team's most-wanted list, first pick in the draft, *numero uno*.

The lieutenant said, "They put some stats together downtown. They don't make good reading, but I'm going to read them to you anyway. They add up to thirty-seven drugstores and mini-markets in six weeks." The lieutenant put her clipboard down. "I want this guy. I want him bad."

There was a chorus of agreement from around the room. As it died down, John said, "Yeah!"

The lieutenant said, "But before we get started, the Captain has some things to report. You don't mind if I tell them that the results of the 'color the police car' contest are in, do you, Cap?"

There were a few catcalls and the captain smiled from his seat at the front of the room.

The lieutenant said, "He's got worse than that for you."

General moans.

"But even before that," the lieutenant said, "I want to introduce Mr. Keith Locke to everybody."

A slight, gray-haired man of about fifty turned in his seat at the side of the room. His mouth formed a smile without his eyes harmonizing above it. He gave the officers a little wave.

The lieutenant said, "Mr. Locke is a writer. He does articles about law-enforcement for all kind of magazines and the Chief's office has asked us to give Mr. Locke a ride tonight. I was told he wants to 'refresh his experience of what real policing in a city like Indianapolis is like.' Did I get that right, Mr. Locke? But I am also assured by his friends downtown that Mr. Locke is one of the good guys. That he's on our side, and that you can speak freely in front of him."

"Why sure, honey," Sondra said to Locke for everyone to hear. "You sure can come ride with me and tell me *all* about your friends downtown."

Many officers chuckled, but the sound was mixed. Sondra was lively and surprising, but she was also newly transferred to North from West. Most of the North personnel did not yet know how to take her ready suggestions of eagerness to shortcut normal promotion channels.

Locke himself did not speak, but his mouth formed the smile again before he turned back to the lieutenant.

"So if you see Mr. Locke taking notes or anything, don't worry about it. If he asks you questions, do your best to help him. Mr. Locke will be riding with John."

John jerked in his chair. "He will?"

"I told you half an hour ago, John," the lieutenant said. "Weren't you listening?"

❖ ❖

Once they were settled in John's patrol car, Locke said, "This smash-and-grab guy sounds very interesting."

"He'll be even more interesting when we catch him," John said. John's mood was heavy. He was depressed at the prospect that his rider might keep him from manufacturing meetings with Lizzie. That he might miss a chance to talk to her alone. He'd decided to say he'd entered a competition for a lake weekend. That he was in the finals. It would test her reaction.

As John pulled on to the main road, Locke continued about the smash-and-grabs. "It seems such a peculiar *M.O.* I can understand why the guy steals cars for his raids, but why does he always steal an Oldsmobile Cutlass? Are there any theories?"

John occupied himself with traffic and lights before turning into a residential area.

"Is a Cutlass easier to get into than other cars?"

"Nope," John said. "The dickhead probably learned on a Cutlass but doesn't have the brain to realize it works on other models too."

"A case of arrested development?" Locke asked.

"I'll arrest his development," John said without realizing his rider had made the joke first. "Just give me the chance."

The car's radio came to life, stopping conversation for a few moments. When the radio was quiet again John said, "Did you get that?"

"Not exactly."

"A stolen car reported on Ditch Road."

"Oh."

"But not a Cutlass."

Just then John braked sharply so the patrol car came to a halt well short of a stop sign. He waved to a woman who stood waiting on the corner with several small ghosts, witches, cowboys and bats. The woman's hair was covered by a scarf and she wore a loose jacket, but she smiled brightly as she mouthed her thanks. Then she ushered her tiny trick-or-treaters across the street. John wondered if the woman had gotten a clear look at him, whether she would recognize him another time, the nice policeman who had put himself out for her. If he'd been alone he could make sure to come back this way a few times while the woman was still out with the children. Well maybe he could manage it anyway. No need to let the rider cramp his style completely.

The woman had a friendly smile, John thought as he drove on. Nice. Not as nice as Lizzie's, of course. But not a smile to say no to.

Then John felt slight guilt at his unfaithfulness to Lizzie. Well, what Lizzie didn't know couldn't hurt her. Time enough for all that when they got it together. And again John recalled warmly the surprise softness of Lizzie's touch when they shook hands two weeks ago. Sixteen days now. Funny how small things like that can start you off. Lizzie acts so tough but feels so soft. And if that's what her hands were like …

"A pirate," Locke said.

"What?"

"I said, maybe this guy who steals Cutlasses will dress up like a pirate tonight."

John nodded slowly and said, "Yeah," though he wondered if maybe he was riding with a lunatic.

After a few quiet moments Locke said, "So do I have this right? The pirate steals a Cutlass and *then* he steals a plastic trash can?"

"Yeah," John said. And enlivened at the memory he added, "One time he even stole a trash can from right out back of the Governor's Mansion!"

"Really?" Locke said.

"Sure thing," John said happily. "The Governor's own goddamn trash can. All his orange peels and cereal boxes, dumped right there in the alley behind the house."

"Do you think there might be a political element to the pirate's crimes?" Locke said. "Could that be why he chose to go to the Governor's Mansion?"

In the face of uncongenial complexity John's spirits dropped again. "Guy wanted a trash can, that's all."

"Mmmm," Locke said. He made some notes.

As they drove on John said, "Now there's a Cutlass, see? Parked behind that rusty pickup. Maybe we should stick around."

Locke was silent for a moment before he said, "Surely the chances of your perpetrator going for this particular vehicle aren't large."

"It wasn't a serious suggestion," John said.

"Ah." Locke turned back to his notes. When he looked up he said, "And the bricks he uses to break the drugstore windows, is there one particular place that he steals them from?"

"There are a whole lot of bricks around northside Indianapolis," John said.

"Still, if they always came from the same place ..."

"They don't."

The radio crackled.

When it was done John said, "Did you get that?"

"Not quite."

"A 'man shot'," John said. "Hold tight." He turned on his flashing lights. He turned on his siren.

❖ ❖

As they drew near to the address given John saw that four other police cars were already there. "Some nights," John said, "whenever there's a decent run I'm about sitting on top of it. And other nights I'm miles away every time."

"A quarter of the city," Locke said, "*is* a very large area to be responsible for out of one station, even if it does make it possible to sustain specialized teams and enjoy economies of scale."

John unharnessed himself and opened the door.

"Shall I come?" Locke asked.

"Up to you." But John didn't wait on Locke's decision. One of the cars already on the scene was Lizzie's. Well, it would be. She was that kind of gal.

❖ ❖

The lieutenant was that kind of gal too and she stood between John and where Lizzie was talking to a middle-aged female civilian. "What's up?" John asked the lieutenant.

"Would you believe ... a b-b gun?"

"A ... ?"

"A goddamn b-b gun. This guy and his brother are playing cards in the kitchen. Mom goes to the door for some trick-or- treaters and while she's away the brothers start arguing. Then Mom hears a bang and one of the brothers squeals, 'He shot me, he shot me.'" The lieutenant shook her head.

From behind her Lizzie's voice carried to them both. "Well I'm telling you, ma'am," Lizzie said, "you did exactly the right thing to call us. You didn't know it was only a b-b gun."

"I'm so sorry to get y'all out here like this," the woman said.

"No problem, ma'am," Lizzie said. "You did exactly the right thing, believe me."

"Time to get back on the road," the lieutenant said to John. "Let the young'uns clean up here. You and me should get out there and find us some *real* bodies."

John hesitated, but he had no choice. He walked with the lieutenant to where the cars were parked. They met Locke coming the other direction. "How's it going, Mr. Locke?" the lieutenant said.

"Fine thanks," Locke said. "Is it over?"

"It never began. But hang in there. Chances are we'll get you something juicy before we all get to go home."

⁘ ⁘

When they were on the road again, Locke said, "I was thinking about roll call."

"What about it," John said.

"How often does the captain talk to the shift?"

"Whenever he wants to."

"But today he had so much to say," Locke persisted. "And a lot sounded important. It can't be like that every day."

"The end of the month," John said. "All the brass — captains and up — they meet with the mayor's people. They go through everything from health care to some idiot's idea to change the color of all our police cars."

Locke took a moment to make some notes. Then he said, "Did I understand correctly what the captain said about the officer named Wilson?"

"What about Wilson?"

"That the department wants him fired but the mayor says no?"

"That's about the size of it," John said.

"Isn't that kind of situation usually the other way around?"

"I wouldn't know," John said.

"If you don't want to talk about it," Locke said.

John considered. Then he remembered the lieutenant's comment about Locke's friends downtown. "I don't mind talking," John said.

"So what's the story with Wilson?"

"It's just that he was involved in three of what they call 'incidents of bad judgment.' And we're worried he might do it again. And if he does, who gets the blame? Morale is low enough around here and it isn't helped by the media jumping on every little thing to make us look as bad as they can."

"What sort of incidents?" Locke said.

John breathed heavily. "Like one time was he chased his girlfriend all over Broad Ripple and he dragged her into the back seat of his car and he beat the shit out of her. All right? You get the picture?"

"Not a pleasant picture," Locke said.

"But the guy's still wearing the uniform, despite what we do to try to clean up our own act. So if this guy off and shoots somebody, is the newspaper going to say the force tried to get rid of him but the politicians wouldn't let them? Is that what they're going to say? You tell me. That's your line of work, isn't it?"

"But what makes the mayor want to keep the guy?" Locke asked.

"You tell me," John said again, uncomfortable now that he had talked about Wilson at all.

There was a moment of silence in the car, but it was broken as the radio came alive. After the message was complete John picked up his own receiver and asked the dispatcher to repeat a number. As the number was repeated, John wrote it on the back of his hand. Then he said to Locke, "Did you get that?"

"Not quite."

"Trick or treat!" John said. "Stolen Cutlass."

⚬ ⚬

For a while they cruised the main arteries of northside Indianapolis talking only about Cutlasses. Then Locke said, "Tell me about yourself, John. If you don't mind."

"Not much to tell."

"How long have you been on the force?"

"Thirteen years."

"Married?"

"Not now."

"Was your being a policeman a factor in the break-up?"

"It didn't help."

"And what do you do for relaxation?"

John thought of Sagamore Lake. The motel by the shore. Of Lizzie.

"John?"

"I fish," John said. "When I get the chance."

"I've met a lot of policemen who fish," Locke said.

"Yeah?"

"I think there's something about the quiet that particularly appeals to policemen."

"Policewomen too?" John said.

"Sure," Locke said. "They need to relax too."

John looked at his watch. "Do you feel like coffee?" But before Locke could answer the radio burst into life again. When it was done, John said, "Forget the coffee. Let's go arrest the suspect in a shooting instead."

❖ ❖

But again there were several cars already on the scene when they arrived. Not, however, including Lizzie's. "Come on," John said as he got out, and Locke kept pace as they went to the open door of the apartment building. The suspect lived on the second floor.

Even before they emerged from the stairwell they heard Maxwell's voice from inside the apartment. "So when does your mother get home, Thomas?"

A younger, fearful voice said, "When the store close."

"What time is that?"

" 'Bout eleven, I guess."

Maxwell was looking at his watch as John and Locke entered. Maxwell said, "And you were going to stay here alone till she came home?"

Three officers were ringed around a twenty-year old man who was kneeling in the middle of the room. The young man was shirtless and handcuffed behind his back.

"Yes sir," the young man said. "To keep the trick-or- treaters from soaping the door and stuff."

Two more officers, Sondra and Vince, emerged from another room in the apartment. They stood with John and Locke. "Rest of the place looks clean," Vince said to Maxwell.

"That's right," the kneeling prisoner said. "Ain't nothing bad in here."

Maxwell said, "And you deny shooting Dexter Hill?"

"I didn't even know he was shot," the prisoner said.

"But you know him?"

"Sure I know him. But I didn't know nobody shot him."

"When was the last time you saw Dexter?"

"I saw him this morning."

"Where?"

"Over outside his place. He owe me some money and I went to get it, but 'bout the time I got there, I saw him leave out the back."

"You didn't talk to him?"

"No sir."

"You didn't threaten him?"

"No sir. Well, I did shout after him to stop, 'cause I wanted my money, but it didn't look like he heard me none."

"And you didn't see Dexter again after that?"

"No sir."

"Not outside the 500 Liquors on 38th Street?"

"No sir."

"And you didn't shoot him?"

"No sir."

"So why do you think he says you're the one that shot him, Thomas?"

"I don't know. Except maybe he think that's how to keep from paying me back the money he owe."

Behind John and Locke the lieutenant appeared. Vince saw her and nodded to the hall outside the apartment. Sondra, John and Locke followed them.

"What's it look like?" the lieutenant asked Vince.

"Maybe he's good at playing the innocent," Vince said, "but this kid was watching TV alone in the apartment when we got here and he answered the door with a bag of candy in his hand. Didn't seem like he had anything on his conscience."

"Let them sort it out downtown," the lieutenant said.

"Pity," Sondra said, "because Dexter Hill needed shooting. I knew him from out West. Whoever did shoot him, if he'd done a better job he'd have done the city a favor."

"How bad is Hill?" the lieutenant asked. "Could he still kick it?"

"No idea," Vince said.

"Hi, Mr. Locke," Sondra said. "John treating you OK? You getting what you need?"

"Just fine," Locke said.

Vince said, "Lieutenant, I was thinking."

"See, Mr. Locke?" Sondra said. "You're bringing out the best in all of us."

"About the smash-and-grabs," Vince said.

Suddenly everyone was attentive. "What about them?" the lieutenant said.

"I was driving past a Hooks a while ago and I got to wondering why the smash-and-grab guy hadn't hit it yet."

"Where?" the lieutenant said.

"49th and Pennsylvania," Vince said.

"It hasn't been hit?"

"I checked that list downtown gave us. He's done seventeen Hooks, but he hasn't done this one."

"He sure likes a good Hooks, this sucker," the lieutenant said.

Vince said, "There's a gas station, Pete's Service, across the street. It's dark and there are other cars. I could watch from there."

The lieutenant said, "I'll arrange cover for you. Go on. Get out of here."

Vince turned and went down the stairs. The lieutenant returned to the apartment. Sondra, John and Locke followed. As they entered, Maxwell was saying, "You do understand, don't you, Thomas. I got a call from downtown and they said, 'Arrest Thomas Banks.' They may have made a mistake, but that's not up to me. They tell me to arrest you, that's what I got to do."

"I understand," the young man kneeling on the floor said.

"OK," Maxwell said. "I'll call your mother at the store and let her know what's happening. Then I'll take you downtown so we can get this sorted out."

"Yes sir," the young man said.

John whispered to Locke, "We might as well go."

Locke nodded. He led the way out of the apartment, but as John followed to the stairs he heard Locke gasp and say, "Jesus!" There was also a fierce snarl.

John turned the corner on the stairwell and saw a German Shepherd baring its teeth. Behind the dog John saw Andy, one of the K-9 officers.

"This guy with you?" Andy said.

"Yeah, a rider," John said. "Y'all didn't scare him none, did you?"

"I didn't," Andy said, "but I think Baby Fritz mighta done."

✜ ✜

When they got back on the road John said, "Now, how about that coffee?"

"Sounds good to me," Locke said.

It sounded good to John too because it gave him an excuse to cruise through the residential area where he'd stopped for the woman with the scarf and the nice smile.

But although the evening was warm and there were a lot of trick-or-treaters out John didn't see the woman. Ah well. He pulled into the parking lot of a Pantry Pride.

He bought a coffee for Locke and a diet cola for himself and then passed a few comments with the owner. But John drained his cola quickly and encouraged Locke to drink up.

When they were back in the car Locke said, "What's the hurry?"

"You heard when Vince said he was going to stake out a Hooks on 49th and Penn?" John said.

"Yes," Locke said.

"Well he's lucky, Vince. Some guys are like that. It wouldn't do us no harm to wander up that way, just in case."

At that very moment the car radio burst into life with Vince saying, "I'm at 49th and Pennsylvania, outside a Hooks Drugstore. There's been a smash-and-grab raid here. Can't have been more than a few minutes ago."

✜ ✜

"Vince, are you psychic or what?" Lizzie said.

"It's just a pity you didn't get your idea a little earlier," John said. "We'd have nailed the bastard."

Vince said, "He doesn't usually go to work till later on. Has he ever hit one this early?"

"I don't think so," Lizzie said.

"So damn close," John said. "I suppose you're sure it was him?"

"I didn't get an autograph," Vince said, "but there's a couple of bricks inside the front door and the cigarette cabinet is bust open. Is that good enough for you?"

"If we get him tonight," Lizzie said, "you're definitely down for a psychic assist, Vince."

The lieutenant came up behind them. "What are you all doing here?" she said. "There's a Cutlass with a trash can full of cigarettes out there someplace."

❖ ❖

When they were on the road again John said, "I was hoping to get a chance to introduce you to Lizzie, the policewoman we were talking to."

"Oh?" Locke said.

"She's only been with us a couple of years, but she's good. Always quick on the scene, not afraid to bust a head if it needs busting, but she's also got that softer side they have. Yeah, she's doing good. She'll go far. A credit to her... to her, well, sex."

"You approve of the increasing female police presence on the force, do you, John?"

"Yeah, I guess." Having spoken out loud about Lizzie, John was thinking of something else. He said, "I was meaning to ask you, Mr. Locke, speaking as a guy who gets around a bit. I just wondered what you thought."

"What about?" Locke said. "Females in the police?"

"Not exactly. I just wondered, what do you think women respond to? What, in your experience, is the key to what a woman wants in a man."

Locke, surprised at the subject, hesitated.

"Is that too personal?" John said. "If you don't want to talk about it ..."

"A woman?" Locke said. "Any particular woman?"

"No. In general. But we were just talking about Lizzie. That officer I'm going to introduce you to? Take her as an example. What would you say a woman like Lizzie would respond to in a man?"

"Success," Locke said.

"Success?"

"In my experience women who opt for careers in law enforcement respect success, accomplishment. Someone who has made a lot of arrests, seen a lot of action."

"So you wouldn't say they were looking for someone who was thoughtful about them?"

"I'm just guessing, John. I haven't studied the subject from this angle. Do you like Lizzie? Is that it?"

"Lizzie? You mean as herself? I hadn't really thought about it," John said.

❖ ❖

At first John thought it was just another car running a red light. His instinct was not to bother. But then he realized he had not actually *done* anything the whole shift except arrive at other people's action. While a traffic violation didn't exactly amount to "success" it was better than a blank sheet. John made a U-turn and sped after the car. Only then did he realize he was pursuing was an Oldsmobile Cutlass.

In another minute — by checking against the number on the back of his hand twice — John established it was *the* Cutlass. "Jesus God!" he said aloud, and he reached for his radio.

He broadcast his location. He broadcast the plate number of the car he was in pursuit of. He requested back-up. He requested the K-9 officer. He requested anybody else who was out there.

Then the Cutlass turned off the main road onto a residential street. John followed.

The Cutlass screamed through a 4-way stop. So did John.

And then the driver of the Cutlass suddenly braked and slid and turned into an alley.

John tried to follow. But as he swung into the alley his car spun and he lost control. John's car came to a stop sideways across the alley mouth. Miraculously, it hit nothing in the process.

From his seat John could see the Cutlass, fishtailing away on the alley cinders.

But then, as John watched, the Cutlass braked hard. It skidded to a skewed halt and it hit a telephone pole. Then it began to back up.

John knew stories of drivers who intentionally ran into police cars so that the officers inside would be immobilized by their airbags, but John's car was already immobile.

Then, a few yards away from them, the Cutlass stopped.

The driver's door opened. A man got out with his hands in the air. As John got out of his own car all he could hear was the man saying was, "Don't shoot. Don't shoot. Don't shoot." Over and over.

Behind the man, blocking the other end of the alley, John could see a party of little figures, some dressed as cowboys, other as ghosts.

"Come and look at this, John," the lieutenant said.

John was in a daze from the sea of flashing police lights that now swarmed around the scene of his arrest, but he followed the lieutenant back into the alley, past his own car to the Cutlass. The lieutenant pointed to a dark object beside the captured vehicle. The object was a trash can. "Take a look inside," she said.

John looked while the lieutenant illuminated the can's interior with her flashlight. John saw cigarette cartons. He saw liquor bottles. He saw a bag of candy corn. He took the candy corn out and held it up.

The lieutenant said, "The sucker was taking it home to give to trick-or-treaters. That's probably why he went out early."

Maxwell walked by and patted John on the back. "Well done!" he said.

The lieutenant said to Locke, "I wanted this Cutlass sucker *so* bad, you wouldn't believe it."

"Thirty-eight more clear-ups for the month too," Locke said.

Several officers approached, all smiling. The three closest patted John's shoulder, ruffled his hair, congratulated him.

The lieutenant said, "I thought we might come up with something juicy for you, Mr. Locke."

"It was very exciting," Locke said. "But when he turned into the alley, I knew John had him."

"You did?"

"We drove by those kids partying in the alley earlier on so John knew all he had to do was block off this end. Very cool. That's what you were thinking, wasn't it?" Locke smiled at John, and this time his eyes smiled too.

John said, "Yeah."

"I look forward to telling the Chief all about my ride tonight and what a great job my new friend John here is doing," Locke said.

"Well done, man," Vince said.

"Thanks."

"Good arrest," Lizzie said.

John blinked as he picked her out from the crowd. "Thanks, Lizzie," he said. Then, "Will you come fishing with me at Sagamore Lake?"

After everyone was silent for a moment, Lizzie said, "Are you kidding?"

"No. Will you?"

"Get a life," Lizzie said. She turned and walked away.

But before John could quite take in what had happened, Sondra stepped forward and took his arm. She said, "I like fishing."

John looked at her. "You do?"

"Sure do, big boy," Sondra said, smiling first at John and then his well-connected friend, Locke.

Boss

ONCE ONLY, on the way to the funeral, I stopped to look at my breath and wonder that it didn't freeze and fall to earth. But as I watched what I had exhaled I began to shiver beneath my thin coat and then I cursed myself for wasting time on such impractical considerations as frozen breath.

As I walked on I turned my curses toward my dead boss. "Cheapskate. Thatcherite. Exploiter." No sorrow for his demise but anger at the memory of his clench-fisted running of the company. And anger that my need for a job, even this job, was so great that I felt obliged to be seen grieving at the funeral and at the widow's afterwards.

If the dead man had paid me half what I was worth I would be driving to the funeral, or at least walking inside the skin of a warm coat.

"Dearly beloved," the cleric began, but that is what none of us from the company were. Nonetheless we cried, because no one, not even the managers, knew who would take the business reins, who was favoured in the widow's mind.

"He was so young!" I cried when there was a lull. Several heads turned my way and I was satisfied.

At her house the widow wore dark rings around her eyes. She welcomed every one as we arrived, shook every hand. For just a moment I felt sad for her. It was not her fault that the dead man screwed every penny out of the factory that was his living and our existing.

Though I had not planned to do so, I said, "It is such a tragedy, but worse for you than anyone."

She said, "Thank you," but could not raise a smile.

But inside the house I grew angry again. Perhaps it was the widow's fault after all. The house she lived in, now owned, was as lavish as the factory was bare. No comfort spared, even the wallpaper was soft. She was the cause of our misery. The dead man drew our blood to transfuse her. No wonder her pampered grief was deep.

✥ ✥

I ate what I could and then watched for ways to take home more. I stood aside to await my chance. I hung in the shadow of velvet curtains. Having drawn the attention that would serve me, now I avoided eyes. It was a practised skill.

✥ ✥

The tide turned. Having completed obeisances, it came time for company employees to leave the widow to her darkness.

From my shade I saw the widow thank each in turn for coming. But I was not the only employee who lingered A man I knew only by name held back too, but the feast he planned was not the same as mine.

The widow turned to him. Her black grief broke and she smiled with bright warm relief. He winked. They thought they were alone.

Then the widow saw me in the velvet ripples. I had to leave, without food in my pocket.

But I was no longer angry, for was I not the only witness to a murder?

Wrong Number

I T IS SATURDAY. She is late rising and it is after ten when she opens the apartment door to bring the newspaper in off the mat. "Municipal Official in Bribe Allegation." "Fifth Woman in Brutal Random Murder String." "Sewage Peace Formula Clog." Not uplifting headlines to begin a lonely weekend.

She carries the paper to the kitchen table in her small kitchen. She opens to the more mellow news inside; drama reviews, foreign travel. She finishes assembling breakfast.

The telephone rings.

She looks up at first and puzzles. One knows when people are likely to call, when a call is unusual.

She goes to the telephone and answers it.

"May I speak to Liz, please?"

The man's voice is not quite clear. She furrows her brow. "Who?"

"Liz. Is she there?"

"I think you must have the wrong number."

"Oh," he says without hesitation, as if it happens to him often. "That's not a very good omen for the rest of the day."

He waits, as if for her to answer.

She says nothing. She has nothing to say.

He says, "Sorry to have troubled you."

"That's all right," she says. Then, "No trouble."

He hangs up.

A minute later, the telephone rings.

She rises evenly from her kitchen chair and answers it.

"Oh my, I haven't done it again, have I?"

"If you were trying to get, Liz, then you have," she says after a momentary hesitation. She wonders if she is being saucy.

"I dialled 886 1091," he says. "At least I thought I did."

"This is 886 1001," she says.

"That's the problem. Either I misdialled or it's a strangled line."

"Oh."

"I knew I was wrong when I heard your voice," he says.

96

She doesn't know what to say to that.

"It's so pretty," he says. "May I say, you have a lovely telephone voice."

" I ... Well, thank you."

"And if the rest of you is as lovely, your husband must be a lucky man. Sorry to have troubled you."

He hangs up.

She replaces her receiver slowly, stirred slightly by his unfamiliar familiarity.

She returns to the company of her newspaper, but at first cannot concentrate on what it has to say.

✛ ✛

Sunday morning. She thinks of him when she brings in the newspaper. "Inflation Shock," "Cabbage Cancer Connection."

✛ ✛

Sunday in the late afternoon she is watching television.

The telephone rings.

She rises and turns down the volume before answering.

"Liz?"

"Who?" she asks, although she knows full well who it is.

"I haven't got the wrong number again, have I?" he asks without surprise.

He waits for her answer, though it is obvious. She opts for safety and says, "I think you have. This is 1001 and you want 1091, don't you?"

"That's right," he says. "You remembered."

"Yes."

"I have the most terrible trouble with this telephone."

"Telephones are such a problem."

"I never had any difficulty with the old one, one of those lumpy black ones, you know? But now I have this blood-red one and it's terrible. Unless I dial very articulately, it doesn't seem to understand the number want."

"Yes." she says, unhappy to have no other words.

He continues easily. "Yet I hear your lovely voice again. So it's not all bad. Unless I've disturbed you in the middle of something. I'm very sorry if I've inconvenienced you."

"I wasn't doing anything," she says instinctively. Then adds the pigmentless camouflage, "Nothing that couldn't easily be interrupted."

"I'm sure you are always fully occupied."

He hesitates. Is he fishing for her to say something?

"It varies," she begins.

But he is already saying, "Sorry to have troubled you."

"That's quite all right," she says. "It's something one doesn't expect, so it is sort of a surprise."

He says, "I'll try not to let it happen again, as hard as I can," and hangs up.

She holds her telephone receiver for several seconds. How awful! What other kind of surprise can there be but one that one doesn't expect. What a stupid thing to say!

✤ ✤

Sunday evening she is in the bathtub, soaking and reading and humming. The weekend is nearly over.

The telephone rings.

She spends a moment deciding whether to make the effort to answer it. She feels warm and comfortable.

But then, in a wet hurry, she makes it to the telephone by the end of the seventh ring.

"I was afraid you weren't there," he says. It is him!

"This isn't Liz," she says, hoping it sounds light and playful, not stark.

He laughs lightly. "I know. This is 1001, right?"

"Right," she says, and tries to echo his laugh.

"Isn't life unpredictable?" he says. "I just wanted to see who I would get if I started out by trying to dial 1001."

She could feel diminished. But she doesn't. "Now you know," she says. Thinking, "Me! You got me!"

"I guess I do."

She says nothing.

"Are you there?"

"Yes. I'm here," she says. She smiles. She wishes he could see her smile, At the office they say her smile is sweet.

"You're not offended by my calling you like this, are you? It's just I feel, somehow, that I already know you."

"Yes, I understand."

"Yes, you're offended?" he persists. "Or yes, you're not offended?"

"I'm not offended."

Suddenly there is a silence. She feels desperate.

She almost says again, "So now you know." Unable to think of anything else. Now he knows she's not offended, like now he knows what happens when he dials 1001. But she doesn't say it. It makes sense, but it is too stupid. Of course he knows now. Whatever it was.

"Well, lady with the lovely voice, what I wondered was whether you would come out with me."

Suddenly, there it is.

You Man. Me Lady. Me Lady, someone's loving wife? Lady, widowed grandmother of seven? Lady, leprous drug addict?

Lady with a lovely, voice.

Lady, lonely girl. How could he tell?

"Are you there? You're not offended, are you?"

"Yes, I'm here. Yes. Yes."

"Yes, you're … ?" He is not clear what she is saying.

She knows this and helps. "Yes, I'll come out with you."

"You will? Oh, that's great. How about tomorrow night?"

Monday. Monday. How late does she have to work on a Monday? On tomorrow Monday? If she goes in early …

"That's … that's all right."

"We'll have something to eat and maybe take in a movie?"

"Yes. Fine."

"About seven-thirty?"

"That will be all right."

"Great. That's great. I have to go now."

"Oh. OK."

"Bye." He hangs up.

She stands, smiling. Still wet, but not cold.

Monday the newspaper rests unconsulted on the breakfast table. "Oil Price Rise Imminent." "Sewage Hopes Rise With Backlog."

Monday evening she is home from work before six.

She walks straight to the telephone. She looks at it, distressed.

She doesn't know whether to get ready to go out or not. They've made no arrangements. She doesn't know his name. She cannot contact him.

He'd said he "had" to go. Where? Why? Why then?

She hasn't slept.

She looks at the phone. Her hand drops slowly. She picks up the receiver and dials 886 1091, the number he was trying to get. At first. Liz's number.

To remain uninvolved, she holds the instrument well away from her ear.

After several rings her call is answered. By a man. He says, "Hello." Coldly. Martially.

She dashes the phone back to its cradle.

Her conceits, her hopes, her babies all rest there.

She breathes heavily.

It wasn't the same man, not her man. But she knows that "her" man could be someone's grandfatherly husband. Husband.

Suddenly, sharply, she hits the side of her thigh with a fist.

And the telephone rings.

She answers it. "Hello," she says, still sharp.

"It's me," he says.

"What? Oh!"

The voice is altogether different from what she has just railed at. Oh God!
I've not even taken off my coat.

"Hello," she says again.

"It is tonight we're going out, isn't it?" he asks.

"Yes, yes. I'm sorry. I was thinking of something else."

"We didn't fix our plans. You didn't tell me where you live."

"I know." She explains where her apartment is.

"I'll be there at seven-thirty."

"Fine."

They hang up. She flies around her rooms, bewailing the time she has
wasted.

✜ ✜

Monday evening at seven thirty-five her doorbell rings.

✜ ✜

Tuesday morning, a few minutes after eleven, her telephone rings. And rings.
She does not answer it.

✜ ✜

Tuesday night martial men cross the newspaper on her threshold. None thinks
to cancel the order.

✜ ✜

Wednesday morning a new paper is on the mat. It bleats silently, "Sixth
Woman Slain: When Will It Stop?"

✜ ✜

Elsewhere in the city a telephone rings. The caller apologises.

The Hand That Feeds Me

I WAS DOWNTOWN on a hot, windless, humid, summer evening. I was grazing the alleys. There was plenty of food to be had — the amount that human beings throw away never ceases to amaze me and there's even more when the temperature is high. This particular evening the only obstacle to a full belly was the competition.

When the temperature goes up some dogs go crazy. I've seen fights to the death over a burger roll. I can fight, and win, but I don't see the point of spilling blood over scraps. On hot summer nights, if I meet a contentious dog I go elsewhere.

There was still a little light in the sky when I left one alley, entered another, and found an old human male poking in a barrel. Heat can have the same effect on humans that it does on dogs so I gave him a wide berth, but the old male began to talk to me. I didn't understand a word, of course, but I could tell that he meant to be friendly. And then he threw me a piece of meat.

It's not smart to take meat from strange men, but this old male seemed genuinely amiable. What he threw was most of a well-done sheep chop. I prefer meat rare but I sniffed the chop carefully and it seemed OK so I ate it. It tasted good.

I stayed with the old male for a while. I'd root a bit, and he'd root a bit, and then we'd move on. Whenever he found meat on the bone he gave it to me. That puzzled me until I realized he had no teeth. So I began to push bread and unfinished burgers his way. He seemed pleased.

He even tried to make things easier for me. Behind a restaurant he took the top off a garbage can and then knocked it over so I could get in. And in an alley where two dogs were already ripping through the contents of a plastic bag, the old male shooed them away. It's not that I can't do such things for myself but it made a pleasant change to be looked after.

Finally the old male decided he'd had enough to eat. He took a blanket from a plastic bag he carried and spread it in the gap between two garages. He stretched himself out and patted the space beside him. But I wasn't ready to sleep, so I left.

✤ ✤

I didn't return to the old male's alley on purpose. Things just worked out that way a couple of hours later.

He was still between the garages, but I saw immediately that something was wrong. The way he lay on the blanket was wrong. The lack of sound was wrong.

I approached him cautiously. Nothing happened. But nothing could happen. The old male was dead.

There was blood on his face. There was blood on his clothes too. Someone had given him a terrible beating.

I licked one of the wounds. The blood was dry on top, but still runny under the crust. And the old male's body was warmer than the ground it lay on. He hadn't been dead long.

I picked up three human scents, all male. The odors were fresh, hanging in the sultry air. Three males together. Three against one. One old male with no teeth who gave meat to stray dogs.

I set out to find them.

✤ ✤

The three-male pack had headed away from the center of town. They stuck to the alleys, though they hadn't stopped at any of the places I, or my dead benefactor, would have.

The only time their spoor veered from alleyways was when it turned along a sidewalk toward a couple of stores. There the mixture of human scents became confusing, but I guessed that they'd gone to buy something. And, sure enough, when I checked the alley on the other side of the street I got them again. After another two blocks I began to find discarded beer cans.

I set one can from each of the men in a place where I could find it again. Then I concentrated on following the trail. I did so with increasing confidence. I figured I knew where they had gone.

There is a long, narrow park on the banks of a stream on the southern side of town. It is popular on a summer's night and not just with humans. But my trio made finding them easy. When I arrived by the waterside, they were whooping and hollering. They were throwing stones into the air and swinging thick sticks at them. They were drunk and unsteady and they all made a terrible din to celebrate if a stick connected with a stone.

Nearby they had made a fire. A fire! On a hot night like this. Its flames reflected on the wet sides of beer cans which lay next to a pile of jackets.

I crept toward the young males. I wasn't quite sure what I would do. I only knew that I would do something.

It wasn't until I was close to the fire that I realized that they were burning the plastic bag that belonged to the old male who gave me meat. The old male they had beaten to death.

I felt a strong impulse to attack these young killers. I wanted to sink my teeth into each of them.

But just as I was about to make my move, one of the louts spun as he swung his stick and he saw me in the firelight. He yelled to his friends, and they reeled toward me.

For a moment I considered taking them on. But they all had heavy sticks, and I am considerably bigger than a stone. So I settled for grabbing a jacket from the pile, and I ran.

They roared as one, and began to give chase. But there was no way they would catch me, even though I was lugging the flapping jacket, a heavy, leather thing and not clean.

The last I heard of the three young killers was what I took for swearing as their noise floated, loud and angry, on the humid night air.

⁜ ⁜

I went back to the old male. I laid the jacket by one of his hands. I pushed a sleeve as best I could into its forceless grasp.

I left the old male to make three trips, returning each time with a beer can. Each can reeked of a killer and probably also bore paw marks.

Then I sat and surveyed the scene. To me it looked as if the old male had grabbed the jacket of one of his beer-drunk attackers and not let go. Perhaps the contents of the jacket would name its owner even if the beer cans did not identify the killers. Cowards that they were, if one of them was captured he would surely squeal on the other two.

I was pleased with my justice. I was pleased for the dead old male. I had given him teeth.

I raised my eyes to the sky, and I cried to the moon. I cried and cried until I heard human beings open their doors. Until I heard them make their way into the hot summer night to see what the fuss in the alley was about. Then I set off into the hot darkness.

The Hit

THE MAN WALKED slowly along the aisle and then stopped. "Excuse me."
The woman looked up from her book. "Yes?"

"Is this seat taken?" He pointed to one of two empty across the table she was resting her elbows on.

"No," she said, without betraying her annoyance. The carriage was by no means full. Elsewhere there were empty pairs of seats, even another table. Oh well, it happens. She could always move to another seat herself. A pain. A fact of life.

The woman picked her book up.

Inevitably the man spoke again. "Are you enjoying it?" The woman said nothing. The man, however, persisted. "The book. Is it good?"

"Fine," the woman said without raising her eyes.

The man said, "It's just that I have been waiting my whole career for this moment."

Still not raising her eyes, and despite her expectations, the woman felt a flicker of curiosity as she digested what he had said. She said, "Oh yes?" in a way that could equally be the prelude for a go-away-and-leave-me-alone outburst.

"My whole career," the man repeated easily. "It's been sort of a dream. A career target. And now it's happened."

The woman put her book down. "What *are* you talking about?" she said.

"I wrote what you are reading," the man said.

"You ..." She looked at the cover of the book.

With a modest laugh, the man said, "I am Clive Kessler. I've always hoped that one day I would see someone reading one of my books on the train and now it's happened. I suppose it's a rite-of-passage event for a writer. A coming of age." He grinned good-naturedly.

The woman smiled. "You're Clive Kessler?" Once the question was out she felt stupid to have asked it.

Kessler reached across the table asking to shake hands. In a mock-American voice he said, "And you are my one millioneth customer so you win the grand prize."

The woman shook hands. "What prize?"

"A cuppa coffee and a Briddish Rail doughnut. D'ya take sugar?"

"Yes," the woman said after a moment. "Thanks."

✤ ✤

By the time Kessler returned with two coffees and two jam doughnuts the woman had read what little there was about the author on the jacket of her paperback thriller.

"I didn't know how much sugar to bring," he said. "If one of these mingy little packets isn't enough you can always scrape some off a doughnut. Here, use mine." He began to scrape sugar onto a serviette.

"No no," she laughed. "This is plenty."

"If you're sure … As my one millioneth customer I want to see you're treated right."

"I must say," she said. "You're younger than I would have expected, for having written eight novels."

"And you're younger than I expected my millioneth reader to be," Kessler said quickly. "No, in fact I am older than I look."

"Are you?"

"Thirty-four. Do I look thirty-four?"

She shook her head. Although his hair was beginning to recede she would have guessed late twenties. Not an unpleasant looking man, and when he joked his face lit up.

"And you're what? About forty-five?"

"Thank you *very* much."

"Fifty? Fifty-five? It's just that my publisher tells me I particularly appeal to the older reader."

"Really?" she asked.

"So I was told."

"I'm surprised."

"I will fax my publisher immediately and have my image corrected," he said. "Conductor? Conductor? I want to send a fax. Where *is* the conductor? They're never around when you need one. So, how old are you? It's not that I would ask on my own account, but if I am to prove my point with the publisher …"

"Twenty," she said.

"Twenty," he repeated. "And lovely with it. And did your parents give you a name, or do they just call you what mine used to call me. 'Oy, you. Come here. Clean this mess. No I don't believe your brother did it.' I was fifteen before I realized that my name wasn't 'Oy, you'. "

"Really?" she asked.

"All those years thinking I was Japanese. Sounds Japanese, doesn't it? 'Oy, you'. People teasing me because I lost the war. I never understood."

"You're joking, aren't you?"

"Let's just say that I lead a rich fantasy life. But of course I have to, don't I?"

"Where do your ideas come from, then?"

"From the very air we breathe. They're all around us."

"No, really."

"Really? Well, as you're a prize-winning reader, I'll tell you. They come from paying attention to what I see and what I read and what happens to me. And then I try to think of different ways it might have happened."

"Different ways?"

"If I do it the same way everybody else does it then there's no point, is there? If I write the three little pigs, who cares? But if I write a story called the three little wolves, then I'm on my way. See?"

"I think so," she said.

"So," Kessler said. "Do you have a name?"

"Catherine. But people call me Cat."

"So, Cat, are you married? Do you have children?"

"Give us a chance!" she said.

"I keep forgetting. You're not one of my typical readers. You're my one millioneth reader."

"Am I? Really?"

"I hereby pronounce you Clive Kessler's official one millioneth reader. If you accept this official position, you must shake my hand again."

They shook hands again but this time the man did not release the woman immediately. "You have nice hands," he said quietly. "But I expect everybody tells you that." Then he let her go.

She said, "No, they don't."

"Well they should. Because you do. And that's official too. But to make your hands official we must shake books on it." He picked up her book. Instinctively she grabbed it too. He shook the book up and down. "There, we've shaken books on it, so it's settled."

"You're weird," she said.

"I'm sorry," he said quietly. "I didn't mean to upset you."

"You didn't upset me," she said.

"I was just a bit lonely. I saw you reading the book. And, well, the rest is history."

"Lonely?" she said.

"A writer's life is a lonely one," he said. "You have to do it by yourself."

"Oh, I see."

"And you never meet any of the people you do it for," he said. "They may buy the book, and eventually the publisher tells you how many you've sold. But normally you never meet anybody who ever reads them. The people who, after all, are the people you wrote the book for."

"I never thought of that," she said.

"Did you ever meet a writer before?"

"Only in school. They had a poet come in. It was in primary school and most of the kids thought her jokes were pretty naff. I kind of liked her though."

"And so you continue to read. And here you are, on the train today, reading one of mine. So, where are you going?"

"To Reading. I'm visiting my dad's mum."

"Do you like her?"

"Not much."

"So, it's a duty visit?"

"Yeah. I go about every couple of months."

"You're a very good granddaughter, Cat."

She laughed. "Dad gives me a tenner and pays the train fare."

"And you make an old woman happy."

"She doesn't usually know who I am, to tell the truth. But it's a day out."

"I'm going to Reading too," the man said.

"What for?"

"Research."

"Oh."

"For my next book. I'm going to have a look at Reading Gaol."

"The gaol. What for?"

"Because famous people have been incarcerated there. Oscar Wilde, for instance."

"Yeah?"

"And Stacey Keach. He's an American actor. Played Mike Hammer on the tele."

"What was he in gaol for?"

"Drugs."

"Oh."

"He's out now though."

"Who's Mike Hammer?"

"Mickey Spillane's psychotic, misogynist private eye."

"Oh."

"Not your thing, private eyes?"

"They're OK, but I like books with more romance in them better."

"And sex?"

She smiled. "Don't mind."

"Like my books?"

She hesitated.

"You haven't got to the sexy bits then?" He nodded at the open book on the table between them.

"What sexy bits?" she asked.

"I don't want to spoil them by telling you," he said easily. "Surprise, unexpectedness … They make sex so much more exciting, don't you think?"

She frowned at him across the table.

"I'm sorry if I've upset you by referring to sex," he said gently. "You said you didn't mind. I didn't mean to offend you. All I mean to do is chat." He raised one of his hands and counted off on his fingers. "One, chat. Two, see Reading Gaol. Three, invite you for a meal after you see your gran. Four, walk around the park. *Then*, if we get to the thumb, then maybe we can talk about sex before the last train home. Something like that."

The man spoke lightly, playfully. But the woman's mood had hardened. He saw it, recognized it, and said, "What's wrong, Cat?"

She picked the book up. "I've read this book before."

"A real fan. That's great. Do you want me to sign it?"

She pulled the book to her chest. "There are no sexy bits in it."

"There aren't?"

"None."

"It's amazing that someone can write a book, can spend all the time and energy it takes to convert blank sheets of paper into something interesting, and then not remember what he's written."

"Yes. It is hard to believe," she said.

"It happens though."

"So tell me the story of the book."

"The story?"

"What is it about?"

"You can write a book," the man said, "and then once you start on another you can't remember a single thing about the first. Not a single thing."

The woman was not impressed with this insight about writers. She and the man looked at one another for a number of seconds.

Then the man said, "I *am* a writer."

"Congratulations."

"My name is John Leith. I'm twenty-seven years old. I've written three novels, and finally one of them got published last summer. Actually published. That's quite a big deal these days. It was called *Winter Rain*. It came out in June. It went back in again in July. I've written another novel since then, but the publishers don't even want to read it. I have always wanted to be a writer, since I was about twelve. I have always wanted to be on a train or a plane and see a beautiful woman reading one of my books. I've wanted to know what it would be like to introduce myself and to see what she felt about what she was reading. Because when I write, the way I do it is by writing as if it's a letter to a woman I love, by writing as if I am making love to her."

So you tell lies to the women you make love to, the woman thought. She said, "And so you made all that stuff up."

"Yes. To find out what it would feel like. To see if it was worth my continuing to write. To see if it was worth keeping on trying."

"And is it?"

"It was very nice while we were talking, while we were getting along. Extremely nice. I liked it."

"Even though you were lying through your teeth."

"You wouldn't have talked to me otherwise, would you?"

"No."

"I have no regrets," he said.

"How did you know there was nothing in the book about the real Clive Kessler?"

"I study the book racks in railroad stations. I make a list of books with no picture of the author and nothing saying he's sixty-five, gay and a leper."

"You make a list?"

"I'm a very organised person."

"Did you really write a book called *Winter* ... whatever it was?"

"*Winter Rain*."

"Yeah."

"No," he said. "I've never written a book. But I'm only twenty-four. I have time."

"Never written a book," she said, "but you have picked up girls this way before."

"Yes," he said.

"Really?"

"No," he said. "In fact, this is the first time I've tried it. I was in Taunton station and I saw you buy a copy and so I looked at another copy and there was nothing about the author, and then I saw you sitting alone." His voice tailed away.

She smiled and raised one eyebrow as she watched him think.

"You said you'd read it before."

"Yes."

"But you bought a new copy."

"I read a library copy," she said, "but I wanted one of my own."

"Oh," he said.

"Or I read a mate's copy, and wanted one of my own. Or I lost my first copy. Or I just wanted two."

He stared at her.

"No more questions? I thought authors were always full of questions."

"*Have* you read it before?"

"Trash like this? Certainly not." She laughed.

"Oh," he said.

"And I don't have a grandmother."

"You don't?"

"I am going to Reading to meet my boyfriend."

"You are?"

"To tell you the absolute truth," she said, "he and I are going to sort out how we can get rid of his wife."

"I don't believe you," the man said. "You're just getting back at me."

"It is the truth," the woman said. "And it's such an exquisite relief to be able to tell someone, someone who can't possibly hurt me."

"I can't?"

"For one thing you're a complete stranger. For another you're a liar and a fantasist. Nobody would ever believe you. I feel really good for having said it out loud now. Not that I am getting cold feet. I'm not. My boyfriend — well he's a little old to be called that — but he's exactly what I have always wanted in a man. He's mature. He's exciting. And he is extremely rich, or at least he will be if his wife dies by accident. My only worry is that he'll chicken out, so chances are I'll have to do it myself. I won't mind that. She's a bitch and a ball-breaker. She deserves to die. I figure I'll run her over. She jogs, so it shouldn't be hard. God, I hate joggers. Don't you?"

"You're making all this up," he said.

Her look at him was the coldest he'd ever seen. "Yeah," she said. "Making it all up. Just don't read the papers for the next few days."

"That's awful," he said.

"That's what I hate about men," she said. "Under the bluster they're so soft. You only go round once in this life, right? Well, this is my chance to get the gold ring."

The man sat staring at her, silenced.

The woman said, "Hey, talking about finally being rid of *her* is making me moist in my tufty club. You fancy a quickie? We could do it in toilet at the end of the carriage. You're not HIV positive, are you?"

"No," he said.

"I didn't think so. I can usually tell by looking."

The man said, "Come on, it's a joke, right?"

"You go first. I'll knock twice when I want to come in."

The man rose unsteadily. He left the carriage without looking behind him.

At his fleeing back the woman made a heartfelt 'V' sign. She finished her coffee. She picked up her book.

If the Glove Fits

I TRIED TO get out of it. I did. For instance, I said, "Look, there's no way — not under any circumstances — I would vote to send someone to the gas chamber. You could show me a video of a guy taking an axe to a dozen five-year-old nuns and feeding the bits into a wood-chipper and I still couldn't put up my hand to put him down."

Something of an exaggeration, but hey ... Being a juror was *not* what I wanted at that point in time and, when you have a clear objective, you take whatever steps you have to, right? "It's a matter of principle," I told the selection clerk. "I just couldn't do it. Sorry." I spread my hands, doing my best to make it look like it was out of my control.

"They ain't asking for the death penalty on this one," the clerk said, "so you'll be OK."

"But it's a First Degree Murder trial."

"That don't mean that they gotta ask for the chamber, and they ain't doing it." He looked at his clipboard. "And you'll get a choice of Second or Manslaughter One on this one too."

"Look," I began again.

"Look yourself, pal. You've already put it off twice on the deferrals, ain't you?"

"Yes, but that's not the issue."

"It is for them. You run out on it and they'll persecute you — jail cell, mug shot, fingerprints, DNA, the whole shooting match. Is that what you want?"

"Well, no."

"Unless you got a baby on the tit, which I don't see, or mental derangement *with* a doctor note?"

I shook my head.

"Then your only chance — and don't tell 'em I said so — your only chance is to go into the selection room and give the defendant a big 'Hiya Jack, long time no see!' "

"It's Charles, isn't it?" I said. "I mean, I have read about the case in the papers. Charles Allen Hall, something like that? Not that I've ever met the man." Which was true, I hadn't.

"There's been so much publicity on this one, just saying you read about it ain't going to be enough to get you sent home, in my opinion," the clerk said. "But you can try the 'I read about it in the papers' route if you want, pal."

✛ ✛

When it was my turn to be questioned by the District Attorney I told him about reading the papers about the case.

He looked me in the eye and put his hand on his hip. "This is the kind of case and the kind of community where it would be hard not to have prior information, Mr. Albertson. The question is, have you in any way come to judgement about the guilt or innocence of the defendant, based on your reading?"

"On my reading?"

"Or any other media source, of course."

"A judgement about the guilt or innocence? No," I said. Which was nothing more than the truth.

And then the DA sat down and said, "No objections to this juror, Your Honor." I never got another chance to talk my way out. I shouldn't have been surprised, though, I guess. Word is that prosecutors like thirtysomething white guys who wear ties.

The defense guy didn't bother getting up from his chair. "Mr. Albertson, do you know what circumstantial evidence is?"

"Well, I think so. It's when what you see — or hear, or whatever — implies what happened instead of being a fingerprint, or somebody who saw you, or it was your blood or whatever."

"Mmmm," he said in a way that sounded like he was impressed with my answer. He looked at the papers on the table in front of him. "And you're a … What is it you do for a living, Mr Albertson?"

"I'm a photographer."

"What do you photograph?"

"I photograph children. In a mall. I'm one of *those* guys." It crossed my mind to add that a photograph was an example of evidence that wasn't circumstantial. But I hesitated because one of life's lessons is, "Don't answer what you're not asked." Although another is, "He who hesitates is lost."

"And do you like your work?"

But the District Attorney butted in before I could answer. "Your Honor, I think my esteemed colleague is going on a wild goose chase here."

The judge, a woman, good looker for her age, she said, "What is your point here, Mr. Mockton?"

Mockton, the defense guy said, "I'm trying to establish Mr. Albertson's attitude to circumstantial evidence, your honor."

"By asking him if he likes his work?" she said, and the tone was pure put-down.

But I thought I saw what Mockton had been getting at. If I like pictures then maybe I don't trust circumstantial evidence.

From what I'd read, the prosecution case against Charles Allen Hall was all circumstantial, which was hardly surprising, especially considering that Westgate & Davies didn't even have closed circuit TV — what a cheap company! But it meant there was no video of Nat Byrd being bashed to death. And there were no witnesses either, at least none I'd read about.

I was formulating what I would say about whether I liked my work when Mockton surprised me by changing the question. He asked, "Do you have previous acquaintance with the defendant, Charles Allen Hall? Or the deceased Nathaniel Byrd?"

The DA jumped to his feet to interrupt. "I object to my esteemed colleague referring to Nathaniel Byrd merely as 'the deceased', Your Honor. By any accounting of the facts in this case, Mr. Byrd is unquestionably the *victim* here."

"Save it for the trial, Mr Valentine," the judge said sharply. Whew. Cute, but I'd hate to pass her strawberry jam for her breakfast toast if what she asked for was raspberry.

"Yes, Your Honor," Valentine, the DA, said, and he sat down.

Mockton for the defense said, "To repeat my question, Mr. Albertson, do you have previous personal acquaintance with the defendant, Charles Allen Hall? Or the late Nathaniel Byrd? Or with anyone else related to this case insofar as you know through your reading or any other source?"

Well, I wasn't going to answer yes to that, was I? "No."

"The defense has no objection to this juror either," Mockton said.

Which was the last thing in the world I wanted to hear. How do I let myself get pinned into the situations where there's no reasonable way out? Man! Story of my life.

✦ ✦

However, by the time they'd picked the rest of the jury and we were all sworn in, I'd come to terms with the fact that I was going to have to serve on this jury and do my level best to do my civic duty. As I said to Juror 6 — I was Juror 5 — when we were having lunch before the tip-off, "It all sounded like a wedding, didn't it?"

"How do you mean," she said. Nice looking girl. Year or two older than me, maybe.

"When the judge said, 'Do any of you know of any reason why you would not be able to come to a fair and just judgement in this trial based solely on the evidence presented?' "

"You've got that down pat," 6 said with a smile, and it was really nice. It transformed her face into a friend's. "Are you a lawyer or something?"

"No, a photographer."

"Oh right, I remember. Kids, in a mall."

"And I do like it," I said, smiling back. "Even though I never got a chance to say so."

"You got kids of your own?" I took it she was half-asking if I was single.

"Me? No. I'd never do that without getting married," I said. "You?"

She shook her head. "Not without Mr. Right there to change some diapers. And when I look out the window I don't see anybody who even resembles Mr. Right."

"Have you checked the door?"

"The ...? Oh, I get it," 6 said. "Windows, doors."

"It's just that I always think, if you're not finding what you want in one place, then maybe you should try looking someplace else."

She raised her eyebrows as if she was saying, And does that mean I ought to be looking in the jury box? What she actually said was, "So tell me, how did you mean it was like a wedding?"

"Like when the priest or whatever says, 'Is there anyone here who —' "

"Oh I get it. Is there anyone with a just cause or impediment. Yeah, I see what you mean now." The smile again.

I've always been a sucker for a nice smile. That's one of the first things that attracted me to Annie.

✜ ✜

In the afternoon the facts of the case were laid out straight-forwardly, if a touch ponderously, by the DA, Valentine, in his opening statement.

The *victim*, Nathaniel Byrd, was the night watchman at a building that included the offices of Westgate & Davies, an accountancy practice with nine employees. Or rather ten employees, until the day of the murder or, possibly, manslaughter.

Charles Allen Hall had been fired by Dan Westgate in the afternoon, for a series of increasingly serious errors and because he'd failed to pull himself together after repeated warnings.

We would be undoubtedly be told by the defense, Mr. Valentine said, that Hall had been under what would be called "stress" because of problems at home. But surely no domestic upset could justify or excuse what he had done that night, beginning with a return to the offices of Westgate & Davies in order to "wreak havoc."

But, Valentine said, while Hall was trashing the very office area he'd worked in, the true *victim* of these events — night watchman Nathaniel Byrd — had interrupted him. With a fury possibly augmented by alcohol Charles Allen Hall had bludgeoned the unfortunate Byrd to death with a blunt instrument.

We, the jury, would be shown police photographs of the *victim* and his horrifying injuries. We would hear how the defendant had at first provided no alibi when questioned by police, and had then offered an alibi that was in many ways demonstrably unsatisfactory. We would also hear from police witnesses that there were no signs of forced entry to Westgate & Davies, a telling detail because it strongly implied the use of a key to enter the premises, which the defendant still had when he was arrested. And further, we would be shown that the defendant already had a history of violence.

At that point the defense guy, Mockton, objected and we were sent out to the deliberation room while the lawyers talked their problems over with the judge.

When we were settled at the big table, I said to 6, "I think if that Valentine guy says the word 'victim' in that pious way one more time I'm going to puke."

But it was an old guy across the table — Juror 11, I think, another suit and tie, like me, but sixty, easy — who said, "We're not supposed to talk about the case."

"I wasn't talking about the case," I said. "I was talking about puking."

6 laughed, but a couple of old biddies next to 11 — they looked like they'd have brought their knitting if they'd have been allowed — one of them clucked and the other tisked and said I should show more respect.

Well, I wasn't going to be put on the defensive. I said to 11 and the biddies, "If I was to say that maybe the prosecutor was making a big emotional deal about the victim because he knew his case was weak, then *that* would be talking about the case and something I shouldn't do. But if I say I am having waves of nausea, then that's about me and not about the case, so it's OK."

As I was talking I saw that everyone at the table was looking at me, except for a young black guy who never seemed to look at anybody or make a sound. So I looked up and down the table. "I hope you all have that straight now." Which I thought was making pretty good use of the opportunity. And nobody said anything back at me, because it was then we got called back into the courtroom.

Once there, the judge said that the reason we had been sent out was so that she and the lawyers could discuss Mr. Valentine's assertion that the defendant had a history of violence. The reason Mr. Mockton had objected, she said, was that he feared Mr. Valentine would try to leave an impression that the defendant was violent in our minds without offering any evidence to back the assertion up. And to do that was wrong. If Mr. Valentine brought up a supposed history, it would be up to him to prove it, and Mr. Mockton promised that he would deny any such history vigorously. Meanwhile she was instructing us all to ignore Mr. Valentine's misplaced reference. So I made a note on my pad to do just that.

Then Valentine began again. Almost at once he said *victim* in that special way, and I nearly laughed, and I knew I couldn't look at 6 or any of the other jurors, so instead I concentrated on Charles Allen Hall's face.

The guy had hardly moved during the whole thing so far. He sat there, looking down at the table in front of him, only there were no papers or anything there. He looked pale, though for all I knew that was the way he usually looked because I'd never seen the guy before that day. But to tell the truth, he didn't look like a violent man to me. I wrote a note on my pad saying, "Look at Hall. He looks more shocked than guilty to me — the way I'd look if I was being tried for something I didn't do. What do you think?" and I pushed it in front of 6. But then I saw that the court official who had led us in and out of the deliberation room was frowning our way. 6 saw it too, and she put her hand on top of my pad and didn't look down.

✥ ✥

When Mockton got up to talk about the defense case, the main thing he said was that Charles Allen Hall had not killed Nathaniel Byrd and nobody could prove that he did.

It was true that Hall had been fired that afternoon. And, also true, he was upset about it. He had worked for Westgate & Davies for more than four years, most of that time without complaint. But in this last half year he'd had a run of bad luck. First his mother had died and then his wife had left him, and he had also endured a number of other difficulties in his private life of which we would hear more later. Ideally, Mockton said, he would have been able to separate his domestic life from his professional life but Charles Allen Hall was not the first — and would not be the last — who couldn't keep the different parts of his life comfortably compartmentalized.

However on the night he was fired Hall had not, repeat *not*, returned to the offices of Westgate & Davies. And he had most certainly *not* been involved in any way whatever with the killing. Charlie Hall commiserated, deeply, with Nathaniel Byrd's widow and with all his other grieving relatives. But what had happened was, simply, nothing to do with him.

When Charlie Hall left Westgate & Davies that afternoon he had gone to a bar. Not an ideal response to his misfortune, but an understandable one. Then — reprehensibly one admits — he had driven around the town despite his inebriated state. His route was aimless and covered a long period of time, and neither Charlie Hall nor the police could altogether reconstruct it. But one thing Hall did remember was that late in the night he had parked on a bridge, and contemplated jumping off and drowning himself.

However unconstructive his drinking, aimless driving, and suicidal thoughts might have been, however much they reflected on the accumulation of problems in his life and, perhaps, his own contribution to them, Charles Allen Hall had *not* returned to the office. He had *not* killed Nathaniel Byrd or anyone else — not even himself. And he should certainly *not* be convicted of anything whatever.

It was *not* the job of the defense, Mockton said, to prove that some other specific person had killed Nathaniel Byrd. And it was *not* the job of the defense to prove that Charlie Hall was innocent of the killing, although by the end we might well decide the defense had done that anyway.

The only job the defense needed to do was underline the extreme weakness of the so-called evidence — all circumstantial — that the prosecution would parade before the court.

Was there a witness to the killing? There was not. Was there a murder weapon for us to see that could be tied to Charlie Hall? There was not. Was there even a witness to place the defendant's car outside Westgate & Davies at the critical time? There was not. Indeed, was there any single piece of direct evidence to link Charles Allen Hall with the crime? There was *not*.

About that time 6 pushed a slip of paper to me. It read, "Is he going to tie himself in 'nots'?" I didn't think it was very funny. In my opinion Mockton was doing pretty well. Even so, I smiled at 6 and she smiled back — that lovely smile — and it felt like we were in school and passing notes and would maybe go to the prom.

When I turned my attention back to Mockton he was saying that the only reason he could make out as to why this prosecution was taking place at all was that it was an election year and Mr. Valentine wanted to keep his name on the front pages.

Not surprisingly, Mr. Valentine got all heated at that point. For a moment I thought they'd be sending us to the deliberation room again, and I was trying to work out how best to use that time — cement things with 6, or apologize to 11 and the biddies or introduce myself to some of the others.

But we never retired again. Mr. Mockton withdrew his remark about a political motivation to the case, the judge told us to forget it, and the trial moved on.

⁕ ⁕

Mr. Valentine started his apolitical prosecution with a parade of policemen. The first, the guy in charge of the investigation, whose name was Proctor, he went through uncontroversial details like how the police had been called to the scene at Westgate & Davies early in the morning and what they'd found there, like the battered body and the wrecked office. "But not," Valentine stressed, "signs of a forced entry?" What he was getting at was it looked like the perpetrator had entered with a key, and even though it sounded like speculation to me, Mockton didn't object.

Valentine gave Proctor a rest and called a forensic guy who said how the damage to both Byrd and the office was consistent with the use of a baseball bat.

And there was other stuff but, frankly, my mind wandered. Mostly I was thinking of Annie and of how happy we would be once this was over and I got off the bad luck of being on the jury duty and we could be together and get on with our lives. I also replayed some of our happier times past, with full X-rated imagery.

It's not that I didn't pay any attention to the case at all, but what was being covered was not what was at issue. After the last cop — a woman policeman, and not pretty at all, though some are — it was the dead man's boss, and he talked about what a reliable employee Nathaniel Byrd had been and what his duties at Westgate & Davies were. All pretty standard stuff.

But then Valentine surprised me, because he put Byrd's widow on the stand. I mean, the guy was dead, right? And he was killed at work. So what the *hell* does the widow have to do with it? Why drag her in?

About the time she was saying her full name was Bernice Joann Regina Byrd — a mouthful for anyone, even someone without as beautiful a mouth as hers — 6 tapped my elbow and slipped me a note which said, "Are you all right?"

I frowned, and crossed her question out, and wrote, "Sure," and if we'd been talking I would have asked her why she asked, but I left it at that, and turned back to the widow.

She was a sad sight in the black dress, but gorgeous at the same time with her sleek brown hair and smooth, pink skin. I would have bet my last dollar that every man in the courtroom was thinking the kind of X-rated stuff I had been thinking about before — at least every man who was a man, if you know what I mean. But I was trying to work out why Valentine had called her.

What he asked about was her husband, and his medical history, because Nathaniel Byrd wasn't always a night watchman. When they met — before he came down with the manic-depression — he was one of those number crunching guys who seem to be inheriting the earth. But then when he when did get his manic-depression he turned out to be one of the few who the L-dopa doesn't work all the way for. The medication fixed the up-down part, but it left him so he couldn't do the numbers like he used to. He had good insurance from the company he'd been crunching for, but life for him and his wife was nothing like what it used to be. And eventually Byrd did the night watchman work to supplement their income, as well as to make him feel that he was bread-winning.

I finally realized what Valentine was up to when he said, "So despite all these problems at home, Mrs. Byrd, your husband performed his job reliably?"

And she nodded and said, "Very reliably. It was a matter of great pride to him."

What Valentine was doing, apart from underlining the Byrd-the-*victim* thing again, was making the point that that Charles Allen Hall wasn't the only guy in the world with problems in his domestic life.

When it was Mockton's turn I saw — at least it seemed to me that I saw — that he considered asking her all kinds of questions, like was the marriage happy and how did you cope when his condition meant he wasn't the guy you married. But that might have strengthened Valentine's point, so instead what Mockton said was, "Mrs. Byrd, please accept sincere condolences for your loss from those of us on this side of the courtroom."

"Thank you," she said. It was only quiet but we all heard it.

Then Mockton said, "No questions for this witness, Your Honor."

✣ ✣

After that, Valentine really got to work on his case. He had Westgate of Westgate & Davies testify about Hall's reaction to being fired — he didn't like it. And he had Westgate say that the bulk of destruction in the office had been to Hall's desk, Hall's computer, and to a filing cabinet which contained the files of clients Hall had worked for. And that the only way into the offices was with a key.

On his turn Mockton asked if any other employees' records had been damaged, and Westgate said they had, how many other employees' papers were affected? To which Westgate could only say that it was several. And while it was still clear that most of the damage was to Hall's stuff, the impression left after Mockton got through was a lot different than the one Valentine left. Mockton also asked how many keys to the office there were, and Westgate said every employee had keys so he — or she — could come in to work nights and weekends.

Then Proctor, the policeman in charge of the investigation, was called back, and he said that it was the Hall-centered focus of the destruction that had made them think of questioning Hall in the first place, especially when they heard he'd been fired that day.

Proctor said that when they got to Hall's apartment he was asleep, dirty and unshaved. They asked him about his movements the previous night but he'd claimed not to remember anything, only after a while he'd come up with the went-to-a-bar, drove-around, stopped-on-a-bridge story.

As well, in Hall's apartment they'd found a metal softball bat that fit the injuries to Byrd and which also fit a lot of the dents in equipment around the office. Moreover, Proctor said, the forensic people had found hairs and flecks of skin belonging to Hall on the dead man's clothing. Valentine said he'd be calling the forensic people back to confirm that.

When it was Mockton's turn he asked Proctor if the search of Hall's apartment, or car, or garage, had turned up any blood-stained clothing. Proctor agreed that it hadn't.

"But there would have been a lot of blood spattered from Mr. Byrd's wounds, wouldn't there?"

"Yes," Proctor said.

"Some of which *must* have gotten on the killer and his weapon."

"In all likelihood, yes."

"So Hall would have had either to dispose of all the clothes he wore, or clean them extremely thoroughly, if he was to leave no trace of the blood on them?"

"Yes."

"But isn't the dirty, disorganized state you found Hall in more consistent with the actions of a man who came home and just fell into bed? Isn't it inconsistent with the actions of a man who had to either throw away every scrap of the clothing he was wearing — including his shoes — or wash them thoroughly?"

Proctor said, "He might have thrown away his clothing and changed into dirty clothes. That could explain it too."

"And what about the bat you found? Did it have traces of blood on it?"

"Well, no. But a metal bat is a lot easier to clean than clothes."

"So you're suggesting that Mr. Hall threw away his clothes, including his shoes and probably his underwear in case a stain had come through. And then he cleaned his bat thoroughly, changed into dirty clothes, and went into a deep sleep. Is that what you're suggesting?"

"I'm not suggesting anything," Proctor said. "That's for you lawyer guys. But it could have happened that way. Or it could be that Hall used another bat entirely and dumped it with the clothes. The fact that he had one bat makes it more likely that he had two."

"Thank you, Mr. Proctor. No more questions about bats or clothes just now." And it was obvious that Mockton had scored good points.

"Instead," he said, "let's turn to the hairs and flecks of skin ..." and he went on to say that hairs and skin cells are only to be expected where a guy has worked for more than four years and that they could easily have gotten on Byrd that way.

The cop agreed it was possible, but it felt to me like Mockton did less well with this one.

Then Mockton asked Proctor if he himself had ever gotten drunk, or known anyone who had, and wasn't Hall's condition and response when the police found him consistent with someone who'd drunk himself stupid and had a very bad hangover. Eventually Proctor said it might be.

"Finally," Mockton said, "after the decision was made to interview my client, did you or anyone in your investigative team actively consider looking for any other possible perpetrator of this crime?"

Proctor squirmed a bit on this one, I thought, and said, "We followed up on every bit of evidence we found. There just wasn't any that pointed in another direction."

"No other keyholders of Westgate & Davies who owned one or more bats?"

"I … don't know," Proctor said.

"No other keyholders without an airtight alibi?"

"I couldn't swear to that either."

"So is the fact of the matter that there was no evidence pointing at anyone else, or that you and your team didn't bother to look for it?"

But he didn't make the cop answer that question, he just sat down. And I thought that was pretty smart. And I was relieved, because if he'd followed through on the whole thing he'd have had to say something like, "Did you explore who might have benefitted from Byrd's death?" and that would have led to questions about whether the widow would get any life insurance, which the jury probably would have found pretty insensitive after having seen her and her grief themselves. No, I thought that Mockton dealt with the police evidence pretty well on the first day.

❖　❖

I said as much to 6 that night at dinner, but before she could give an opinion there was loud tut-tutting from the biddies across the table, and then the court official who was with us stuck his nose in and said, "Mr. Albertson, you must not to talk about the case with anyone, including other jurors."

"Sorry," I said, "but I thought that meant we shouldn't talk about whether he's guilty or not. I didn't think getting the facts clear about what we heard today counted."

"Well, it does," the court official said. "It all counts. You're not to talk about the case at all."

"How about to give the lawyers points for style? Because that Valentine's voice really gets up my nose."

There was a lot of reaction at the table to that but I said, "Hey, hey, I hang on every word Valentine says. It was just my little joke. I'm funny that way."

"As in 'not'?"

The voice came from down the table, and everybody noticed, because it was the first thing the young black guy had said the whole day. He had a strong, rich voice and the way everybody turned to him made me wonder if he was going to be a player after all.

But the court official took the edge off it all by saying, "And may I take this chance to remind everyone that because you are not to watch any news coverage of the trial, the television sets in your rooms have been removed. There is, however, a jury lounge and you may watch television there until ten o'clock."

"Boring," I said. "Who's for the bar?" I turned to 6 and she flashed me one of those smiles.

But the court guy said, "Sorry. There's a TV in the bar so it's off limits."

"Well," I said, "what say we all just vote the guy 'not guilty' now, so we can go home and catch ER?" I only gave it a moment before I said, "Hey, hey, joke, joke."

✢ ✢

But there was no joke when 6 slipped me a napkin with her room number on it. When I saw what it was and glanced at her she gave me a little nod.

Which put me in something of a quandary. I was not *looking* to cheat on Annie. Sure, I do notice women and maybe I flirt a little bit, but nothing serious. I'm not one of these guys for whom commitment is like Buffy to a vampire. I don't think you can get much more committed than I am to my little Annie.

But on the other hand when a woman, like 6 in this case, misunderstands your intentions, I know enough of the world to be careful how I respond. A carelessly spurned woman is a loose cannon and all that.

So in the end the way I worked it out was, if I was to say to 6 "Sorry, but I've got a steady girl friend," that would be fine in itself, no problem. But what she would do is say, "Tell me about her," which I did not want to get into.

I could have lied and made up stories or a different girlfriend, of course but, to tell the truth I've gotten into trouble before telling lies and I don't like to do it unless I really have to. So the way I saw it, I really didn't have much choice — unless I was going to tell her I was a fairy, which didn't appeal to me either.

What I did was go to the TV room after dinner. All the jury were there except 6 and the young black guy, and I made a point of saying nothing at all, just to prove to them I wasn't one of these gotta-be-the-center-of-attention types. I stuck it out through a couple of sit-coms. But about nine I left and what I did was go to 6's room.

She pretended to be surprised to see me. She *said* she only gave me the room number so I could call her on the hotel phones. "But you're here now, so come in."

For a while we did talk about the case. She agreed Mockton had done pretty well today, but that Valentine had his moments too. Then she asked me again if anything had been wrong with me when Byrd's widow was on the stand.

"Only that I could see all the guys ogling her when they *ought* to be ogling you," I said.

"Men talk such shit," she said, but she smiled that smile, and it served to get us onto more personal matters. I didn't know if the court guy would have approved, but I didn't have *his* room number so I couldn't call and ask him.

✛ ✛

Valentine began the next day with the forensic guy who repeated what Proctor the cop had said the day before about dents fitting the bat and how there was hair and skin, only the forensic guy took longer about it. He also took longer to concede Mockton's hair-in-the-air point. But maybe it just felt longer because I was so tired.

Then Valentine brought Proctor back and they went through what Charles Allen Hall had said when he was questioned. And I had to concede it was true the story didn't make Hall look very good.

To begin with he hadn't been cooperative — but hey, who is when they're innocent *and* hungover? Then Hall'd said that after he got fired he guessed he went to the West End Bar and got drunk. But when the cops came back saying nobody at the West End remembered him, Hall said he remembered now, he'd thought about going to the West End but instead he went to a package store and bought a bottle of Scotch and he drove around and around in his car drinking it.

"Where did you go on this drive?" he'd been asked.

"I don't remember exactly, except I stopped and got gas, and then I stopped and bought another bottle — and some nuts, I remember peanuts in there somewhere — and then I drove around some more until I ended up on the Marianne Bridge and I sat there drinking and I was thinking about throwing myself off it. But while I was thinking that, the sun came up, that made me think different. It made me think, 'Maybe I can get through this,' so I chucked the empty bottles over the railings and went home again and I went to sleep and that's where I was when you guys showed up." The way Proctor read it from the transcript of the interview tape made Hall sound pretty unreliable. I wonder if they teach them that at the Police Academy.

It also did not help Hall when Proctor went through how the police had not found any bar or liquor store in town which could confirm anyone buying

Scotch whiskey at the times Hall gave, nor could they find a gas station where anybody remembered him.

"How hard did they look?" I asked 6 in a note. But I agreed that it sounded bad and even worse when Proctor said that when the police looked at Hall's car it was nearly out of gas. And it didn't sound any better either when Proctor said that they'd found not two but three empty Scotch bottles in Hall's apartment.

When Mockton questioned Proctor about this phase of his testimony, he didn't begin with the whiskey. Instead he asked, "Did you, in the course of your investigation, look for any witness to place either Mr. Hall or his car at the scene of the crime that night?"

Proctor said they did look, but hadn't found anyone.

"And may I assume," Mockton said, "that because Mr. Hall was your only suspect, and because you knew that your evidence against him was weak, that your team tried very very hard to find such a witness?"

Valentine didn't like that question, and eventually Mockton had to change it, but the gist was that the cops had tried to find a witness to put Hall at the scene but couldn't. "You must remember," Proctor said, "that the crime took place at 3 a.m. and that witnesses are always thin on the ground at that time of night."

Mockton got the judge to remind the cop to answer only the questions he was asked, but Proctor had made his point, and I saw Valentine smile.

And the truth of the matter is that there wasn't a whole lot more of the trial after that. Mockton didn't contest the gas station, bar or liquor store evidence — so the cops hadn't found anyone, so what? And Valentine didn't have any more case to make. So he said, "We have no need to call any more witnesses, Your Honor. The Prosecution rests."

So it was Mockton's turn, and the first thing he did was to move that the case be dismissed for lack of evidence. I thought that was pretty smart, because it helped underline his point that there wasn't much evidence against Hall.

The judge wasn't playing, however. She said, "Let's let the jury decide on that point Mr. Mockton. Proceed, please."

What he did first was to call the secretary from Westgate & Davies, and he asked her what Charles Allen Hall was wearing the day he was fired.

His point was that if he was still wearing the same clothes when the police picked him up, then where was the blood?

However Valentine got the secretary to say that Hall seemed always to wear the same kind of clothes to work and that if he had two blue shirts she didn't know Hall's clothes well enough to say on that day he was wearing one rather than another. So he could perfectly well have thrown one set of clothes away and still looked pretty much the same. I thought Valentine did pretty well there.

The next person Mockton called was a truck driver who said he'd seen a car like Hall's parked on Marianne Bridge about five in the morning.

But Valentine got him to say that he couldn't be certain it was Hall's car or even that there was only one person in it.

Then Mockton called Hall's landlady who said what a nice man Charles Allen Hall was, how he always paid his rent on time, and also how badly his wife had treated him by running off with a dog groomer.

When the judge asked Valentine if he had any questions for the witness, Valentine just a gave a big, theatrical shrug and shook his head.

"In that case," the judge said, "we will break now for lunch."

❖ ❖

I had missed breakfast, so I was starving. And I also made a point of drinking a lot of coffee so I'd have a chance of paying attention to whatever happened in the afternoon.

So I was feeding my face and trying to think of something to say to 6 so she'd understand that after the trial finished, that was it, when from down the table I heard the young black guy say, "It'll be interesting to see what Hall has to say for himself if he takes the stand."

The court guy said, "Please," and raised a finger.

The black guy nodded, and didn't even say, "Sorry." I scrunched up my nose, thinking that if it had been me saying that, the court guy would've given me another big lecture. They get it easy these days, black guys, I think sometimes. Although I also had to concede that what little this particular guy had said made sense each time. It would be interesting to see how he played out in the jury room, for or against, which might end up being quite influential.

It was then that 6 passed me a note which said, "Cat got your tongue?" It wasn't till I thought about it later that I realized she was making her own joke about what we got up to during the night. At the time I just smiled.

❖ ❖

When the trial reopened after lunch, the first thing Mockton did was put Charles Allen Hall on the stand.

"Mr. Hall, did I advise you to testify in this trial?" Mockton asked him.

Hall cleared his throat and said, "No. You said that there wasn't enough evidence to convict me, but I insisted anyway." Here he turned to us in the jury box. "I wanted to tell them for myself that I'm innocent."

It turned out that Hall had a high, nasal voice. If Valentine's style of talking was irritating, with Hall it was the voice itself. I could see in a minute why Mockton had advised him to keep quiet, and it had nothing to do with the strength of the evidence. Maybe it's just we're all so used to seeing trials on television that it catches us by surprise when someone takes the stand and sounds awful. I knew it couldn't help Hall any no matter what he said.

In fact Mockton's questioning dealt only with Hall's having gotten drunk after he was fired, with his inexperience with large quantities of hard liquor, and with his innocence of all the charges.

"They offered me a deal," Hall said — God, the whine! — "but I'm not going to plead guilty to anything when I am completely innocent. That would be wrong."

Mockton left it at that. Valentine didn't.

We spent more than half an hour listening to Valentine make Hall display his vagueness. The poor guy got more and more rattled the longer he went on. As well as the voice, what we, the jury, got treated to was Hall's growing edginess, which he expressed by rocking in his chair and not seeming to be in control or able to concentrate.

It sure made *me* think that the guy was perfectly capable of doing something violent. God help his cellmate if they ever did send him to the slam. Or God help Hall, depending on who his cellmate was …

On his redirect Mockton had Hall say again what a bad year it had been for him, and how he was innocent and shouldn't have to prove it. That wrapped up the trial, except for the closing statements.

With them, unsurprisingly Valentine went the *victim* route. Mockton went the he-may-have-behaved-stupidly-but-he's-innocent-of-all-charges route. The judge reminded us what the charges were and what Mr. Valentine had to prove for us to convict, and then she sent us to our deliberations.

❖ ❖

The young black guy was elected as our foreman. It happened so quickly that it felt like they'd all decided it ahead of time. Maybe they did, last night, in a commercial after I'd left the sit-coms to visit 6.

"My name is Darryl Jackson," the black guy said. "And our concern here is to come to a just verdict, assessing whether the accused had motive, means and opportunity to commit the crimes he is accused of, assessing whether the prosecutor proved these three things, and assessing whether there is any reasonable doubt about the defendant's guilt."

Looking back, it seems like the black guy, Jackson, kidnapped the whole session. Or maybe it was just the contrast between the way he spoke — which was articulate and direct — and our recent memories of Hall's voice and the way he got rattled. It was like Jackson snowed us. That's my best "assessment" of what happened, looking back.

To begin he had us vote. "It's pretty clear," he said, "that Mr. Hall is not guilty of First Degree Murder, because as the judge said, that requires premeditation. Speaking personally, it didn't sound to me like Mr. Hall could premeditate his way out of a paper bag. But perhaps others of you have a different opinion?"

Well, who's going to put a hand up for Murder One after that?

"No?" Jackson said. "No one wants to argue that taking the bat with him implies premeditation? Well, I agree. The bat need only mean that he planned to smash up the computer. So now that we're down to the nitty-gritty, I suggest we have a secret ballot and consider the charge of Murder in the Second Degree: did he know what he was doing might kill poor Byrd, but he didn't plan to do it? Shall we vote?"

After that, to tell you the truth I was surprised that as many as three of us voted, "Not Guilty."

Jackson said, "Well, three quarters of us feel that the correct verdict in this case is guilty of Murder in the Second Degree. Given that the balance of our opinion is so one-sided, I think it my help if our next step is to invite our three not-guiltys to identify themselves and tell us what their reservations are. So, who voted 'not guilty'?"

I felt guilty just putting my hand up.

"Predictable," Jackson said. "Who else?"

6 put her hand up and, to my surprise, so did one of the biddies.

Jackson turned to 6 and the biddy first. "What did you feel was the weakness of the prosecution case?"

They both said, in essence, that they didn't think the case had been proved beyond reasonable doubt.

"Would you favor convicting him for Manslaughter?" Jackson asked. "Or is it your opinion that Hall should be set free?"

The biddy went for Manslaughter like a shot. 6 dithered, saying she'd consider it, but that she'd need to think about it, and that she thought we ought to discuss the evidence more. And as she said that, she turned to look at me.

Jackson too. "And you, Juror 5?" he said. "Do you think Manslaughter is the correct verdict?"

I could almost hear him think, "Which might get us out of here in time to see ER? Oh, no. That was last night." Sarcastic bastard.

Showtime. I took a breath. I said, "My feelings about the verdict seem to be stronger than those of the others. I don't feel that the prosecution has proved its case at all."

"Hmmm," Jackson said. "All right, let's consider motive … If we have to believe that Hall was angry at being fired, decided to take revenge, got interrupted and struck out and the person interrupting him, then motive is OK by me. Or do you think he had no motive?"

I said, "He had possible motive, sure."

"Okay, let's consider means. You don't go for the bat?"

"The bat's not the problem."

Jackson raised his eyebrows. "Opportunity?"

"Obviously he had the opportunity," I said, "but what I'm worrying about is what wasn't presented."

Jackson said, "But we are charged to evaluate what they gave us."

"I'm saying there could easily be reasonable doubt."

"Go on."

"There could be any number of other people out there who might have done it. Like, for instance, it could have been a burglar who was interrupted."

"A burglar with a key?" Jackson said.

"Or what about other possible disgruntled employees? I'm not at all convinced that the police explored the other possibilities."

"I think that's a fair point," Jackson said. "Anything else?"

"Isn't it smart when someone is killed to ask who benefits from the death?"

"You're accusing Mrs. Byrd?" Jackson said. His expression said he found what I was saying hard to believe.

"No," I said. "But we don't know it was her, or only her, who might have gained from Byrd's death. Byrd might have had other relatives who had problems with him, or he might have owed money, or ..." I could feel myself running out of steam. "The point is that there are so many possibilities that weren't raised, and therefore weren't eliminated."

It was 6 who turned to me and said, "There's still the key. How did anyone else get in?"

"All those employees had keys. And it's not just them. How about whoever does the cleaning?" I said. "Like, a cleaner could have a key and a relative, say, copies it, and uses it to go in to look for money, and, say, Nat Byrd interrupts him, or her, and Byrd gets killed and then the person smashes up the place to make it look like ... something else. And maybe it was only accidental that what got smashed was what Hall worked on."

There was a silence in the room. Then Jackson said, "Something like that could have happened, I suppose. But we had no evidence from the defense to make any such suggestion."

"How much money did they have to check stuff like that out? It's not like Hall is OJ."

"And, two," Jackson said, "it's quite a coincidence that Hall's stuff is damaged the very same day he gets fired, don't you think??"

"But coincidences happen," I said. "They do. They really do."

"Hmm," Jackson said.

"Look," I said, "give me a few minutes to think about this. All right? All right?"

"Well …"

"Where's the john? I need the john."

And I left the deliberation room to lock myself in a cubicle and think it through.

✣ ✣

I don't like injustice. I never have. I never understand how people can say, "No reasonable doubt," so easily. Just about everything has doubt. You never know. Not really.

I never asked to be on this jury. What I did was ask *not* to be on it. Not. But then it happened.

So what was I supposed to do? I'm part of a jury. I'm supposed to listen to all the stuff and scratch my chinny-chin-chin and say yes he did it or no he didn't do it. And that's all right, I can play that game. For a while.

But then, then Valentine rolls in the widow.

And that's what finishes it off. Kills it stone dead, like Nat Byrd. Poor old dumb innocent Natty Byrd. The *victim.* Yep. He was that all right.

And what am I supposed to do? What are my options? Like, suppose I stonewall it. Suppose I say to the other jurors, "Say what you like, but I'm voting Hall 'Not Guilty' to everything." And then we go a few rounds with them trying to convince me, and I hold out. And maybe if I get to sleep on it I can be more convincing tomorrow about why he shouldn't be convicted, and maybe I get a few of the others to vote with me. Or maybe I don't.

But I can still hold out, and then Jackson would tell the court guy go back to the judge and say, "The jury's split and no, there's no chance of a unanimous verdict."

So the judge declares it hung. And Hall is not convicted. Which is no more than justice, because the guy is innocent.

And what happens then is that maybe there's another trial and maybe there isn't. But probably there is. That's because the vote is probably eleven to one "Guilty," and because it *is* an election year.

So chances are there's another trial, and another jury. A trial and jury that is without me. But it *is* with the widow.

The poor, grieving widow, who would have to go through the whole business again. Testifying, answering questions.

And maybe, just maybe, she would be asked different questions. Worse questions.

Like, did your husband have any life insurance you are beneficiary of.

Yes, she would say. A lot. A whole lot.

Like, did you make a copy of your husband's keys and give them to your lover?

Not that she would answer that truthfully.

Like, was the plan that your lover would kill your husband and then make a mess so that it looked like your husband had interrupted a burglar?

If anyone ever asked her such a question she'd just sit there silent, and beautiful. But in her heart she'd be saying, "He was *supposed* to break a window so it looked like a break-in, only he forgot, the dummy, what with the distraction of just having committed his first murder."

No, those would be bad questions to be put to Bernice Joann Regina Byrd, my Jo-Annie.

Despite the surprise — and shock — of her being called to give evidence this time, those questions weren't put to her. And they can't be put to her. And I can't act in such a way that makes it possible for them to be put to her. I just can't.

⁂ ⁂

Poor Charles Allen Hall. It certainly has been a bad year for him. He's a *victim* here too, isn't he? Coincidences do happen.

But I have no choice. I have to change my vote and find him guilty, of something. When all he's really guilty of is being unlucky.

I didn't have the slightest idea whose computer I was pounding on with *my* aluminum softball bat. Or whose desk. Or whose filing cabinet.

Annie and I never once expected someone else to go down for the murder. But, for sure, we had no intention of going down for it ourselves.

What we expected would happen was that the police would come to her, that they would check her out. And they would find big life insurance policies, all right, but they all dated from before she and her natty Natty first married. He was an important number cruncher. The company valued its young, healthy important number crunchers. The medical and life policies came as part of the Natty package.

Years pass. Natty has his bad luck. And one fine day Annie and I meet in a mall when she laughs at me for failing to be polite to the mother of an unphotogenic little monster. And we go for a cup of coffee. And together we dream about living somewhere else, comfortably.

Which now we will.

There's a knock on the cubicle door. I hear Jackson's rich voice. "Are you all right in there?"

The true answer is that I don't know. But I say, "Fine. Out in a minute."

Which is more than poor, unlucky, nasal Charles Allen Hall will be.

Oh well. Maybe Mockton will appeal.

You Pay for Everything

"**S**OMETHING HAS TO be done, Eugene."

"I know," I said.

"Now," Sarah said. "It has to be done now."

"I *know*."

"A child who shoplifts needs to learn from the experience, needs to know from day one that actions have consequences and that he isn't going to be protected from those consequences all his life. Roy is fourteen years old."

"I know how old the boy is," I said.

"*I* can talk to him, of course." She looked at me. "But ..."

"I know," I said.

"When we agreed that you would have more to do with his discipline I had no idea that — "

"I know," I said.

"Mind you, I should have known something was up. That girl. Those kids. But I had no idea."

Neither had I. "I ... I'll talk to him."

"Now?"

"In ... I need a little time to think what I'm going to say."

"He's going to go back to the shops and apologize to the shopkeepers and work it off."

"I need a little time."

"But tell him now."

"I said — "

"I mean, tell him now that you're going to talk to him in a few minutes."

"I ..."

"You have to, Eugene."

"All right, all right. Where is he?"

"In his room."

"All right."

She stared at me.

"I'm going," I said.

I went.

At the bottom of the stairs I called, "Roy."

131

"He'll never be able to hear you over that racket."

I went upstairs. I knocked on his door. Eventually he opened it "Oh. It's you."

"Who did you expect? The laughing policeman?"

"It had to be somebody, I suppose."

"Roy ..." I said.

"Right first time."

"Roy, I expect to see you in the dining room in an hour exactly."

"What about?"

"What do you think 'about'?"

"Yeah. All right." He looked at me as if he were a little bit puzzled.

I turned and left him.

Sarah was waiting at the bottom of the stairs. "Well?"

"I'm seeing him in the dining room in an hour."

"An hour!"

I raised my voice slightly and said, "If he has time to stew and get worried, it will be more effective."

"Honestly!"

"Let me do it my way."

She turned without saying anything more and went to her study.

I went to the dining room to think about how, exactly, I would say what I had to say.

2

Roy turned up three minutes late. That he came at all, without my having to call him, I considered to be a good sign. He came into the dining room. He stood inside the door.

"Close the door. Then sit down across from me."

"Look, I did it and I'm sorry, all right? It wasn't the smartest thing in the world, especially to get caught. I know that."

I stood up and said, "Close the door, and then sit across from me."

He was surprised.

He shrugged. He did it.

"I want to tell you a story," I said.

A smirk.

"What's funny?"

"You reminded me of a comedian all of a sudden."

"I can see to it that your life is made very unpleasant," I said.

Neither of us knew how true that was, but the idea wasn't so funny. "Say what you have to say," he said.

"I want to tell you a story that an old man told me once."

Roy sat motionless.

"This old man was in a British Home Stores one day. It was a long time ago. Well, quite a long time ago. It was a wet day. One of those days that you think, 'If God meant people to live in England he'd have given them gills,' you know what I mean?"

Seemingly not. A mistake. Never mind.

"And the old man was drying himself off. He had just come in and he stood to the side, a few rows into the store, and he was drying himself off, as I said, and he suddenly noticed a girl. The girl turned out to be about your age, but she looked older, about seventeen. She had long straight hair the colour of summer sand and she had chocolatey brown eyes, the kind that are so rich and warm that they make you wonder why you ever thought eyes any other colour were pretty. A lovely girl. Absolutely perfect and gorgeous. But as the old man looked on he saw her take two cardigans off the counter, and put them into a pocket she had sewn inside her raincoat. The old man couldn't believe it. He stood transfixed. And as he did so, he saw her move along the counter and take two more."

"What colour were they?" Roy asked.

"What?"

"The cardigans. I just wondered what colour they were?"

"How the hell do I know what colour they were?" This was an awful child and I hated him.

"I just thought the old man might have told you."

"He didn't. All right?"

His silence was acquiescence.

"So the old man saw her steal four cardigans and then, then suddenly she looked up as if she had felt him watching her. She turned to face him and all she did was look into his eyes. And they stood for several seconds. That's a long time when two people are looking at each other, but this old man was a very precise person, and if he said it was several seconds, I'm sure it was.

"And then the girl said, 'Are you going to shop me, or what?' But the old man said, 'No. Not if you come with me for a cup of tea. For I have something to tell you.' "

"Well, rather than be turned in, the girl went with the old man to the store's restaurant and they got a pot of tea for two and they found a quiet table and they sat down. And after a few uneasy moments, the old man said, 'Now listen to me. I want to tell you something.' "

I looked at Roy.

He looked at me. But only for a moment.

"Do you see?" I said. "What I want to tell you is what this old man told that girl."

"Yeah all right. Get on with it, will you?" But he didn't say this last bit sharply, so I didn't take offence.

I said, "What the old man told the girl was something that had happened to him when he was younger. This old man had had a daughter and *she* had shoplifted once and they found out about it at her school. The man who found out was the Deputy Head and he found out because he was questioning a friend of the girl's about something else and the friend had misinterpreted a question and she answered it in such a way that the Deputy Head became suspicious and asked her more questions as if he already knew and that tricked the girl into telling him everything she knew about the shoplifting. I don't remember the details of what the old man told me, but you know the kind of thing."

Roy sat motionless.

"Well, the point is this. The Deputy Head came to the old man and his wife, just as Mr. Morrison came to your mother and me the other day, and the Deputy Head told them what he had found out and that led to a big family row. Just like the one we had here last night."

I gave Roy a moment to remember.

Then I said, "Only moreso, because the girl was not the type anyone would have expected to get herself involved in something like that. Which is not to say that we don't think highly of you too, Roy, but you aren't exactly serious, quiet and studious — and wouldn't want to be — but this girl was. Anyway the old man said there was a sleepless night or two, and tears and recriminations and apologies and all that. And then, two days later, there was an incident at the school."

I paused for a moment to try to heighten the impact on Roy.

Then I said, "At the school a girl, another girl, went to her teacher and said that some money had been stolen from her bag during P.E. This was not the first time that money had been stolen from children during this P.E. class and the teacher had been keeping a special eye on the comings and goings of the girls in the class. And it happened that the old man's daughter had asked to go to the changing room during the particular class that the other girl said she'd had her money stolen. Well, you can almost imagine what happened. Can you?"

Roy said nothing, but he was paying attention.

"The P.E. teacher told the Deputy Head. And the Deputy Head called the old man's daughter into his office. And he asked her about the stolen money. She denied she had taken it.

"But the Deputy Head didn't believe her. And — with the P.E. teacher there — the Deputy Head questioned the old man's daughter for more than two hours. He tried everything he could think of. He tried shouting at her. He tried saying he *knew* she had taken the money. He tried threatening her with what would happen if she didn't confess. He tried to tell her he understood and if she would only confess, he wouldn't punish her, that the important thing was that she owned up. He talked sweetly to her. He screamed at her. He tried absolutely everything he could think of. But the girl wouldn't admit taking the money."

"Maybe she didn't take it," Roy said.

"That's what she said and kept saying and even though she was getting more and more hysterical as the Deputy Head kept saying 'I know you did it. I know you're guilty.' All the way through she kept denying it. But by the end she was in tears and out of her head and really mixed-up. And finally the Deputy Head realized that he wasn't going to get the girl to admit taking the other girl's money. Now during the time that the old man's daughter was being interrogated she said over and over again, 'Let me call my father. Please call my father,' so after the two hours, when the girl was longer able to do anything but cry the Deputy Head rang the father, who was at home. He explained that the daughter was under suspicion of stealing some money. He explained that the daughter denied it, but that he, the Deputy Head, frankly thought that she was guilty. And could the old man, who obviously was younger then, could the old man come and pick his daughter up from school and perhaps talk some sense into her himself. The old man told me that then he asked to speak to his daughter. The Deputy Head put her on and the daughter said to him, 'Daddy, they say I stole some money, but I didn't do it.' "

It was getting to me. I could hardly swallow or hold the rush of tears from the feeling I had for what I was about to say.

But I stopped for a moment and took some breaths. So I could tell Roy, "And the old man told me that he said to his daughter, 'Confess if you did it.' That's what he said to her. 'Confess if you did it.' "

I didn't cry. But I had to stop again and I blinked my eyes and breathed hard.

Roy was studying me.

It took a long time for me to get going again, but I said, "The old man was crying when he told me what he had said: 'Confess if you did it.' "

"Is that it?" Roy asked.

"No," I said.

He waited for me.

Eventually I said, "I'm not going to drag this out. The old man came to the school and he picked up his daughter and brought her home. What happened was that that night the daughter took her own life."

I waited for Roy.

Roy said nothing.

"Did you hear what I said?"

"Yeah. She topped herself."

"She 'topped' herself. Yes. She topped herself and she left a note for her father and the note said, 'You didn't believe me.' "

"That's pretty tough," Roy said quietly.

"It turned out that the girl at school whose money had been stolen decided next day that it hadn't been stolen at all. But it was too late by then."

"Yeah, tough," Roy said again.

"Well, I was telling you that the old man, a long time after all this had happened, was telling this story to the girl in British Home Stores."

"Is that the one on Market Street?"

"Yes, as it happens."

"And the girl had brown eyes."

"What?" I had made that up, and I couldn't remember what I had said, only that she was pretty. But I've always loved those rich brown eyes, like my first wife had. Only she always wished she'd had blue eyes like her sister. Silly girl.

"Oh yes. Brown eyes," I said.

"So what happened?"

"About what?"

"The girl with the brown eyes that the old man caught boosting sweaters."

"Well," I said, "he took her for a cup of tea."

"A pot."

"Yeah, a pot of tea. He took her for a pot of tea and told her this story and he could see that even though the questions she asked were a bit unfeeling, the story had actually moved her, that she had really taken it in. And the conclusion he wanted her to draw was this: that things that you do have consequences. Like, in your case, *you* are going to have to go back to all the shops you stole from and give back what you stole to the owners and apologize to them."

"There was only the two. There's no point in talking like I'm Al Capone or nothing."

"But it's more than that, Roy. The point is that the consequences of your actions can be bigger, far bigger than ever you think they're going to be. Life is a terribly dangerous place at the best of times. I can go to an appointment on any single day and find out that when I come back your mother has been killed or … or hurt. Or she can find out that I've been hurt or killed, or you have been. All by things we have absolutely no control over. Like a car or a crazy person."

"The world's full of nutters," Roy contributed.

"But the point is that we are all potential victims of things we can't control. So it's just plain crazy for us to take big chances with the things that we *can* control. Do you *understand?*"

Roy blinked. He said, "No. You're saying I've got to keep indoors all day every day in case I get run down by a car?"

"Don't be stupid! You're trivializing what I'm saying to you."

"I'm not stupid. You're just not making yourself clear."

"What I'm saying the old man was saying was this: his daughter shoplifted. *That* was the crazy risk, because she didn't think through the consequences of her action and what it might mean to her. In her case it meant that later, in a critical situation, her father no longer believed in her, and she couldn't live anymore without her father's belief. She never knew that she would die as a result of her shoplifting, but that's what happened. And what was the father supposed to do? Believe her against the opinion of the school? Fresh from the upset and confusion of just having learned that his princess of a daughter — the quiet one, the studious one — had, all the time, been consorting with a little gang of vicious, ugly, crazy children who lured her into crime and smoking and drinking and then, when she was dead and gone, had the nerve, the brazen gall to claim that it was she who had led them, that it was her idea all along. I could have *killed* them when I heard that. *Killed* them!"

After I stopped crying and pounding the table I realized that Roy was looking at me with a degree of fear in his eyes. He shook a little and said, "Look Uncle Eugene, I know I was really stupid to steal stuff. I'll never do it again."

I couldn't speak. I just nodded.

"Is it over? Can I go?"

I nodded again, and he got up and left quickly and closed the door behind himself.

3

A little later I was working in the study when Sarah knocked and came in.

"Hi," I said.

"What are you doing?" she asked.

"Writing a little story."

"Is it all right if I interrupt?"

"Sure. I'm nearly finished and I know how it comes out."

"What did you say to Roy?" There was an urgency in her voice, but it was not a displeased urgency.

I tried to think of how to describe what I had said.

While I was thinking Sarah said, "Whatever it was he came out of the dining room almost running. He actually apologized to me. He was ever so much more contrite than he was this afternoon."

"Good. That's what you wanted isn't it?"

"Well, sure."

"What's a brother for if not to help his only sister out when she's in a tough spot with her eldest child?"

"But what did you *say?* No one's had that kind of effect on Roy since Arthur died. Come on, you've got to tell me what you told him."

"Well," I said, "I told him a little bit about the time Dad found out you'd been shoplifting."

"*I've* told him about that. But having my bottom spanked for picking up comics that weren't mine is hardly the kind of stuff that would affect a hard case like Roy."

"Well let's just say this," I said: "There is hardly any point in being a writer if you can't embellish the truth a bit. Now is there?"

Suicide Note

THERE ARE NOVELS where the wife says of her suicide husband, "He wouldn't have done *that*. You didn't know him like I did." Or where the mistress (even one who used to be a wife) says, "But I talked to him that very afternoon and he was completely normal and cheerful."

Crap lines like that are supposed to inspire the 'tec to traipse around a whole book and lift the coffin lid from the suicide's life. Revelations follow. Surprise, surprise. But it's a crap book that begins that way. I ought to know. I wrote one.

Still, I *was* cheerful on the telephone today. It was with neither wife nor mistress, but my agent and I made him laugh. So when he hears he'll say, "John was so cheerful at three-fifteen."

But it's six o'clock now, and I'm not cheerful.

Haven't I been "not cheerful" before? Of course! What do you take me for, a machine? I've been here many many times.

Ah, but then why the different denouement today? Well, 'tec, that's for you to determine, once your client slaps down hard-earned cash, and instructs you to decrypt the *truth*. Or are you a weary copper seeking diversion, or an inspired amateur with a "hunch"? Well, good luck to you all.

Oh, let's start by dispatching the obvious, OK? The easy handles you'll grasp for by reflex. No, I wasn't a gambler with debts galore. And I had no habit I couldn't afford to sustain. I was not being blackmailed, and no past sins were about to present themselves. Take my word for it, 'tec.

And the domestic life? Well, the (current) wife watches *Neighbours* and sometimes leaves her shoes near the top of the stairs (I always wondered if that was intentional, making it possible for an accident to happen.) But she says she loves me and has steadfastly refused to break the routine of our life by running away with another man, woman, or motorcycle gang. She's OK.

Our sole child is healthy. He passed his exams, and — God help me — cohabits with a social worker. But at least he and Daphne B.A., M.A., C.Q.S.W., eschew pregnancy and thus far feel no need to make public vows of private matters. The lad even rings each Sunday.

Do you enter the (past) wife and current lover under "domestic," 'tec, or does she get a category of her own? No matter, she'll give you no progress. No conscience riven with guilt. No wronged husband. No unattainable quest-unto-death to live together again.

139

Oh, once upon a time she was a love story, *the* love story of my life. We met at college, hate at first sight. A year later I followed her everywhere. Even, gawd help me, onto a stage. I was "Plebeian C" in *Julius Caesar* and spoke a line, and all for love.

Love's a funny bugger, you know, 'tec. Love brings two people together, but then the togetherness kills the love. Do you need me to define my terms? Love is: an illusion with an itch. You won't go far wrong applying that, 'tec, though you'll have to trust me on it if you're under forty.

So you have two people in love. Ah. Hearts and flowers, trumpets and earth-moving equipment. But how — tell me — how do you sustain *illusion* when you live with someone? When you share nooks and split crannies. When you get up in the middle of the night to go to the bog and she's there sitting on it? You do *not* thus sustain illusion, young 'tec. And as the illusion, so the itch. Ways part. She was an actress, you know.

But no, 'tec, ours was not a "love" rekindled thirty years on. What happened was she got a disease (and *that* is truly none of your business.) I read about it in a magazine and wrote. She wrote back. I called, first on the phone and then the old-fashioned way. We talked. We touched. And lo it came to pass that we traded comforts, 1st Widow and I. But you won't solve your case with her, 'tec. Like as not she'll be the one who asks you the loudest.

How about health? You'll enjoy my GP, 'tec, if you invite him for a drink and ask him about his ten years in India. But he won't open his file on me and hint, with professional discretion, at AIDS or a hypochondriacal obsession with motor neurone disease. My knees creak and I get someone else to mow the grass because of "the back." But the salt still has some savour. I am mobile. I make occasional laughter, occasional love. Look elsewhere, 'tec!

So where *do* you look for clues? At the method?

Now there I nearly succumbed. It was a sore temptation to go out with a splash. And I had a plan, one that befits my craft. I would write a story, then publish, market and promote it myself. It would be called "Islam Sucks."

Oh come on, 'tec, don't go priggish on me. Islam does suck. Just like all the other holy hoodoo that masquerades as verity.

After publication of my story, I would do the rounds. Copies to everyone! A vellum copy to Iran. Then I'd sit back to await my fatwa.

Elegant, eh, 'tec? I kill myself by inspiring others to murder me. But, alas, chancy. And time-consuming. To keep the pot boiling I'd have to produce sequelae: "Islam Still Sucks"; "Islam Keeps on Sucking." To mobilize the media, I'd have to initiate book burnings of the Koran. Of course to make sure there was an adequate supply of Korans to burn, I'd have to publish them.

I could have made a mint out of killing myself, 'tec. Do you sense, as I do, how the Amereichans would *love* a chance to burn some books? There is an untapped moronic rabidity in that country that would be just suited by self-righteous destruction of printed words. They are deeply suspicious of books over there because there are no commercials between chapters.

Chances are, before the muslims got to me, I'd be killed by an assassin's Bible. Some enraged bermuda-shorted bigot would "bean" me with it because the Koran was outselling his own restrictive justification to do down to others. Amereicha has truly taken religion to its bosom. How they brag on "freedom" but punish non-confomity.

But I am revealing myself, 'tec. Yes, our brothers across the water never took to my books. They couldn't cope with words they hadn't learned to spell from cheerleaders. They failed to understand that last chapters can be free from mind-gagging sentimentality. They thought irony was a laundering term. But I did well enough without them, 'tec. They are not why you are here.

The splashy end *was* tempting, and it would have moved my backlist (death is so often a good career move.) But I couldn't be bothered and I settled for pills today instead.

Why? You keep asking that. Solely on behalf of your clients, of course. Or are you involved? Perhaps. So perhaps I'll give you a clue. I came close to doing this once before, you know, a year ago. What happened was that I failed to recognize a beautiful woman who recognized me. Does that help you?

Do you need more? Yesterday I read a diary and found that when I was nineteen I took a cricket ball and a bat onto a playing field. Over and over I threw the ball up in the air and I drove it, elbow high and bat straight. I *felt* that I did not want to die without having improved my straight drive.

It's a long time since I was nineteen. I was married less than two years later.

I grow tired, 'tec. The act is upon me. It is happening so perhaps it's time to offer some truth.

Why today? The *real* reason is … Wait for it. Because there *is* no reason.

See, one time or another I'd have ended like this anyway, 'tec. So why not now?

And I have always been resolved *not* to footstep other people completely. I'm not ill. I'm not broke. I am not celibate or completely cerebrate. Even the weather is good today, springlike. Why not now?

I chose today because it's time. I never left a library book to overdue.

"He was so cheerful this afternoon. What terrible and dramatic and secret thing could have happened to lead him to this?"

You'll have to make it up, 'tec, write that fiction, because the answer is that nothing happened. Nothing. The vast void, sensation in its absence.

That, 'tec, is what you have to work with. You'll earn your fee. "He says that the absence of a reason was the reason." Explain *that* to the widows.

Family Business

A T 09.38 HOURS Gina heard footsteps on the stairs. She sat up from the typewriter and ran a hand through her hair. When the door opened she was ready with businesslike attention.

In the old days the door had the words "Please knock before entering" lettered at the bottom of the glass. When Gina took over as receptionist/secretary she pointed out that nobody could come up the stairs without being heard and suggested that the door could do without being knocked on. The Old Man, of course, hadn't changed the door, but one of the first things Angelo had done was get the sign painter in. The lettering was altered to "No need to knock before entering." It was longer and that disturbed the symmetry and the Old Man didn't like it and Gina's idea had been to paint out all the stuff about knocking, but Angelo had gone one better and that was Angelo for you.

When the door opened a woman looked hesitantly into the room.

"Hi," Gina said. "Come in."

The woman was about forty with graying brown hair. Despite the invitation she was still uncertain. "Is this the detective agency?" she asked. "The private detectives?"

"That's right. Can we help you?"

The woman looked as if she were reminding herself of a decision already made. She stepped in and closed the door behind her carefully. Then she turned to face Gina. "Is the detective in?"

"We have a number of operatives," Gina said, "but they are all out working at the moment."

"Oh."

"Mr. Angelo Lunghi is the head of the agency. I can call him on his car phone if it is an emergency."

"I know all about car phones," the woman said. But it didn't sound like an emergency.

Gina said, "Hey, why don't you sit down and tell me what the problem is."

"You?" The woman's face said, "You? The receptionist?"

"That's right. What you say to me is entirely confidential, I promise you. And although Mr. Lunghi supervises all our cases personally, I can certainly assess whether we are likely to be able to help you with the sort of problem you think you might want us to work on."

"I see," the woman said.

"As well as being receptionist and secretary here," Gina said, "I am also Mr. Lunghi's wife."

2

Dinner was served at 19.10. It was the Lunghis' traditional Thursday evening meal, a hot chili made by Rosetta, Angelo's sister. Rosetta's domestic duties doubled with a part time role as agency bookkeeper. Thursday was a full family evening. The Old Man and Mama came down from their apartment, and the two children, David and Marie, were expected to organize their school and social lives in such a way as to be there. Only Sal — Salvatore, Angelo's older brother the painter — was not regularly there on Thursdays, Sunday afternoons and Tuesdays. But quite often he came and sometimes he brought one of his models, as he called them. It was not an issue.

Gina's parents lived in another city.

Tonight Angelo rubbed his hands together as he sat down. "Good good good."

"Hey, and what's wrong with spaghetti?" the Old Man asked. But it was in a friendly way and he said that sort of thing often. Spaghetti, or some other pasta, was on Sunday.

"Sorry I didn't get back to the office," Angelo said.

"We coped," Gina said.

"You know that guy Hardwick?"

They all knew that guy Hardwick, as various bits of investigation for Hardwick's lawyers had formed the major part of the agency's work for more than four weeks.

"Suddenly Hardwick decides that he *does* remember where he was on the night of April 18th."

A groan went up from around the table.

"If he's going to be stupid enough to plead amnesia," the Old Man said, "then he ought to smart enough to remember that he has amnesia."

Everybody laughed.

"So what came into the office today?" Angelo asked.

"We were pretty busy."

"Good good good," Angelo said and rubbed his hands.

David mimicked his father a moment after. "Gooda gooda gooda."

"Smart alec." Angelo swatted David on the top of the head.

David reconstructed his hair. It was all good-humored.

"The main thing was a woman whose son has too much money."

"We should all have such a problem," Mama said.

"But as far as the woman can tell, the son doesn't work for it. He doesn't have a regular job and he won't explain where it comes from."

Everyone was listening now. Most of the agency's work was done for lawyers or involved missing relatives or related to faithless spouses. The Old Man had once had a murder and would only too happily tell the whole thing yet again, but by normal standards a son with too much money was unusual. The diners began to vie gently for the chance to ask Gina questions.

Angelo held up his hand and established chairmanship. "Marie."

"How old is the son?" Marie, fourteen, asked.

"Too old for you, my girl," Gina said.

Marie blushed, but smiled. She enjoyed her position as the family heartbreaker.

"The boy is twenty-two."

"And he still lives at home?" Angelo asked.

"You still live at home," the Old Man said.

"Our situation is not an ordinary one," Mama said.

"That's right," David said. They all looked at him. "Our house is bigger than most people's." David was a pretender for "family wit."

"Twenty-two years of age." The Old Man looked thoughtful. "So what does he do that his mother doesn't know what he does?"

Gina said, "Well, he goes out evenings and nights and then sleeps late into the days. His last job that the mother knows about was helping a friend paint a house, but that was more than a year ago." Gina's face suggested that there was some unusual bit of information about the boy that was awaiting the right question.

"He's got boyfriends?" Mama asked.

"No."

"He's not a goddamned artist?" This was the Old Man.

Gina shook her head.

"He's enrolled in night school and that's why he stays up late?" Rosetta, the bookkeeper, offered.

"That's pretty tricky thinking," David said with admiration.

Rosetta smiled.

Angelo considered, staring at his wife. "So what's it going to be?" he asked himself aloud. "So what's it going to be?"

"Give up?" Gina asked.

"Never," the Old Man said.

Gina said, "This unemployed lay-about kid has a one year old car and a car telephone. And when he goes out at night and his mother asks him what he's been doing, all he will say is, 'Driving.' "

"Well well well," Angelo said. He looked around the table. Everyone else was looking at him. It was a matter of who had driving licenses. And who could be asked to stay up all night to follow the son.

"We could ask Salvatore," Mama said. She didn't like the Old Man to be out at night. There'd been enough of that, one way and another, when he was younger.

Gina said, "Yes. He'd be interested in the work."

"Work? He wants work, he can come here to work, he wants work. Right, Angelo?"

"Sally knows he's always got a place here if he wants it, Papa," Angelo said. "But he'll never do it."

"Never is a long time," the Old Man said. "But while I'm alive I think I agree with you."

"That'll be forever," Marie said and the Old Man, who doted on his only granddaughter, beamed and said, "There. Now there's a child!"

"I'm glad you like my handiwork, Papa," Gina said.

The Old Man looked at Gina for a moment and then burst into loud laughter. He also liked his daughter-in-law.

"So how's it left with this woman?" Angelo asked.

"It's left I got the car and its plate number and the address, the car phone number, the names, all that."

"You mean we're on tonight?"

"I already called Salvatore. He's happy to do the night, or split shifts if you prefer. I didn't know exactly what you had to do tomorrow about the Hardwick."

"Right," Angelo said. "Or we could use Max, or Johnny."

"Outside ops are expensive," Rosetta said.

"Salvatore ain't cheap," Angelo said.

"At least he's family," Mama said.

"I'm family," the Old Man said. "Huh! What's this you treat me like I couldn't follow a giraffe in a herd of mice? Am I not here? I got bad breath from the chili?"

"I haven't forgotten you, Papa," Angelo said.

"You're on shoplifting at Quicks again tomorrow," Gina said.

"Cheaper to get a store detective replacement for me daytime than hire an outside op short notice tonight."

"We're not going to hire anybody tonight except Sal," Angelo said. "I don't know what we're fussing about. We can cover it. We can cover most things."

"Dad?" David asked.

"Uh huh?"

"Can I come out with you tonight?"

"I don't know I'm going out."

"Can I go out with Uncle Sal, then?"

"Not on a school night," Gina said.

David said, "I could try to spin you a yarn about not having school, the teachers having one of those funny days they have or something, but it *is* a school day tomorrow."

"Is that supposed to be news?" Angelo asked.

"But it's not an important day, Dad. No tests and I've got no homework. It's a good day for me to be out the night before."

"Nice try, kid," Angelo said.

"Aw Dad!"

"If we're still on it tomorrow night, maybe then. A Friday or a Saturday night."

"Or both?"

"We'll see. We'll see." Angelo turned back to Gina. "What's the financial?"

"The mother has some money an aunt left her. She intended to fix the house up, but she's too worried about this kid. She's sure he's up to no good."

"What's the name?"

"The boy is Richard Hopkins."

"He has a police record?"

"I rang Charlie. It's mixed. He had some juvenile for a couple of muggings. The last few years he was arrested twice again, for burglaries, but the charges were dropped."

"What does she say about if we find he's engaged in criminal activities?" Angelo asked.

"Of course, she wants a chance to 'handle' it herself. I told her that really depended on what we found out, if we found out anything."

"Sal will find out tonight whether the kid is going to be easy to tail or whether we'll need a team."

"So you want Sally on all night. No shifts?"

"Not unless he needs it. If he does then maybe Papa will cover him." Angelo looked at his father. The Old Man looked at his wife. Mama looked at Gina. "I'll talk to Sally," Gina said, "but we left it that he would do the night unless he heard different.

"So," Angelo said, "you said it was busy. What else came in?"

"Well," Gina said, "there was this woman who found a comb in the back seat of her husband's car. She wanted *him* followed."

"Suddenly it's follow follow follow," Angelo said.

"But she didn't realize how expensive it was or how long it might take."

"To follow a comb?" David asked.

"She went home to think about just how bad she wants to find out who belongs to the comb."

"You should get paid, all the good marriage advice you give out for free," Angelo said.

"Free free free," David said.

3

At 10.55 the next morning Salvatore dropped in to report to Gina on his night's activities.

"Going to need me again tonight?"

"I don't know yet, Sal," Gina said.

"It's just I got a model booked. I can unbook her if it's important."

"I'll call him on the car phone."

Gina tried to get Angelo, but he wasn't in his car. "Sorry," she said. "I'll try him later."

"I thought it through," Sal said, "and this one it isn't that important I know ahead. Just let me know around dinner time, eh?"

"You want to come here to eat tonight?"

"No thanks, kid." In a playful way he said, "You ever done any modeling?"

"Only in my spare time." A joke since everyone acknowledged that Gina never had spare time.

"Get hard up, give me a call."

"You want the money for last night now?"

"Yeah, I'll take it now, now you mention it." He laughed. They both knew who was hard up for what.

Dinner was early on a Friday night to make it easier for David and Marie, who liked to go out. Rosetta went out Fridays too, with her fiancé of the last four years who was agonizing over the morality of divorce, if not necessarily over other moralities. Gina usually cooked on Fridays, unless it was busy.

Angelo was already in when Gina made her way to the kitchen from the office. He had scrubbed some potatoes.

"So what did Sally have to say?" Angelo asked.

Normally they would have waited to talk till mealtime, but with the possibility that David would be riding if Angelo went out, they needed to plan ahead.

"Sally said that Richard Hopkins didn't have a clue he was being followed and that he should be easy for one car."

"That's something."

"What did he do?"

"That's on Morris Street, isn't it?" "Sal got there about 20.00. 21.35 Hopkins left his home address alone. He drove downtown and went to a back street cafe called Henry's. Do you know it?"

"That's it. Do you know what it is?"

"Give me a clue."

"Stays open all night."

"Cabbies?"

Gina smiled.

Angelo considered the information. "How long was Hopkins there?"

"Only about half an hour. Then drove around till 2 a.m."

"Just drove around?"

"That's what Sally says. He took down the street names for a while, but the kid didn't stop anywhere. He just drove till 02.08. He might have been making calls from his car phone but Sally didn't think so."

"If he did, who to?"

Gina shrugged.

"And what happened then?"

"He picked up a prostitute at 02.08."

"I see."

"Dropped her off again at 02.32."

"He may have too much money but he doesn't like to waste it on frills, eh?"

"And then he went home," Gina said.

"Hmm."

"His mother said he usually stays out till 5 or 6, so this probably wasn't typical. I don't know what he does during the days. It was the evenings and nights that really worried her and I told her that's what we would concentrate on."

"I think we stick at that for the time being. What she's worried about is how he makes his money, not how he spends it."

Gina nodded.

"I'll take him tonight. Maybe Sally again tomorrow."

"And David?"

They looked at each other. Angelo said, "I more or less promised him."

"Yes," Gina said. "All right."

4

Angelo and David arrived at Hopkins's house at 18.30. Their car was well stocked for a long night. Thermos flasks, cassette tapes, food, blankets. Specimen bottles in case of emergency. David had been out before and knew the routine.

"Which car is it, Dad?"

"The Rover across the street. Under the light."

"I see."

"How're your eyes these days, son? Can you read the plate?"

David read the plate. Then he said, "Grandad told Mum that he wanted to come along tonight."

"She didn't say anything to me."

"I think Grandma talked him out of it."

"More likely there's a private eye movie on TV. He loves to pick holes in the stories."

"Coincidences like that don't happen in real life," David said, mimicking his grandfather.

Angelo smiled. "That's it."

"Did you ever think of being something other than a private detective, Dad?"

"I didn't get much choice once Uncle Sal went to art school."

"Do you mind?"

"I don't think about it."

"What else would you have wanted to do?"

Angelo considered. "I don't know."

"A painter like Uncle Sal?"

"You got to be able to draw," he said.

"Uncle Sal's stuff doesn't look like you have to draw so well."

"You've got to be able to draw to make it look like you can't," Angelo said.

"Oh," David said. Then, "What time do you think this Hopkins guy is going to come out of his house?

"Not for a while yet," Angelo said. "He didn't go out till 21.30 last night."

But Angelo was wrong, because three minutes later, 19.22, Richard Hopkins left his mother's house and got into his car.

"Write it down," Angelo said to David as he started his car.

David took up the clipboard and wrote a note of the time that they had begun the active phase of their surveillance.

5

Hopkins's night began much as the previous night had begun. He drove to Henry's Café, parked and went in.

The windows of the cafe were large and clear enough that Hopkins could be seen going to the counter, placing an order and then moving to a table where another man already sat. Hopkins had entered the café at 19.49.

The man behind the counter carried a tray to Hopkins at 19.53. The man sitting with Hopkins rose and left the cafe at 19.59. This man got into one of the taxis up the street.

"Glasses," Angelo said with some urgency, but David already had the large lens binoculars out of the case and resting on the dashboard for support.

When the man pulled his taxi into the road, David read out the vehicle's license plate number and the name of the taxi company. Angelo recorded these on the clipboard sheet.

The large lens binoculars intensified light from dim images. It was as if one's eyes were suddenly five times as big: more light from the object was caught.

At 20.06 Angelo took some money from his coin purse. "What say you go in and ask for a couple of doughnuts?"

"Really?"

"See whether Hopkins is talking to anybody else, but if he gets up to leave, just walk back to the car."

"Okay, Dad."

"And don't tell your mother."

David winked and put out his hand for the money.

By 20.13 he was back in the car. "Hopkins isn't talking to anybody else. What he's got left is some French fries on a plate and he took a drink from whatever he had a cup of."

Angelo began to speak but David interrupted him. "There was a mirror behind the counter," he said. "I watched him in that."

"Good boy," he said. Then, "Hang on. I think we're rolling."

Hopkins had risen from his table and was walking toward the café door.

"Got a time for me, Dad?" David asked.

6

Hopkins drove to a petrol station. Angelo pulled into a street on the opposite side of the road, turned around and waited, ready to go in whichever direction Hopkins chose after his stop.

Hopkins filled his Rover. David practiced with the binoculars and saw that that the car had taken 18.3 gallons.

Angelo wrote it down.

Hopkins left the petrol station and drove around for about half an hour. Then, at 21.02, he pulled over to the side of the road suddenly. Angelo had to drive past him. David turned to see what was happening in the Rover.

"It looks like he's talking on the phone, Dad," David said.

Angelo again used a side street and turned around quickly. They could just make out Hopkins's car.

After another minute, Hopkins put the phone away and made a squealing U-turn. Angelo followed and already it was obvious that the car was being driven in a much more positive manner than before.

This went on for thirteen minutes as they followed the Rover across town. Then suddenly Hopkins slowed down. Taking a chance, Angelo — who felt he was lucky still to be with the car — slowed down too rather than pass it has he had done the time before.

Hopkins did not *seem* to notice them.

"If he'd been looking for us," Angelo said to his quiet son, "he'd have spotted us a dozen times."

Hopkins appeared instead to be intent on finding a house number. After a few moments of slow cruising, he parked. Angelo pulled past him and parked on the other side of the street.

"Stay here and stay low," he said to David.

Angelo got out of his car. As he pretended to lock the vehicle door he saw which way Hopkins had turned. Angelo turned in the other direction and walked till he found a telephone pole. In a sideways movement he dropped into its shadow and turned back to watch Hopkins.

Hopkins had not moved far. For several seconds he studied the front of a pebble-dashed house. Then he began to walk. Angelo followed at a distance and was not seen.

Hopkins walked around the block. When he got to the front of the house again, he walked up the path and then through a passageway between the house and its garage.

Angelo slipped back to his car where David waited eagerly.

"What's up, Dad?"

"I think he's committing a burglary," Angelo said. "If I had to guess, that would be it." He started his car.

"Where we going?"

"I want to get in a better position in case he leaves fast."

Angelo turned around in the street and reparked several yards behind Hopkins's Rover.

They waited for nearly an hour, but eventually Hopkins reappeared. He carried two suitcases and was not in any apparent hurry.

"A cool son of a bitch," Angelo said tensely.

David was pleased that his father used such language with him. Gina would have disapproved.

Hopkins did not have to unlock his boot. A push of a button and the lid flew up. In a moment the cases were in and the lid back down. Hopkins got into his car then, and, still without seeming to rush, he drove away.

"What do we do now, Dad?"

"Follow follow follow," Angelo said. He pulled out to do just that but he was in deep thought.

7

Angelo and David came home when Hopkins finally returned to his mother's house, parked and went in. David, who knew he had been along for something unusual, *said* he was too excited to sleep. But when Angelo sent him upstairs the boy went with a yawn, not a murmur. He was too tired to be too excited to sleep.

Angelo left a note on the kitchen table for Gina to wake him at 08.00 and to get the Old Man down. On another day Rosetta would have been summoned, but normally she stayed out on a Friday night and did not return on Saturday until noon.

At 08.22, when everyone was together and Angelo had had a cup of coffee, he said, "It's tough to know exactly what to do."

He explained what they had done and seen. That Hopkins had pulled up to use his car phone a second time and had driven to look for and find a second address after that. But something had perhaps looked wrong to him. He had not stayed long and had not gone onto the property at the second address.

"And then," Angelo said, "cool as can be, he drives back to Henry's and has some more food. This is at 04.12 in the morning. He's got two suitcases of stolen goods in the boot of his car and he still hasn't locked it because when he finally went back to his mother's house, he locked it before he went inside. We have to decide what to do."

"What does the client want you to do?" the Old Man asked.

Gina said, "She said she wanted to know if there was anything criminal before we told the police."

"How much money have you had?" the Old Man asked.

"Fee for three nights, but no expenses."

"She seem flush?"

"She didn't hesitate writing the cheque," Gina said.

"Our responsibility is to her," the Old Man said.

"I am tempted to follow Hopkins this morning," Angelo said. "To find out what he does with it all. He must be going to take it to a fence today."

"Who's paying you to do that?" the Old Man asked. "Suddenly you're an independent working on commission from the police?"

"I know I know I know, Papa," Angelo said. "All I said was that I am tempted. How often do we get something like this?"

"Not often, but so what?"

"Who paid you to solve the murder of Norman Stiles?"

"At least I was being paid to check a suspect's alibi. So I stumbled onto a different way to alibi him. At least I was being paid."

"You never got paid."

"So at least I was owed," the Old Man said with dignity.

"I know I know I know," Angelo said. "But I am still tempted."

"I think we should contact Mrs. Hopkins," Gina said. "She is the client."

The Old Man looked at Gina fondly.

"I was also tempted to try to look in the boot while Hopkins was in Henry's."

"Not with David there!"

"But Hopkins parked right in front of the café a second time."

They sat quietly for a moment. "We have an obligation to the client," Angelo said. "And an obligation to the police. But if it came to it I think I could deal with the police."

At the time they didn't ask him what he meant by that.

Instead, Gina said, "How tired are you?"

"I'm all right."

"This is what we do," Gina said. "We drive two cars to the Hopkins's. I go up to the door to see if I can talk to Mrs. Hopkins myself. You wait outside and you follow the son if he goes anywhere. Papa mans the office."

"Who's paying, he goes anywhere?" the Old Man demanded again.

"Maybe if we recover what's in the suitcases the owners will pay us," Gina said.

8

Gina and Angelo arrived at 09.49. Before Gina went in, Angelo slipped into her passenger seat. "I'm not that happy about you going in cold," Angelo said.

"I'll be all right."

He raised his eyebrows. "Tell her you're there only as a courtesy. We have to tell the police. We have no choice."

She nodded and got out.

And it was true enough. Police everywhere are territorial. It is not enough that justice be done in the end. If it's their justice, they are loathe for anybody else to administer it. The bulk of a detective agency's business may not require direct involvement in or knowledge of illegality, but to be in the bad books of the local police can obstruct detective work a hundred times in a year. It is not something to risk casually.

But Angelo was still tempted to let Hopkins have a little rope and to see where he would take the suitcases.

In the end, however, stronger forces determined his actions.

Gina went to the door of the house at 09.54. She was admitted to the house at 09.55 by Mrs. Hopkins.

By 10.15 Angelo, who was tired anyway, was tired of waiting. He sorely wished he had put a wire on Gina. Or at least a call device, a button to be pushed in case of emergency. They had relied too much on the assumption that the young Hopkins's routine of sleeping late would be followed. Angelo felt he had been careless from fatigue. He felt that he had put Gina at risk. He began to think that he should go to the house himself.

Having begun to think that, he began to decide to do it.

He got out of his car. He walked toward the house. He stood by the Rover. Gina did not emerge.

Angelo looked at the house. Then he began to walk up the path.

Suddenly the front door burst open. Richard Hopkins ran out.

Angelo froze. He was in no man's land. He couldn't get back to his own car to follow without it being obvious. And Gina still did not appear.

So Angelo tackled Hopkins himself as the young man ran by.

The act was a surprise to both of them. But with Hopkins on the ground, Angelo knew enough to keep him there.

The young man swore and spluttered and made enquiries as to what Angelo thought he was doing.

Angelo informed him that he was making a citizen's arrest, something he was perfectly entitled to do as long as he was willing to take the consequences of the risk of a false citizen's arrest.

Angelo fretted, however, because all he could do was sit there holding Hopkins immobile when what he wanted to do was go into the house to make sure Gina was all right.

Why had Hopkins come out running? What had he done? What had happened to the two women inside. Angelo at first asked for answers from Hopkins. Then he screamed at his prisoner.

9

Rosetta served Sunday dinner at 14.00 sharp. It was an even numbered Sunday in the month so her "fiancé," Walter, was in attendance. Salvatore was there too, with a model named Carol.

"This is my father," Sal said, introducing her to the Old Man. "And my mother. And this is Carol. She models for me."

"Hello," Mama said tersely. Carol didn't *look* like a potential wife.

"Welcome and make yourself at home," the Old Man said. He shook Carol's hand warmly.

"My niece and nephew, Marie and David."

"Hello."

"Hello."

"Hello."

"Gina you met at the door. That's Rosetta behind the salad bowl and Walter next to her. And the man with the black eye is my brother Angelo. He's about to tell us how he got it."

Carol exchanged greetings with the rest of the family and everyone sat down.

In fact the one thing that Angelo didn't remember was when he had been hit in the eye. "I was just worried that the creep had done something to my Gina."

Gina said, "The boy's mother was crying. I was trying to console her. She was a client after all."

"But I didn't know."

"No."

"So there I was sitting on this kid," Angelo began, "having made a citizen's arrest."

"Tricky," the Old Man said. "Very tricky."

"I thought I had him bang to rights," Angelo said. "I thought he had two suitcases of stolen goods locked in the boot of his car. I had seen him put them there. I had seen him lock it. I thought ..."

"But it was hours later."

"I know I know I know. Nobody was more surprised than me when the police opened the boot and it was empty."

"That was a very tense moment," Gina agreed.

"I was thinking I'm going to go down for assault and battery," Angelo said. "A friend Charlie may be over there, but he's not going to be able to get me off assault and battery."

Angelo paused to look around the room.

"So come on," Salvatore said. "Get on with it. How come you're here and smiling instead of being held without bail because you're a menace to society?"

Gina said, "My Angelo did say before we went out that he thought he could deal with the police."

Angelo said, "I was bothered by this Hopkins's car telephone."

"He didn't use it the night I was out," Sal said.

"But with David and me ..." Angelo turned to David who beamed at the guest. "With David and me he used it twice. Each time he then goes to a house somewhere. First time it's suitcases. Second time nothing. But it bothered me. And then I'm thinking, each night he's down at this taxi drivers' café. First night he eats alone. Second night he eats with a cabby. You see, the problem about these phone calls is who is it he's talking to?"

"So my boy puts two and two together," the Old Man said to Carol proudly.

"And he got twenty-two," David said.

"And this time I am lucky," Angelo said.

"Who was it then?" Carol asked.

"What I decided was that Hopkins was working with a taxi driver. The driver picked up fares from a house. He noticed whether they locked up when they left, whether it looked like it was empty. Then after he took them to their destination, he telephoned Hopkins. Gave him the address. Hopkins went to the address, confirmed to his own satisfaction that the house was empty. And burgled it if he thought it was right."

"Wow," Carol said.

"Some nights the driver got no appropriate fares or maybe he was just off work — that's what I think happened your night, Sal."

Salvatore nodded.

"But Friday night they had a big score. The police figured there was nearly three grand's worth in the suitcases. When they recovered them from the cabby. Who drove home at the end of his shift via Hopkins's house. Duplicate key to Hopkins's boot. Takes the cases at six in the morning. Who sees?"

"They were still in his taxi when the police got there," Gina said.

"And how did you know who the taxi driver was?" Carol asked.

"Ah, that was down to David," Angelo said. "He was the one who spotted the man's taxi ID number when he went on shift. A word with his dispatcher and he was dispatched."

"All in a night's work, ma'am," David said.

Carol smiled.

"The police say they think it will resolve about forty outstanding burglaries," Gina said.

"Well done, brother," Salvatore said with genuine pride.

"Thanks."

"Are people ready to eat?" Rosetta asked.

"So what's today?" the Old Man asked.

"Linguini, with my special sauce," Rosetta said.

"That's Italian for 'little tongues'," the Old Man said.

"Oh," Carol said.

"So," the Old Man said to Rosetta, "what's wrong with some chili?"

There was a quiet groan from several places around the table.

"A family joke," Salvatore explained.

"You know, Carol," the Old Man said, "one time, one time only, I was involved in an actual *murder* case."

"Gosh," Carol said.

"The man's name was Norman Stiles and he was a small-time bookmaker."

A second, louder groan was heard. But not by the Old Man.

Wedding Bells

THE CASE CAME into the office because of Salvatore, the artist.

One of Sal's models — a real one this time, in that she did actually model for him as well — took Sal home for a meal, to meet her father. The meal was a *disaster*, a real-thing double-dyed wave-the-flag disaster, at least for the purpose it was conceived for. Salvatore and "Daddy" did not hit it off.

"I don't know why I agreed to go in the first place," Sal said when he talked about it next afternoon at the Lunghi family's Sunday dinner.

Mama had a theory. "Maybe, just maybe, this girl you thought she was something special, like you were thinking serious."

"We'll whip her with the vermicelli," David, Salvatore's nephew and Mama's grandson, suggested.

There were a few titters around the table.

But not from Mama. Her preoccupation, re Salvatore, was to get him married. To anybody. "We'll whip her into shape once we know what we're dealing with," she had stated in his absence once. The "whipping meal" was what David was referring to.

Nevertheless everyone was impressed to hear that Sal had actually gone to this girl's house. How many he got up to in his studio there weren't records, though Sal did bring quite a few of his "models" to his home. Home not being where he lived, but where he grew up and where the family's detective agency was based.

But bringing a girl to meet the Lunghi family was a whole different issue. Knowing the family was part of knowing Salvatore.

"You wouldn't believe," Sal said. "I didn't believe. This guy started cross-examining me as soon as I got through the door. How much do I make in a year? What are my prospects? That whole archaic business"

"He raises two daughters alone after a wife divorces him. I can understand he'd be concerned," the Old Man said. But his mind was on other things. "Hey, Rosetta!" the Old Man called. "My plate's starving to death out here!"

Rosetta was Salvatore's baby sister but it was his brother Angelo's wife who spoke next. "Some people," Gina said, "they still expect their daughters to keep company with civilized people." But the comment was not being offered to

Salvatore. Gina directed the remark at Marie, her own fourteen year old who was hanging around with an earring and a nineteen year old earring at that.

"Ollie, Ollie Ollie," Marie's brother David taunted.

Marie blushed, to her great annoyance, but lifted her nose as an act of disdain and self-control. "Oliver is very intelligent," she said.

"I tell you," Sal said. "I told this guy, my intentions for your daughter are to get her to move less when she is posing and to pose less when she is supposed to be moving."

The Old Man — Salvatore and Angelo and Rosetta's father — laughed. Mama, their mother, did not.

"So anyway," Sal said, "I told this guy about the agency and how I do a bit of private detecting for the family business to supplement my income. I *thought* it would rattle him even more. I can tell you I was already fed up and getting sick to my stomach even before the cook trotted out this weird stuff they said was veal."

"Veal they serve you," Mama said. "What's this girl's name again? Susie?"

"No need to remember it anymore, Mama," Sal said.

"Oh, poor girl!" Mama said.

Rosetta served the roasted chicken. "Use it right, Mama, and veal doesn't have to cost that much." As well as organizing household domestic functions, Rosetta was the family business's bookkeeper. She knew how much things cost.

Angelo, now head of the Lunghi Private Detective Agency that the Old Man had started, said, "You said there was something coming to us in a business way."

"That's right," Salvatore said. "I thought when I said 'private detective' the guy might take it as the last straw and kick me out then and there and tell me never to darken his daughter again."

"But he didn't?" Gina asked.

"Instead he looked at Susie and then he looked back at me and he started crying."

2

"My brother Salvatore said that you would probably be contacting us, Mr. Notice," Angelo said. "But before we start I want to introduce my wife, Gina."

Howard Notice was a small, lugubrious looking man who revealed an extremely expensive suit when the Lunghis finally prevailed on him to take his overcoat off. He and Gina shook hands.

"Gina is our receptionist and handles agency correspondence. This is a family business and I like, when I can, to have Gina present at initial interviews. It saves time later on."

"I understand," Notice said.

"Salvatore did not tell us what it was all about," Angelo lied. "Only that you had a problem, that it was a delicate family matter and that you felt in desperate need of help. Desperate was the word he used. I don't know whether that was accurate."

"It was an accurate use of the word," Notice said.

"Perhaps then you would explain the situation. I can assure you that anything you tell us will be kept in complete confidence. My father once went to jail rather than betray something he was told in confidence in this office."

The exaggerated assurance seemed to have the desired effect. Notice said, "I have a desperate problem with my daughter."

"Would that be Susan?" Angelo asked.

"No. With my younger daughter, Barbara."

"I see."

"She wants to get married. She *insists* on getting married." Howard Notice was suddenly breathing heavily. He had to pause.

Angelo and Gina exchanged glances. "Uh huh," Angelo said, to invite a continuation.

"A marriage must be prevented. It must not take place. The man she wants to marry is an opportunist. It is obvious to anyone with an ounce of sense that he is only after what he perceives as her money, that is, her share of my money."

"I see," Angelo said.

"Of course I could tie the actual cash up so he can't get hold of it, but even more than the money I am convinced that a lasting and legal entanglement with this man will ruin my poor Barbara's youth and possibly her life. It's already bad enough that she wishes to see this man, to spend her time with him. At least, thank God, she is sensible enough to know that she is too young to have children."

"How old is Barbara?" Gina asked.

"Eighteen years of age. She is in art school, like Susie. With her whole life in front of her. A wonderful girl. Well, they both are."

"And the man?" Angelo asked.

"His name is Maurice Franklin. He is a so-called student himself, although he is twenty-six years old and has been enrolled at the school for seven years. Seven years! He has a veneer of maturity that is, no doubt, attractive to a child of Barbara's age. But he is a sponger. He is the type to live off older women, but he has latched onto my little Barbara for some reason and I intend to make him let her go."

"I see." Angelo's voice was thoughtful.

"I *cannot*, I *will not* let this marriage take place. Legal entanglements have ruined vast tracts of my life and I will not let that happen to my children. I am just about prepared to commit murder, I'm that determined."

"I see," Angelo said. His voice was calm but his face showed clearly the surprise he felt at hearing such a threat.

For the first time Notice smiled. "I would prefer, of course, to avoid such an extreme. Which is why I have to come to you."

3

"So this Susie of Salvatore's has real money?" Mama said. "Oh dear, oh dear."

"It wasn't Salvatore the father disliked, Mama," Gina said. "He was upset about the younger daughter's boyfriend."

"At least my Salvatore is an established artist. Not some *student* of twenty-six years old."

"What does the father do?" the Old Man asked Angelo. "Is he good for the bill?"

"He owns some farms and other property. He got started with inherited money but he's been successful in his own right too." After a dramatic pause he added, "And we're to spare no expense." Angelo knew that would impress the Old Man.

"He actually said that?"

"Yes."

"I one time had a guy say that, but what he meant as it turned out was that I should spare none of my expense. He never paid up."

"Yes he did," Mama said. "Eventually."

"Not everything. Not everything."

"But most."

"All right. He paid most. But it was a struggle."

"Howard Notice gave us a retainer of a thousand pounds."

"I like your no expense better than mine," the Old Man said. "What do you think he's going to be worth to us, Angelo?"

"That's the problem."

"What problem?"

"I'm not all that sure what we can do for him."

"We can lighten his wallet a little, we can do that."

Gina said, "At eighteen the girl is old enough that the father can't prevent her from marrying, if she doesn't care what he thinks."

"Maybe this Maurice Franklin is already married," the Old Man said.

"That's one place to start and I thought you might check that out tomorrow, Papa."

"Right. Is he already married. I got it."

"Otherwise I think we're looking to turn up information that will show this Franklin in a bad light and put Barbara off. That could be his personal past or it could be other women that he is seeing now. But at the moment we are just fishing around for a real angle."

"Are you going in gang-busters," the Old Man asked. "Or do you wait till I find out about the marital?"

"The client is very upset," Gina said. "We'll explore all the possibilities as fast as we can. He even threatened to kill Franklin rather than see him marry the girl."

"We can't have that," the Old Man said with concern.

"No," Gina said.

"If he kills we never get paid."

4

Gang-busters it was. Salvatore was booked to follow Franklin. The Old Man worked on marital status, police record, credit rating, educational history, bank balance and all the other information held on the various computers that long-established Lunghi contacts might be able to get at.

Angelo himself went to the art school to talk to administrators and secretaries and to get what he could generally from school sources.

And Gina decided to have a go at Maurice Franklin himself. "I'll go in as a rich woman thinking about enrolling as a mature student. I'll sound him out to ask if there are any special problems about being older than the other students. I'll flirt outrageously and see if he'll propose to me on the spot."

Angelo was not altogether taken with the idea, but Gina insisted. "The client said spare no expense and I've been dying for an excuse to buy a mini skirt."

5

After two days the gang-busters knew a lot about Maurice Franklin. They knew he was twenty-nine and not twenty-six. They knew that his mother was a widow. They knew he'd had hi-fi equipment repossessed, but was not now in debt.

Paid off by Barbara?

They knew that he was five feet seven inches tall and they knew that a number of the girls at the college admired his wiry-but-muscular physique, front and back.

They knew that he liked green socks and lived in a room alone.

They knew his status with the school was ambiguous but since he was "helpful" with the students and didn't cost anything, the teaching staff was happy enough to have him around.

"Some kind of 'helpful,' " Gina said dismissively. She'd met Franklin easily, but mini skirt and the recent death of her extremely rich husband notwithstanding, he had not displayed the slightest interest in her.

However a sculpture teacher who dressed like a cowboy begged her to model for him so Gina did not return dispirited. The cowboy had been steered to talk of Franklin. He obviously disliked "the lecherous bum," and had referred to him as a womaniser. But pressed, the cowboy had conceded that these days Franklin seemed totally occupied with Barbara Notice. "Personally I just can't see it," the cowboy had said.

"No?" Gina asked.

"She's a mere child! Pleasantly enough composed, but an empty well, a nothing. Me, I always respond more powerfully to mature beauty. To a woman who has seen life, suffered despair and known exultation. A woman who — "

"All right, all right, all right!" Angelo said. "I get the sculpture."

Salvatore, in his turn, reported a particularly boring two days tailing Franklin. He confirmed that there was no hint at any time that there was any woman in the target's life but Barbara.

"The mail at his place gets left on a table but all he gets is junk and bills. Nothing billet. Nothing doux. I talked to the janitor's wife even."

Mama's eyes narrowed. "Stay away from wives already."

Nothing they had assembled suggested to Angelo that Franklin was either a very special or a very evil character.

A teacher Angelo had talked to at the college himself summed Franklin up as "a man with some talent who had trouble disciplining himself enough to develop in one direction to the exclusion of others." The teacher had also talked of Franklin as, "from a rather difficult background and a man who had trouble sustaining relationships."

6

"It's not going very well," Angelo said when the Old Man asked about the case at breakfast on the third day of active investigation. "We're having trouble coming up with a strategy. As far as we can tell, the relationship between Franklin and the girl is *likely* to peter out. But, on the other hand, it's just possible that Barbara is the right girl for the guy and will be the making of him."

"Sometimes it happens," Mama said.

The Old Man snorted.

Angelo said, "But we've got nothing that looks like being any use to prevent a marriage."

"When is the client coming?"

"Day after tomorrow, unless we call him."

"So in two days," the Old Man said. "What you doing?"

"Sal's still following him. And we've hired in a female op for the day. I doubt she's going to get any farther than Gina did, but if his current taste is in young ones, we can but try."

"Young and pretty and female and wired?"

"That's the idea," Angelo said. "See if she can do anything to entice him into some unaffianced proposals for a tape we can play to the daughter."

"One day soon Marie will be able to do that kind of work," the Old Man said.

"Not this kind, Papa. The op will imply she's up for anything. Bondage, S&M, whatever."

The Old Man doted on Marie, but he also worried about money. "Even so, it's expensive, hiring outside ops."

7

The outside op was a failure and knew it after a day. "No interest at all. I felt I would have had better luck with a statue," she said. "I'm happy to go back tomorrow to try again but I don't want you to waste your money."

"You should meet my father," Angelo said.

"Only if he's easy," the girl said. "My confidence is shattered."

Just then Salvatore returned to the office. "Hello," he said. "What's this about confidence?"

At dinner Angelo passed on Salvatore's report. "He feels we're getting nowhere," Angelo said. "With following the target, that is."

"So where is this Salvatore that's got opinions for us?" the Old Man asked. "I thought he was eating here tonight."

"He got inspired to do some painting," Gina said. "But he thinks we either tell client that this Franklin is not as bad as he thinks or we tell him to try to buy Franklin off."

"Has anybody else got another suggestion?" Angelo asked.

Gina, who often had ideas, was blank this time.

The Old Man wanted to meet the wired female op.

Rosetta was out with her fiancé.

David and Marie were just out.

"So, nobody asks me?" Mama said after suffering through a long silence.

"Mama, if you have an idea of what to do ..."

"I don't know about this or that," Mama said. "But I tell you something for nothing. You want to get the dirty laundry on a son? Go see his mother."

8

Angelo prepared a couple of ways to get Grace Franklin to talk about her son.
They never left the rehearsal room. Grace Franklin needed no excuse to talk
about anything.

"Coffee, Mr. Lunghi? Would you like some coffee?"

"That would be nice, thank you."

"Only the instant. My finances don't run to better but, you know, I always
think about coffee that unless you're going to have cream with it, and I mean
double cream, then it tastes just as good, or just as bad, to have instant anyway.
That's what I think. Of course," she added with a long-suffering tilt of the head,
"I can't afford the cream either."

Finance proved to be one of the two major themes in Grace Franklin's
conversation. The other was her ungrateful only child.

"You have a child?" Angelo asked. "No! You're too young! You must
have been a child yourself." But the pump had hardly needed priming.

Grace Franklin explained in great detail what a disappointment Maurice
was to his widowed mother. Best in his class in maths at primary school the boy
had spurned the opportunities such talents opened in order to become "a
so-called artist." Clearly there was no money in being a so-called artist.

As well the son never telephoned or wrote or visited. "And now he's got
some rich little girly on the boil. Not that I hear from his own lips, but I have
a few friends to tell me, even now, in my distress. But will I see a penny if he
hooks her? Not in a month of Saturdays. I say 'Saturdays' rather than Sundays
because I've always liked Saturdays better than Sundays. You know?"

"So I figure I got flirted with too," Angelo said when, finally, he managed
to escape the extended accountings of Maurice Franklin's mother.

"To have stayed there so late, it might have been more than a flirtation,"
Gina said. But she was wearing a new nightie and she also had that rare quality
of complete confidence in her man.

"I got more than flirtation, all right," Angelo said. "I got an idea."

9

Howard Notice was on time the next morning and struck Gina as having a
strange look on his face. She read it as a mixture of tension and expectation,
and wondered if it made Notice dangerous. The man *had* threatened Maurice
Franklin on his last visit to the office. The man seemed ready for extreme
behavior. Well, he'd come to the right place.

This time when the client took off his overcoat and sat down, Angelo got
quickly to the matter in hand. "Mr. Notice, just how serious are you about

wanting to prevent a marriage between your daughter Barbara and Maurice Franklin?"

10

The wedding took place the next Saturday. Angelo and Gina served as witnesses but came home straight afterwards. Not that they missed anything. There was no reception. Nor, indeed, did the happy couple plan a honeymoon.

But the couple was happy, no doubt about it.

Grace Franklin could hardly get the words "I do" out of her mouth fast enough, what with wanting to get on with spending some of her new lifetime income.

And Howard Notice, if not exactly wreathed in smiles, certainly felt relief and satisfaction that he had succeeded in preventing Barbara from *marrying* Maurice Franklin. Although to do it he had had to marry Franklin's mother himself.

"So, is there nothing Barbara and Maurice can do about it?" Marie asked at dinner. "Their parents may be married but *they* aren't related in any way at all."

"Nothing, as long as the parents remain married," Rosetta said. She was passing on the information that had been provided by Walter. Walter, Rosetta's fiancé — ish — was a lawyer and provided the family with legal information when needed.

"Oh that's *sad!*" Marie said. "That's really *sad.*"

Gina studied her daughter, but said nothing.

"Has he paid his bill, this groom?" the Old Man asked.

"He paid it before the wedding," Angelo said.

"Ah, weddings," Mama said.

"It isn't going to be that kind of marriage, Mama," Gina said.

"Who knows, who knows," Mama said mistily. "Maybe she'll whip him into shape."

Angelo and Gina exchanged smiles. "Somehow I doubt it, Mama," Angelo said.

"You never know," Mama said irrefutably. "So, what do you think Salvatore's up to tonight? What is this detective girl *like*, who is supposed to be up for anything?"

Gains and Losses

"I T's NOT MY case," Walter said. "I mean, she's not one of my clients. I do conveyancing. I don't handle criminal cases for the firm."

"But Walter happened to be there when the woman came out," Rosetta explained. "And she was so upset. Crying, wasn't she, Walter?"

"Copious tears," Walter said.

"He couldn't just walk past her as if she didn't exist," Rosetta said. "That's not your nature, is it, Walter?"

"So what did you do?" Gina asked.

"I said 'There, there,' and I offered her a cup of tea."

"Even though he was very busy himself," Rosetta said. "Weren't you dear?" She patted her sort-of fiancé approvingly on the shoulder.

"I was meeting a crucial deadline for an exchange of contracts," Walter confirmed. "A big deal. Hush hush."

Gina and Angelo exchanged glances. Angelo said to his sister Rosetta, "I don't mean to hurry you, Rose, but I've got an appointment."

Rosetta said, "Tell them, Walter."

Walter said, "So I took the woman to my office and asked her what the matter was. She said she was crying because nobody was going to *do* anything. The 'nobody' being Kirsten Boyle, our criminal specialist."

"What's the case?" Gina asked.

"The crying woman's brother was arrested and nobody cares," Rosetta said.

"The father is rich, but he won't pay for a solicitor," Walter said, "and the brother has no money of his own. Kirsten got the case on the rota. She is very good but she's, well, I shouldn't say notorious exactly, but her reputation is that she can't be bothered unless she thinks she has a chance."

"The brother is pleading guilty," Rosetta said, "but he told his sister he is innocent."

"The sister says he has no self-esteem," Walter said. "It sounds a very sad case."

"But I still don't understand what you're asking us to do," Angelo said. He looked at his sister. He looked at Walter. He looked at his watch.

Walter said, "Would you see the woman about her brother? I told her I knew these wonderful detectives who wouldn't charge the earth. Would you talk to her? Evaluate the facts?"

"Of course we'll see her," Gina said. "That's our business."

"But Walter wondered if you'd see her and maybe make a telephone call or two, for free," Rosetta said.

"Oh," Angelo said.

"Just the first interview," Rosetta said. "And checking details with the police. We *can* afford it."

Rosetta's opinion on the financial aspect was definitive. She was the family firm's part-time accountant.

2

"No money," the Old Man said at dinner that night. "Start doing charity cases, you end needing charity."

"She sounded a sweet enough young woman, Papa," Gina said to her father-in-law. "And she's very concerned about her brother."

Marie, Gina and Angelo's daughter, stuck out her tongue but so that only Gina could see. Marie's brother, David, was away, on a school trip to a conservation park, but the concept of "brother" was too powerful for Marie not to acknowledge it.

"Sweet don't pay the rent," the Old Man said.

"Fortunately," Gina said, "my brilliant father-in-law had the business acumen to buy his premises outright when he got the chance. That was a very clever move and it also means we don't have any rent to pay."

"Soft-soap don't wash, young woman," the Old Man said. But in truth he was pleased by any flattery.

"Let her tell the story," Mama said. "Have you finished your pie?"

"Is it gone from my plate?"

"No."

"Well I haven't finished it, then, have I?" The Old Man picked up his knife and fork. Mama winked at Gina.

"There isn't much more to tell," Gina said. "The sister made the appointment for tomorrow morning."

"What was her voice like, Mum?" Marie asked. "That's a good thing to ask, isn't it, Granddad?"

The Old Man smiled benevolently and nodded at his granddaughter. Marie could do no wrong in his eyes anyway, but when she joined in conversation about the family's cases he was more pleased with her than ever.

Only the four of them were at table. Angelo was not due back from a medical claim surveillance until, perhaps, ten. Rosetta was out with Walter.

And Salvatore, the eldest, appeared or not for meals solely at his own convenience.

Gina said, "Her voice was on the plummy side. You know, saying 'tine' when she means 'town.' 'I shall come to tine for ten on Tuesday.'"

"Did she say what her brother is supposed to have done?" Marie asked.

"He works in a hospital and he stole morphine from the drug cupboard." The Old Man groaned.

"What's the matter, Granddad?" Marie asked.

The Old Man said, "Druggies. Terrible payers. I lost more money working for druggies than any other kind of client."

"Oh," Marie said, "I thought you were in pain. I'm so glad you're not."

Gina and Mama looked at each other.

The Old Man said, "Three women in the room, but who hears my pain? Only Marie."

3

When Sandra Summerson climbed the stairs to the Lunghis' office she was late by nearly half an hour. Although Gina would shortly be due elsewhere, she was pleased to be able to meet the woman who had so moved Walter.

Sandra Summerson was small, fine-featured, about twenty, and she was expensively dressed. To Gina's eye she did not carry herself like someone who cried easily.

"Ms Summerson?" Angelo said.

"I am."

"I am Angelo Lunghi and this is my colleague and wife, Gina."

Sandra Summerson did not offer to shake hands. Instead she sat and said, "I must have walked down Walcot Street a hundred times before today without ever noticing this doorway or your sign."

"The firm has been here since 1947," Angelo said, "but most people are either on their way into town or looking at the shop windows."

Gina found herself growing uneasy with Sandra Summerson. It was the way she sat, which struck Gina as in charge, when the fact was she was receiving a favour. Gina also heard a harshness in the voice that she had not felt on the telephone, even at 'tine.' Gina said, "About your brother, Ms Summerson."

Angelo was about to offer tea, the Lunghis' usual practice to help clients relax. Then he remembered Gina's imminent appointment and thought he understood.

Sandra Summerson said, "I do so admire people who come straight to the point, Mrs. Lunghi. My poor brother Thom is accused of stealing twenty ampoules of morphine. But he isn't guilty. I know it sounds odd, but although the morphine was certainly in Thom's flat, it was nothing to do with him."

"How does he come to have access to morphine?" Angelo asked.

"He doesn't," Sandra Summerson said. "He works as a hospital orderly, but he doesn't have a key to the drug stores."

"But this morphine came from the hospital?"

"Yes."

"And am I right that your brother is planning a plea of guilty?" Angelo said.

"He's never admitted stealing the morphine," Sandra Summerson said, "but the police also charged him with 'possessing' it, and since it was in his flat he says he must have possessed it, because that's what the word means."

Gina and Angelo exchanged glances. They could get the police side from their friend, Charlie.

"How long has he worked at the hospital?" Angelo asked.

"Since he was sixteen."

"And how old is he now?" Gina asked.

"Twenty-two, Mrs. Lunghi."

The way Sandra Summerson said, "Mrs. Lunghi" particularly annoyed Gina. It seemed to define, diminish and age her.

"Where is your brother?" Angelo asked. "Is he in custody?"

"No, I sold some jewellery to put up his bail so he's at his home."

"And where is home?" Angelo asked.

"Thom has a flat in the Royal Crescent."

Angelo and Gina exchanged glances again. You could get very long odds locally against any hospital orderly's home address being in the Royal Crescent.

Sandra Summerson said, "Thom inherited the flat from our Auntie Beatrice. Apart from that, he's skint. He hardly earns anything at the hospital. If it comes to that, I'm skint too."

Gina could not help letting her eyes run over Sandra Summerson's clothes again.

Sandra Summerson said, "I know I dress well. That is because Daddy allows me clothes on account. I can also charge food and drink. But he starves me of cash."

"So you don't have a career?" Gina said.

"A job, Mrs. Lunghi? Certainly not. I was brought up to expect that I would never have to work. I have no occupational qualifications or skills whatever, bar a native capacity to organize other people. I assist a few medical charities, because Daddy approves of them, and I make an effort on behalf of the Festival each year."

"I see," Gina said.

Picking his words carefully, Angelo said, "Is it, perhaps, a little unexpected that your brother should choose a career as a hospital orderly?"

"He is the family rebel," Sandra Summerson said. "And he is paying for his refusal to bend to Daddy's expectations at this very moment. If anybody else in the family were in trouble, Daddy would hire a fleet of lawyers and gold card investigators to 'beat the rap.' But he won't lift a finger for Thom, who is his only son. And it's not fair. It's not bloody fair."

4

"It turns out," Angelo reported at dinner Tuesday evening, "that the father is a doctor. A surgeon."

"Cosmetic surgery," Gina said.

"He is world-renowned in his field," Angelo said.

"And his particular speciality," Gina said, "is giving people interesting-looking scars. He was the first in this country."

"It's to give their faces, or other parts of their bodies character," Angelo said. "It's supposedly becoming even more fashionable than tattoos

"Good heavens," Mama said. "He *scars* people?"

"On the private or the NHS?" the Old Man asked.

Salvatore snorted tiredly and said, "Trust you to go straight for the credit rating, Papa."

"There speaks someone who has no credit rating," the Old Man said. Salvatore was a painter and only occasionally a detective in the family firm. The friction between him and his father was chronic, especially when Salvatore did not make the effort to lubricate their contacts.

Gina said, "Sleeping badly, Sally?"

"I was up all night."

"I thought painters needed light," the Old Man said. He appealed for support from the rest of the table. "Or were you just studying the model?"

"My father always taught me," Salvatore said, "that time spent planning work saves working time."

"Be quiet, you two," Mama said. "I want to hear about this poor innocent boy and his sister." Then to the Old Man she said, "My Salvatore is tired. Let him eat."

"He started it," the Old Man said.

"That's right," Marie said. "Uncle Sal started it."

The Old Man beamed at Marie. Salvatore added rice to his curry.

Angelo said, "This cosmetic surgeon was already a success when he inherited a lot of money from his wife."

The Old Man wanted to ask how much money, but hesitated.

Angelo said, "The son, Thomas, was fifteen when his mother died and, although he was academically gifted, he dropped out of school at sixteen. He's twenty-two now and the father considers him to be wasting his life."

"You talked to this rich doctor?" the Old Man asked finally.

"No," Gina said.

"Maybe he'll pay for this free work you do," the Old Man said.

"I doubt it, Papa," Gina said. "He and his son are estranged."

Salvatore began to make a comment, but stopped. Then, because he had attracted everyone's attention, he asked, "Does he have a police record, the kid, or is this arrest his first?"

"Good question, Sal," Angelo said with a smile.

"Previous drug offences?" Salvatore asked.

"No, but Charlie says that four years ago the son received a police caution. Care to guess what for?"

Salvatore considered the challenge, and that it had been addressed directly to him. "Painting pictures without parental permission?"

"For harrassing his father," Angelo said.

"Just a caution?" the Old Man said. "He didn't get life?"

Salvatore managed a smile, but it was Mama who asked, "How did he do that, harrass his father?"

Angelo said, "Thomas Summerson filled out hundreds of coupons. He enrolled his father for courses, got firms to send him further particulars, subscribed him to magazines, pledged contributions to charities. And for each of them he gave his father's name as 'Dr. Scar.'"

"Good heavens!" Mama said.

"Charlie says that since the son was cautioned, there have been no further complaints about him. The only other thing anybody knows is that he writes poetry."

5

When Angelo opened the post the next morning, he examined the addresses on the envelopes more carefully than usual. But at nine he heard footsteps on the stairs. Alone in the office, he scooped the buff pile into an empty drawer and sat up straight.

Sandra Summerson swept in. She stopped directly in front of the desk and slapped a stack of twenty pound notes down on it. She said, "I know I'm a bitch, but I respect Thom and the sacrifices he's made for principle. That's five hundred pounds. Don't ask how I got it, but it's yours. Your fee or retainer or whatever you call it. Please, please help Thom. Gaol would destroy his innocence, no matter what he says!"

Angelo hardly knew where to begin. He said, "Would you care for a cup of tea, Ms Summerson?"

"I'd *kill* for a cup of tea," she said. "Do you have Darjeeling?"

When their cups were full Angelo said, "I'll make out a receipt for the money."

"I don't *want* a receipt," Sandra Summerson said.

"That's as may be, but I want to write you one. Perhaps while I do it you could tell me more about your brother. When did Thom inherit his flat?"

"About two years ago."

"Where did he live before then?"

"At home."

"So," Angelo said, "your brother left school to work at the hospital, but despite your father's disapproval, he continued to live at home."

"Daddy did more than disapprove," Sandra Summerson said.

"What did he do?"

"He convinced Thom that he — Thom — was dying."

"Excuse me?"

"He told Thom that he only had a few months to live. And Thom believed him." Sandra Summerson burst into tears.

✤ ✤

"I suppose you put your arm around her and stroked her hair," Gina said over coffee at eleven-thirty. "And promised you would make it all better for the poor ickle girl."

"No," Angelo said. "I started crying too, so she stroked my hair."

"You, I don't know," Gina said, "but her I wouldn't put it past."

"You don't like Sandra, do you?"

" 'Sandra,' is it?" Gina said as she poured the coffee. "The tears flow when she's with Walter, and then again alone with you. No, I don't trust your Sandra."

"Mmmm," Angelo said.

"Her brother Thomas, on the other hand, seems an inoffensive boy. He told me all about a butterfly he rescued when he was seven. Or was he eight?"

Angelo took a Bourbon biscuit.

"But he was not very helpful about his crime," Gina continued. "The police showed up and found the ampoules of morphine on a shelf in his kitchen. He said he didn't know they were there, but neither did he have an explanation."

"What's the flat like?" Angelo asked.

"It's on the first floor," Gina said. "It's almost empty apart from the futon he sleeps on, but it has spectacular views."

"Good looking boy?" Angelo asked.

"Oh yes. And *very* friendly," Gina said. "But he has a fatalistic attitude about going to gaol."

"It wouldn't come to that, would it?"

"Perhaps not," Gina said. "But he plans to plead guilty to possession and he's been suspended from his job. More coffee?"

"Thanks."

Gina warmed both cups.

Angelo said, "Did he say anything about his family while you were there?"

"He says his sister is a bitch, his father is the devil and that I am a warm person."

"He didn't happen to mention melanoma, by any chance?" Angelo asked.

6

"What's melanoma?" David asked.

"It's a kind of skin cancer," Angelo said.

"The exact same kind computer freaks get when they go outdoors," Marie said to her brother. "That's why they have to stay in dark rooms all their whole lives. And why they should never to go conservation parks, or pop concerts."

"I wouldn't want to go to a pop concert anyway," David said. "All those sweaty people herded together? Ugh!"

"You," Marie said with venom, "have no appreciation of what's important in life."

"Yes I do," David protested.

"Nerd," Marie said. "Dag."

Mama and the Old Man were eating in their own flat.

Angelo said, "So when Thomas was seventeen, the father convinced him that a rash was a melanoma and that he, the son, had only a few months to live."

"And it wasn't true?" David asked.

"It wasn't true," Angelo said.

"But why did the father do it?"

"He thought once the son found out he wasn't dying after all he would value life more. That it would make him more ambitious, make him decide to go back to school and have a career."

"I hope he didn't," Marie said. "I hope he told him where to stick it."

"The episode made the son start writing poetry," Gina said.

"Good!" Marie said.

"What a tragic family!" Rosetta said. "And so do you think it was the father who planted the morphine in the son's flat?"

The dinner table conversation stopped dead. Everybody turned to Rosetta who, alone among the family, almost never made suggestions about cases.

"What did I say?" Rosetta asked. "Is something wrong?"

"Not at all, Rose," Angelo said. "Go on. Why do you think it might be the father?"

"Because being a doctor I suppose he could have access to hospital morphine. Because he didn't like the way the son harrassed him. Because he still didn't like what the son was doing with his life and maybe *this* would shake him up."

"Possible," Angelo said. "Possible, possible. I think maybe someone goes to see Dr. Daddy tomorrow."

David said, "I want to know what this boy did when he found out that he didn't have melanoma."

"That's when he harrassed his father with the Dr. Scar junk mail," Angelo said. "Otherwise he just stayed at his job with the hospital and spent more and more of his time writing poetry."

"Good!" Marie said.

❖ ❖

"What's up with Marie?" Angelo asked Gina when they were in bed. "Some days she's nice as could be and other days you could cut a finger, she's so spikey, spikey, spikey."

Gina believed that these days Marie was only "nice" when the Old Man was around and that she was cultivating her grandfather for a purpose. But she answered more generally. "Marie's just being an adolescent. I know I was moody at her age."

"I find that hard to believe," Angelo said.

Gina *thought* this to be a compliment about her equable nature but did not make further enquiries. She said, "With an adolescent the key is to pick your battles. Let them win some minor ones, but hold out if it is something major."

"And if she wanted to drop out of school to become a hospital orderly would that be major or minor?" Angelo asked.

"Marie? An unglamorous job? If she did that I'd send her straight to a doctor," Gina said. "But not," she added quickly, "to a cosmetic surgeon."

7

To her surprise, Gina had only to tell Dr. Summerson's secretary that her visit would be about Thom to get an appointment next morning. She arrived on time and was shown in promptly. Summerson was a slim man of about fifty with protruding eyes that seemed always to stare. His face bore no suggestion whatever of wrinkles caused by frequent laughter.

Gina began to explain who she was when Summerson cut her off. "You think I don't know? Pah! You work for my daughter to assist my so-called son. Of course I know! Where do you think she got the money to hire you?"

"I didn't realise you gave it to her," Gina said.

"Give? Pah! She stole it from me."

"I didn't know that either," Gina said.

"Ah!" Summerson said, "but how do you think I knew to leave it out where she could steal it?"

"I have no idea," Gina said.

"The telephones!" Summerson said. "She rang you, right?"

✜ ✜

"He bugs his own home telephone?" Angelo said at lunch. "That takes the biscuit," he said, taking a biscuit.

"He is not the world's most pleasant man."

"So is Rose right? Did he plant the morphine at Thom's flat?"

"When I suggested it he said I was absurd. But I said that anyone who diagnosed a false melanoma for his son could hardly accuse me of absurdity. He said I had a point."

"You sound like you got along with this 'devil'," Angelo said.

"I understand him better now. He struck me as someone who sees his family problems as things he can solve by a simple, direct intervention. Surgically, you might say."

"If only a family were simple," Angelo said with feeling.

"That's the point," Gina said. "Dr. Summerson is just not equipped to deal with adolescents and adolescence on his own."

"So he's still on his own?"

"Yes," Gina said. "Though I wouldn't say that was by choice."

"No?"

"He strongly recommends a three-inch rising scar above my left eyebrow. He says it would lend an air of mystery and allure. What do you think?"

8

Angelo called Charlie after lunch to ask how the police had come to raid Thomas Summerson's flat in the first place. While Charlie checked, Gina went to the Royal Crescent.

Thom answered the door wearing swimming trunks and a T-shirt decorated with the image of a sumo wrestler. "Oh," he said, when he saw who it was. He turned and went back upstairs.

Gina took the "oh" as an invitation and followed.

"It's not that I want to go to gaol," Thom said as they sat facing each other on the floor of his front room. "But the police say the morphine was here, and I can't deny that, can I?"

"But who put it here?"

"I have no idea."

"Why was it put here?"

Thom shrugged.

Gina said, "If you're not defending yourself because you want to go to gaol, say for the experience, that probably won't happen. Not for a first offence. Most likely you'll be fined, though chances are you'll lose your job."

"I'm already suspended," Thom said. "I wrote a poem about it this morning. Would you like to hear it?"

"Please," Gina said quickly, if without conviction.

"Suspension," Thom read. "By Thomas Summerson. Suspended, from my vital thread/Suspended from my daily bread/Hanging as the sun goes past/Doubtful of my next repast ..."

Thom read slowly. The poem lasted for five minutes.

"Interesting," Gina said when it was over. "Is any of your poetry published?"

"No," Thom said, and for the first time he was not languid. "I don't think poetry publishers can be bothered even to read verse that's in the poet's own hand, verse that isn't typed out prettily. But I'll never stoop to that. Word processors only give you processed words. And that," he said sternly, "can never be *good*."

"It must be frustrating for you," Gina said.

"What must?" Thom asked, with an abruptness that suddenly put Gina in mind of the young man's father.

"It can't be easy to write and not have your work read. To put in all that effort and have no appreciation back from the like-minded. There must be people out there who *would* appreciate your work." Gina swallowed and added, "Lots of them."

"Publication," Thom said slowly, obviously mulling over Gina's words. "I do certainly find that reading a poem aloud to other human beings helps me to find its pulse, its heart."

"So you read your work to people?"

"Oh yes," Thom said. "I hold readings here. Sandra lays on food and drink and I provide the entertainment."

"And who comes?"

"I invite everybody I know. I know you now. I invite you. The next one is on Friday evening. I've invited the policeman who arrested me too. I invite absolutely everyone I know. Except father, of course."

9

Over dinner it was Rosetta who picked up the case baton. "The key," she said to the table, "is to identify someone who both attends the poetry readings and who works at the hospital."

"It could be a patient," David said. "He might know some of them too."

"But a patient wouldn't be able to steal the morphine, stupid," Marie said. "Would he, granddad? Not as easily as someone who worked there."

"Good point, Marie," the Old Man said.

"Charlie says the police got an anonymous tip-off that the morphine was there," Angelo said.

"Whoever phoned the police, that's who did it," Rosetta said.

"How about the sister?" David said. Everybody stopped eating and looked at the youngest member of the family. "At least if she made the tip-off phone call, then there would be a tape recording of it at Dr. Scar's house."

After a moment of consideration, Gina said, "I think if he knew Sandra was responsible, Dr. Summerson would have told me."

"Besides," Marie said, "why would she do it, except that it was her brother?"

"Good question," the Old Man said. "Why? Why did whoever did it do it?"

"It's all so obvious," Mama said impatiently.

"Is it?" Gina asked.

"So take off our blinkers," the Old Man said. He winked at Marie. "What's the answer?"

"Someone who works with your Thomas is in love with him, but he spurned her. She did it to get him back."

"Interesting," Angelo said.

"Or maybe someone is jealous of him," Rosetta suggested.

"Jealous? Of a penniless poet?" the Old Man said dismissively.

But Angelo said, "His workplace. His workmates. Good, good, good."

There was a pause in conversation around the table.

Marie said, "Grandad?"

"Yes, my dear?"

"Do you think music is important?"

"Important?"

"To make someone a complete and rounded individual." Marie smiled invitingly.

"I suppose so," the Old Man said. "Why?"

"Oh, I just wondered," Marie said.

10

"At least we've solved one mystery today," Gina said to Angelo when they were in bed.

"What's that?"

"Why Marie has been cuddling up to Papa."

"Has she?" Angelo asked. He considered. "Why?"

"She's going to ask him for the money to go to a pop concert."

"Is she?"

"You heard about music and the rounded individual at dinner."

"I thought she was asking for a school essay or something."

"Marie? Talking about school work voluntarily?"

"Good point," Angelo said.

"The Mordant Wits," Gina said.

"What?"

"In Birmingham, at the NEC. A month ago she asked if she could go if she saved for the ticket from her allowance. I said we'd talk about it when she'd saved the money."

"And has she?"

"Marie? Save money?"

"Mmmm," Angelo said. "So when is it, this concert?"

"I don't remember, but soon."

"And tell me," Angelo said, "if she gets the money from Papa, will this be a minor adolescent battle you can let her win, or a major one she has to lose?"

"What do you think?" Gina asked. "Could she handle herself at something like a pop concert?"

"If she can get money for something like that out of Papa, she can handle herself anywhere," Angelo said.

11

"Sandra Summerson!" Gina said suddenly. She and Angelo were sharing a pot of coffee, after the children left for school but before time open the office.

"What about her?"

"If she can get money out of her father to pay for us, she can help us solve the case."

Angelo understood the reference but not the point.

"She organizes food and drink for her brother's poetry readings. So she must attend them. She's also the busybody type who would have to know who everyone was. She would know if Thomas had spurned the affections of someone at work."

"I'll phone her," Angelo said. "And see if I can get her to come to 'tine' again this morning."

✣ ✣

"Oh God!" Sandra Summerson said when Gina and Angelo explained what they were thinking. "Regis Woolwich."

Angelo turned to Gina. "Not a spurned girlfriend. A spurned boyfriend."

"I tell them," Sandra Summerson said. "I do tell them. But I can't help it if they don't pay attention, can I? Is that my fault? What am I supposed to do?"

Sandra Summerson paused but Gina and Angelo both opted to wait her out.

Sandra Summerson said, "Should I stay in my room at home? Should I not come out of doors? Am I supposed to ignore my only brother as he strives to improve at the only thing that means *anything* to him? How could I do that? Is it my fault if soft, daft people like Regis fall for me? Is it *my* responsibility?"

"Who exactly is Regis?" Angelo asked.

"I told him. I told him as soon as he took my hand for the very first time, I said, 'Regis, don't get involved with me. I am bad news for people who fancy me, because I am a *bitch*. I only like men who are *very* rough. That's just the way I'm made. I am bad news.'"

"But he didn't take the warning?" Gina said.

"No," Sandra Summerson said. "He didn't. And he was *so* bitter."

12

"So it was a case of the bitter bit," David said.

"Very *amusant*," Marie said acidly, but she smiled at her grandfather. "That's French, in case you didn't know, little David."

"So this Regis, he was in love with this Sandra?" Mama asked.

"Desperately," Angelo said. "He met her at one of the poetry readings."

"Salvatore, you like poetry, don't you?" said Mama, who yearned to see her eldest paired.

"Not a lot," Salvatore said.

"But such an attractive sister, by all accounts," Mama said.

"Salvatore wouldn't like this one, Mama," Gina said.

"Whoever knows about the path of love?" Mama said. "She's single, right, this girl? Let him make up his own mind. And free food and drink, on Friday night. Am I right?"

Rosetta said, "So in his bitter frustration, Regis tried to hurt her by hurting her brother?"

"It was the only way he could think of," Gina said.

"Charlie says Regis confessed immediately when the police interviewed him this afternoon," Angelo said.

"And will the doctor father be grateful when he finds out?" the Old Man asked. "Maybe offer a bonus?"

"He may be more grateful than he knows," Gina said, "but not if he finds out."

"Is that a riddle?" the Old Man asked. He turned to Mama. "Does she ask a riddle?"

"It means that Thom has decided to give up his job at the hospital," Gina said.

"To be a poet?" Marie asked.

"When did he decide that?" Rosetta asked.

"When Charlie called us about the confession," Gina said, "I went over to tell Thom. That's when he told me he plans to sell the flat and use the money to go to college."

"Why?" Marie asked.

"He says he needs a job that will give him enough money to publish his poems himself."

Marie was relieved that artistic integrity remained intact.

"But," Gina said, "he doesn't want his father to know."

"Why not?" the Old Man said. "A father would be interested in a son who decided to make something of himself. He might even want to help him."

"Ah," Salvatore said, "that's *why* he wouldn't want him to know, Papa. He would want to do it himself. Am I right?"

"I'm impressed, Sally," Gina said. "Thom says that his father would butt in, give him money, interfere."

"You should tell the father," the Old Man said. "Even if he is a scar doctor. What if he died tomorrow? He would want to know this so he could rest easy."

"We can't tell the father, Papa," Angelo said. "He's not our client. It wouldn't be ethical."

"But," Gina said, smiling, "we should tell Sandra Summerson about her brother. I can ring her on her telephone at home."

This met with approval around the table.

Then Rosetta said, "If Thom is going to sell his flat …"

"He promises he will use Walter to do the conveyancing," Gina said.

"Oh good!" Rosetta said. She clapped her hands. Then she brought herself under control and said, "Of course, it's not just because we're engaged. Walter really *is* very good at his work."

"That's what I told Thom," Gina said.

"Granddad," Marie said.

"What, my dear?" the Old Man said.

"Would you help me after dinner? For school."

"How can I do that?"

"I'm writing an essay for English about your murder case," Marie said. "The one you solved."

"You are?" He beamed. "About Norman Stiles?"

"That's it," Marie said. "Would you mind telling me how you did it again?"

"Well," the Old Man said. "I don't know. It's a pretty violent story for a young lady." He looked to Marie's parents.

Gina gave a tiny nod.

The Old Man said, "Well, if you say 'please' …"

"Oh, please, Granddad," Marie said sweetly, winning her minor victory.

Travel Plans

"SLOW, SAL," Angelo said as he wound spaghetti onto his fork. "Slow, slow, slow."

Salvatore Lunghi looked suitably grave and decided to shelve his good news. "That's too bad, bro," he said.

"Bro? What's this 'bro'?" The Old Man had suffered from dyspepsia all winter. "In my day a man spoke the Queen's English at his father's table and was proud to use it."

But Gina had seen something flicker across her bro-in-law's face. She said, "How about you, Sally? Anything new?"

"You know," Salvatore said.

Gina was not made of the stuff one fobs off. "Are you seeing somebody?"

"Not especially," Salvatore said.

Gina studied him and persisted. "So what *is* it?"

Salvatore, never good at delaying gratification, grinned.

Mama perked up. Angelo's marriage to Gina was a long-standing success. And Rosetta was at least engaged, even if the engagement was in its fifth year and her Walter was somewhat married. But Salvatore ... A mother despairs. "Don't tell me. At last!" she said.

"No no, Mama. Nothing like that," Salvatore said.

"So like what?" Mama said.

"I've got an exhibition." Salvatore was a painter.

Mama's disappointment was silent, but Gina said, "That's *wonderful*. When is it? Where is it?"

"I open in June. It's a gallery called The Academy. Do you know it?"

"No," Gina said. Everyone looked around the table. Nobody knew The Academy. "So what street is it in?"

Salvatore grinned again. "It's not in a street."

"He's up to something," the Old Man said. He rubbed his stomach.

But everybody understood already that Salvatore was throwing down a deductive challenge to the family.

Gina said, "So, it's not in a street. Where else could it be?"

The thoughtful pause was broken by David, Gina and Angelo's younger child. "I know. Uncle Sal is going to sell his pictures on the pavement, like a busker."

This speculation was considered least amusing by the oldest members of the family.

"No," Salvatore said. "Strictly indoors."

"But not in a street," Gina said. "What else have we got? A road?"

"No."

"A lane?"

"A mews?"

"A close?"

"A crescent? Is it a crescent?"

But it was none of these, offered from various positions around the table.

Then Angelo said, "A passage." There were galleries in a number of the city's tourist-targeted passageways.

Instead of saying a simple, "No," Salvatore said, "Good try. Warm."

"Warm," Gina repeated. "Does this mean that your gallery is not accessible to motor vehicles?"

"It does."

"Mmmm," the Old Man grumbled.

Angelo said, "How about in one of the buildings at the edge of the Abbey's forecourt?"

"Forecourt, he calls it," the Old Man said.

But Salvatore's grin broadened. "Spot on, bro."

"Wow," David said. "They get the best buskers in front of the Abbey."

"That's wonderful, Sally," Gina said.

"That's in the middle of town?" Mama asked, for confirmation.

"The middle of the middle," Salvatore said. "A mate of mine bought what was a souvenir shop and he's turning it into three floors of paintings. Including a generous and reasonably-priced selection of beautiful works by yours truly, June to September."

"But that's tourist season," Mama said.

"Oh, is it?" Salvatore winked at Gina.

"Yes," Mama said slowly, thinking it through. "But do you have enough of your paintings in stock, if suddenly they are going to sell?"

"Paintings you call them," the Old Man said. These days he had kind words only for Marie, his granddaughter. But Marie was out with a girlfriend agonising about her boyfriend, Brian. At Sunday dinner time!

"Shouldn't you paint some more, Salvatore," Mama insisted. "For the demand?"

"I plan to do exactly that," Salvatore said.

"Good," Mama said. "Very good." Because for Salvatore to paint meant that he would hire models, meet women.

"There's no pleasing you," the Old Man said to his wife. "When he brings one home she isn't good enough. When he doesn't, you want him to find another." The Old Man beseeched the skies for relief.

"One day my Salvatore will find the right woman," Mama said. "When it happens, he'll know. He'll know."

Salvatore said, "I was hoping there would be a little work you could put my way. I need money to buy paints and canvasses."

"When he needs money, the agency is good enough for him," the Old Man said.

"Hush," Mama said.

Angelo said, "Business is so slow."

"It's true," Gina said. "I can't remember it this bad. Even the legal work has tailed off."

"Ah well," Salvatore said philosophically.

Then David said, "I put a case your way, Dad."

Everyone looked at David. "Not funny," Angelo said to his thirteen-year-old son.

"It's no joke. Do you know Ben Smith?"

"No."

"He's in my maths class. His family went on holiday over Christmas and while they were away his house was robbed. They had pearls and silver and all stuff like that. Well, on Friday he was talking about how his dad said the police were useless and how some of the most expensive things weren't insured. So I told him my parents were private eyes and that he should tell his parents our family was a hundred times better detectives than the police."

"Pearls and silver," the Old Man said. "They sound like payers."

2

To Gina and Angelo's great astonishment, Ben Smith's parents did come to the office on Monday afternoon. Moreover, the Smiths hired the Lunghis to investigate the burglary.

When she heard about it at dinner, Marie threw up her hands. "You are going to be insufferable," she said to David. "In-bloody-sufferable."

"Marie ..." her mother said.

"I'm sorry, but he's bad enough at the best of times. All la-di-da because he thinks being good at maths and computers is so important when at the same time he has no more personality than a single-celled organism."

"School work is important," Angelo said.

"Amoeba, amoeba, amoeba," Marie sang in her brother's ear.

But David's excited mood could not be quenched. "You're just pissed off because Brian is taking Ellen to the cinema tonight," he taunted.

"As a matter of fact," Marie said, "I *told* him to."

"Children ..." Gina said.

"That statement would have more evidenciary credibility if you'd said it *before* he asked her out."

"So how are you getting along with the lovely *Lisa* these days?" Marie said cruelly. "Shared any good floppy disks lately?"

"None of your business."

"Freaky, battery-powered, Miss Personality *Lisa!*"

"Children, that's enough!" Gina said. The siblings resorted to girning , but at least they were silent.

"So tell about the Smiths," Rosetta said. Angelo and Salvatore's only sister, Rosetta was the family business's accountant, part-time.

Gina said, "Mrs. Smith said that it wasn't the value of the missing property that mattered most. They were family heirlooms and it was the sentimental loss that counted."

"*He* was sentimental about the money," Angelo said.

"But they were both furious that it happened despite the precautions they'd taken," Gina said.

"How long were they away?" Rosetta asked.

"Two weeks," Angelo said, "skiing in Switzerland."

"Oh lovely," Rosetta said, her own ambitions for such things having increased following the success of a recent weekend away with Walter.

"They followed all the advice in a police leaflet. They stopped the milk and the papers and the post," Angelo said.

"And left a key with a neighbour who looked in every day."

"And they bought gadgets to turn lights and radios on automatically in the night, like there were a dozen insomniacs in the house."

"But they were robbed anyway," Gina said. "We called Charlie and he's checking the files, but he wasn't aware of anything special about the police investigation. All he said was that it wasn't a typical target for a burglary."

"Neighbours close by," Angelo said. "Well lit. Neighbourhood Watch."

"The opportunistic thefts happen in dark places, or where the house is isolated."

"So does Charlie think it was organised?" Rosetta asked. "Or maybe somebody who knew they were away? Who knew they were away?"

"No one apart from close friends and family," Gina said. "No one who could possibly be involved. They were very positive about that."

3

However it was about the matter of who knew the Smiths were away from home that Angelo made his first enquiries. Tuesday morning he called at the Owl and the Pussycat, the travel agents with whom the Smiths had booked their holiday. He spoke to the manager in her office.

"I have complete faith in my staff," Nora Henryson said. "We give the best and most personal service in the city. We make every effort to get the right holiday for every customer. And I know my people well. There's not one I wouldn't trust with my own cash."

"It's not that I think any of your employees moonlights as a burglar," Angelo said, "but they *do* handle information that burglars could make use of."

"As a matter of fact," the manager said, "my boyfriend happens to know about these things. He's told me all sorts of stories about how devious burglars can be and because of that my staff helps our clients to take all possible precautions. Even so, it can happen to anyone, you know. Even policemen get burgled."

"Do you have the impression that there's been an increase in burglaries while people are on holiday?"

Ms Henryson considered. "As a matter of fact I *have* heard of quite a few recently."

However when Angelo returned to the office Gina reported that Charlie, their police contact, had quite a different impression. "Charlie says the local police have concentrated on fighting burglaries this year. It's been a point of pride that we've done better here than anywhere comparable in the country."

"Interesting," Angelo said.

"Charlie also said that there was nothing unusual about the Smith burglary, except that everything taken was small. Portable. And that some of the valuable things were well hidden. The Smiths didn't have a safe but some jewellery was kept in a hollow bedpost. Even so, the burglars found it."

"What do you mean, portable?"

"There were valuable items of furniture that weren't touched."

"What did Charlie make of that?"

"He thought maybe the thieves parked some distance away. Maybe too far not to be conspicuous carrying a Sheraton table."

"Or maybe they just didn't know a valuable table from an MFI one."

"Maybe," Gina said.

"I think next I'd better have a look at the Smith's house and the neighbourhood," Angelo said.

"It's in hand," Gina said.

"It is?"

"After I talked to Charlie, I rang Salvatore."

4

Salvatore reported what he learned at dinner. "The house," he said. "Anybody who found the hollow bedpost either knew it was there or went over the place with a fine-tooth comb."

"Who knows about bedposts?" the Old Man asked. "Who does this woman invite to her bedroom?"

Salvatore said, "They don't think anybody knew."

"So it's the comb," the Old Man said. He turned to his plate. "Curry, I get? What's so hard about making lasagne?"

"Curry comb," David said. Marie stuck out her tongue at her brother. Neither contribution drew response.

"A search so thorough as to try bedposts takes time," Salvatore said.

"So we have a burglar with a lot of time," Angelo said. "Mmmm. What else, Sal?"

Salvatore described his exploration of the Smiths' neighbourhood. "I don't go for this parking problem idea," he said. "There's an alleyway behind the house and everybody has garages anyway. There would be plenty of places to park inconspicuously, close enough to carry out furniture at night, if they wanted to."

"So they didn't want to," Angelo said. "Why wouldn't they want to?"

"The table you mentioned," Salvatore said. "It's worth at least five thousand itself."

"Maybe they didn't know the value," Gina said.

"Or they don't have anybody to sell tables to," Salvatore said. "What did Charlie say about recovery of the jewellery?"

"Nothing has turned up in the month since the burglary. All the usual outlets have been checked."

"So," Angelo said, "maybe our burglars have fences outside the area."

"Which suggests organisation, big time," Rosetta said.

"Yet, they don't take a valuable table," Gina said.

"There were other good pieces too," Salvatore said. "Chairs and some so-so pictures. It could all have been carried."

"They had time to look," Gina said.

"Yet such things were left," Angelo said. "And that suggests no organisation, small time and local. Mmmm."

Then Angelo recounted his meeting with the travel agency manager. This led to a number of questions and Angelo decided to return to talk to Nora Henryson again the next day.

5

On Wednesday morning, however, the first thing Gina did was to ring Charlie. She asked him to find out from the officers in the anti-burglary campaign whether there had been an increase in the proportion of the city's burglaries that had occurred while property occupants were away on holiday.

Charlie returned the call before lunch. The police were adamant. Burglaries of all kinds were down in the city.

Armed with this information, Angelo returned to the Owl and the Pussycat. Ms Henryson seemed surprised to see him but again she took Angelo to her office and this time offered him a drink.

Angelo declined.

"So what brings you back to us so soon, Mr. Lunghi?"

"Your boyfriend," Angelo said.

"Steve? What about him?"

"It's a matter of putting a few facts together. You said yesterday that you'd heard of an unusual number of holiday burglaries. That's burglaries of your clients, I presume."

"Yes," she said thoughtfully, "I supposed that's right."

"Well, I checked with the police, and they say that burglaries are down in the city. Not up." Ms Henryson was about to speak, but Angelo held up a hand. She shrugged. Angelo said, "And you trust your staff completely."

"Yes, I do."

"Yet you also said that your boyfriend has special knowledge about burglaries. What I need to know, Ms Henryson, is more about your boyfriend. How he's gained his knowledge, and whether it might be he, in fact, who is somehow connected to the incidents we're talking about."

"Steve can be extremely awkward, as I am only just beginning to realize, but you can't be suggesting that he might — "

"The connection could be unwitting. I'm not accusing him of anything. But I really do need to know more about him."

"This is ridiculous," Ms Henryson said, but just at that moment her telephone rang. "Excuse me."

"Of course."

She answered and said, "I'm busy now. Who? Oh. Yes. Send him in."

Angelo was puzzled, but in a moment the door was opened by a large man with a rumpled suit and with a tie loose at the collar. "Nora?" he said. "I go to work this morning and the first thing I hear about is the Owl and the Pussycat. Somebody's got the bright idea to go back to some of our victims and see if they got their tickets from you. What's this all about?"

"Steve, let me introduce Mr. Lunghi. Mr. Lunghi, this is Steve Nelson. He is a police sergeant assigned to the city's anti-burglary task force."

6

"I was so embarrassed," Angelo said. "Are you going to have that teacake?" Gina passed the plate and Angelo took the last toasted teacake. "I'm all but accusing this guy of accessory, and he turns out to be someone Charlie is getting his information from."

"So," Gina said equably, "if it isn't him it must be someone else."

"You think?"

"Charlie rang while you were out. Five of the seven holiday-burglaries in January were of people who booked with the Owl and the Pussycat."

✛ ✛

By Thursday morning Charlie telephoned the further news that the police had belatedly established common factors in the way the five Owl and the Pussycat burglaries had been committed. In particular, at each house only small items had been stolen, and the thieves seemed to have plenty of time. The police were reopening the five investigations as a group. The suggestion, therefore, was that the Lunghis should suspend their own work so as not to interfere with the police operation.

But Gina and Angelo had hardly put the phone down, and certainly had not had time to think through what they would do, when there were footsteps on the stairs to the agency office.

A moment later, Sergeant Steve Nelson entered.

"You don't have to tell us," Angelo began. "We know that you are reopening the cases."

"What I came around for," Nelson said, "was to apologize for yesterday. I was a little steamed. I didn't know what was going on. But I've gone through it all at work now. I understand that you were hired by the Smiths."

"Will you have a cup of tea, Sergeant?" Gina said.

✛ ✛

Over tea the Lunghis learned that Nelson had only been with the new burglary task-force for two months. They also found that he had known Nora Henryson for less than a year. "She's made that travel agency into the best independent in the city. I doubt any mere man could come first in her life, but I have hopes. I'm crazy about her, I really am."

7

It was Nelson's enthusiasm for Ms Henryson and his related frustration that was the focus of conversation at the family dinner Thursday night.

"A man in love," Mama said. "A man who has found the right woman and knows it," she continued, looking at Salvatore. "Such a man would do almost anything to win his mate."

"And lose the rest of his life," the Old Man said sourly.

"Do you think the policeman is responsible?" Rosetta said.

"Someone must have given these criminals their information," Mama said. "Maybe if he undermines her business a little she'll begin to depend on him more. Love knows no rules. As you already know, my little one."

Rosetta blushed.

"So we're agreed," Angelo said. "The burglars received information about who was away from home and for how long. That's how they knew they were safe in the house and could spend a long time looking for hidden money and valuables."

Though no money had been taken from the Smiths, small amounts were lost in other burglaries, and in one house nearly a hundred pounds in twenty pence coins had been taken from what looked like bags of flour in the pantry.

"But why only very small things?" Gina said. "Some of the paintings they left were easy enough to carry."

"Paintings!" the Old Man snorted. "Don't tell me paintings."

Salvatore said nothing in response to this any more than he had responded to his mother's musings on love. Indeed, everyone paused to think.

David broke the silence saying, "It doesn't have to be someone giving."

"What are you talking about?" Angelo asked.

Marie made circular motions with her index finger, pointed at David's head. Screwy. Crazy.

"Go on, David," Gina said. "Don't mind your sister."

"It doesn't have to be that someone gave the information about the travel agent customers to the burglars."

"How else did the burglars know where to go, stupid," Marie said.

"I mean it could be that someone took it. Not an employee or a boyfriend. Someone from the outside."

8

"I'm beginning to think these visits are more than just business," Ms Henryson said. "Not that I'm complaining. Are you sure you won't have a coffee?"

"No, thank you," Angelo said.

"So, you wanted to see me?"

"On business, I assure you."

Ms Henryson sighed. "The signals men give can be so confusing."

"I always thought it was women who were confusing," Angelo said with a smile.

"You think? Well I can't make men out at all."

"Is that Sergeant Nelson in particular?"

"It certainly is," she said. "All I do is make a little joke about commitment and he practically breaks down my door to get married. But I don't want to marry. I like Steve, but I've got a life without him. I've got a lovely house of my own. A business. I'm perfectly happy with things the way they are."

"Sounds ideal to me," Angelo said.

"Not to Steve Nelson," Ms Henryson said. "Men!"

Angelo waited a respectful moment before he said, "It was rather about the breaking down of your door that I've come."

❖ ❖

The door, however, drew a blank. Nevertheless when Angelo returned to the agency office a few minutes after eleven he strode positively. He found Salvatore with Gina, and tea in the pot.

"Hit me," Angelo said. "I've worked it out."

Gina poured him a cup of tea and then offered the brothers biscuits.

"No chocolate ones?" Salvatore asked.

"Cheek."

But Angelo said, "When there's no milk chocolate it doesn't mean there's no plain."

"This business slump's getting to him," Salvatore said.

Angelo said, "Nobody burgled the travel agency."

Gina frowned. It had been the family's working hypothesis that the burglars broke into the Owl and the Pussycat and stole information about customers' holidays.

"But," Angelo said, "it came to me as I was leaving."

"What did?"

"Travel agents book tickets by computer. The computers are connected to airline and holiday companies by telephone links. Nobody broke into the shop, but someone broke into the shop computer."

"Go on," Gina said.

"I had Nora Henryson go through it for me. All the basic travel information is there. And the best part is that the Owl and the Pussycat prides itself on personal service. You call up a customer's name and you even get personal details the agent has found out in chatting. And they make a particular point of asking whether the house will be left unoccupied *because* they have special leaflets prepared by the police anti-burglary task force."

Gina said, "So all we have to work out is who broke into the computer."

9

David, who was on a roll, cracked it at dinner. "Kids," he said.

"What?" Angelo said.

"Kids. Kids are the ones who know about computers. At school they even talk about how to hack into them."

"Such an ugly word, 'hack'," Rosetta said, but she was in a bad mood because Walter had cancelled the cinema.

"Kids, kids, kids," Angelo said.

David was particularly sorry that Marie was not there to envy his triumph. Though on Friday evenings dinner was held early to facilitate family members going out, Marie had gone out even earlier. Brian had rung. They were making up.

Then Rosetta asked, "If it's kids, why have none of the stolen goods turned up? You're not suggesting that these children have fences outside the city, are you?"

"I suppose not," Angelo said.

"So where are Mrs. Smiths' pearls and the other valuables?"

"I don't know," Angelo said.

David said, "Maybe they don't know how."

"How what?" Gina said.

"Suppose it's kids. My age or maybe older. They might know how to hack into a computer, and they might be able to sneak out of their houses to do the robberies. But would they know how to sell stolen things without getting caught? I wouldn't."

"I should think not," Rosetta said.

"What would they do with the things they stole then?" Gina asked. "What do you think?"

"Give things away at school?" David suggested. "To girls they want to impress, if they're immature."

10

As a special treat, and because it was a Saturday, Angelo took David with him to the police station. They asked for Sergeant Nelson at the desk and thought they were lucky when told he was on duty.

They were less certain of their good fortune when Nelson came to meet them. The man looked awful, tired and unkempt. He also behaved gruffly, saying, "Not more about the Owl and the Pussycat and flaming Nora, I hope."

Angelo was surprised. "I thought you and Ms Henryson were close."

"Women are supposed to want commitment, right? So you offer them commitment. But no. That's not good enough. That won't do. Suddenly they want to keep their freedom instead. Women!"

"Have you two broken up?"

"After a lengthy discussion, I decided to reconsider my position," Nelson said. "And I started reconsidering it with some mates at the Star last night, and I shall renew deliberations again tonight at the Hat and Feather."

"Oh."

"So. What did you want, Mr. Lunghi?"

"We've come to solve your case for you," David said.

"What?"

"Nothing," Angelo said. "We just wondered if there had been any progress on solving the case."

"Progress?" Nelson said. "Give us a chance. We only just reopened it."

"Dad, I thought —"

"In that case we'll be on our way," Angelo said. "Sorry to have bothered you. And good luck."

As they left, Sergeant Nelson stood watching them, scratching his unshaved chin.

David's chin too was unshaved, though considerably smoother than Nelson's. David, however, was just as puzzled. Even so, he knew to wait until his father was ready to explain.

Back in the car Angelo said, "He was too sour to work with Ms Henryson. We'll handle it differently, that's all."

11

David was the only Lunghi who expected that anything would happen that night, but when you're on a roll, you're on a roll. For David the case *had* to break immediately because the five nights after Saturday were school nights and he would hardly be allowed to go on a stakeout on a school night.

Sure enough, Salvatore, from his position at the Owl and the Pussycat, rang through that an illicit call had been made to the travel agency's computer. That news sent the family to action stations, bar Rosetta, who was already committed for the evening — deliriously and to everyone's relief — with Walter.

Marie and the equally rehabilitated Brian agreed to stay by the phone at home, where Mama was assigned to keep a discreet eye on them.

Like David, the Old Man was allowed to take part in the stakeout. He was in such a foul mood, maybe a little action would cheer him up. Alone in his car what trouble could he get into with kids? Angelo too drove alone. David went with Gina in Rosetta's car.

❖ ❖

It seemed hardly credible that the hacker-burglars would go the same night to the address that had been freshly planted in the Owl and the Pussycat computer. But at two-fifteen Gina interrupted a walkie-talkie game of In My Grandma's Suitcase to say, "There are two cyclists coming down the street. Over."

"Cyclists," Angelo said. "Do you mean motorbikes? Over."

"Push bikes," Gina said.

"I see them," the Old Man said. "Over. And you forgot to say 'over' last time, Gina. Over."

"Over," Gina said.

"How big are they, these cyclists? Over," Angelo said.

"Small," Gina said.

"Say 'over'," the Old Man said. "That's how it's done. Over."

"Over," Gina said.

"Girls!" the Old Man said.

"I am *not* a girl," Gina said. "And if you call me one, you'll be over and out. Over."

"Not you," the Old Man said. "Them. The bikes are girls' bikes. Both the riders are girls."

"He didn't say 'over'," David whispered to his mother.

Gina shook her head. "The cyclists are female, confirmed. Over," she said.

"Well, well, well," Angelo said. "Over."

Suddenly David was agitated. "Mum!" He said. He pulled at Gina's sleeve.

"What *is* it?" Gina said.

"I know one of them."

"Who?"

"One of those girls. It's Lisa!"

12

"Go on," Mama said, beaming. "What happened then?"

"The last thing in the world I expected," Salvatore said, "was to have to subdue two thirteen-year old girls as they climbed through a smashed-out window frame. Especially when we left the windows unlocked on purpose, so they wouldn't have to break them. Didn't we, Nora?"

"We certainly did," Nora Henryson said, returning Salvatore's broad and friendly smile.

"Have some more fettucine, my dear," Mama said.

"It is very good," Nora said.

"Little ribbons," the Old Man said.

"Excuse me?"

"In Italian. That's what fettucine means. Little ribbons. Little slices."

"Oh."

"Good for you," the Old Man added.

"I'm sure," Nora said.

"So go on," Mama said. "You'd been waiting in this lovely, successful young woman's own house for how long?"

"All evening, Mama," Salvatore said.

"And at two-thirty in the morning these burglar girls break a window."

"And climb in."

"And one of them is Lisa," Marie sing-songed. "Little David's nerdy computer-mad ex-true-true-true love."

"Shut up!" David said. It should have been a triumphal Sunday lunch for him, but he was agitated, twitchy, lorn and without wit.

Marie giggled happily.

"And you know the rest," Angelo said. "What they stole had to be small enough to be carried on bikes. And the police recovered everything from the girls' rooms at their homes."

"Except for the money," the Old Man said.

"Except for the money," Gina agreed. "And so tomorrow we'll be able to let the Smiths know that they can have their family heirlooms back, once the police are done with them."

"That's wonderful," Nora said. "You've done such brilliant work."

"You know," Mama said, "my Salvatore is a painter really. A very successful painter with an exhibition this summer near the Abbey."

"Yes, I know, Mrs. Lunghi," Nora said.

"Mama, Nora has agreed to model for me if she can find the time," Salvatore said.

"One time," the Old Man said.

"Excuse me?" Nora said.

"Just the one time did I ever get hired to solve a murder. Norman Stiles was the victim. Did you ever hear about that? It was in all the papers."

Angelo and Gina traded glances. David and Marie weren't listening. Nora said, "I don't think I saw that, Mr. Lunghi. What happened?"

"I don't know," the Old Man said unexpectedly. "They've all heard it before, these." He waved a hand, indicating the family.

But Mama, experiencing a satisfaction with life she had not felt for months, said, "Go on. You tell the nice young woman about Norman Stiles, Papa. You tell her all about it."

Pay Phone

"**I** LAID IT all out for them," Nigel Bartolome said. "I used simple, declarative English. I even made enlargements of the bills and highlighted them in three colors."

Angelo Lunghi glanced at his wife. Eyes lowered, Gina appeared to be focussed on her notebook and pencil but from Angelo's vantage point he could see she had written almost nothing.

He turned back to the pleasant-looking man in his early forties who was a prospective client. He'd walked into the Lunghi Detective Agency office with a light step and a smile on his face. There had been nothing to warn them that he was an obsessive. "So I take it that the police did not respond in the way you hoped?" Angelo said.

Bartolome shook his head sadly. "If a tax-paying member of the public brings in unambiguous proof that a crime's been committed, you'd *think* the police would be interested. I even went to the police station myself, so as to obviate the necessity of an officer having to find 3 Ayling Close. Would you believe, some of the maps of Bath omit our little cul-de-sac altogether. Including the map that's distributed for free at the tourist office. You'd expect *them* to want to be accurate, of all people, though you'd be disappointed, I promise you. Not that I *want* tourists coming to gawk at our little Grade II listed cottages, but right's right and there's not much point having a map if it's wrong. Call me old-fashioned if you like."

"Excuse me for interrupting," Gina said. "But do you live alone in 3 Ayling Close?"

"Alone, yes." Bartolome folded his hands together. "Alone in the sense of no one living in the house with me. At least not for the last seven years, which is when my then-wife chose to depart."

Angelo watched as Gina wrote "alone" and "wife 7 years ago" below Nigel Bartolome's name, address and telephone number. "But you did actually see a police officer?" he asked.

"I saw, briefly, Detective Constable Dolores Palmyra. They tried to palm me off with a uniformed officer but I insisted on seeing someone from CID because they're the ones with the power to investigate and because 'uniformed' normally means 'uninformed'."

"And what exactly did DC Palmyra have to say?" Almost immediately Angelo added, "The gist of it, please. I don't need all the details." He saw Gina's shoulders give a little twitch, then another. She'd better not laugh. Bad Gina. That would be terribly unprofessional. What would Papa say?

❖ ❖

"So can he pay, this Nigel?" the Old Man said.

"He left a deposit, Papa," Gina said to her father-in-law.

"If he can pay, who cares that he fusses?" The Old Man took a pickle from his plate and studied it. He didn't remember pickles on plates. Why suddenly were there pickles? Was it somehow to do with Mama being away, shopping with that Gabriela? Were they sneaking pickles past her? "Huh!" he said, unable to remember whether his wife liked pickles. He took a bite.

"How is it, Papa?" asked Rosetta, Angelo's younger sister, who looked after the agency's accounts. "There's a new pickle stall in the market and I thought I'd try it out."

There was a pause at the table as everybody turned to the Old Man. "It's a pickle," he said, frowning. But as he spoke he noticed a lingering taste of chili. And was that ginger? "Huh!" He took another bite.

"Let me get this straight," said Salvatore, Angelo and Rosetta's older brother. Although Salvatore was the one family member who no longer lived at home, he did work for the family agency occasionally and he ate at the family table often.   "This Bartolome guy thinks someone is making calls on his telephone, and he came to you because the police won't investigate it for him?"

"That's the gist of it," Angelo said.

"Making what calls? Like ordering pizzas, or what?"

Marie, Gina and Angelo's teenage daughter, said, "Why doesn't Mr. Bartolome just unplug his telephone and lock it away? Or does he think that such a thing is immoral and a denial of the basic human right of communication?" Marie glared briefly at her mother.

Gina said, "When you convince us that you can keep your telephone calls under control we'll talk about basic human rights."

"She lacks self-control," said David, Marie's younger brother, to no one in particular. "And she doesn't have the money to pay for her appetites."

"You *could* pay me for the work I do around here," Marie said as she took three slices of ham from the serving plate.

"What work?" Angelo said.

"You can tell she lacks self-control by the way she eats," David said.

"Control *yourself*, please, David," Gina said.

Marie picked up a slice of ham and rubbed it on her brother's face. As he sputtered she said, "You're so right, Parma-nut. I have no self-control whatsoever."

"Marie Lunghi —" Angelo began.

"I'm going. I'm going. I'm going." Marie got up. "I deserve to be punished. I'll lock myself in my room. *Without* a telephone." She left the kitchen.

"I don't know what's got into her these days," Gina said, with a sigh.

As David wiped his face with a napkin the Old Man said, "So why not lock up the telephone for this Nigel client?"

"He's already tried that, Papa," Angelo said. "He has two telephones. One is combined with an answering machine and the other is a cordless. Since the illicit calls began, he carries the cordless with him all the time. He tried locking the other one in a box while he was out at work, but it had no effect."

"Not surprising, since it was a pointless thing to do in the first place," Gina said. "Why lock up handsets and do nothing about the plugs in the wall? All someone would have to do is bring in a handset of his own."

"Or her own," Angelo said. "But please, nobody tell Marie that."

"What does Bartolome do for a living?" Salvatore asked.

"He works for HTV as a continuity announcer. You know, the voice that comes on between programmes to say what's next, or to apologize because something's gone wrong."

"And how long have the calls in question been going on?"

"All this calendar year," Angelo said. "And we're not talking chicken feed. In the six months since January there have been more than eight hundred pounds worth of unauthorized calls on his line."

"Eight hundred," the Old Man said. "Huh!"

"Sounds about what Marie would spend in a week if you let her," David said.

❖ ❖

After the dinner dishes were cleared the family retired to the living room except for the self-excluded Marie, and Rosetta, who went line dancing Wednesday nights at the Pavilion.

"So when is Mama due back?" Angelo asked his father.

"Tomorrow on the train," Papa said. "Such a palaver about sinks and ovens." His wife's trip to London with her friend, Gabriela, was for the purpose of selecting kitchen equipment for Gabriela's daughter's new café venture.

"So do you have plans for tonight, Papa?" Salvatore asked. "You going out to play while the cat's away?"

"What cat?" the Old Man said. "You call your mother a cat? And what play? How should I play when I have a wife in London and a son whose idea of work is to paint pictures? Huh!"

"You want me to work on the case?" Salvatore said. "OK, let's work." He turned to his brother and sister-in-law. "This Nigel, he has itemized bills for his phone?"

"Itemized, enlarged and highlighted in three colours," Gina said.

"The unauthorized calls in yellow," Angelo said, "the calls he made himself in pink and the calls his sister made in green."

"He can attribute every call?"

"It's like reconciling a checkbook," Angelo said, mimicking their client's precise enunciation. "How else can one know whether the telephone company is adding fictitious calls to augment its already excessive profits?"

"You should show respect," the Old Man said, "if this client can pay."

"Maybe the phone company *is* adding fictitious calls," Salvatore said.

"Bartolome has had exhaustive dealings with the phone company," Gina said, "and he's finally satisfied himself that is not what's happening."

"So we respect the client's assessment," Angelo said.

"Huh!"

David said, "May I ask a question?"

"Certainly, son," Angelo said.

"If Nigel's sister doesn't live with him, why does she make calls from his phone?"

"Good question." Angelo applauded his son. "We asked that."

"The sister lives next door with her son," Gina said. "She cleans Nigel's house and in exchange she uses the phone there to ring her husband, who is working in the Middle East."

Salvatore shook his head. "All this counting up …"

"Counting up ensures you keep something to count," the Old Man said. "Or am I wrong all these years, because I counted for my children? You could learn from such a client, Salvatore."

In the pause that followed, David said, "You can tell who's been rung from itemized bills, can't you, Dad?"

"Of course."

"So are the unauthorized calls long distance? Or maybe premium numbers? Chat and sex lines can run up big bills fast, can't they?"

Everyone turned to David.

"What?" David said. Another pause followed as his face turned bright pink.

"There were a lot of premium calls in the first couple of months," Angelo said.

"I heard about them on TV," David said. "Honest."

"But," Gina said, "Nigel had them blocked. So don't get any ideas."

"Mum!"

"Since then the calls have been to various overseas numbers — some of them sex lines too — and more recently there have been long spells on the Internet."

Angelo said, "Nigel — and the phone company — tried tracking the numbers but none of them produced any clues about who was calling."

"There's no pattern at all?" Salvatore asked.

"Only that the calls are always made when Nigel is out of the house."

"How does the call-poacher know when Nigel is out of the house?"

"We think," Angelo said, "that it could be from watching HTV. If Nigel's voice is on television, that means he's in Bristol and at least twenty minutes away."

Gina said, "Nigel's even tried ringing home from work, getting an engaged signal, then ringing his sister to get her to rush next door."

"And have her son go to the back door. But they've never caught anyone."

"Although apparently the sister refused to search through cupboards and under the bed and such, in case she *did* catch someone. Running up phone bills is one thing. Running *into* a stranger is quite another."

"Sensible woman," Salvatore said, "compared to her brother."

"So," Angelo said, "Nigel went to the police to get them to stake the house out while he was at work."

"Only they wouldn't."

"So he came to us."

✧ ✧

"You know I'm going to fail my exams, don't you?" Marie said at breakfast.

"Do I?" Gina said.

"You had a point to make about my telephone calls, I admit that, but if I can't talk on the phone with Cassie I don't have a hope in hell of passing."

"Pity."

"Do you *want* me to fail? Is *that* it? You can't bear for me to be an academic success just because you weren't?"

Wasn't I? Gina thought. Funny, *my* parents were pretty pleased. She rose to put a slice of toast in the toaster.

"All I want is to have the opportunity to accomplish more with my life than going to art college and dropping out. Is that too much to ask?"

Dropping out to marry your father and spawn you, Gina thought. She said, "Life is so beastly unfair," and sat at the kitchen table.

"Do you think *I* could have a piece of toast, or is that too expensive too?"

"So what's happening about Nigel's phone today?" David asked as he came into the kitchen. "You going to bug it?"

But before Gina could respond, Rosetta came into the kitchen from the landing.

"Morning, morning everyone." She stopped inside the door, crossed one leg over the other and then spun around. "That's called an 'unwind'."

"Ooo-la," Marie said. "It's nice that someone's happy around here."

"What's this about bugs? Do we need to call the exterminator?" Rosetta took a cup and filled it from the teapot.

"David asked if we're going to bug the phone-client's own phone," Gina said, "but before we start things like that we're going to talk with his sister."

"His sister?" Rosetta sat. "Is she a suspect?"

"Seems unlikely. But she is the only other person with a key to the house."

"Is there anything you want me to do?"

"Well, you might look at the itemized bills. Maybe you'll see a pattern that the client missed."

"Can I help?" David said.

"Let him, Mum," Marie said. "The nerd's got a special affinity for numbers. It's not like they're *human*."

⁜ ⁜

Angelo's first stop in the morning was at number 5, Ayling Close, the home of Fiona Castle, Nigel's sister. He got there about ten. A tall, very thin woman answered the door. "Mrs. Castle?"

"Who wants to know?" the woman asked, but Angelo soon established who he was and what he wanted to talk about. She found it hard to believe. "Nigel has actually gone and hired someone about this telephone business?"

"That's right."

Mrs. Castle snorted. "Poor you. I've heard nothing but bloody telephone bills from Nigel all year long. Sometimes I want to run an extension from my phone through the wall so he can unplug his telephone line altogether."

"Would that work, do you think? Because he has changed his telephone number."

"Twice." Mrs. Castle sat down with a sigh, facing him.

She struck Angelo as exasperated with her brother rather than sympathetic to his problem. "As I understand it, only you and your brother have keys to his house."

"That's right."

"Could someone have copied your key without your knowledge?"

"Without my knowledge?" Mrs. Castle smiled. "How would I know?"

"I apologize for being inexact," Angelo said.

Fiona Castle raised a finger. "I'm *not* like my brother, all right? Inexactitude is not a crime with me. But we did share a father who loved twisting people's words, if they gave him a chance. When your language is being examined all the time, awareness of such things becomes automatic."

"What I'm asking is whether you have, perhaps, lost your handbag with the key in it, or ..."

"I know what you're getting at, Mr. Lunghi, but it won't help you. I don't carry Nigel's key. I keep it in a bowl by my phone. So to copy it without my knowledge someone would have to have broken in here and then returned it. But doing all that just to enter Nigel's house to use his telephone but not for any other purpose doesn't make sense. Besides, Nigel's changed the locks twice."

"I take your point, but if it was someone who came into your house regularly ..."

"There are no regular visitors here who would know about Nigel's key, unless you count Robby, my son."

"Could your son be involved?"

"I can't imagine Robby going into Nigel's house voluntarily. He thinks his Uncle Nigel is creepy. But you can talk to him about it yourself, if you come back after school."

"How old is he?"

"Seventeen in a couple of weeks."

"Ah. So he's a mystery. I sympathize."

"Well, there's no need," Fiona Castle said with a laugh. "Robby's pretty quiet, at least around here. Maybe the computer generation is going to be as quiet as ours was loud."

Angelo scratched his chin and thought about David. He was by far the more computery of his children. Was he quiet?

"In my family the troublesome one is Nigel," Fiona Castle went on. "He thinks nothing of ringing me at midnight so I can run into his house and face down some complete stranger. 'Take a poker,' he tells me, even though I don't have a poker because we've been on the gas here for years, which he knows full well."

"Nevertheless, you have gone into the house?"

"Robby came with me. He's soft as warm butter, my son, but he's six-feet-six so he might look scary."

"But you never saw anyone."

"No. Nor heard anyone. Nor detected a trace of anyone."

"Although you got into the house pretty quickly?"

"Within a few minutes of Nigel ringing. But after rushing next door three times in one week, I told Nigel to stuff it."

✤ ✤

"After I left the sister I toured our client's house," Angelo told Gina later at lunch. "And I checked where the phone line comes in, and so on. It felt like a waste the client's money since it's all exactly as he described it yesterday. What's the soup?"

"Which is no surprise. Tomato with basil. Shop-bought."

"Not bad." Angelo slurped happily. "Not bad at all. Did you know that Bartolome's even fingerprinted his phones? Wiped them before leaving for work and then dusted them when he got home."

"I'd suggest that he cover his phone with his own fingerprints and check whether they'd been wiped when he got home if it weren't stupid to assume someone breaking in wouldn't bring his, or her, own handset."

"As you observed last night. There's more bread?"

"Sure. Would you like a pickle?" Gina asked. "I'm getting one."

"What's with Rosetta and the pickles?"

"Your question should be, 'What's with Rose and the pickle-seller?' "

"Sorry to be inexact." Angelo thought for a moment. "I guess I wasn't inexact. I was exact, but asking the wrong question."

"Isn't that probably our client's problem too? Surely it's wrong to assume someone's breaking into the house rather than tapping into the line somewhere outside. I know he's had the phone company check the wiring outside but I think we should check it again to see if someone is getting physical access to his line somehow."

"Makes sense to me," Angelo said. He bit into a pickle. "Mmmm, spicy. Want a taste?"

✤ ✤

"Welcome home, Mama," Rosetta said when the family assembled for dinner that evening.

"Such a trip," Mama said. "Such cooking machines they have these days. You put in a seed at one end and you get out tomato sauce. Though not such a sauce as this one, my own Rosetta's." Mama smacked her lips.

"At what cost your machines?" the Old Man said. "You see chip wonders on the television, but never the price."

"For chips you need potatoes, not tomatoes," Mama said.

"I meant the microbe chips."

"I know your meaning. After all these years I shouldn't know your meaning?"

"Huh!"

"So did Gabriela buy a lot of equipment for her Nina?" Gina asked.

"Gabby buys brochures, and prices, and she makes calculations. Nina and the husband will decide later what they can afford and order by telephone. But such things we saw in London even on the streets. A woman with blue spikes for hair and nothing else, and horse tattoos all over her arms, she calls to a little one, 'Come to Granny!' Never in my life would I imagine such a granny. I should go to London more often."

"Are you going to get tattoos, Grandma?" David said. "And punk hair?"

"So go to London," the Old Man said. "Punk your head. Who stops you?"

Mama hugged her husband. "My oldest baby, this one."

"Get off, old woman."

"So how are my other children? Did you miss me, or were you so busy?"

"We all missed you lots, Grandma," Marie said.

"Oh, so sweet, my Marie, to say."

"She just wants to use your telephone," David said.

"My telephone? What about it?"

"Nothing about it," Marie said. "Wonk-head is just obsessed with telephones because we're working on a new case."

"What case?" Mama turned to Angelo. "And where is my Salvatore tonight?"

"He told me he's painting tonight," Rosetta said. "He sends his apologies."

"Painting is good," Mama said. "It's what he does." She turned to her husband. "Nothing to say?"

"I say, 'Have a pickle.' "

"What pickle?"

"In fact, have Salvatore paint one and say, 'It's a pretty pickle.' "

"What are you talking about pickles?"

"Now we have pickles sneaked in behind your London. But they're not bad. Me, I'll have another. See?" The Old Man took a pickle. "Mmmm."

"The case, Mama," Angelo said, "concerns a client's telephone. Someone has run up big bills without the client's permission. We had someone check today that nobody is running a wire from the phone line, but nobody can work out how the illicit user is getting into the house."

"Who needs to get into the house?" Mama said. "All over the train and pavements there are telephones with no houses. Telephones with no wires that ring all the time and people talk as if no one can hear them so they must shout."

"Those are mobile phones, Mama," Angelo said. But he turned to Gina.

"The cordless?" they said together.

✥ ✥

After the dinner dishes were in the machine, Angelo decided to call his client. He wanted details of the cordless telephone, its make and model. But the line was engaged.

From the kitchen he went into the living room where Rosetta and Gina were talking about Mama. He turned the television on to HTV.

A few minutes after the closing strains of the "Coronation Street" theme song faded, Nigel Bartolome's voice urged viewers to stay tuned for an episode of superb Victorian police detective series, "Cribb".

Angelo turned the set off and dialed Bartolome's number. Still engaged.

"What?" Rosetta asked.

"I think the telephone bandit may be using our client's line even as we speak."

Gina said, "Do you want to go over there?"

"Yeah," Angelo said. "I do. Fast as we can."

✥ ✥

Seventeen minutes later the three Lunghis were in front of 3 Ayling Close. The house was dark, but when Angelo called Nigel Bartolome's number on his mobile phone the line was still engaged.

"What now?" Gina asked.

"I'll go to the alley where I can see his back door. I'll call you when I'm in position. Then, one of you go next door to ask for the key."

"Be careful," Gina said. "If this does involve some kind of cordless connection then the bad guy could be hiding somewhere outside, like in the bushes."

"It's only a phone-time thief." But Angelo nodded. Someone committing a comparatively petty crime *might* turn violent if surprised. And surprise was what they were aiming for. "You guys be careful too." He left for the back of the house.

✥ ✥

Gina had to ring the bell at 5 Ayling Close twice before she heard sounds inside. Then the door was opened to the extent of the the gap left by the door chain. "Mrs. Castle?"

"Who wants to know?"

After explaining who she was Gina said, "I'd like to borrow the key to your brother's house, please. The phone there is being used now although your brother is at work."

Fiona Castle undid the chain and opened the door wide. "Yeah? And you're going in?"

"My husband is at the back and my sister-in-law is with me at the front."

"Would you like Robby and me to come too? Just in case …"

"Good, yes."

"Come in while I get the key."

Gina took a step into the house as Mrs. Castle took a key from the bowl by her telephone. "Robby!" she called up the stairs. "Robby!"

When Mrs. Castle called a third time Gina heard a door opening upstairs. "What is it, Mum?" a boy called. "Cause I'm on the phone."

Mrs. Castle was about to explain when Gina put a hand on the woman's arm. "Do you mind if we go up?"

❖ ❖

When Marie emerged from her room she was surprised to find the living room and the kitchen empty. Not that her parents were obliged to tell her where they were going when they went out or what time they'd be back. Oh no, such things were for children only, one-way traffic, do-what-I-say-not-what-I-do. Life was *so* unfair.

She'd intended to ask permission to go over to Cassie's house, but if they *were* out, then she could ring and no one would know. Cautiously, before making the call, Marie went to Rosetta's room to see if she was out too. But instead of her aunt she found David. He was hunched over Auntie Rose's desk studying some papers marked in various colors. "I'm going to tell," Marie said.

David jerked upright. "Go ahead. I have permission."

If he was lying, Marie thought, she could neutralize David if he caught her on the phone. "Do you know where Ma and Pa are, Breathosaurus?"

With his attention split between Marie and the colored papers, David could only manage a negative grunt.

"Thanks, Shakespeare," Marie said, pleased with her own wit. She swanned out of Rosetta's room and headed back to the kitchen telephone. It would be wise to keep the call short. Getting caught would be *bad*.

❖ ❖

"Where have you been?" Rosetta asked as Gina returned to the front of 3 Ayling Close.

"Slight alteration in plan. This is Mrs. Castle, the client's sister, and her son, Robby."

"Hello," Mrs. Castle whispered from slightly behind Gina. Over Mrs. Castle's shoulder Rosetta saw a very tall, thin boy — a slouching, reluctant shadow. Wasn't he the one who'd helped out before when the sister had been sent to catch the phone-time bandit?

Gina said, "I'm going unlock it now." When she opened the door all four crept into the house. "Mrs. Castle, could you lead me to the back door, please? You two stay here, to block this way out."

"OK," Rosetta said. When the other two women had left them, she said, "I'm Rosetta Lunghi," and stuck out her hand to the boy.

He shook hands weakly, and grunted.

❖ ❖

Marie had been on the telephone with Cassie less than five minutes when she heard the outside door open downstairs. "Bugger," she said. "I think they're back."

"See you in school tomorrow. Bye," Cassie said.

Marie hung up the kitchen phone. She could hear only one set of footsteps. It might just be one of her grandparents, in which case maybe she would call Cassie back. She sighed as she listened. Sometimes it seemed that her grandparents were the only people in the family who loved her.

But as Marie sat at the kitchen table trying to look wistful and virtuous, her uncle Salvatore came in.

"Anybody home?" he asked.

"Just me and David," Marie said. "Feel free to use the telephone if you like."

"I will." Salvatore looked puzzled. "Are your parents likely to be back soon?" He opened the refrigerator.

But before Marie could answer, David came in. "Are Ma and Pa here? Because I think I've found something in these itemized telephone bills."

"What?" Marie said. "Drool, because they're all numbers?"

❖ ❖

When Angelo came in through the back door of Nigel Bartolome's house, the first thing he did was go to the telephone and answering machine. Standing beside it he dialed his client's number on his mobile. The line was still engaged. "OK, someone's using the line, but not the phone." He looked at the boy who was towering behind the three women. "You are … ?"

"Robby. My son," Mrs. Castle said.

"Hi."

" 'Lo," Robby said, his eyes on the floor.

"Geronimo," Angelo said, and he picked up the receiver of the phone and put it to his ear. And he frowned. There was no sound except "noise" — like when you hit a button on the television's remote control for which there was no channel. "I don't understand." He passed the receiver to Gina. Then to the others.

Robby only needed to listen for a second. "Internet," he said.

❖ ❖

"You see," David said, "the earliest time in the afternoon that there were unauthorized calls was 4:32."

"Oh yeah, Mr. Smarty-specs?" Marie said, pointing to a 1:13 pm call marked in yellow. "What about there?"

"But that was on a Sunday."

Salvatore said, "The unauthorized calls were all made when Nigel was out. That's the key, isn't it?"

"Yes and no," David said, leaning back. "The client being out is what we call 'necessary, but not sufficient' in symbolic logic."

"We do?" Salvatore said.

"It's necessary for Mr. Bartolome to be out, but it's not enough for him to be out. The phone bandit has restrictions on the times he or she makes calls too. For instance, Mr. Bartolome sometimes works Saturday daytimes but there aren't any unauthorized calls then. Well, except once. But there *are* calls on the Saturday nights when the client is working. Why nights, but not mornings and afternoons?"

"So you're saying the bandit may not always be able to get to the equipment he or she needs to tap into the phone line with?"

"Or the bandit might be doing other things."

"So you're saying that the timing of the unauthorized calls tells us something about the bandit's movements?"

❖ ❖

Fiona Castle made tea as the Lunghis and Robby sat around Nigel Bartolome's kitchen table.

Angelo said, "Having now witnessed the fact that the unauthorized caller doesn't need to come into the house, and having eliminated the possibility of a tap into external wires, the only possibility we're left with is that someone is able to get into the line via the cordless even though the client carries the phone with him wherever he goes."

"If you buy another cordless telephone of the same brand and model, would it work on this phone line?" Gina asked.

"No," Rosetta said. "Each cordless is coded to prevent that. They have, like, sixty-four thousand different codes. It is possible to set it up so two cordless phones can use the same line, but you need to program both phones at the same time."

"And that couldn't be done without Mr. Bartolome knowing. Unless ..."

"What?" Angelo said.

"Maybe the phone broke and was taken in for repair. Maybe someone at the repairer coded a second phone."

"But even if you have a second cordless phone programmed to use this line, it has to be somewhere close by. Like within a hundred feet of the base unit. And then to use the line to go on the net we are talking about someone hiding in the bushes with a second cordless phone, a computer, and the adaptor to make them work together."

"Unlikely, I agree," Angelo said.

"Honestly," Fiona Castle said, "if it's the ruddy cordless telephone that's been causing *all* this trouble I sincerely wish that I'd never given it to Nigel."

The Lunghis all turned to face her.

❖ ❖

With Bartolome's sheets of itemized calls spread out on the kitchen table David showed Salvatore and Marie what he'd found. "I've listed the times of all the unauthorized calls, breaking them down by days of the week."

Frowning, Salvatore said, "It's not all that cut and dried. There are those two Monday mornings though, I agree, otherwise, there's nothing before 4:32."

"Uh huh," David said.

But he was smiling, which Marie knew meant her brother had something up his sleeve. "There's something he hasn't told you yet, Uncle Salvatore."

"There is?" Salvatore turned to his nephew. "Do you have an idea about the caller?"

"My theory is that none of the calls were made during school hours, Uncle Sal."

Salvatore considered. "But the Monday mornings?"

David smiled even more broadly. "It's a case of what we call in science, 'the exception proves the rule.' That means when something that seems to contradict the theory actually fits with it."

"And the meaning in this case?" Salvatore said with a sigh.

"Those Monday morning calls were on Bank Holidays." In case his uncle hadn't recognized the significance, he added, "No school."

"So you're saying the phone bandit is a school kid?"

"I think so, yes," David said.

"But why aren't there any calls Saturday daytimes?" Marie asked, impressed, despite herself.

"Well, that would be explained if the kid has a Saturday job."

"And that one Saturday call?"

"Off sick?"

❖ ❖

"It was a Christmas present," Fiona Castle said. "I asked Nigel what he wanted and he told me, including the make and model. He said that he'd looked in *Which?* and that it had the best range for the money."

"So where did you buy it?" Gina asked.

"Argos. Well, I mean, it was bought at Argos. I didn't do the actual buying of it myself." She looked at her son.

Robby, who had not yet said an intelligible word, cleared his throat twice and said, "Adge."

"What?"

"It's his friend," Mrs. Castle said. "Billy Padgett. P*adge*tt, hence Adge."

"And what is the significance of Adge Padgett?" Angelo asked.

"He works at Argos on Saturdays. He gets an employee discount. He got the phone for us."

Gina and Angelo exchanged a glance. "I think we'd better talk with young 'Adge'," Gina said. "Where does he live?"

"Next door," Mrs. Castle said. "At number 1."

✤ ✤

"I tell you, Cassie," Marie said on the telephone the next evening, "it was like the answer to a prayer."

"All because they caught this kid on the phone?"

"That, and because I threatened them." Marie put her feet up on the windowsill and swept her hair back with her free hand. Yes! Life was sweet again.

"How?"

"OK, what happened was this kid who works at Argos on Saturdays was asked to get a cordless phone for a next-door neighbor."

"Yeah …"

"But what he did was get *two* cordless phones, and then he did some nerdy thing to make it so that both phones will work on the same line."

"OK …" Cassie said.

"So when the neighbor got his phone, the kid used the second cordless to make free calls on the neighbor's line right through the wall! Is that heaven, or what?"

"Wow!"

"And then," Marie said, "while our very own nerdy-trog David has gone blind by working out that it was a school kid who made the mystery calls, Ma and Pa and Auntie Rose had already caught the kid themselves, so all little Davy's numeracy went to waste."

"Wicked," Cassie said.

"It *was* a detail that gave me extreme pleasure of nearly orgasmic proportion."

"But I still don't understand how that meant you got your telephone privileges back."

"Personally, I think communication is a right, not a privilege."

"Right on."

Marie laughed. Someone knocked on the door to her room. "I'm on the phone," she called.

From the hall Angelo called back, "What kind of homework involves hysterical laughter?"

"Drama homework, Pa. We're working on the practical for the humor module. How can you work on humor without laughing?"

"Just don't take liberties, young lady."

"Go away, Pa. I need to concentrate." Marie heard Cassie giggling in her ear. "You heard that, huh?"

"But Marie, you said something about a threat."

"Yeah. What I told them was, if my phone calls were so expensive, then I'd have to get a part time job. And I said, 'I've heard that there's a Saturday job about to open up at Argos.' "

Gunpoint

A S ANGELO WALKED up Walcot Street, he felt stupid. In fact he felt worse than stupid. He felt ineffectual. He felt unmanned. He felt ashamed. He felt ... *stupid*.

And it wouldn't even be late enough when he got home for there to be any chance that everyone would be in bed. There was little that he wanted more than to be able to slink into his place beside a sleeping Gina and hide from reality beneath a duvet.

In the event Gina was in the kitchen, alone — which was something. She was reading a catalogue at the table. "The wanderer returns," she said with a glance up.

"Sorry I'm late. I got held up."

She pointed to a picture and Angelo saw the catalogue was for surveillance equipment. "What do you think about this?" she said. "You wear it on your wrist and then using a satellite and the accompanying CD-rom computer map I'll be able to locate you wherever you are anywhere in the world."

"No you won't."

"It says here I will. Only twenty-four easy payments."

"What you'll locate," Angelo said, "is where in the world my wrist is. Who can tell about the rest."

"That's a cheery thought," Gina said.

"I'm going to make tea. Do you want some?"

❖ ❖

When Angelo set the mugs on the table Gina closed her catalogue and threw it in the paper recycling bin. She wasn't sure why she even read them. The agency wasn't at the high-tech end of the private eye market and, anyway, it was her sister-in-law, Rosetta, who bought their equipment. "Thanks," she said and blew across her mug to cool the tea off. "So, where were you?"

"I told you. I was held up."

"But where?"

"About twenty yards down from the cash point on Green Street."

"What's there?" He seemed to be playing a game about his later-than-usual return. There was a pub on Green Street wasn't there? The Green Tree? So had he stopped for a drink, was that it?

211

"Nothing is there except a shop doorway," Angelo said, "and, like I said, I was being held up."

"Held up?"

"Yeah. As in robbed. Deprived of a portion of the cash form of our hard-earned wealth."

"Good heavens. Are you all right?"

"Only on the outside."

She saw that he looked a bit pale, now that she studied him. "But... what happened?"

"Well, like I told the police," he began.

✦ ✦

The CID officer who interviewed Angelo was not one of the many he already knew and it soon became apparent that DC Bainton was a newcomer to Bath. "Walcot Street …" he said when Angelo gave his address. "Don't tell me. I know. I'm sure I know."

If he didn't know Walcot Street already he soon would — just as soon as he wanted the best burger in town, at Schwartz Brothers, or some second-hand building materials, at Walcot Reclamation, or leather jackets, or used books, or a bicycle, or even the YMCA. Walcot, originally a village, had long since been subsumed into Bath proper. An arty-hippie area from the '60s, it was now becoming fashionable since it was so close to the centre of town. And, of course, the street was the site of the Lunghi Detective Agency, founded 1947. What street needed a greater claim to fame.

"Got it, got it," Bainton said. "Cadillac's Nightclub, right?"

Initial paperwork completed, Bainton asked Angelo to go through what had happened, but when he began to explain that twenty or thirty yards down Green Street from the cash point he'd been shown a gun and deprived of his fifty pounds, Bainton exclaimed, "Oh God. Not another one."

"Another one?"

"You're the fifth victim, all in the last two weeks. And of course there could well be more that weren't reported."

"So," Angelo said, "*is* the gun real?"

"Nobody's been stupid enough to find out, so far, if I may put it that way. Tell me, were you robbed by a man or a woman?"

"A man. You mean that there's a woman doing it too?"

"At least one," Bainton said. "In fact I'm not at all certain just how many of them there are who're at it."

"More than two? All with guns?" It was barely conceivable. Yet there *were* shooting incidents sometimes in Bath. And kidnappings. And even murders.

"That all the robberies have been at gunpoint is one of the few things that the incidents have in common. Please, Mr. Lunghi, describe the man who robbed you."

"Well, he was about five-ten, I'd say. Thirty-five, give or take a few years. Medium build, on the thin side if anything. He wore a navy donkey jacket. Jeans. Blue — denim coloured — trainers. I didn't see a brand logo, but they didn't look new. And the guy ... Let's see, he had an egg-shaped face in that it was narrower at the bottom than the top but with smooth curves, not angular. He hadn't shaved for a few days and as well he had a light-brown moustache, covering his upper lip but not long, so either well-trimmed or newly grown. Brown hair too, I think, under a navy — as in the colour — knit hat. I couldn't see the eyes. Sorry."

"Nevertheless," Bainton said, "a very good description."

"Thank you."

"Part of your professional training, I daresay."

"I've never been as observant about people's appearances as I'd like to be," Angelo said. "So for the last seven months I've been going to a life drawing class once a week, and it's helped a lot. That's where I was tonight."

Bainton made a note. "And what about the man's accent?"

"Geordie. I can't say Newcastle or Gateshead or Durham specifically, but it was definitely north-east. He even had the gall to call me, 'Pet'."

Bainton smiled.

"So, is it the same man who committed the other robberies?"

"I don't know."

Angelo frowned. "Why not?"

✤ ✤

"Do you want mustard in your beans?" Gina's poor Angelo. He needed comfort food after a shocking experience like that so she was making him beans on toast.

"Yeah, please," Angelo said.

"So why didn't Bainton know whether it was the same man or not?"

"My description was different from what the other victims have given."

"If one of them was robbed by a woman, fair enough."

"But even the guys seem to have been different from each other. They've ranged — according to the descriptions — from five-seven to 'about six feet.' They've had different builds, different hair colours, and the clothes have been different each time — I mean different in style. Like, one wore a suit and tie. Another looked like he'd been out for a run. And there was also one in 'smart casual' trousers and a polo-neck shirt and with a Welsh accent."

Something sweet to follow the beans would be good for him too, Gina thought. But what? She opened the refrigerator door. "What about the woman?"

"She was five-eight, blonde curly hair and wore a beret."

"Five-eight's quite tall for a woman."

"It used to be," Angelo said, "but I'm not so sure these days."

"There's some chocolate cake in here."

"I don't know."

"I think you should," Gina said. She took it out.

"Well, if you insist," Angelo said. "And the accents have all been different — or at least not Geordie. One of the victims said he couldn't tell what accent it was except that it was 'posh.' "

"But your guy wasn't posh if he called you 'pet'." Gina cut a big slice from the cake and put it on a plate. Then she considered having a piece herself.

"No. My guy wasn't posh. And that's not just from how he talked. It was the way he held himself, you know? The way he walked. He's done heavy labor in his time. I'd bet on it."

"That's good observation. Your classes are working."

"I'm just trying to use my eyes more."

"And succeeding." Gina felt a certain amount of pride in the transformation since she'd been the one who originally suggested that he sign up for the drawing classes.

But she did not cut a piece of the chocolate cake for herself. Her mother had a widow friend who would talk about her late husband. "Whenever he bought me a dress," the widow would say, "he always bought a size too small. He never *saw*, you see." If Angelo was going to start "seeing" it was definitely not the time to snack on cake she wasn't even sure she wanted.

"I just wish I'd stood up to him instead of saying, 'Yes sir, please take my money, sir'," Angelo was saying.

"Stood up to a man with a gun? For fifty quid?"

"How much would it have had to have been?"

"At least sixty-nine ninety-five." The beans were ready and Gina dished them out onto the toast.

"The more I think about it, the less I believe it was a real gun."

"No?"

"Thanks, love," he said as she put the plate of beans before him. "It wasn't that it didn't look real, because it did. And he even cocked it, and that sounded real enough for me. But could it really *be* real? Especially if there are several of them out there all robbing people after they've been to cash points. The one thing they have in common is the gun. Surely there can't be that number of *real* handguns, all being used in this comparatively petty way all at the same time.

If you had a real handgun would you risk going down for armed robbery for fifty quid?" Angelo took a forkful of the beans. "Mmm, delicious."

"Thanks." She put his slice of cake on the table and then her temptation back in the fridge.

"To me," he said, "it sounds more like somebody came to town with a box of good replicas and flogged them off in a pub."

"Buy now and I'll throw in an instruction sheet called, 'How to rob people, California style', no extra charge."

"Yeah," he said with a chuckle.

But it was a bit hard for Gina to visualize someone in a Bath pub saying, "Get your replica gun here!"

❖ ❖

David, at breakfast, asked, "So what exactly did he say to you, Dad? Was it, 'Make my day?' "

"You've been watching too many violent videos," his older sister, Marie, said. She turned to Gina. "He isn't anywhere close to eighteen, Mum. How come he gets to watch 18-rated videos and I don't?" It was a current household issue, ever since Gina caught Marie and her friend Cassie in the act.

"Tell me this, face-waste," David said. "How come *you* know that's from an 18-rated video? I don't recall our celebrating *your* eighteenth birthday lately."

"Stop straining your brain against the grain," Marie said. "With a brain like yours, it's obvious you're only cut out to be a *tree* surgeon when you grow up. If you grow up. Mum, do they let people be tree surgeons who can walk under a table without having to bend over?"

"Stop it, both of you," Gina said. "Show some respect for the fact that your father has suffered a shocking and humiliating experience."

"But that was last night," Marie said. "It's morning already."

"But," Angelo said, "old people don't recover as quickly from shock — and humiliation, thank you dear — as you youngsters."

It should have been a cue for the Old Man to make a morning entrance from the flat above, but he didn't. Instead it was Mama who entered the kitchen. "Whose humiliation dear did I hear?" she asked. "Not Marie in trouble again."

"*No*," Marie said.

"It was Dad," David said. "He was about to tell us what the man said last night when he pointed the gun at him and took all his money."

Mama frowned. "What man? What gun?"

"I don't know if it was a real gun, Mama," Angelo said. "In fact, I'm all but certain that it wasn't."

"Do you want tea, Mama?" Gina asked. "There's some in the pot."

"Yes, thank you, Gina. I'll sit down to hear this." Mama pulled out a chair and lowered herself onto it. "Ah."

"But what did he *say*?" David asked. "What exactly?"

"Why do you care so much, feather fur?" Marie said.

"For school," David whispered. "Tell you later." He turned to his father. "Dad?"

"What he said was, 'Ay pal. D'ya not see what I've got pointed at yer jaw here?' "

"Ooo, gross accent," Marie said.

"Is Papa coming down?" Gina asked.

"Ay pal, 'e is," Mama said, with a laugh.

"Even Gran's better than you, Dad," Marie said.

"We were not all privileged enough to go to a secondary school which offered Drama," Angelo said. "And what opportunities we did have we appreciated."

"Do you children want to hear about this or not?" Gina asked.

Marie turned to David and leaned to his ear. "It's for your drama project, isn't it?"

"It's on violence," David said, flicking her a nod and speaking almost too quietly for her to hear. "Go on, Dad. So what did you say?"

"Well, I said, 'Is that a gun?' and he said, 'Put it this way, pal. It's a banger you canna eat,' and then I said, 'No, it can't be.' And he said, 'If it looks like a gun, pal, and if it quacks like a gun ...' And he pulled the hammer back and it made that cocking sound, you know? And then he said, 'Worth finding out, d'ya think, pet? Because I know in yer position, me, I'd hand over the cash and not make the nasty man any more impatient than he already is.' "

"Wow," David said. He wrote furiously in a notebook.

"So I gave him the money and he walked away."

"You shouldn't have given it to him," Mama said.

"You'd have had me risk my life for fifty quid?"

"What risk?" Mama said. "Such a gun can't be real. Not in England. Not in Bath. It's not like there are guns here to murder people every day, like other countries."

That was when the Old Man came in. "Murder?" he said. "What murder?"

"No murder, Papa," Gina said, "unless you could 'murder' a cup of tea."

"The only murder I know is the Norman Stiles."

Everybody else in the kitchen groaned. The Old Man's willingness to reminisce about the agency's one true murder case was legend.

✣ ✣

The Avon and Somerset Police were notable by their absence during the rest of the day. What with having his time filled to brimming with routine work, Angelo didn't tell the story of his "shocking and humiliating" experience again till the whole family was at the dinner table in the evening. Three times a week the Lunghis had big, sit-down meals, usually including Angelo's sister and brother, Rosetta and Salvatore.

Rosetta had her own room in the Walcot Street complex and slept there, but, having dumped one long-standing boyfriend, she was diligently searching for another so she was often out. Except for afternoons, when she did the agency's financial business, and for the big meals.

Salvatore actually lived out, being a painter and only a family detective part-time, when needs-must. But the food at home was good and plentiful, not always the characteristics of the meals he took with, or from, the women who modelled for him. Guests were also always welcomed at the Tuesday and Thursday evening and Sunday afternoon gatherings, but this Tuesday evening only Lunghis were present.

"So was this gun a revolver or an automatic?" Salvatore asked.

Angelo paused to revisualize what he had experienced. "A revolver."

"Did you see bullets?"

"Ah," the Old Man said, "because for a revolver, a real revolver, one that's loaded, you would see bullets. This Salvatore of mine is not just a painter of pretty faces."

"Faces are the least of it," Gina said, "unless you've changed your style recently, Sally."

"I'm quite into faces at the moment, as a matter of fact," Salvatore said.

"And when the man cocked the revolver," David said, "the chamber would have rotated one bullet, that's right, isn't it, Granddad?"

"They rotate," the Old Man said. "David's right."

"Are you going to finish your manicotti?" Mama asked him. She began to take his plate.

"My plate needs a stop watch all of a sudden?" the Old Man said. "Huh!"

"Was it playing with cap guns that made you such a weapons expert, David?" Marie said

"Careful," Salvatore said. "That's Davy The Kid you're talking to there. You used to dress up and everything, didn't you, David. Do you remember?"

"*Please*, Uncle Sal," David said.

Angelo said, "It was too dark for me to see whether there were bullets or not."

"Well *I* think it's all shocking," Rosetta said. "My own brother, robbed at gunpoint."

"So, a real gunpoint," the Old Man asked, "or a plastic gunpoint?"

"It wasn't plastic," Angelo said. "There was a metal sound when he cocked it."

"That could be metal workings inside a plastic exterior," Salvatore said. "True."

"So are we going to catch him, Dad?" David asked.

"That's the police's job, surely," Gina said.

"But if the police need help," Marie said, "they can always call for Davy The Kid."

"Shut up, Soup-For-Brains," David muttered.

Rosetta said, "It's one thing to face a man with a gun when you can't help it, and quite another to go looking for him."

"You want to look for these gunpoints?" the Old Man said to Angelo. "Who pays? Who's the client? Do we hire ourselves now? We'll starve to death."

"We'll all starve to death if you don't either eat your manicotti or let me take the plate away," Mama said. "We're waiting for you to finish so we can have these nice cannoli Gina made."

"I didn't make them today, Mama," Gina said. "I was too busy so I bought them at Waitrose. I don't know if they're nice or not."

"We'll never know till this old man makes up his stomach."

"So take the plate away," the Old Man said. "I'll sacrifice, for my family, like always."

Immediately Mama took the plate away. "They *look* nice," she said.

"It hadn't occurred to me that *we* might try to find this guy," Angelo said, "although now that you mention it ..."

"There's always the fifty quid he took off you, Dad, if you get it back," David said.

"I'll go looking for him if *I* can have the fifty quid," Marie said.

"You will *not*," Gina said.

"You wouldn't know where to start," David said. "That's what happens when you have slop for brains. Sad but true."

"Well," Mama said taking a cannoli, "*I* would like to find this Gordie who stole from my son."

"He was a Geordie, Mama, not a Gordie," Angelo said.

"Whatever he calls himself, I'd tell him a thing or two." She took a bite. "Not bad. Not so bad."

"It's just we've been so busy," Gina said.

"I'd start with the police," Marie said. "I'd start by going to Charlie and asking him exactly what the police know about it, so far."

"These robbers ought to be caught," Rosetta said. "I hate the idea that someone might point a gun at me. Did the cop — "

"Bainton," Angelo said.

"Did Bainton say whether any women had been robbed?"

"I didn't ask. And all he said was that one of the robbers *was* female."

"Making her a robb*ess*?" said Salvatore, whose interest in feminine endings was long-established.

"Charlie would have it on his computer," Marie said, "including where the victims were robbed, which might be a clue too."

"Well," Salvatore said, "counta me in iffa we gonna revenge-a my brother. Eh, whata these robbers they thinkin'? Messa with my brother, you messa with me, you messa with my whole-a family."

"Ooo, gross accent, Uncle Sal," Marie said.

✛ ✛

In fact it was Rosetta who went to the police station the next morning, not Marie. And it was DC Bainton she asked for, not the family friend, Charlie, who worked on the police computers.

Bainton was on duty and happy to talk to her but he didn't have much to add to what Angelo had already reported. "Except," Bainton said, "that there was another robbery last night. It was …" He consulted his notes. "At about a quarter to ten. A woman had just taken money out of a machine at the railway station and was on her way to the bus station to catch a bus."

"A woman?" Rosetta said.

"It is," Bainton said. "The first female victim."

"But that's awful," Rosetta said.

"And embarrassing," Bainton said, "considering that it took place only a few meters from where we're sitting now."

"What description did the victim give last night?"

"Male, Afro-Caribbean, five feet-nine, twenty-five to thirty-five, heavy, 'Built like a rugby player,' was what she said."

Rosetta shook her head. That could hardly be the man who robbed Angelo.

"The only other thing," Bainton said, "is that when she handed over the seventy pounds she'd just taken out of the machine, he gave her thirty back."

"He what?"

"He told her he only needed forty and said, 'Thanks just the same.' "

✛ ✛

"That's a new wrinkle for a stick-up artist," Gina said when Rosetta came back to the office before lunch. "Angelo's going to want a refund."

"And Bill agrees with us that the guns probably aren't real," Rosetta said.

" 'Bill'?" Gina asked.

"Bill, DC Bainton."

"So what's he like?"

"Well, he *is* kind of cute. But younger than me. Is that important, do you think?"

"For him to be so much younger than you that it mattered," Gina said, "he'd have to still be in primary school."

"Yeah, I do hate to go lower than middle school," Rosetta said. Then she blushed.

The cheeks told Gina that her sister-in-law was interested. "Is he single?"

"I think so. I do know he's only been in Bath a few weeks. Do you think he'd like someone to show him around?"

❖ ❖

Angelo missed lunch at home but returned to the office early in the afternoon. Gina brought him up to date.

"Bainton may be new to town," Angelo said, "but he's already managed to find his own way to Cadillac's."

"I don't think Rose had the top-of-a-bus tour-guide kind of show-him-around in mind herself."

Angelo filled the kettle with water so he could make tea. "So are we really working on this case now?"

"Rose wants to. And she did get details of all six incidents."

"So it's Rose on the case, not Marie?"

"Or David," Gina said. "For the moment."

❖ ❖

But when David got home from school he found Rosetta waiting in the kitchen to meet him. It was an unusual thing for his aunt to do. "Is something up, Auntie Rose?"

"I've been working on the gunpoints."

"Oh yeah?"

"I went to the police this morning and I've been putting the information I got onto the computer. Do you want to see?"

Computer and detection was too heady a mix for Davy The Kid ever to turn down. Even though he had a lot of homework to do and a difficult question to ask someone.

But maybe Auntie Rose was the person to ask. Especially if it was before Marie got back from hanging out after school with all those ugly pierced friends she seemed to think so highly of. "Actually, Auntie Rose," David said, "there was something I wanted to ask you."

"What?" Rosetta said as they went down the hall toward the room that doubled as her office and her bedroom.

"Do you have a dress that might fit me? I mean, like an old one. One you wouldn't mind me borrowing?"

✣ ✣

Dinner on Wednesday nights was made from cold or reheated foods, but as Gina and Angelo were getting the last of what was available onto the table only Marie was at the table.

"What's the time?" Angelo asked. "I thought we were already late. Am I fast?"

"Marie," Gina said, "will you go call your brother and your aunt?"

"My brother is an ant." Marie got up, but before she left the room she said, "Dad, do you want to know why your only begotten son was so eager for you to tell him exactly what your robber said?"

Angelo was surprised by the question. What why could there be? David was interested. He was always interested. "Why?"

"Because the little worm has a *drama* project on violence."

"On violence?"

"It's the kind of thing they assign beginners in Drama," Marie said. "Especially boys. They don't understand dramatic nuances, so the teachers assign them subjects with hitting and shouting. It's all they understand, the poor dears." Marie tossed her hair with a sweep of her head. "So Davy, Davy The Kid, and his little-boy cronies are putting together a drama project that will reinact what happened to you and what happened to some of the other victims. And, because they can't make up dialogue, Davy had you say it all for him. Didn't you see how he was taking notes?"

"How do you know all this?" Gina asked.

"One of the girls in my — advanced — Drama class has a little brother in Davy's. In *my* class subtlety is the name of the game. They are *so* young, these little boys."

Marie left the kitchen to fetch the in-house little boy.

✣ ✣

But Marie only got a couple of steps into the connecting hall when David burst past her, shoving her against the wall as he passed. More surprising was the way Rosetta followed him, moving almost as quickly.

"Mum, Dad," David shouted. "Auntie Rose and I think we've got it."

"I think you got it this morning," Angelo said. "You were taking notes weren't you?" He was cutting tomatoes and did not turn around.

Gina was putting olive oil and bread onto the table. She was in a good position to see that her son was wearing a full skirt and a peasant blouse. "David?"

"See, Auntie Rose and I were talking it through," David said. "All the guns and all the people robbing people."

"Men, women, Geordies, Welsh, West Indians," Rosetta said, nearly as animated and breathless as her nephew.

"David, why are you wearing your aunt's line dance clothes?" Gina said.

Angelo cocked his head. "He's what?"

"I was just trying them on," David said. "But see it just doesn't make sense for there to be all those different guns in Bath."

"So we followed the logic of the thing," Rosetta said. "If it doesn't make sense for there to be lots of guns, then maybe there *is* only one gun."

"It suits you, Davy," Marie said, returning to the kitchen. "Davy the Ewe."

"Only one gun?" Angelo said.

"One gun," David said, "but lots of people sharing it. Do you see? A bunch of friends, maybe. Or a commune or something. When one of them needs some money he — "

"Or she," Rosetta said.

"Whoever, the person takes the gun and robs someone of whatever he or she needs."

"Which is why the one last night gave some money back."

"Hmm," Gina said, sitting down, "that makes a certain amount of sense, I suppose. A commune ... Hmmm."

"But then," Rosetta said.

"It was when I tried on one of Auntie Rose's dresses," David said, "only it was too long."

"Yes, what is that for?" Angelo asked.

"His drama group is all boys," Rosetta said.

"We've been hearing about this drama group."

"So if one of the characters in their scene is female, one or other of them has to pretend."

"They call it *acting*," Marie said, "when the students reach a higher level of maturity."

"Acting. That's it exactly," David said.

"Because when we talked about what kind of people might be in this group of friends who shared the gun, and went through the details of the descriptions given by the victims, it doesn't make sense."

❖ ❖

"Their point," Angelo said later when Salvatore dropped in to see if there was any work, "is that groups tend to get together because they are similar. They're all from one place, or they're all in the same job, or they're all homeless."

"Or they're all from the same family," Salvatore said.

"And the witness descriptions were so different," Gina said. "Angelo's Georgie, a posh guy, a jogging guy, a woman, a West Indian. There was also a smart-casual Welshman."

"So you're saying this group of people wouldn't be a group?" Salvatore asked.

"It's hard to see what kind of group they would be," Angelo said, "especially if they're also a group which puts guns under people's noses and demands money."

"So, if I understand this properly, Rosetta and David's breakthrough ... Where are they, by the way?"

"Rosetta's changing clothes because the policeman she likes is coming," Gina said. "David's upstairs because he wanted to explain it to Mama and Papa."

"What he's explaining," Salvatore said, "if I've got it right is that, on the one hand, there can't be a lot of guns, so there must be a lot of people sharing one gun. And on the other hand there can't be this particular group of people sharing the gun because they're too diverse."

"That's it exactly," Angelo said.

❖ ❖

When Bill Bainton arrived at the Lunghis's flat it was Rosetta who ushered him into the living room. There Gina, Angelo, Salvatore, Marie and David were waiting. "So this is the family that runs the Walcot Street detective agency," Bainton said. "How do you do?"

"Grandma and Granddad live upstairs," David said, "but they'll be down in a second."

And it was only a moment later that everyone heard the eldest Lunghis on the stairs. When the Old Man entered he was saying, "So who is it to tell the policeman about the ducks?"

"David will, I'm sure. Not you," Mama said. "Oh look. He's here already."

"Ducks?" DC Bainton said.

"It's a syllogism," David said. "We were talking about them in maths at school."

"Oh," Bainton said.

"It goes like this. If you know that all ducks quack, and that Marie does not quack — "

"Keep me out of your sillyisms," Marie said.

"If all ducks quack, and Marie's friend Cassie does not quack," David said, "what can you deduce?"

DC Bainton looked distinctly uncomfortable.

Rosetta said, "The conclusion is that Cassie is not a duck, Bill."

"Wouldn't you know that by looking at her?" Bainton said.

"The way it applies here," Rosetta said, "is that if there can only be one gun, and there can't realistically be so many different people sharing it ..." She opened her hands which everyone but the detective constable knew to be an invitation to draw a conclusion or make a speculation.

Bainton just waited.

Rosetta said, "Then the conclusion is that maybe only one person is using it after all."

"One person?" Bainton said.

"One person who dresses up in different clothes. One person who speaks in different accents."

"And who does different walks," Angelo said. "Because the guy who robbed me *walked* just the way he would if he had the voice he had."

"What?" Bainton said. "You mean an actor?"

❖ ❖

Even after Rosetta and David's breakthrough, it was not obvious how the police should proceed. Staking out all the city cash points day and night was impossible from a manpower and police budget point of view. And finding one particular actor in Bath was almost as daunting. The place was teeming with actors, especially if you counted amateur dramatics participants, students, and residents who naturally made dramas out of molehills.

"But the guy who robbed you is good, right?" Salvatore asked Angelo, when the family repaired to the kitchen for a cuppa after Bainton left.

"He certainly convinced me," Angelo said.

"And none of the other victims said, 'He sounded like he was putting on an accent,' did they, Sis?"

Rosetta's mind was on other things, but after the question was repeated she agreed that none of the victims had reported any doubt that the robber was what he, or she, appeared to be.

"Doesn't that make it likely that he's a pro?" Salvatore said.

"That makes sense," Gina said. "So are you suggesting that the police contact Equity for names of all their members who live here?"

"Mightn't that be what we would do next if the case was ours?"

"What ours?" the Old Man said. "We have a client, all of a sudden?"

"I think it's better to make the actor come to us," Marie said. "Are there any biscuits, Ma?"

"Of course," Gina said. She put biscuit tin on the table.

"How do you mean, 'come to us', Marie?" Angelo said.

"Well, not everyone interested in the thespian arts is a show-off," Marie said, "but the ones interested in *violence* and guns usually are." She stared at David.

"What does she thespian art at?" Mama said. "I don't understand." She opened the biscuit tin as Gina began to fill cups with tea.

Marie said, "Why not announce in the papers that the police are going to do a reconstruction, like for *Crime Watch*. Announce that they're auditioning for actors who live in Bath who can do different accents. I bet this gun actor couldn't resist being first in the queue, thinking he was putting something over on us."

"What *us*?" the Old Man said. "Who pays? That's what I want to know."

"You know, it's not a bad idea my niece has there," Salvatore said. "It should at least be worth passing on to our new friend, Bainton."

"I'll do that," Rosetta said quickly. "In the morning. First thing."

"If they do catch him that way," Marie said, "does that mean I get the fifty quid?"

✠ ✠

In the event, however, the police got their actor by different means. Saturday after the match, he dressed as a Harlequins supporter and waved his gun under the nose of a young woman near the rugby ground. However it turned out that the young woman not only watched Bath Rugby Football Club, she played flanker for the leading local women's team. The actor ran but was no match for her. She delivered him to the police station personally.

Bill Bainton rang the Lunghis in the evening to let them know, and that made it natural for Rosetta to invite him to Sunday lunch. This time when he surrounded by the family he was much more comfortable. "This is delicious, Mrs. Lunghi," he said. "What is it again?"

"A kind of lasagne," Mama said, "with a special sauce they make only in the village from which I came. A sauce that passes from mother to daughter. They never write it down. You have to marry into such a sauce. Like he did." She nodded toward the Old Man.

The Old Man had his mouth full but began to speak.

"Hush," Mama said. "This nice young man doesn't want to hear your mouth." She beamed at Bainton.

"So it *was* an actor?" Angelo said.

"He is indeed," Bainton said. "He spent last night in the cells. And, you'll be relieved to learn that the gun he used was a replica. A very good replica, but replica nonetheless. He got it from the prop department of a movie he was in, apparently."

"He's been in movies?" Marie said.

"Not many," Bainton said. "He's been most successful at things like radio plays and voiceovers on commercials. Because he is very good at different accents."

"If he's so successful," Salvatore said, "then why in the world was he robbing people at cashpoints?"

"Last Christmas he was arrested for drunk driving and he lost his licence," Bainton said. "Being unable to drive has hit him hard financially. He can still get to London, but now he has to take the train instead of going on his motorcycle."

"He has a motorcycle?" Marie said.

"And with the cost of train travel, he all but loses money every time he works. Or so he says. To listen to him it's been a very rough year for him."

"But not so rough that we feel sorry for a man who robs," Angelo said.

"Of course not. Or a man who drinks and then drives," Bainton said. "But his idea was that the police wouldn't work out his modus operandi if he was a different person each time who committed the crime."

"He convinced me," Angelo said.

"Well, he'll have plenty of opportunity to keep in practice while he's in prison," Bainton said. "My fiancée is a probation officer and she tells me that virtually every prison in the country has a drama group."

"Your fiancée?" Rosetta and Mama asked at the same time.

"Yes, Beryl," Bainton said. "She'll be moving here as soon as she can get reassigned. Which it can't be too soon for me. It's tough, living alone. Let me tell you."

"Would you care for another helping of this lasagne, Mr. Bill Bainton?" Mama said. "So the memory of what it tastes like will last you?"

Mr. Hard Man

IF I WAS BEING interviewed about what I do … By someone I respected, say… Like, if Dolly Parton had a chat show, and she was asking me about the job I'd just done what I'd tell her is, "Dolly, some things about it were typical of how I work and some weren't."

For one thing, very little of my business arises locally yet this commission began when I arranged to meet a woman at a pub in Bath, which is where I live. How the woman — Tricia was her name — how she knew to contact one of my sites I'm not certain of, even now. Sure, I know what she *said*, but — as I'd tell Dolly — the day I start believing what people tell me, that's the day I'd better order my coffin suit.

But events took their course and Tricia found me sitting at a table in the Star and what she said was, "I need help." This before she even sat down.

I said, "I help people sometimes."

"I also need a drink."

Now if Dolly was interviewing me she might comment that a pub sounds like a risky place to talk business, but in fact it isn't. Old pubs, like the Star, are made up of little rooms connected together. They remind me of rabbit warrens in the culvert banks back in some of the places where I grew up, and as long as you avoid Friday and Saturday nights, you can be private. So, when Tricia returned with a glass of wine, we had a room to ourselves and I asked her, "What exactly is it that you want?"

She sat down and took a deep breath. "There's this guy."

Isn't there always a guy? I picked up my glass. "Here's to guys." But I didn't drink. I only sniffed. My tipple now is a malt whisky and I love the way it smells.

"Don't toast this asshole," Tricia said. "He's hunting me and if he finds me, he'll take my kid."

✣ ✣

Having a singer's ear, Dolly would probably be able to tell right away that I'm American. Tricia was too, which maybe wouldn't be surprising if we were sitting in Bath, Indiana. But we were in Bath, England — an uptight olde English city that's got a bucket full of uptight olde English charm, if you go for

227

that stuff. Why I came here is a long story, but neither Tricia nor I were tourists.

So, there was a guy who would take her kid. Heart-breaking stuff. It could make a song. "I don't take checks," I said, "or IOUs or major credit cards." The money side can be a deal-breaker. It's important for us to be clear from the get-go.

"I can pay cash, within reason."

"Okay, let's talk. Why do you think there's a guy after your kid?"

"Because he showed up at the apartment of friends I was with in London."

"And?"

"Janny and I weren't there — thank Christ. We were at London Zoo, but when we got back there was an ambulance outside. Neighbors heard the screaming and called the cops."

"Screaming? This guy killed your friends?"

"He put Rafe in the hospital and scared Sally half to death, but neither of them knew where Janny and I were or when we'd be back. They'd gone to work before we decided."

"So, you came home and saw the ambulance. What then?"

"I grabbed our stuff and took a cab to the only train station I knew the name of."

"Why Bath? You know somebody here too?"

"I came to Bath because I *don't* know anybody here."

Which, as I would tell Dolly, was an interesting point. "You're saying the guy who's after you knows every single place where you know people?"

"His brother does. His brother, Tim, is my husband."

Ah. "And where is Tim?"

"St. Louis."

"Where you resided?"

She nodded.

"Until?"

"Recently." She took a deep breath. "Look, can you get rid of Larry for me or not?"

"Rid, in the sense of … ?"

"In the sense of getting him off my back so that I have the peace of mind to start over and bring my kid up."

" 'Peace of mind'?" I laughed.

"I'm sorry if peace of mind is a joke to you."

"Hey, I'm for peace of mind." I lifted my glass. "Here's to it. Whatever it may be. Wherever it may be found." I smelled the malt again. The air above The Macallan is the cleanest smell I know.

"Are you not up to the job? Is that it?" She stood. "Well fuck you, Mr. Hard Man. I hoped you wouldn't turn out to be all fuse and no explosion, but I'm not the least little bit surprised."

It goes like that sometimes, as I'd tell Dolly. People come to me for help, which means by definition that they can't help themselves. But then they behave as if it's a favor to me if I get involved. The truth is, not everybody's up to letting him or her self be helped. So I told her, "Have a good life, lady. And if you can find peace while you still have your mind, you're a better man than I am." I lifted my glass to her and this time I drank, and it was *good*. But when my eyes came up again she was still there. I said, "Show me some cash."

While she fiddled with a belt around her waist I mused about what she'd look like naked. The sandy hair might prove to be real. The tits probably wouldn't — which is not to say I'd hold that against her. However the face was too "interesting" for my taste, which was just as well, because work is work and play is play. That's not to say that I don't get pleasure from the workplace sometimes, but that's more along the lines of job satisfaction than jollies.

And anyway, that day my type was more bright-red-lipstick and a police uniform. Yeah, that would have done it for me. Or maybe a traffic warden, if her skirt was real short.

Men are like that — as I'm sure Dolly would already know. They get things a certain way in their heads, even though on another day it could be completely different — say, dark-haired and a hippie and with glow-in-the-dark tattoos on her butt.

But then an old guy carrying a pint and leading a dog came into our little room. "Excuse me," he said. "Anyone here?" He pointed to the other table.

"No," I said, "but the lady and I will be lying on it in a minute, if she manages to find her johnny."

"Excuse me?"

"No, I won't excuse you, old man. I don't like watch-em-at-it perverts."

"I say," he said while he tried to think of something to. But his dog was smarter. She jumped for the door and dragged the old guy away by his leash.

When I looked back at Tricia, she was holding a roll of bank notes.

✛ ✛

Tricia's sad story was that hubby Tim was a psycho — amazing how many husbands are, if a wife's trying to get you to help her. Tim, it seems, beat her up and worse — see previous comment. She took it and forgave and took it some more, boohoo, until Terrible Tim began on Janine, the kid. That was too too much, so one afternoon Tricia hoiked Janny out of school and ran.

Tricia *didn't* say that she'd emptied Tim's bank accounts that morning, having sold off everything she could lift the day before, but I took it as read. And so Tricia and Janny hied them to the airport and flew away. Now, if it was *me* bailing from St. Louis I'd take a steamboat down the Mississippi, but I'm a romantic.

Tim, it transpired, did not approve of his wife and daughter's relocation. For a while he chased them around Tricia's friends in the States, and in Denver, it seems, he got close enough to scare her into running farther and better. But not so much better that Tim's ex-con baby brother Larry couldn't find Tricia's London pals and make some work for the National Health Service.

That was her story as she told it to me and, as I'd tell Dolly if the subject came up, quite often significant parts of what they say is true. But total truth is not important to me. All I need is enough to work out a plan I'm happy with.

Anyway, once Tricia had fetched up in Bath by pure chance — yeah, right — she worked out that she would need help if she was ever going to live without looking over her shoulder every day — and she wasn't wrong about *that*. But how do you get heavyweight help in a strange town?

According to her, she tried a detective agency from the Yellow Pages. But, as she soon found out, Bath so-called detectives are pussies who wouldn't know how to begin. What she did then was to ask around in some pubs. In one of them, she said, a guy suggested searching the net. And I *am* out there if you look hard enough.

Whatever.

Tricia's roll of notes was only tenners, but even as I was counting I was developing an idea of how to get more.

✛ ✛

When Tricia left the Star — and her fate in my hands — I went to the little ground floor apartment (every room with windows I can fit through) that I call home. From one of the phones there I put a call in to Tim, the husband.

St. Louis is six hours earlier than Bath, so I got him at work. I told his secretary that I had news about Tricia and Janine. She put me through.

"Who is this?" Tim sounded normal enough when he came on the line. Women with a grievance so often exaggerate.

"I know where Tricia and Janine are, Tim. Interested?"

I heard an intake of breath. Good.

"Where?" he said.

"Inside the building we'll be standing in front of when you give me the ten thousand dollars."

"What ten thousand dollars?"

"I have information. You want it. That's the basis of a transaction where I hail from. And believe me, Timmy, this is information that you won't be able to get without me." I gave him a moment before I sealed the deal by adding, "And neither will Larry."

One of the important things I'd explain to Dolly is how much it helps for them to think you know everything about everything. When they think you're God they're a hell of a lot less likely to try to take advantage.

I said, "I know what Larry did to the couple in London, Timmy."

"Where are you calling from?"

"Somewhere in Britain."

The pieces were beginning to fit for him, each one increasing my credibility. He kept with the questions but the tone of his voice showed more respect. "And who exactly are you?"

"I'm the guy you're going to give ten grand to so that you can engage in reasoned, face-to-face debate with your missus about her future, or lack of it. Also about Janny's future."

"Is Janine all right?"

"I didn't see her. I only saw Tricia."

"The bitch left the kid on her own?"

"I didn't check the child-minding arrangements, Timmy," I said. "But before you make the trip over here, I can understand that you'll want proof that Janine is okay. So why don't I take a picture of her and her mother and e-mail it to you?"

✛ ✛

I took the snap the next morning. Tricia didn't like that I wouldn't explain why I wanted it, so I went the if-you're-not-going-to-trust-me-then-solve-your-own-fucking-problem route. We met in the middle of town in the Parade Gardens which overlook the river. No way would Tim be able to tell one watery background from another when he got the idea to try to cheat me out of my money.

The kid turned out to be maybe seven. She wouldn't smile for the camera or hold up the newspaper I was using to prove the date with, but Mommy held the paper and who cares about smiles anyway.

I took the picture with a digital camera — Dolly might tease me about "boys and their toys" but I'd have to confess to her, I *am* a number one sucker for anything high-tec or new-tec — and I left Tricia and the kid to pass the day however they passed days. I went home and e-mailed Tim. Then I called him. Woke him up. "Oh, sorry," I said. "I forgot you're on different time."

Yeah, right.

So while he was checking the picture, I sent another e with his instructions:

```
Tonight you will fly to London.  When you get there, find
a hotel and sleep.  In the evening, go to the Paddington
Station and buy a ticket on the 20.00 train to Truro.  The
cars on Brit trains are lettered and you will travel in
car B.
```

Whenever the train stops at a station, get out and stand
on the platform. As a point of information, to get out of
a British InterCity train you have to open the window in
the door and use the handle on the *outside* — and they
wonder here why they lost the Empire …

Somewhere between London and Truro I will greet you by
name. That's when you'll show me that you have the money
— American dollars in used twenties and fifties. We won't
move another step until I know you're carrying the ten
large.

Then, we'll go to a telephone and I will call a hotel.
Within your hearing I will ask the clerk to confirm that
your wife is currently in residence. At that time — and
without delay or I'll hang up — you'll hand me the money.
I'll hand you the phone so you can ask directions to the
hotel, or ask the clerk to call the room — whatever you
want.

You will come alone. No Larry. That's the deal. I will
not communicate with you again.

It was full of holes, of course. Like the "hotel clerk" might be a friend of mine playing the role. That's probably the first thing that would occur to Dolly, what with all the acting she's done herself, though neither she nor Tim would know I don't have friends to trust with something like that.

But even if my "deal" did look like a slice of Swiss, it was still the only cheese in town.

❖ ❖

I had more than a day before crunch time. And so did Timmy and Larry. The former would probably get the latter to spend his time calling hotels in all the cities along the Paddington-Truro line on the principle of find-the-hotel-and-save-ten-thousand-bucks. But I doubted Larry would make the right call. Bath isn't one of the stops between Paddington and Truro. We would be doing our bit of business at Westbury — it's only about twenty miles from Bath but it's on a different train line.

Larry might waste his day, but I couldn't. This may be a squishy soft country — which makes it possible for someone hard to make a real nice living — but the locals *will* cause a working man no end of tedious trouble if stuff gets put under their noses. And since my plan is to continue living in this land of milk and money without let, hindrance or incarceration, I always plan what I do very carefully.

That included a call to Tricia the next morning. "I expect to be seeing Larry later today," I told her.

It was bound to be Larry, who was already in the country, and not Tim. Bet ten grand on it. I'd even have bet that Larry'd traveled here on Timmy's passport. That way when he found Janny he could bring her home saying he was her daddy. A few knockout pills would take care of any protest the kid might make. At least that's the way I'd have done the job, if Timmy had hired me.

"You're *seeing* Larry?" Tricia asked. You could almost see her eyes widen into ashtrays over the phone line. "Where?"

"Not in Bath."

"But *why* are you seeing him?"

"I thought it was only fair to engage in carefully reasoned discourse designed to convince him of the rectitude of leaving you and Janine to pursue your new lives."

"*Discourse*? The guy can barely keep his knuckles from dragging on the ground when he walks."

"Yeah? Well, grounded knuckles can get stepped on." Clients love it when you talk tough. Maybe there are equivalents in Dolly's business too.

"Larry is a dangerous guy," Tricia said.

"He beat up your Mr. & Mrs. friends in London, I know."

"No, I mean he's *dangerous*. He's killed people. It's what he was in jail for."

"Murder?"

"Manslaughter."

"Doesn't really count," I said. "There was no intent."

❖ ❖

At nine twenty-two a guy got out of the front end of car B and stood by the door. He was bigger than I expected. Ah well.

I approached. "Tim?"

"Yeah."

"Let's see the money."

"Give me ten feet clear."

"I don't have a spotlight. I'll need to see it, or you might as well get back on the train and enjoy the delights of Cornwall."

A kid with a knapsack was walking past. "Excuse me," "Tim" said. "Could I ask a favor?"

The kid stopped. "Sir?"

"Sir" — don't you *love* soft countries?

"Tim" took out an envelope. "Would you mind counting this money for me?"

The kid looked from "Tim" to me and back. "Why not?" He took the envelope and counted. "I make it ten thousand American dollars."

"Tim" said, "Pick one of the bills at random and give it to that guy."

The kid handed me a fifty. "What's this all about?"

"Just a bit of fun," "Tim" said. He gave the kid something from his pocket. "Thanks a lot. Buy yourself a hot dog." He turned to me. "All right?"

It was always possible that the kid was a plant, but the fifty looked and felt kosher. "All right. Let's go."

At the top of the stairs at the Westbury Station there's a public phone. I placed "Tim" beside the hood where he couldn't see what I was dialing. As the number rang, I said, "You seem to have stood up to the jet lag pretty well."

"Not bad."

A hotel clerk answered. I asked him to put me through to Tricia. As the room was ringing I passed the phone to "Tim." "You know her voice, right? Listen to her, then give me the phone back."

He took the phone and listened. The hotel had one of those systems where Tricia could leave a message in her own voice. I watched as "Tim" listened. He passed the phone back to me. I hung it up.

"Her, yes?"

"Yes."

"What happens now is that you give me the money. After I've checked that you haven't pulled a switch, we'll trade places. You hit redial and ask the clerk how to get to the hotel."

"Tim" hesitated.

I said, "I won't leave until you're happy about how to get there."

"Tim" aimed a finger at me. "Just keep away from the stairs."

Gee, are you threatening me? I thought. But I smiled and nodded. He gave me the envelope. The money was okay, so I gave him the phone. Although he probably didn't know enough about British telecommunications to appreciate it, I'd left my phone card in so he could make the call.

"Tim" talked to the clerk and wrote down directions. Then he asked to be put through to Tricia's room. I could tell by watching that he got Tricia's voice on the message system again.

"Happy?" I said as "Tim" hung up.

"How do I get to Bath?"

"There's a train from here in about twenty minutes, or you can get a taxi downstairs."

"Where are you going now?"

"Not with you." I unzipped my jacket far enough to show him the butt of a gun. And I walked away.

Ten grand. Handsome pay for a couple of days' work in anybody's country.

⁓ ⁓

Forty-five minutes later I was back in Bath watching television with my feet up.

There was no way Tricia would have given me as much as ten thousand dollars — even though I'd have bet that she had it. I did take seven-fifty off her, which someone as kindhearted as Dolly might think was greedy since I was going to score ten grand anyway. But, as I'd explain, Tricia needed to pay me that money, because she needed to believe that I wasn't going to doublecross her. So, really, I only took her money to help her peace of mind, which was what she was after, right?

And all in all, I was pleased with the way things had gone. The only pity was the programs on the TV weren't better. Even with all the cable that Bath can muster, there wasn't anything I wanted to watch. Still, there wasn't much else to do.

✜ ✜

Two and a half hours after I left "Tim", there was a knock. I hadn't said a word in all that time, so my high voice was squeaky when I went to the door. "Yes?"

"Bellboy, ma'am. We found a sweater downstairs. They said for me to bring it up and have you check if it's your little girl's."

After midnight? Yeah, right.

"Just a minute," I said, keeping my voice high.

I positioned myself against the wall across from where the door would swing open. Larry would be coming in fast once I turned the handle.

I turned the handle.

✜ ✜

If Dolly Parton *was* interviewing me on a chat show, chances are she'd ask, "So, what does it feel like when you kill somebody?" But what I'd say is, "Dolly, you don't think about what you're feeling. You think about how you're going to do it, things like does mess matter, or are there witnesses, or do you have to keep it quiet. Take Larry, for example."

And I'd tell her how I stuck my foot out so Larry tripped when he rushed into the room, and how that was the critical moment. Because if he only stumbled, or if he racketed around the room breaking stuff, then people in the rooms either side might have heard and they might even have called down to the desk.

"But practice makes perfect, Dolly," I'd say, "as you know from your own line of work." In this case I'd dragged the mattress off the bed and Larry fell onto it as neatly as a hooker in a hurry. I kicked the door closed and was on top of him before he could turn over. The gun was at the back of his head and the pillow in place on top of it in another second. One shot and it was all over.

I only stayed long enough to make sure he was dead. And then I left the room, which Tricia had booked in the afternoon. No need to wipe fingerprints and all that palaver. The kid gloves never came off.

Nor did I head for home, which is what a lesser practitioner of my art might have done, but which would only have given people in the hotel a chance to notice my departure. I went up a flight to the room I'd booked for myself, and I slept like a baby.

Tricia would be all right as long as she followed instructions. As long as when she booked the room she'd said her boyfriend was going to join her later ... As long as when she left the hotel earlier she'd done it in such a way that she and Janny would be remembered ... As long as she boarded a bus to somewhere in the same way ...

So what would happen when the local cops got called to the body the next day by the screeching chambermaid? Even Bath pussy-cops would recognize the work of a pro, but with the woman who booked the room securely alibied by the times of her hotel and bus departures, their ABC thinking would turn to the body. The ID they found would connect Larry to Tim. Was brother Larry over here because he'd run away with the wife? Did Timmy wreak revenge? Or would they plump for something else?

Whatever. Tricia would be away. With no need to look over her shoulder.

"So," I'd tell Dolly, "you don't think about what you *feel* until later." And then? How did I feel about killing Larry? Well, Dolly, I felt like it was a job well done.

Story Notes

The Reluctant Detective

A central origin of this little tale was the discovery that, for tax purposes, I am not a writer at all. I'm a small business. The translation of that fact to Freddie Herring's career as a detective is clear from the story — and not uniquely my own, as Lawrence Shames' recent novel, *The Naked Detective*, establishes.

But the story had another source too because Freddie already existed, not in a crime story but in a basketball one, "How I Won the Cup and Achieved a Place in the Frome Basketball Hall of Fame." It appeared in a British basketball magazine in 1980. (Writers are such scavengers ...) That doesn't mean I have to give the Edgar nomination back, does it?

Rainey Shines

This was written about the same time as "The Reluctant Detective" and is a variation on the theme of an American living in Frome (where I lived then). One of the pleasures of Rainey for me was having a character who could happily bitch about living in Britain. I'm not, however, sure of the significance of the fact that both these Americans hit their heads on doorways. Sounds more like Danny to me.

The Dannys

In 1990 I toured in the US with Peter Lovesey (and Liza Cody and Paula Gosling.) Remember 1990? Remember who was VP?

On the tour Peter was touting a novel about Queen Victoria's son, Bertie, acting as a not entirely intelligent sleuth. I got to thinking that if he could have a dumb prince to write about, so could I. After all, Dan Quayle was from Indiana, so I was entitled to him.

"Danny Gets It Right" and "Danny Pulls His Weight" were the offspring of these musings along with a few unpublished — not very crimey — further adventures. Another result was that for a while I was a bit of a Danny buff. As a matter of awe-inspiring fact, I visited The Dan Quayle Center and Museum in Huntington, Indiana, a full week before He ever did.

The Stranger

Speaking of royalty… I was invited to write a story for *Royal Crimes* and was rather stuck until I remembered a newspaper story I read years ago. In my youf there was a TV program called *Have Gun, Will Travel* that made a star out of a craggy actor called Richard Boone. This newspaper story was about some guy who traveled the boondocks passing himself off as Mr. Boone. It was a scrap of newspaper information that I hung onto for a long time before it had any use.

Night Shift

Mystery conferences loom large on the mystery writer's calendar and the biggest annual version is the moveable feast called the Bouchercon — after a prominent mystery-friendly writer of last century who reviewed as Anthony Boucher. Bouchercons — and other conventions — give writers and readers an opportunity to meet and talk and they also draw people from all parts of the mystery biz — publishers, agents, editors, booksellers, academics, stalkers …

Sometimes the business contacts lead to projects — indeed, this book was first mooted at a Malice Domestic. The story that became "Night Shift" arose from a conversation I had with Hiroyuki Chida, the editor of the top mystery magazine in Japan, *Hayakawa Mystery Magazine*. We were at the Bouchercon in Philadelphia in 1998. Well, on the street outside the Bouchercon hotel in Philadelphia, but same difference.

Happily, my books sell well in Japan. The word on the street was that I would write a story for which the first-ever publication would be in *HMM*. "Night Shift" is that story, and the circumstances of the commission are the origin of having a Japanese visitor to Indianapolis.

She shares a name with my translator's wife, by the way. Details in stories and novels often arise like that. A police officer, Lieutenant Turk, named in this story is also real. She's a friend I met while researching the police in Indy and the job Powder is doing in the story is, roughly, the last job Sheryl did before leaving IPD.

Other details came my way originally from a correspondence I had for a couple of years with a then-fan of mine in Kobe. The letters we exchanged gave me a lesson about how little we in the US/UK understand about what real people in Japan are like and how they live. And, I originally met my correspondent at a Bouchercon.

What a Woman Wants

You'll suspect — seeing that I again focus on having a civilian "rider" with a police officer — that this kind of thing actually happens in Indianapolis, and you're right. It's something I've done several times in over the years and the experiences continue to feed the stories and novels I set in Indy. Often that's in a background way but this story of the Cutlass bandit is a true one — although the officers are made-up, it didn't happen on Halloween, etc. I happened to be riding with Sheryl the night her shift finally caught the sucker.

Boss

Yasunari Kawabata, the winner of the 1968 Nobel Prize winner for Literature, wrote a series of stories called "Palm of the Hand" stories. They are short in words but long in story. After I read them, I wanted to try the form for something mysteryish. It was hard to write …

Wrong Number

I described why this became a crime story in my introduction. It's not as short as "Boss," though its got a succinctness of its own. It was an early marker of the way I hear stories in dialog.

The Hand That Feeds Me

This too is short, and the most crimey of a series of stories about a problem-solver published as *Rover's Tales*.

In many ways Rover is the product of my co-editorship of the CWA's annual anthology, shared with Liza Cody for the '92 and '93 collections, with Peter Lovesey coming aboard for '94. From the time the new editors were announced, I read more crime short stories with more critical attention than I ever had before. That put my brain into a short story mode and in the spring of '92 I wrote a dozen stories of my own — many are in this collection. In the summer of the same year, while I was working on a stage play during the day, I began writing Rover stories at night.

The Hit, If the Glove Fits, You Pay for Everything, Suicide Note

Rover, though he doesn't know it, prowls Indianapolis (where I grew up and where much of my mystery fiction is set). Of course, having lived in the UK for 30 years I've written some things set here too, long and short. Among them are

"The Hit," "If the Glove Fits," "You Pay for Everything," and "Suicide Note."
I won't comment about them in detail, except to note that, like many of my
stories, these all began with a key image or phrase or situation and were then
developed. When "Suicide Note" was published, the then-editor of *The Armchair
Detective* said some extravagantly nice things about it. Then in the next issue
TAD stopped publishing fiction …

The Lunghis

I've already described how the family arose and the only specific note is about
"Gunpoint." This tale arose when an actor friend of mine lost his driving
license for 18 months. I'm sure it made that time easier for him to know that
his difficulties were good for something …

Mr. Hard Man

This story is published here for the first time and I wanted to include it because
it's recent work. Like the Lunghis, my Hard Man, lives in Bath — indeed, on
the same Walcot Street — but he is as far from the family down the road as he
could be in all other ways. He is my version of Unfamily Man. And the less
human because of it? Sure, but … There's maybe not so much "but" in this
inaugural story of a new series, but there'll be at least another nine stories for the
character, and his circumstances, to develop.

MZL in the Mystery Field

The Case of the Money Murders, with Harold York. 1953 (approximately).
   This 7 act stage play was the second production of the 411 East 50th Street
   Basement Theatre in Indianapolis. Scheduled to run for two performances,
   it enjoyed an encore performance the following week in a classroom of PS
   70. No copies of the script are known to have survived.

BOOKS

Novels:

Ask the Right Question. Putnam, 1971.
The Way We Die Now. Putnam, 1973.
The Enemies Within. Knopf, 1974.
Night Cover. Knopf, 1976.
The Silent Salesman. Knopf, 1978.
Outside In. Knopf, 1980.
Missing Woman. Knopf, 1981.
Hard Line. Morrow, 1982.
Out of Season. Morrow, 1984. (UK title: *Out of Time*)
Late Payments. Morrow, 1986.
And Baby Will Fall. Morrow, 1988. (UK title: *Child Proof*)
Called by a Panther. Mysterious, 1991.
Underdog. Mysterious, 1993.
Family Business. Foul Play, 1995.
Cutting Loose. Holt, 1999.
Family Planning. St. Martin's, 1999.

Story collections:

Telling Tails. PawPaw, 1994. (Marginally mystery)
Rover's Tales, illustrations by Karen Wallis. St. Martin's,1998. (Marginally
   mystery)
The Reluctant Detective and Other Stories. Crippen & Landru, 2001.

Novelization:

The Next Man. Warner, 1976.
This was a movie starring Sean Connery. Although I was carefully instructed to make sure the end of the novel did not rule out a sequel, the movie's release was not a success. Part of the *New York Times* review read that it was "made by people whose talent for filmmaking and knowledge of international affairs would both fit comfortably into the left nostril of a small bee." In the novelization, the story is the screenwriters' and the jokes are mine.

Audio book:

Rover's Tales. Blackstone Audio Books, 1999. Unabridged, read by the author.

Non-fiction:

How to Beat College Tests: a Guide to Ease the Burden of Useless Courses. Dial Press, 1970. Even today college students find many tests to be a mystery — especially the badly written ones.

TV Movies

Missing Woman. In Japan in the late 1980s.
And Baby Will Fall. Japanese TV deal for 90 minute adaptation signed in 2001.

Short Stories

[*= stories in *The Reluctant Detective*]

"The Loss Factor." UK: *Penthouse*, 1975
"Students of Disaster." First in the Swedish *The Enemies Within*, 1978; UK: *Match Me Sidney*, No Exit, 1989; US: *Ellery Queen's Mystery Magazine* [hereafter, *EQMM*], January 1994.
*"Wrong Number." *Crime Wave*, Swedish Academy of Detection, 1981; London: Collins, London, 1981.
"Silent Testimony." *Alfred Hitchcock's Mystery Magazine*, March 1982

*"The Reluctant Detective." *The Eyes Have it,* ed. Robert J. Randisi, Mysterious, 1984.

*"Family Business." UK: *Winters Crimes 20,* ed. Hilary Hale, Macmillan, 1988; US: *Alfred Hitchcock's Mystery Magazine,* March 1994.

"At Home." *New Crimes,* ed. Maxim Jakubowski, Robinson, 1989.

*"Wedding Bells." *New Crimes 2,* ed. Maxim Jakubowski, Robinson, 1990.

*"Danny Gets It Right." *Crime Waves 1,* ed. H.R.F. Keating, Gollancz, 1991.

*"You Pay For Everything." *EQMM,* December 1992.

"The Truth." *EQMM,* March 1992.

*"Danny Pulls His Weight." *1st Culprit,* eds. Liza Cody and Michael Z. Lewin, Chatto & Windus, 1992.

*"Rainey Shines." *EQMM,* July 1993.

*"Gains and Losses." UK: *Midwinters Mysteries 3,* ed. Hilary Hale, Scribners, 1993; US: EQMM, July 1994.

*"The Stranger." *EQMM,* Sept 1993; *Royal Crimes,* ed. Maxim Jakubowski and Martin H. Greenberg, Signet, 1994.

*"Boss." UK: *2nd Culprit,* eds. Liza Cody and Michael Z. Lewin, Chatto & Windus, 1993; US: *EQMM,* February 1995.

"Kitty Kitty." Japan: *Hayakawa Mystery Magazine,* 1993.

"In Mitigation." UK: *New Crimes,* ed Maxim Jakubowski, Constable, 1993.

*"Travel Plans." *Alfred Hitchcock's Mystery Magazine,* April 1994.

*"Suicide Note." *The Armchair Detective,* Winter 1994.

*"What a Woman Wants." *Murder for Halloween,* ed. Michele Slung and "Roland Hartman," Mysterious, 1994.

"Blood Blue." *EQMM,* June 1994.

*"The Hit." *EQMM,* October 1994.

"Cormorants." *London Noir,* ed. Maxim Jakubowski, Serpent's Tail, 1994.

*"The Hand That Feeds Me." *3rd Culprit,* eds. Liza Cody, Peter Lovesey and Michael Z. Lewin, Chatto & Windus, 1994.

"Dr. Bud, CA." *Crime Yellow,* ed. Maxim Jakubowski, Gollancz, 1994.

"Cross, Rems Of." *EQMM,* April 1995.

"Albert's List." *No Alibi,* ed. Maxim Jakubowski, Ringpull, 1995.

"Oil and Water." *EQMM,* May 1999.

*"Night Shift." Japan: *Hayakawa Mystery Magazine,* 1999; US: *EQMM,* July 2001.

"Backwater." *Diagnosis Dead,* ed. Jonathan Kellerman and Martin H. Greenberg, Pocket Books, 1999.

*"Gunpoint." Japan: *Hayakawa Mystery Magazine,* September 2000; US: EQMM, Dec 2000.

*"Pay Phone." *Alfred Hitchcock's Mystery Magazine,* March 2001 .

*"If the Glove Fits." *EQMM,* Sept/Oct 2001.

Competition Mystery Story:

"Murder in the Library." *Indianapolis Star*, 1993.

Drama

Crimey Radio Plays:

"The Loss Factor." 1974. 45 minutes. BBC. Adapted from my story of the
  same name.
"The Way We Die Now." 1974. 90 minutes. BBC. Adapted from my novel.
"The Enemies Within." 1976. 90 minutes. BBC. Adapted from my novel.
"Arrest is as Good as a Change. 1982 45 minutes. BBC. Original play.
"Rainey Shines." 1987. 55 minutes. BBC. Adapted from my story.
"Ask the Right Question." 1988. 60 minutes. Germany, then later by the
  BBC, adapted from my novel.
"Missing Woman." 1991. 60 minutes. BBC. Adapted from my novel.
"Keystone." 1991. 90 minutes BBC. Adapted from Peter Lovesey novel.
"Rough Cider." 1993. 90 minutes. BBC. Adapted from Peter Lovesey novel.
"Cross, Rems Of." 1994. 30 minutes. Belgium. Adapted from my story.
"Wrong Number." 1994. 20 minutes. Belgium. Adapted from my story.
"The Silent Salesman." 1999. 90 minutes (in 2 parts). Germany, Adapted
  from my novel.

Competition Radio Play:

"Who Killed Gnutley Almond?" Five 5 minutes episodes of this original play
  were broadcast on consecutive days on the BBC for a week leading up to
  the 95 Bouchercon in Nottingham. Listeners were invited to provide a
  solution. All the episodes plus my solution were then broadcast as complete
  30 minute play.

Vaguely Mystery Radio Plays:

"Place of Safety." 1985. 90 minutes. BBC. Original play.
"The Interests of the Child." 1987. 90 minutes. BBC. Original play.
"Jingle." 1999. 45 minutes. BBC. Adapted from the story "Backing."

Crime Stage Plays:

"Deadlock." Written on commission for and with Dr. Fosters Travelling Theatre. British-set small-cast multi-role whodunnit. Toured in the UK for 8 weeks in October/November 1990.

"Who Killed Frankie Almond?" Based on the competition radio play of similar name. This version was first staged as a competition library event in the fall of 1995 for the Indianapolis and Marion County Public Library.

"Whooodunnit?" Episodic play structured in a competition format, like "Frankie Almond." First staged in Indianapolis and Marion County Public Library in fall of 1998.

Non-Fiction

"Soft-Boiled But Still An Egg." *Murder Ink*, ed. Dilys Wynn, Workman, 1977. How Albert Samson originated.

"Afternoon by the Pool." Ross Macdonald, *Inward Journey*, ed. Ralph Sipper. Cordelia Productions, 1984. About meeting Ross Macdonald.

"Liza Cody's Anna Lee." *100 Great Detectives*, ed. Maxim Jakubowski, Xanadu, 1991.

"Foreword" to Marcia Muller's *Edwin of the Iron Shoes*. Chivers, 1993.

"Chandler from the Perspective of a Working Detective Writer." *Raymond Chandler Jarhbuch 1*, ed. William Adamson, Germany: Andreas-Haller-Verlag, 1996. Published in English.

Awards Type Stuff

Edgar nominations: 1971 for *Ask the Right Question* for best first novel; 1984 for "The Reluctant Detective" for best short story.

International Short Story Competition: 1981 got "Wrong Number." One of fifteen equal winners after 1st, 2nd & 3rd in the competition run by the Swedish Academy of Detection in association with the International Crime Writers Conference in Stockholm.

Falcon: 1987 for *Hard Line*. Best foreign novel of the year in Japan. Awarded by the Maltese Falcon Society, it's a beautiful carved and painted falcon that adorns my office even as I write this.

North Central High School Hall of Fame: 1991. I was one of the ten inaugural inductees, all recognized for our "outstanding achievements and the honor [we] bring to [ourselves] and our school." Other inductees have included Kenneth "Babyface" Edmonds, an astronaut and a former Indiana Supreme Court Justice. But not Dan Quayle, 'cause he didn't go to North Central.

Marlowe: 1992 for *Called by a Panther*. Awarded by the Raymond Chandler Society of Germany for the best PI novel of the year.

The Detection Club: 1993. Doug Greene, the publisher of this book, tells me that I am only the third American to be invited to join this distinguished dining club since it was created in 1930.

Mystery Masters Award. 1994. Awarded by the Mid-America Mystery Conference "in recognition of [my] distinguished career as an outstanding writer of crime and detective fiction and [my] numerous contributions to the genre."

The Reluctant Detective

The Reluctant Detective and Other Stories by Michael Z. Lewin is printed on 60-pound Glatfelter Supple Opaque Natural (a recycled acid-free stock) from 11-point Baskerville, a computer-generated version of a typeface designed by John Baskerville in 1757 (and which has nothing to do with a famous hound).   The cover painting is by Carol Heyer and the design by Deborah Miller.   The first printing comprises approximately in one thousand copies in trade softcover, and two hundred fifty copies sewn in cloth, signed and numbered by the author. Each of the clothbound copies includes a photocopy of a 1987 page of notes by the author about the Lunghi series.   The book was printed and bound by Thomson-Shore, Inc., Dexter, Michigan.

The Reluctant Detective and Other Stores was published in October 2001 by Crippen & Landru Publishers, Inc., Norfolk, Virginia.

CRIPPEN & LANDRU, PUBLISHERS

P. O. Box 9315
Norfolk, VA 23505
USA

Crippen & Landru publishes first editions of short-story collections by important detective and mystery writers. Most books are issued both in trade softcover and in signed, limited clothbound with either a typescript page from the author's files or an additional story in a separate pamphlet.

☞This is the best edited, most attractively packaged line of mystery books introduced in this decade. The books are equally valuable to collectors and readers. [*Mystery Scene Magazine*]

☞The specialty publisher with the most star-studded list is Crippen & Landru, which has produced short story collections by some of the biggest names in contemporary crime fiction. [*Ellery Queen's Mystery Magazine*]

Books are available by the following authors: Doug Allyn, Lawrence Block, P.M. Carlson, Hugh B. Cave, Max Allan Collins, Michael Collins, Susan Dunlap, Michael Gilbert, Joe Gores, Ed Gorman, Ron Goulart, Edward D. Hoch, Clark Howard, H.R.F. Keating, Michael Z. Lewin, Peter Lovesey, Ross Macdonald, Margaret Maron, Patricia Moyes, Marcia Muller, Bill Pronzini, Ellery Queen, Peter Robinson, and James Yaffe

E-mail: CrippenL@Pilot.Infi.Net
Visit our web site for full descriptions of books:
www.crippenlandru.com